Why read *The Clara Conjecture?*

By the year 1939 it had become widely recognized among scientists of many nations that the release of energy by atomic fission was a possibility. … The possession of these powers by the Germans at any time might have altered the result of the war and profound anxiety was felt by those who were informed.

Winston Churchill in the *New York Times,* August 6, 1945, following Hiroshima.

The SIS file on Ian Fleming is classified if one exists (p.191). Ian was party to the top-level panic that the Germans had succeeded in developing the atomic bomb (p.331). Ian's last duty in Room 39, following VJ Day, was to sign a pledge never to reveal what he had done there (p.204). Nicholas Shakespeare, *Ian Fleming: The Complete Man,* New York: Harper Collins 2023.

In *The Clara Conjecture* Jack Ondrack has made the most plausible reconstruction of why Nazi Germany did not come up with the atom bomb first. It is a very important Canadian footnote to the Second World War. I strongly suspect Ondrack has it right.

Ian Winchester, Professor, University of Calgary; BSc (Honours) Physics, University of Alberta; BPhil and DPhil Oxford University, Philosophy of Science.

Winston Churchill once said, "In wartime, truth is so precious that she should always be attended by a bodyguard of lies." In this remarkable book written by Jack Ondrack, the author explains how two women, taking on the role of "bodyguards," were instrumental in saving the world's democracy. Anybody interested in a James Bond-like story, but an adventure that's not fiction, will be fascinated to follow this tale.

Manfred F.R. Kets de Vries, DBA Harvard, Distinguished Clinical Professor of Leadership Development and Organizational Change, The Raoul de Vitry d'Avaucourt Chaired Professor of Leadership Development, Emeritus, INSEAD The Business School for the World. Member, International Psychoanalytic Association, Canadian and Paris psychoanalytic societies.

Combining deep scholarship and high intrigue, *The Clara Conjecture* unveils the role of two women in preventing Hitler getting the atomic bomb. Could a Canadian psychoanalyst and an Austrian physicist have tipped the balance of World War Two? Author Jack Ondrack has a credible response while providing a wealth of insights into the world of spies and nuclear secrets in wartime Europe.

David Halton, journalist (senior CBC foreign affairs, retired), author of *Dispatches From The Front,* a biography of his father Matthew Halton, the "Voice of Canada" during World War Two.

A ripping yarn! Jack Ondrack's singular mind and razor-sharp research skills have produced this riveting account of how two women likely helped stop Nazi Germany winning the race to develop the nuclear bomb. Had Hitler succeeded the consequences would be unspeakable. The Clara Conjecture is a must-read, and I can't wait for the movie.

Graham Dalziel, former Editor-in-Chief, Edmonton Sun newspaper.

Jack Ondrack's, *The Clara Conjecture,* is more than a comprehensive and often riveting story of Germany's race to get the bomb. It's all there: Commandos in German-occupied Norway, Ian Fleming, women James Bond-like characters, and a spying adventure worthy of scholars. Worth reading for those seeking a well-told story of what happened, and importantly for us, what may have happened in the world of spying and the development of the atomic bomb. This is an indispensable book, curated masterfully by Ondrack.

Col. Christopher P. Costa, USA (ret.), Executive Director, The International Spy Museum, Wash. D.C., former career intelligence officer and former special assistant to the president and senior director for counterterrorism at the U.S. National Security Council from 2017 to 2018.

I am very proud to learn of Jack's efforts in producing the text of this Book, which is a wonderful Historical Read. It certainly causes me to recall our delightful discussions in this regard a few years ago.

Donald G. Bishop, K.C., Second Secretary, Canadian Embassy, Warsaw Poland 1966-68, Honourary Consul for Sweden, Edmonton, Alberta, Canada 1994-2007, Swedish Royal Order of the Polar Star 2003, University of Alberta Distinguished Service Award 2006.

Interesting read. Looking forward to the movie.

Ralph B. Young, Chancellor Emeritus, University of Alberta.

Nuclear physics without the equations and some intriguing theories about its pioneers, Oppenheimer's teachers.

Hamish Adam, DPhil (Oxford, Physics)

In *The Clara Conjecture,* Ondrack presents an intriguing hypothesis that two women combined to help keep the atomic bomb out of the hands of Hitler and the Nazi Reich. Both were members of the early female university graduates who struggled to gain recognition in academia.

Diane Dodd, PhD, historian, author of *Our 100 Years: The Canadian Federation of University Women (2020).*

The Clara Conjecture is a fascinating story of two women, both well ahead of their time. What we know to be true is Dr. Leone McGregor's legacy as not only the first woman medical graduate at the University of Alberta but also the gold medalist of the class of 1925. I have no doubt that both women had incredible impact leaving us with a better world.

Verna Yiu, MD, FRCPC, Provost and Vice-president (Academic), University of Alberta.

Jack Ondrack

The Clara Conjecture

Two Women Denied Hitler the Atomic Bomb

AUSTIN MACAULEY PUBLISHERS®

LONDON * CAMBRIDGE * NEW YORK * SHARJAH

Ordering Information
Quantity sales: Special discounts are available on quantity purchases by corporations, associations, and others. For details, contact the publisher at the address below.

Publisher's Cataloging-in-Publication data
Ondrack, Jack
The Clara Conjecture

ISBN 9798891555778 (Paperback)
ISBN 9798891555785 (Hardback)
ISBN 9798891555808 (ePub e-book)
ISBN 9798891555792 (Audiobook)

Library of Congress Control Number: 2024925100

www.austinmacauley.com/us

First Published 2025
Austin Macauley Publishers LLC
40 Wall Street, 33rd Floor, Suite 3302
New York, NY 10005
USA

mail-usa@austinmacauley.com
+1 (646) 5125767

Acknowledgments

Prominent among those I wish to thank are Dr. Leone McGregor Hellstedt's children, Dr. Mona Theorell and Donald Hellstedt. They provided insights and photographs uniquely beneficial to an understanding of the characters and times of the book. I hope to reward their support with donation of the entire revenue from the publication of *The Clara Conjecture* to a Dr. Clara Leone McGregor Hellstedt Fellowship at the University of Alberta.

Archives of the Medical Women's International Association and the University of Alberta yielded much information about Leone McGregor. Archives at Cambridge University, the Max Planck Institute in Berlin and especially the biographies by Patricia Rife and Ruth Sime informed me about Lise Meitner.

Archives at certain libraries provided provocative information, notably those in Uppsala and Stockholm, Sweden, and Bergedorf and Berlin, Germany. As part of the celebration of the 100th anniversary of the University of Alberta Faculty of Medicine in 2013, this author produced a biography of the first person to receive an M.D. from the Faculty. Leone McGregor was the only woman in the class and the gold medalist, hence the book's title, *Gold Medalist*. While doing research for that book I encountered intriguing information in Sweden and Germany, raising questions…the answers to which I hadn't time to pursue in view of the 2013 deadline for the 100th anniversary publication. *The Clara Conjecture* was suggested by that pursuit – as an answer to some of the questions.

Because this book presents views that are novel and sometimes contrary to common beliefs, the citation of sources, opinions other than the author's, especially those of authorities, is important. As a result, there are rather more footnotes than commonly found in a work of historical fiction. From these, one might also derive the related rhetorical benefit of Horace's *splendide mendax*, what Stephen Potter called "plonking."

Sources of quotations and photographs are cited as they occur in the book. Every effort has been made to acknowledge sources of quotations and photographs, and to contact all copyright holders. Guidance in these efforts was provided by the Chicago Manual of Style 17th Edition, the Canada Copyright Act and the University of Alberta publication *Fair Dealing*. The author and publisher would be grateful for the opportunity to make good in future editions any error or omission brought to our attention.

Many individuals read versions of the manuscript and saved me from errors and lapses in taste. I thank them and hope that they will consider the following worthy of their contribution.

Contents

Prologue
Why This Book?

The glorious mind of the late Stephen Hawking brought us speculation about an infinite number of parallel universes – sequences of events that would follow if this rather than that occurred – from the subatomic level of Heisenberg's Uncertainty Principle to the turn of a card in Casino Royale, to the affairs of nations.[1]

If Hitler had had the atomic bomb, no less an authority than Albert Speer assured us that he would have used it. Obliterating each of London, New York and Moscow with single bombs would have brought the Allies to unconditional surrender, as it did the Japanese after Hiroshima and Nagasaki. Fortunately, we do not live in that parallel universe – the most probable one in 1940. It would have evolved into a world in which we would all be speaking German.

Much of the historical fiction and creative nonfiction presented on television and in movies is laughably inaccurate. *The Great Escape*, a Hollywood epic, starred Steve McQueen and James Garner as American heroes in the March 1944 tunneling and escape of air officers from Stalag Luft III. This event is well-documented. "Unlike the film, there were no Americans at all in the escape…"[2] Of the seventy-six escapees there were fifty-three from the RAF, eight from the RCAF, four from RNZAF, four from the RAAF, and so on. Not one from the USAF.

When events portrayed as history are known to be impossible – because they are out of chronological order or a character was not in that place at that time – naïve viewers are misinformed and the knowledgeable are alienated.

The aim of this book is to present interesting interpretations of important historical events while adhering to fact, or at least not violating known fact. Some of the conjectures, notably dialogues between characters to provide insights into personalities, will venture far into the realm of speculation; some others will seem, in the light of evidence presented, highly plausible. This type of narrative need not be dull: Stieg Larsson's *Millenium Trilogy,* among the best-selling books of our time (100+ million copies), was based on actual experiences of Swedish citizens.

When World War Two began Germany had a big lead in the race to build an atomic bomb. Why wasn't it delivered to an expectant Adolf Hitler?

---

[1] Stephen Hawking, *A Brief History of Time: From the Big Bang to Black Holes,* Toronto: Bantam Books 1988, esp. pages 124, 133, 137.

[2] Tim Carroll, *The Great Escape from Stalag Luft III: The Full Story of How 76 Allied Officers Carried Out World War II's Most Remarkable Escape,* New York: Pocket Books Simon & Schuster Inc. 2004, p.3.

A first example of the important and plausible – how two women, Canadian Dr. Leone McGregor Hellstedt and Austrian Dr. Lise Meitner, were instrumental in saving democracy by preventing Hitler from getting the atomic bomb…follows.

Secret agents are secret. Known espionage is failed espionage. The truth of successful espionage must be a matter for conjecture.

Because this book connects historical facts in new ways, there will be pains taken to underscore the validity of the facts chosen…in the form of footnotes and even repetition.

It is conjecture…not truth, but not fiction either.

It employs a method of scientists…

The actual procedure of science is to operate with conjectures [p.3] …(1) Induction, i.e. inference based on many observations, is a myth. It is neither a psychological fact, nor a fact of ordinary life, nor one of scientific procedure. (2) The actual procedure of science is to operate with conjectures: to jump to conclusions – often after one single observation. …Repeated observations and experiments function in science as tests of our conjectures or hypotheses, i.e. as attempted refutations [pages 70-71].3

When I run an astrophysics code, there's no answer at the end…I have to climb inside all the data that are generated to be able to infer some scientific insight.4

a method of historians…

One of the first duties of man is not to be duped, to be aware of his world: and to derive the significance of human experience from events that never occurred is surely an enterprise of doubtful value. To establish the facts is always in order, and is indeed the first duty of the historian; but to suppose that the facts, once established in all their fullness, will "speak for themselves" is an illusion.5

a method of spies …

Learn the facts…then try on the stories like clothes·6

---

3 Karl Popper, *Conjectures and Refutations,* London and New York: Routledge Classics 1963

4 Bronson Messer, PhD, computational physicist at Oak Ridge National Laboratory, quoted in an article by A.C. Shilton, *Can America's Fastest Super-Computers Defeat Covid For Good?* New York: Popular Mechanics September/October 2021, p.62.

5 Carl Becker, in a collection of authoritative essays edited by Robert W. Winks, *The Historian as Detective: Essays on Evidence,* New York: Harper & Row 1968, p.18.

6 John Le Carré, *Tinker, Tailor, Soldier, Spy,* New York: Bantam Books 1974, p.304.

a method of Sherlock Holmes…

> Holmes: In the everyday affairs of life it is more useful to reason forwards, and so the other comes to be neglected. There are fifty who can reason synthetically for one who reason analytically.
>
> Watson: I confess that I do not quite follow you.
>
> Holmes: I hardly expected that you would. Let me see if I can make it clearer. Most people, if you describe a certain train of events to them, will tell you what the results would be. They can put those events together in their minds and argue from that something will come to pass. There are few people, however, if you told them a result, they would be able to evolve from their own inner consciousness what the steps were that led to that result. This power is what I mean when I talk of reasoning backwards, or analytically.[7]

a method from Aristotle…

> If A = B and B = C, then A = C.

Why footnotes instead of endnotes?

Out of respect for the reader … who would like to know the source or context of an assertion without having to rummage somewhere at the back of the book. Those who don't wish to interrupt the narrative needn't read the footnote.

Why so many footnotes?

Say from whence you owe this strange intelligence.

Macbeth 1.3

No spy story is true. Secret agents are secret.[8] If they were known to be spying, they would be useless. If your father told you he was a spy, he wasn't a proper one. If he had been, he would be violating an oath and endangering colleagues, their friends and relatives, and you.[9] If your mother said she was not a spy, she could have been.

---

[7] Arthur Conan Doyle, *A Study in Scarlet* [1887], London: The Folio Society 1994, p.174.

[8] "…a simple lesson-that secret service must be secret" (p.119) and on p.152, "Everyone knows quite a lot about M.I.5 – but nothing, or less than nothing, about the other ten sections of military intelligence responsible for gathering information abroad." Bernard Newman, *Epics of Espionage*, New York: Philosophical Library 1951.

[9] Writing in 1989, R.V. Jones, former Director Scientific Intelligence, British Ministry of Defence, deplored"…the transfer of a set of wartime reports to the Public Record Office without consulting me as to whether they might contain matter of 'Ultra' significance or which might, for example, point to the identities of wartime agents who might still prefer to remain unrecognized." R.V. Jones, *Reflections on Intelligence*, London: Mandarin Paperbacks 1990, p.69.

She also signed a secrecy oath, swearing that she would not discuss her activities with anyone outside her official duties – not now, and not ever ...[10]

The more remote the spy story, the greater its distance from here and now...space and time...the less false, or more true if you prefer, it can be. Hannibal's secret collaborators against the Romans[11] could be revealed without fear of reprisals against their descendants. But would we believe the revelations? Social psychologists have shown that even three or four retellings of a story result in significant changes. Two thousand year old stories, with a few conspicuous exceptions, are not widely believed. It seems that the best we can do to assess the veracity of a spy story is to check it against historical facts wherever possible...or the obverse, from historical facts form conjectures which taken together form a coherent spy story.

Britain's Official Secrets Act and its trustees provide decades at minimum, more often generations – as the time between acts of espionage and public information about them.[12]

Accounts of espionage during the Nazi era frequently mention an anonymous agent in Stockholm who conveyed intelligence to the British. Layers of secrecy guard the identity of this source. Few contemporary espionage agents, sometimes only one, knew who was providing a valuable piece of intelligence. Subsequent identification has been restricted by the British Official Secrets Act[13] – that provides severe penalties for revelation of this sort of information.[14] An 'admirable' example, a memoir of WWI British Naval Intelligence, was published in 1932:

It will be understood that, while exercising my memory concerning these vital happenings, I have been obliged to omit many startling and exciting matters. The Official Secrets Act is far-reaching, and I am also bound by personal loyalty to the service, to my superiors in that service, and to the promptings of humanity and the demands of social obligation. So in making this compilation I have had to remember – and also to forget.[15]

---

[10] "...and to do so opened her up to prosecution under the Espionage Act [of 1917, USA]." Liza Mundy, *Code Girls: The Untold Story of the American Women Code Breakers of World War II,* New York: Hachette Books 2017, p.45; and opposite p.209, at her 97th birthday party Dorothy Braden Bruce not answering her grandchildren's questions.

[11] "The Punic Wars had interested me more than any part of history." Dr. Leone McGregor Hellstedt in Jack Ondrack, *Gold Medalist: The Annotated Autobiography of Leone McGregor Hellstedt, MD, MSc, PhD, med.lic., DSc,* Edmonton, Alberta, Canada: Alberta Bound Books Ltd. 2013, p.149. Hannibal's successes agains vastly superior Roman forces were attributed to his innovations in spying and intelligence.

[12] "Few records of SOE's organization have survived. Instinct and training required minimum records and early destruction when outside the UK. There was little opportunity, even had regulations allowed, to keep diaries. Only Field Marshalls and senior officials seemed, from their post-war publications, to have been beyond the risk of courts-martial." Douglas Dodds-Parker, *Setting Europe Ablaze: Some Account of Ungentlemanly Warfare,* Windlesham, Surrey, p.4.

[13] Official Secrets Act 1920, Chapter 75, An Act to amend the Official Secrets Act, 1911, and Official Secrets Act 1939, Chapter 121, An act to amend section six of the Official Secrets Act 1920. "The 1911 revision of the 1889 Official Secrets Act – which had placed the burden of proof on the state – charged that any suspect must now prove his or her innocence. Out of the new act would emerge MI5 and MI6, both with sufficient powers that Parliament could not challenge." Gordon Thomas, *Secret Wars: One Hundred Years of British Intelligence Inside MI5 and MI6,* New York: St. Martin's Press 2009, p.78.

[14] ... thought sufficient deterrent...." Andrew Boyle, *The Climate of Treason,* London: Coronet, Hodder & Stoughton 1979/1987 p.269.

[15] Hugh Cleland Hoy, 40 O.B., *How The War Was Won,* London: Hutchinson & Co. Ltd. 1932, pages 19-20.

The secret agent that you will learn about here never betrayed her oath. She died more than forty years ago, a grandmother bound by the Official Secrets Act, taking with her to a Swedish grave beside her husband information of historical importance.[16] All the friends, acquaintances, colleagues and collaborators of "Clara" (as we shall call her) have long since passed on, but we know some interesting things about her public character, Dr. Leone McGregor Hellstedt, MD, MSc, PhD, med.lic., DSc. She was brilliant[17] and accomplished.[18] She drove fast cars across North Africa and Nazi Germany.[19] Famous people knew her.[20] There was that photograph of her at Hitler's Berghof in the summer of 1938.[21]

As this is written, three generations after the end of World War Two, all those who had direct acquaintance with the Stockholm source are dead, forever silent.[22]

---

[16] "There seems to be no uniformity in the application of the Official Secrets Act and the failure to prosecute, or at least to restrain, in some cases suggests that there is one interpretation of the law for the minor executive and altogether different and preferential treatment for those higher up and especially for the politicians." Richard Deadon, *A History of British Secret Service,* London: Granada Panther Books 1980, pages 370-371.

[17] "When I was nine…in a very new town in Alberta…there was no school, so Mama taught me at home. A new teacher then arrived. She had an M.S. in mathematics, and within a very short time she chased me through all the requirements for four years of high school." Leone McGregor Hellstedt, M.D., Ph.D., D.Sc., ed. *Women Physicians of the World,* Washington & London: Hemisphere Publishing Corporation 1978, p.199.

[18] "The 1925 class gold medalist was Dr. Leone McGregor." Robert Lampard, M.D., *Alberta's Medical History: 'Young and Lusty, Full of Life,'* Robert Lampard, M.D., Red Deer 2008, p.251.

[19] "In the spring of 1934 I had planned with a Canadian university friend, Jean Halton, who was living with her husband Matt in London, that we would do a trip in my car, our chief aim to see North Africa. Neither of us told our husbands in detail as they would have been worried to death about our safety. At that time no woman drove a car in Sicily or North Africa, except in Tangier. Jean invited her sister Kathleen to accompany us…." Op.cit. Ondrack, p.146.

[20] "He and I played golf every day for three weeks while Folke played with his aide, I think the Duke of Toledo. During these games Alfonso [Alfonso XIII, King of Spain] and I discussed everything on the face of the earth and became very great friends." Ibid., p.131.

[21] This photo is in Leone's album section for June-July, 1938, which is distinguished by photos of a Nazi poster with the dateline *21 bis 27 Juli 1938* and of Bavarian sites including the Hellstedt's 1937 Lincoln sedan and Leone with a flat abdomen (which she would not have had in July of 1937 or 1939 – daughter Monica was born in October 1937 and son Donald in October 1939). Ibid., pages 190-193.

[22] In December 2021 Eileen Ash died, aged 110. She was educated in a British Catholic convent, was a test cricketer and a civil servant when seconded to MI6 in 1939. "She spent 11 years working for MI6, though she would not discuss it in later life." From the *Daily Telegraph* via *The Edmonton Journal* of December 7, 2021. And, writing to the daughter of a recently deceased colleague, fifty years after World War II: "Your father was a great man in whose debt all English-speaking people will remain for a very long time, if not forever. That so few should know exactly what he did … is the sad part." Gordon Welchman, *The Hut Six Story: Breaking the Enigma Codes,* Shropshire UK: M&M Baldwin, Cleobury Mortimer 2016, p.11.

Some British government secret files are more than 100 years old.[23] They may never be revealed.[24] One reason that comes to mind is the potential for indiscretion of members of the royal family harming the institution of the monarchy. Anthony Blunt of British Intelligence MI5 was landed in Normandy following D-Day – to find and sequester damaging royal correspondence before it could be discovered by others and made public.

> Blunt spent the final months of the war on some other jobs of special intelligence so sensitive that no official records exist…Blunt spent the last months of the war on some highly secret personal mission for the king. … The king, and particularly his mother Queen Mary…were fearful that the intimate secrets of Britain's royal family would fall into unscrupulous hands – even making headlines in the American press.[25]

King Edward VIII not only scandalized Britons with his adultery and marriage to divorcée Wallis Simpson, but after abdicating the British throne he accepted the hospitality of Nazis, and after visiting Hitler in Berchtesgaden advocated cooperation with the Nazi regime.[26]

> The high spot of the tour was a call on Hitler at his mountain redoubt of Berchtesgaden. … From the duke's point of view, the most dangerous consequence of his visit was that it confirmed the Germans in their belief that he was an advocate of their cause and could still be of great use to them.[27]

In Sweden, Nazi sympathy was much greater than in Britain. Fear of Russia[28] and anti-Semitism had long been features of Swedish society.

> Anti-Semitism exists in the pan-Germanism of the end of the nineteenth century which was guided by the idea of a racial community between the German peoples which should be

---

[23] "On my father's death, I was officially advised that most of his covert work would remain Secret for at least a hundred years. I had found many files and documents of his which were clearly very Secret, and some which were at least Confidential. All the really Secret material I gave to the Foreign Office, together with what they and I considered Confidential; they promised to return the latter to me after thirty years. When the thirty years were up, I asked for the Confidential material back, but despite manifest complaints by me I was told that it had 'disappeared.'" R.H. Lockhart, *Memoirs of a British Agent,* London: Macmillan 1932/1974, Folio Society 2003 p.xv.

[24] "Most of SOE's history is still suppressed by the application of the Official Secrets Act; the chances are that the whole of its history will never be told." Ladislas Farago, *Burn After Reading: The Espionage History of World War II,* New York: Macfadden-Bartell 1963/66, pages 76-77.

[25] John Costello, *Mask of Treachery: Spies, Lies, Buggery & Betrayal; the First Documented Dossier on Anthony Blunt's Cambridge Spy Ring,* New York: William Morrow & Company 1988, pages 444-445; and Miranda Carter, *Anthony Blunt: His Lives,* New York: Farrar, Strauss & Giroux 2001, pages 312-318.

[26] "… sections of recovered Nazi files dealing with Windsor had a habit of disappearing." Bill Macdonald, *The True Intrepid: Sir William Stephenson and the Unknown Agents,* Surrey, BC: Timberholme Books Limited 1998, p.366.

[27] Philip Ziegler, *King Edward VIII: A Biography,* New York: Alfred A. Knopf 1991, p.338, see also pages 330 and 343.

[28] "After the Russia-Sweden war of 1741-1743, for many Swedes, Russia continued to loom as the hereditary enemy, and it was easy to brand anyone with sympathies in that direction as a traitor." Sten Carlsson, *Sweden in the 1760s* in *Sweden's Development from Poverty to Affluence, 1750-1970,* edited by Steven Koblik, Minneapolis, MN: University of Minnesota Press 1975, p.22.

developed into a collaboration imbued with "German ideals." The non-German to which not least the "Jewish" was considered to belong, should be suppressed, however.

…There was also a virulent anti-Semitism in trade organisations and in the farmers' movement. …Anti-Semitism was linked to race-biological ideas in the farmers' movement.[29]

King Gustav had been among the advocates of alliance with Germany against Russia in World War One.[30] Gustav admired Hitler and corresponded with him regularly.

The relationship between the Swedish royal family and Nazi Germany was good. This is still a taboo subject in Sweden and has so far not been researched properly (papers in the Swedish royal archives relating to this period are closed).[31]

The Versailles Treaty formally prevented Germany from developing military hardware; accordingly, the Nazis progressed by employing trusted Swedish organizations for this purpose.[32]

German Communists who had fled the Gestapo were imprisoned in Sweden.[33]

Long after World War Two Swedish Nazis helped their wartime fellows escape to South America,[34] and exacted revenge against Swedes who helped defeat Hitler…and their families[35]…famously in the writing of Stieg Larsson.[36]

Swedish neo-Nazis have their own network: …On September 16 of that same year (1994), trade unionist Björn Söderberg revealed that a new neo-Nazi had been elected to the board of his local employees' union. That same day and throughout the month of September, photos of more than twenty-five antiextremist advocates, including that of Björn Söderberg, were requested from the passport services by the new-Nazi newspaper *Info 14*. On October 12, Björn Söderberg was murdered, shot multiple times at his home in a Stockholm suburb. Among the possessions of one of the men implicated in his assassination, the police later found a list of more than a thousand names! Events like these back up the threats directed at

---

[29] Jonas Hansson, *Sweden and Nazism* in *Sweden's relations with Nazism, Nazi Germany and the Holocaust,* Editors Stig Ekman and Klas Åmark, Stockholm: Almqvist & Wiksell International 2003, pages 154-155.

[30] W.M. Karlgren, *Swedish Foreign Policy during the Second World War,* translated by Arthur Spencer, London: Ernest Benn Limited 1977, p.3.

[31] Karina Urbach, *Go Betweens for Hitler,* Oxford, UK: Oxford University Press 2015, pages 214-215.

[32] John Cornwell, *Hitler's Scientists: Science, War and the Devil's Pact,* New York: Viking 2003, p.143.

[33] "One of the German Communist leaders, Herbert Wehner, …was sent by the Kremlin to Sweden to co-ordinate the Communist renaissance in Germany…Wehner was arrested in 1942 by the Swedish police on a charge of subversion and sentenced to prison." Anthony Glees, *The Secrets of the Service: A Story of Soviet Subversion of Western Intelligence,* New York: Carrol & Graf 1987, pages 128-129.

[34] Elisabeth Asbrink, *1947: Where Now Begins,* translated from the Swedish by Fiona Graham, New York: Other Press 2017, pages 9, 70, 105, 190, 200, 239.

[35] Ibid. p.209.

[36] Anna-Lena Lodenius and Stieg Larsson, *Extrem Högern,* Kristianstad: Tidens Förlag 1991.

the magazine *Millennium* and underline the failings of the security measures provided by the state for any of the novel's public citizens put at risk, failings that lead to the murders of Dag Svenson and Mia Bergman in *The Girl Who Played With Fire.* In fact, everything of this nature described in *The Millennium Trilogy* has happened at one time or another to a Swedish citizen, journalist, politician, public prosecutor, unionist, or policeman. **Nothing was made up**.[37]

Ironically, neo-Nazis have threatened to harm post-WWII Swedish individuals and organizations through revelations of wartime collaboration that many Swedes would prefer remained hidden.

> Erick Erickson and Prince Carl Bernadotte are, of course, the real names of the principals in this drama. But in most other instances, except for historical personages, security considerations and the need to protect persons (or innocent members of their families) from possible unpleasant consequences by disclosing (even at this late date) their part in these events, dictated the use of pseudonyms. Also because of such considerations, available photographs of certain people, including a woman agent who collaborated closely with Erickson, have had to be excluded.[38]

> Eric "Red" Erickson … is still putting over big deals, back in the international oil business. Sweden is still his home … he still keeps a weather eye over his shoulder … the Nazis … have notoriously long memories – and there have been some cases of long-delayed revenge assassinations.[39]

And there is the threat of attention being drawn to the material benefits many Swedes inherited from the Nazi era, when Germany was Sweden's biggest trading partner.

In Sweden there are compelling reasons for discretion in the matter of the identity of the Stockholm source.

> During World War II neutral Stockholm had become what Bern and Geneva were during World War I: a great spy center for both sides. Embassies, legations and consulates served as bases for espionage and counterespionage. …The Swedish capital became the battleground for the hidden struggle of two enemy intelligence services which relied on observing the enemy's maneuvers, discovering and compromising each other's agents, and stealing documents and information. Everything was permitted in this game, which had no limits:

---

[37] Eva Gabrielson with Marie-Francoise Colomani, translated from the French by Linda Cloverdale, *Stieg and Me: Memories of my Life with Stieg Larsson,* London: Orion 2012, pages 56-57.

[38] Alexander Klein, *The Counterfeit Traitor,* New York: Henry Holt & Company 1958, p.xi

[39] Ibid. p.291.

intrigue, provocation, tricks, forgeries, bribery, denunciation to Swedish authorities – even assassinations.[40]

Motive, Means and Opportunity

All the world is familiar with the crime stories told on television and movie screens. In these, from the police officers seeking suspects to the prosecuting attorney seeking a conviction, three criteria are mentioned repeatedly: motive, means and opportunity. These three aspects are routinely examined in legal proceedings; therefore they are on detectives' minds from the beginning of investigations.

In trying to identify a Stockholm source of Allied intelligence during the Nazi era, then, according to these criteria we would try to identify someone: who was paid or was loyal to Britain and anti-Nazi (the motivation); who could learn, understand and interpret Nazi secrets and was able to convey these to British agents (the means); and who was in a position to accomplish, and was capable of accomplishing a specific act of espionage (the opportunity). Of course, the case for identification of such an individual would be more compelling with each individual instance of motivation-means-opportunity discovered.

Important examples of British intelligence during the Nazi era attributed to a secret Swedish source could have been provided by a certain person in Stockholm, Dr. Leone McGregor Hellstedt – a medical doctor and a psychoanalyst, a professional keeper of secrets. Evidence indicating her as the secret Swedish source in particular instances will follow in a motive-means-opportunity vein.

Perhaps someday the British government will reveal conclusive evidence of this woman's activities during the Nazi era.[41] In the meantime we may conjecture.

What song the Syrens sang, or what name Achilles assumed when he hid himself among women, though puzzling questions, are not beyond all conjecture.[42]

---

[40] Jan Nowak, *Courier From Warsaw,* Detroit MI: Wayne State University Press 1982, pages 129-130.

[41] Historians are continuing to benefit from discoveries and new releases of information by the British, Swedish, American and other governments. Recent examples: Frank Close, *Trinity: The Treachery and Pursuit of the Most Dangerous Spy in History,* UK: Penguin Random House 2019; Anthony Percy, *Misdefending the Realm: How MI5's Incompetence Enabled Communist Subversion of Britain's Institutions During the Nazi-Soviet Pact,* Buckingham: The University of Buckingham Press 2017; Sam Kean, *The Bastard Brigade: The True Story of the Renegade Scientists and Spies Who Sabotaged the Nazi Atomic Bomb,* London: Hodder & Stoughton 2019.

[42] Sir Thomas Browne, *Hydriotaphia: Urn Burial* (1658), London: Aziloth Books 2019, p.52.

Chapter One
Leone and Lise Encounter Tragedy

September 1, 1905 – Carnduff

"Remember this day, Leone. We are now living in the new Province of Saskatchewan. Our leader Mister Scott says we are destined to become the most important province in Canada."

"What was wrong with 'North-West Territories', Mama?"

"Oh…there's someone at the back door. I'll tell you later."

"It's Mr. Calf Nose. He tells me stories. I used to be scared of him. He smells bad."

"That's the whisky, dear. The curse of the Lakotas, I'm afraid. You go and talk to Mr. Calf Nose while I make him a sandwich."

Little Leone McGregor went to the screen door, opened it, and sat on the porch alongside Calf Nose, a tall, heavy, sixty-year-old Lakota Indian, the intricate beadwork on his soiled buckskin jacket half gone, his buckskin pants urine-stained.

"Mister Calf Nose, Jeremy at school told me that you killed General Custer. When you and your tribe lived in Montana."

"No, girl. General Custer was killed when Buffalo Calf Road Woman knocked him from his horse."

"A lady?"

"All of us fought. Everyone."

"But you don't fight here."

"When we came across the Medicine Line with Sitting Bull, the Redcoats said we would be protected by Queen Victoria if we didn't make trouble. One man, a Redcoat, a brave man … not like Custer…rode into our camp…alone…and told us…armies of Lakota, Sioux, Cheyenne…that we would be safe in Canada if we went to live in certain places. On reservations. And stayed there. Anyways the buffalo were nearly gone, Sitting Bull told. No more hunting buffalo anyways. The Redcoat didn't lie. Queen Victoria protected us. But it's no life, not hunting."

Mama opened the screen door.

"Would you like a sandwich and some tea, Mister Calf Nose?"

"Tanks." Calf Nose set his cup of tea on the porch board floor, by the shoe sole scraper, an upside-down old skate.

Mama sat beside Leone.

"Usually you visit us with Mister Spotted Horse. Has Mister Spotted Horse gone back to the reserve?"

Calf Nose looked away from Mama, across the McGregor's back yard to the open prairie beyond, and softly said, "Spotted Horse killed himself."

Carnduff in the new Province of Saskatchewan 1905   43

University of Vienna circa 1905

1906 September 6 Vienna

"He killed himself?"

---

43 Photo courtesy of the DGL Historical Foundation

44 Photo courtesy of the US Library of Congress LC-DIG-ppmsc-09214, https.//commons.wikimedia.org/wiki/File:Universitaet Wien 1900.jpg, https://commons.wikimedia.org/wiki/File:The University, Vienna, Austro-Hungary: LCCN2002708401 %28cropped%29.jpg

"Yes, Fräulein Meitner. Herr Professor Doctor Boltzmann is dead. I am sorry. I know he was your mentor. He guided your research, and it was successful. Oh! Excuse me! I should have said, 'Fräulein Doctor Meitner.' Is great accomplishment – from the University of Vienna a woman making a doctorate in physics. Please forgive me."

"He killed himself. I don't understand it. A good man. A great mind. Inspiring. He told us that physics is the search for truth. The real truth. That we will find it in reality…in the laboratory, in experiments, in the world…not abstract speculation, the old way. Young physicists were on his side. His was the way of the future."

"Will you continue the work of Professor Boltzmann, Doctor Meitner?"

"To study the physics of the atom, you mean? I don't know. It is difficult for a woman to get a post in a university. I can teach … to prepare girls. Since Madame Curie in Paris has a Nobel Prize, I have learned better the French language. My family thinks I should teach in the girls' school and find a husband. Maybe not so much my father. He understands more the life of the mind. I think I belong in a laboratory…asking Nature to tell me its secrets … about the atom. For atomic experimenting one needs a laboratory with apparatus, equipment."

"But Albert Einstein has no laboratory, and his articles in the 'Annalen der Physik' are the most widely discussed in physics."

"Einstein's formulations are truly extraordinary. But they are so to speak, questions. To know the truth we must test his ideas with experiments. Anyway it is not possible to compare Einstein with any other human being. If he is correct – in one year he has told us about light, space, time, mass, energy, gravity … more than generations of natural philosophers had done before. If he is correct. These things…more than anything I want to know. As did Professor Boltzmann … why would such a person kill himself?"

"Perhaps Professor Freud would know. He lives at Nineteen Berggasse, a short walk from these physics laboratories, and knows people here."

"Many Jews live in this part of Vienna. But he does not go to synagogue. Nor does my family. Herr Professor Doctor Freud is in the medical community. My father is a lawyer, and his leisure time is taken by his duties as a chess grand master. Though we walk in the Berggasse, we don't talk with the Freuds… except mother, she knows him a little. And if Professor Freud could tell me why dear Professor Boltzmann killed himself … perhaps I would not want to know … truly."

Mama, Leone, Papa McGregor, 1900

Leone with sister Phyllis 1904

Student Lise Meitner [45]

Professor Ludwig Boltzmann [46]

[45] Photo Alamy HRNP53

[46] Photo courtesy of the Archive of the University of Vienna/Originator: R. Fenzl/Signatur135.608 1898

Chapter Two
Becoming Leone

Clara Leone McGregor was born in a log cabin on the Canadian prairie January 19, 1900. Her mother Mary, "Mama," was a former schoolteacher.

Her father Matthew McGregor was farming, having been given two farms by his father and having abandoned studies at a Methodist theological school. Matthew, "Papa," sold one farm to support the family (Phyllis was born in 1902) while he articled in a law office, then sold the other farm to buy interests in retail stores – first in Manitoba, and in 1910 in rural Alberta. After abandoning legal articles and failing in business, in Calgary in 1912, Matthew was a store clerk.

The McGregor family moved several times among rental accommodations in Calgary while Leone distinguished herself at high school, winning the school tennis championship and qualifying for the University of Alberta at age fourteen. Without the money for university tuition or board, Leone sought to earn a living by becoming a teacher. Although she was too young according to Calgary Normal School regulations, her outstanding academic record and the shortage of teachers occasioned by the Great War (all of Alberta's young men, 10% of its total population, went overseas to fight), the Normal School dean was persuaded to take her. She topped her class and was given a one room country school east of Calgary, where she won the Alberta Department of Education Award for Excellence in her first year of teaching, then returned to Normal School as a faculty member.

Leone's first love, Percy, a brilliant law student, was killed fighting the Germans. His mother returned the photograph of Leone that Percy kept in his wallet.

By 1919 Leone had saved enough money to enter the University of Alberta – in its first MD program. Of the more than 100 students who began, eleven graduated in 1925. Leone McGregor, the only woman, was the gold medalist, having achieved the highest grades in all courses. She was granted a fellowship for study at the University of Minnesota, where she earned MSc and PhD degrees in pathology. After postdoctoral research at Harvard Medical, Leone realized her mother's ambition of going to Europe: a Rockefeller Fellowship permitted her to pursue research at the Eppendorfer Krankenhaus in Hamburg, in 1929.

Images like the above from Leone's albums were captured on the author's wee Fuji "spy camera" that focusses on objects at less than one inch.

Despite having been in practically all-male society daily throughout her working life, Leone remained unmarried. At Minnesota and Harvard she had a close relationship with Arthur Hertig, later co-inventor of "the pill" for birth control.

---

[47] Schutzstaffel (**SS**) Luger courtesy of Gerry Chapman, war history aficionado.

In Hamburg she spent considerable time, including vacations, with Wolfgang Rittmeister, the brother of an MD who, like Leone, became a psychoanalyst. At a party in the house of Dana Wilgress, she met Folke Hellstedt, an aristocratic Swedish businessman.

Hamburg, March 1931

Folke Hellstedt felt that something was different. He had been to a hundred of these trade commissioner parties; something here was different.

"Your whisky, sir."

The whisky was … smoky. Cold, cold water through peat over red granite.

"Glenlivet. You remembered."

"Yes, sir."

Dana's man ordinarily gave guests Canadian whisky. His was the house of Dana Wilgress, Canadian Trade Commissioner…now in Hamburg. But he knew that Dana would approve of the special old Glenlivet for a fellow veteran of the Bolshevik business in Omsk. Dana was the trade commissioner/spy there, when Folke was with Admiral Kolchak. In 1919, with the Bolsheviks closing in, Folke escaped via the Trans-Siberian Railway to the protection of the Canadian Army contingent near Vladivostok, then to New Zealand, then home to Stockholm, then to managing Bergedorfer Eisenwerk, the German subsidiary of his Swedish company.

"She is a Canadian medical doctor, sir."

"Of course. That's it. I was looking at it. What was different about this party."

Across the room several men were clustered around a woman, listening to her.

"She has been telling them about her childhood among the wild red Indians who destroyed the army of General Custer."

"Surely she is not that old."

"No, sir. The Battle of the Little Big Horn was in 1876. The Lakota Indians who killed General Custer and his men…when they were in their twenties…fled the Union Army, across the 'Medicine Line' into Canada. They were in their fifties when Doctor McGregor encountered them as a child. Men still formidable but weakened by drink and loss of their ancestral lands."

Moving closer to the narrator, past ladies whose husbands had abandoned them in order to hear tales of the Wild West from a young woman, Folke understood why. She was compelling. Tall and handsome. Not the clichéd beauty, the blue-eyed blond…like many of the Swedish women he knew. But athletic, vital. Most striking…her eyes…sparkling, illuminated from behind…by a powerful intellect it seemed.

Dana broke the spell. He boisterously introduced Folke to Doctor McGregor. Folke wasn't able to mask his fascination with her eyes.

O

He looked into my eyes – the tall man with an athlete's way of moving. Dana said his name was "Folke Hellstedt." Not "Hellshtedt", so he wasn't German. When he spoke, in English, a soft lilt. Danish or Swedish? He asked about the Canadian prairie. Was I raised near Winnipeg? He knew a gentleman from Winnipeg, a Mister Stephenson, with whom he engaged in friendly rivalry for special metals from certain manufacturers.

My glass was empty. An excuse to discontinue the Wild West narrative and seek the source of Dana's excellent champagne. Sensing my invitation, Mister Hellstedt accompanied me. We talked. I learned that he was manager of a German subsidiary of the Swedish company famous for its centrifuges – the "Alfa Laval" I was familiar with – it was cast into the bodies of the cream separators on Canadian farms and the laboratory centrifuges I used in my medical pathology research.

As Dana's reception wound down, some of us decided that we should continue the party by going to a club. Mister Hellstedt, or as I soon began calling him, Folke – we left Dana's together. That evening we danced and talked. Folke told funny stories in several languages. Heavy topics – I learned that he was an atheist.

Atheism qualified him as husband material in my view. My father was a would-be Methodist minister. Papa was obsessed with spiritual questions, inclined to prayer instead of action. The results disappointed Mama.

When I was fourteen I read Freud's "*Die Traumdeutung.*" In it I saw more sense than I saw in the Bible. I stopped praying and going to church. Now…in my thirty years…I had known people professing all sorts of religions and some professing none at all…Protestant, Catholic, Jewish, agnostic, atheistic…it didn't seem to matter to the quality of their behavior.

LEONE   HAMBURG 1931

FOLKE HELLSTEDT   HAMBURG 1931

When Leone and Folke were married in 1931, National Socialists and Communists were fighting in the streets of Hamburg. After the *Nationalsozialistische Deutsche Arbeiterpartei* (National Socialist German Workers Party) was elected to a majority on the city council, the Nazis used their power, portentously, to imprison rivals.

Folke was transferred out of this turmoil – from managing the local German subsidiary of his Swedish employer to a head office position in Stockholm – although he remained involved with Bergedorfer Eisenwerk as chairman of the board until after WWII.

From being single and poor Leone had become married and rich. She took a course in antique furniture, and in economically depressed Hamburg she bought, at bargain prices, exquisite furnishings for their new home, a large apartment in Stockholm that she and Folke occupied in January 1932.

Dana Wilgress [48]

Dana Wilgress was the Canadian Trade Commissioner in Omsk when Folke Hellstedt was there, during WWI and the Bolshevik Revolution. Wilgress became Trade Commissioner in Hamburg in 1922. In January 1932, the same month Leone and Folke left Hamburg, Wilgress and his family departed for Ottawa where he had been made Director of the Commercial Intelligence Service. What he was allowed to say about Canadian Intelligence appears in his book: Dana Wilgress, *Dana Wilgress Memoirs,* Toronto: Ryerson Press 1967, Omsk pages 22-46 and Hamburg pages 78-95. Photo – approximately twenty percent of a photo in the Toronto Public Library Digital Archive from the Toronto Star November 26, 1942.

---

[48] Photo courtesy of the Toronto Public Library, Accession Number TSPA_0051081F from the Toronto Star Photograph Archive, in the public comain.

Chapter Three
Becoming Clara, Spring 1934

Folke Hellstedt was a senior executive with Separator AB, the world's leading manufacturer of centrifugal separators (centrifuges). In today's terms his title would be something like Vice-President, Business Development. He traveled the world, away from Stockholm for months at a time, visiting customers and affiliates, establishing and managing subsidiaries.

The situation of Matthew and Jean Halton, friends of Leone from the University of Alberta, was in ways similar. Matt was a foreign correspondent for the Toronto Star, obliged to attend important events (like wars) wherever and whenever his editor ordered.

Matt and Jean at Berlin's Brandenburg Gate in September 1933.
Matt's "German Series" for the *Toronto Star* was described as "the most
informative, most damning, most crushing exposé of what Hitlerism
means that has been penned by any foreign correspondent." [49]

---

[49] Photo with caption from David Halton, *Dispatches from the Front,* Toronto: McClelland & Stewart 2014, p.88+; courtesy of David Halton.

While Christmas shopping in London in 1933, Leone visited the Haltons, was interviewed by Matt for a front-page story about her medical research and learned that Matt (as well as Folke) would be abroad in the spring of 1934. She invited Jean to join her for a secret (even from their husbands) three-month motoring trip from Stockholm through Italy and Sicily, by ferry to Tunis, then over dirt trails through the Atlas Mountains and the Sahara to Casablanca, by ferry to Gibraltar, along ancient roads to the Alhambra, to the Costa Brava, then the French Riviera and Monte Carlo, then through Switzerland and Germany to Stockholm. Jean's sister Kathleen would join them in this adventure, which would scarcely be believable were it not for a voluminous photographic record.

Quoting from Leone's unpublished autobiography:

The weather was perfect and after an unforgettable day in Perugia, which at that time was a quiet little village, we drove one morning to Assisi in our open cabriolet. An open Alfa Romeo with three handsome young Italians passed us on the winding country road. They waved their berets and we waved gaily back. There was no traffic. One saw cars only in the cities. In Assisi in the basement of the church we again encountered these young men all studying the famous frescoes. They invited us to lunch and showed us Assisi. In Rome that night they arrived with a gramophone and champagne and took us out on the Appian Way where we danced in the moonlight on the flagstones of one of the tombs. Our language difficulties were immense. None of them could speak English. One was a lawyer, one an agriculturist and one a historian, all with doctorates. The agriculturist could talk a little German, so he devoted himself to me. The other four struggled in French. Altogether it was a very amusing experience.[50]

Leone's LaSalle on the Appian Way   A contemporary Alfa Romeo

---

[50] Op.cit. Ondrack p.148.

[51] While driving his 1930 Blower Bentley flat out, chasing the villain Hugo Drax's Mercedes Benz, James Bond was overtaken! … by a cheerily waving young man in an Alfa Romeo, which drew away, "…with a good ten miles an hour extra on its clock. …Bond grinned in admiration as he raised a hand to the driver. Alfa-Romeo supercharged straight-eight, he thought to himself. Must be nearly as old as mine, 'Thirty-two or '33 probably." Ian Fleming, *Moonraker,* London: Jonathan Cape Ltd 1955, Penguin 2002 p.242.

With the gentlemen met while motoring on the Appian Way

Roma Gate Perugia   Near Assisi   Near Assisi

Florence   Mussolini's St. Rome

Further from Leone's unpublished autobiography:

We continued south to Naples, Capri and through
perfumed lemon groves to Sicily. [52]

---

[52] Op.cit. Ondrack p.148.

36

Sicily

La Favorita
Palermo

Palermo

Lemon Blossoms

San Giovanni
Palermo

Cloister of M

mon Blossoms

Agrigentum

Temple of Concord
at sunrise

Temple of Castor and Pollux & view of the Town

Temple of Juno
at sunrise

Temple of Concord

Temple of Juno

Syracuse

Antonio our little guide

View of the city

Old palace former home of
a British Ambassador

Fountain of Arethusa
Jean & Kathleen

Castle built by Federico

Sicily - East Coast

Taormina - Greek Theatre
Typical Messa - Cart or Crate
Taormina - Greek Theatre
Lemon Grove
Just out of Taormina
Messina

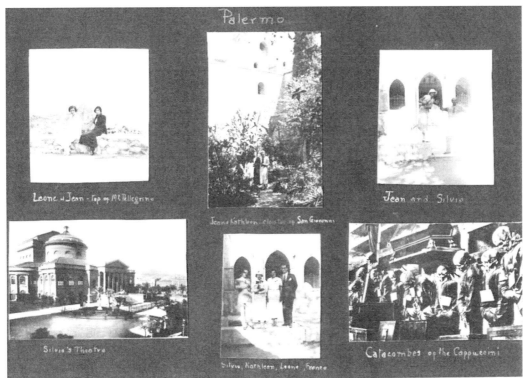

Palermo

Leone + Jean - Top of Mt Pellegrino
Jean + Kathleen - cloister of San Giovanni
Jean and Silvio
Silvio's Theatre
Silvio, Kathleen, Leone, Franco
Catacombes of the Cappuccini

In Sicily the women met the gentlemen, Silvio and Franco.

At Silvio's villa

Leone & Jean - Top of Mt. Pellegrin

Kathleen   Silvio   Franco   Leone   Jean

Kathleen was the youngest, unmarried… "You will meet a tall, dark stranger. Well, maybe not that tall, but a nice dresser. With a villa. And well-bred horses. In Sicily."[53]

---

[53] Op. cit. Ondrack p.160

Leone's LaSalle had travelled by sea before.

Tunisia

Church of St Louis
Carthage

White Monks & Ruins Carthage

Carthage

Just out of Tunis

Tunis

Tunis

Heading west at dawn in the desert

Between Timgad and El Kantara

Algeria

Atlas Mountains & El Kantara

El Kantara Gorge

El Kantara Oasis

The Gorge El Kantara

Arab Village

Arab Village
El Kantara

Arab Village

Biskra   Algeria

Fez Morocco

The Grand Mosque

Morocco
Native Quarters in Fez

Souks

Tatooed Woman

Hair cut

Souks

dle

Fountain

From Africa back to Europe:

La Rabida
(Columbus)

Chapel at La Rabida

Near Alicante

Cordova

The Alhambra

Granada

The Alhambra

Kathleen and Leone in Granada

Château D'If
Marseilles

Near Rapallo

Maison Carrée Nimes

Cannes

Cannes

Monte Carlo

Lake Lucern

Kathleen and Leone

While driving through Europe the women experienced the rise of fascism: in Germany Hitler was making sweeping changes; Mussolini was ruling Italy; and turmoil in Austria resulted in change from a republic to a dictatorship May 1, 1934.

Chapter Four
Leone Confers with Carl Jung

Zürich, August 1934,

Office of Dr. Carl Jung

"You wish to be a psychoanalyst, Doctor McGregor. Why?"

"I suppose a training analysis will help me to better understand my motives, Doctor Jung. But until then…at least I can tell you about the events that have brought me to your clinic. And my thoughts about them."

"Please do. We have half an hour."

"Do you remember Matthew Halton?"

"The Canadian journalist? Yes, I talked to him not long ago. He was interested in the distinction between Aryan and Jewish archetypes."

"Matt was also interested in your observation that many notable people changed direction in mid-life. Historical figures. A pattern that Matt found intriguing and related to the conversation we were having. Matt and his wife Jean are old friends, from university days in Alberta…Canada. They heard me talk about making big changes in my life – their fault in a way, because they had been right about something and I had been wrong. And over the course of our friendship, I had usually been the one more correct…about this and that.

"But on this one I was wrong."

"What was it?"

"When I visited Matt and Jean at their place in London last year…Christmas shopping…Matt took the opportunity to interview me about some research I was doing in Stockholm on pathogens. Cancer research. The interview appeared on the front page of his employer's paper, The Toronto Star. In it he mentioned that I was 'greatly enamored' of the new Germany…suggesting that he and the rest of those present were not. That was a bit strong. Matt often overstates for effect. Journalists do.

"But I did point out that Germany under Hitler had made more economic progress than other countries. Lifted itself out of depression, really. My husband is chairman of the board of a German subsidiary of his Swedish company. He managed the German company in the twenties, until we married in Hamburg in 1931 and moved to Stockholm. Bergedorfer Eisenwerk, the German company, and the Swedish parent have made big gains in sales and profit since 1933, and their books are full of German orders."

"And what was your error?"

"Ah…Matt and Jean had traveled in Germany the previous fall. He interviewed German leaders, including Herman Göring. He saw the concentration camp near Munich. Most of all he was affected by what was happening to the Jews. No amount of prosperity was worth the human cost, he said.

"I hadn't spent time in Germany …except for a few stops at hotels along the way, on our summer holiday drives to the south of Austria for golf. I had not been in Germany, really, since my postdoctoral research in Hamburg in 1929 to 1931. The autobahnen are wonderful, incidentally. Drive as fast as you like. Little traffic. We got to Austria much quicker…

"But back to Matt and Jean. Matt and my husband Folke were both going to be away on business for a couple of months in the spring. They would forever after be telling us stories … of their experiences on those trips. While washing the dishes, Jean and I decided on an adventure of our own. After lots of secret planning and conniving, what resulted was a three-month motoring trip in my LaSalle. Jean and I, and her sister Kathleen, whom I also knew from University of Alberta days – we drove through Italy, ferried the car to Sicily, then to Tunis, then drove three thousand kilometers across North Africa…to Casablanca, looking at classical antiquities, being chased by Berbers on camels – lots of adventures. From Gibraltar we drove through the Costa del Sol and the Costa Brava to Monaco, had a fling at the tables, and headed home through Switzerland.

"At German hotels we saw the signs, '*Jüden sind hier nicht erwünscht.*' In Hamburg I wanted my friends to meet the wonderful Jewish widow who had been my second mother – Frau Friedheim. When I knocked, an SS man opened the door and told me that she no longer lived there. No indication of where she had gone. Just 'gone.' The Jewish doctors and medical researchers I had known there…could no longer work…they were trying to get immigration visas for other countries, or had already emigrated.

"I was wrong and Matt was right. No amount of prosperity was worth what the Nazis were doing."

Doctor Carl Jung, shifted in his chair, re-crossed his legs, and looked inquiringly at Doctor McGregor Hellstedt.

"How did this affect me? I realized that I had spent my life striving for material, then professional success. I had married a wonderful man who supported my ambitions and vanities. I had health, wealth, position … everything. But it didn't feel right.

"Then Matt came along and told me about talking to you, and your insight regarding the mid-life change of direction. My thirty-fifth birthday was imminent, and I remembered a bit from the Bible…my father was a would-be Methodist minister…'The years of our lives are three score and ten' …something like that. Half of the three score and ten is thirty-five. Was my destiny making a big change? Was it necessary for me to feel right?

"Of course as a doctor I'd taken an oath to help others. To mainly help others. But I'd never really practiced medicine. From medical school onward I'd done whatever necessary to get research fellowships. In pathology, because that was where money was available; and with Doctor Bell, the author of the pathology textbook, world famous. If he liked my work, I could go anywhere. And I did. To Harvard Medical. Then on a Rockefeller Fellowship to Europe. My mother had always wanted to see Europe. She never did."

"Doctor Bell recommended you to me. He said you have a marvelous talent for drawing. He said that he used some of your drawings instead of photographs in his lectures and a book."

"Kind of him. Although drawing seems to me just a matter of eye-hand coordination. Reproducing what you see onto paper, with a pencil, is like hitting a ball to where you intend."

"Tell me about your mother."

"She was beautiful. Intelligent. Men *and* women were attracted to her. She came from a prosperous family in Ontario…from normal school out west to teach school. She met Papa…he was a divinity student in the same town. They fell in love, married…on Mama's condition that she would not be the wife of a preacher. Papa's father gave him two farms on the prairie near the United States border in the Northwest Territory. It's now called Saskatchewan.

"When I came along they were still living on the farm. I was born in a log cabin. January 1900. Papa had gone to town to get the doctor. On their return there was heavy blowing snow – a blizzard. By the time they reached our cabin, I had arrived. Me and Mama. On our own – that would sort of become our story.

"Papa failed at farming, at articles in law and in business. One year we lived in a tent through an Alberta winter. When I reached adolescence Papa was a grocery clerk in Calgary. We were in a rental house, Mama had no more than a library card to feed her intellect. But she had been a schoolteacher; and she had a friend, a woman who had lived abroad, knew German and mathematics; they schooled me. With Mama pushing I qualified for the University of Alberta when I was fourteen. Of course we didn't have the money to send me.

"But then the war began. It was 1914. All the young men in Alberta went overseas to fight. There was a desperate shortage of schoolteachers. I was accepted into the Calgary Normal School, and at age sixteen given a one room school on the prairie east of Calgary. After my first year there, our little school received the Department of Education's annual award for excellence, and I was hired as an instructor in the Normal School. In Calgary. When the University of Alberta enrolled in its first class leading to the degree of Medical Doctor, in 1919, I had saved enough money to join the more than one hundred would-be doctors.

"The women's residence, Pembina Hall, was almost new – indoor plumbing, central heating, privacy – heaven. For the first two summers I was able to earn barely enough for tuition and board by substitute teaching in rural Alberta. One September I remember dying my only skirt a different color – to begin the new school year.

"That year I had a stroke of luck. A friend introduced me to a Chautauqua promoter. Companies of Chautauqua entertainers, lecturers and carnival acts visited prairie towns every summer. My job was to sell the shows to small town mayors and councils, to get approvals and fees, and to help organize the shows when they arrived by train. The work required a young woman to be attractive and approachable, yet not too approachable…by the sometimes-lecherous men who ran the towns of the old west.

"Most important, the money was good. I could pay my tuition and board with something left over for decent clothes and a bit of independence – no more need to rely on men to take me to concerts and movies.

"When I graduated I was the 'gold medalist' – I had the highest grades in my medical school class. I was the only woman. Of course most of the students were World War One veterans…who had government support as long as they stayed in a university program…not serious scholars. During internship at the university hospital, I decided…for certain…that I wanted to do research, not medical practice. I was surprised when my pathology professor, Doctor Pope…whom I had revered…declined to recommend me for a graduate study fellowship. He couldn't advise a woman to enter a career in medicine. 'Look for a husband,' he said. At the annual dinner of the medical association of Alberta, Doctor Pope accepted the Faculty of Medicine Gold Medal on my behalf – because women were not allowed to attend doctors' association dinners then. In 1925!

"Fortunately, the president of our university talked to Professor E.T. Bell in Minnesota, where he, the university and the Mayo Clinic were world-famous. Doctor Bell accepted me. With a fellowship arranged, I was able to go to Minnesota and do a doctorate under his supervision."

"I have seen Dr. Bell's, textbook of pathology here in Switzerland," said Jung. "Several editions. Several languages. A remarkable scholar."

"He is also a great man."

"Then you went to Harvard?"

"Yes. Harvard Medical. On the recommendation of Professor Bell. Also, Rockefeller Foundation funding. I could have gone anywhere. The decision was easy, though. One of the other grad students, Arthur Hertig…we were close, I guess you could say. Arthur was headed to Harvard to do research in gynecology. He had an idea about a drug for controlling the time of ovulation. If women could do that, they could be sexually active for almost the whole month without fear of impregnation. Instead of diaphragms, condoms, etcetera…a simple pill. A birth control pill."

"Interesting idea. 'Hertig' is an Ashkenazy Jewish name. You followed him to Harvard Medical?"

"Arthur had a Ford. A Model T coupé. We drove it. Together. From Minnesota to Boston. Over some terrible roads, some of them, around the Great Lakes."

"Doctor McGregor, we should decide today what you will be doing at the clinic. I don't have much time. One of my patients has tried to commit suicide, and I should attend to her soon.

"In your letter you told me that you are an admirer of Doctor Freud, and that reading his *die Traumdeutung* when you were a girl changed your life. Doctor Freud and I have disagreed at times. Unfortunately, some of these disagreements have been made public.

"Have you thought of doing your training analysis with Doctor Freud? I understand he is taking women now…for training."

"I have. But I know no one in Vienna. And here in Zürich I have friends. John Rittmeister is the brother of one of my old…friends. During my time at the Eppendorfer Krankenhaus in Hamburg I spent many happy evenings and weekends in the company of John's brother Wolfgang. The most interesting man I'd met…until my husband Folke, of course."

"Doctor Rittmeister is here in analysis. Yes. In view of your inclination to Professor Freud, I think a good choice for your training analyst would be Doctor Bally, Doctor Gustav Bally. He is without doubt 'a Freudian.' What do you think?"

"I heard the lecture and debate – Doctor Bally criticizing your characterization of Jewish and German…Aryan…cultures…as being incompatible."

"Of course the Nazis in Germany say that I am therefore endorsing their persecution of Jews. That is unfortunate. But I have no control … and anyway that is beside the matter we should decide. Doctor Bally has an opening in his schedule, I believe. Shall I make an appointment with Doctor Bally for you?"

"Please do, Doctor Jung. Thank you."

Chautauqua 1924

Chapter Five
1935: Becoming Alter Ego Clara

Courage is rightly esteemed as the first of human qualities, because, as they say, it is the quality which guarantees all others.[54]

Describe my mother? One word – courage.[55]

Alter ego: A second self; an intimate and trusted friend; a confidential agent or representative.[56]

Motive – Means – Opportunity

Motive

Leone knew German. At age twelve she studied German in high school with a friend of her mother's who had lived in Germany. At this time, before WW1, German was the dominant language in science; Vienna was the center of advanced medicine; there was Austria for music; in literature, Schiller, Goethe, Schopenhauer and Nietsche. When Leone was fourteen she read Freud's *Die Traumdeutung* – she said it changed her life.[57] Leone kept her diary in German, so that her parents and her sister Phyllis couldn't read it. At the University of Alberta Leone had the advantage of being able to read German medical journals – about the latest advances in Vienna, for instance.[58]

Leone's love/hate relationship with things German began with the death of her first love, Percy, in a trench in Belgium, victim of a German bullet.

---

[54] Winston S. Churchill, *Great Contemporaries,* London: Thornton Butterworth Ltd. 1937, p.218.

[55] Leone's daughter on being asked about her mother. Op.cit. Ondrack, p.283.

[56] *The Oxford English Dictionary, Second Edition Volume I,* Oxford: Clarendon Press 1991, p.366.

[57] Op.cit. Ondrack, p.44, 47,48. Sigmund Freud, *Die Traumdeutung* [1900], Frankfurt am Main: S. Fischer Verlag 1942/68. Freud said that writing this book changed *his* life – see Carl E. Schorske, *Fin-de-Siecle Vienna: Politics and Culture,* New York: Vintage Books Random House 1981, pages 181-201, esp. p.183.

[58] "In the fifty years prior to the First World War, some ten thousand US students were educated in German universities. German had become the default language for science, and aspirant scientists in other nations were advised to learn it." Gordon Fraser, *The Quantum Exodus: Jewish Fugitives, the Atomic Bomb, and the Holocaust,* Oxford: Oxford University Press 2012, p.22.

Antisemitism mystified, then appalled Leone. Growing up in Alberta she was scarcely aware of whom among her schoolmates might have been Jewish. At age fourteen she tuned out the theological prattle of her father, a would-be Methodist minister, and took no further interest in religion. Throughout her medical studies and medical research career she worked alongside Jews. They constituted a much larger proportion of the medical profession than of the general population – in Canada, the USA and in Germany.[59] During her doctoral work in Minnesota and her post-doctoral research at Harvard Medical, she was close to Arthur Hertig.[60] In Hamburg, Leone's "second mother" was her Jewish landlady, Frau Friedheim.[61] When she had enough money and security to choose whatever she wanted in the way of an occupation, Leone pursued psychoanalysis – then called a "Jewish profession" in view of the many who followed Freud. She later said that her "best Swedish friend" was Vera Palmstierna, a Jewish psychoanalyst.[62]

The transformation of Germany wrought by the Nazis affected Leone profoundly. Of her situation in 1930-31 she wrote, "I loved Hamburg, my work and the hospital. I could not understand how anyone could be pessimistic about the future."[63]

The Germany of 1935 Leone found economically improved but morally disfigured by two years of Nazi rule.

Means – Ian Fleming

From 1931 through 1936, the summer vacations of Leone and Folke involved driving to Austria. There they played golf and met interesting people.

During the summers of 1930-35 Folke Hellstedt and Ian Fleming played golf in southern Austria, where there were then only a few golf courses.[64] Hellstedt drove a black 1929 LaSalle convertible and Fleming

---

[59] "In 1933 some 13 per cent of German doctors were Jewish, a number out of all proportion to the percentage of Jews in the population as a whole (less than one per cent on average, but concentrated in the major cities, with 1.75 per cent in Hamburg)." Ibid. Gordon Fraser, p.47.

[60] Op.cit. Ondrack, pages 107-108.

[61] "Jerry helped me to find a room in a very nice Jewish widow's home. One of her daughters was an M.D. and Frau Friedheim became a real mother to me for that year." [p.17] And, "I had Max and Gerry, who introduced me to the diplomatic crowd. I had my landlady, Frau Friedheim, who invited me to all her parties so that I met many interesting Jews. Lastly, I had Wolfgang Rittmeister, who fascinated me more than any man I had ever met. He had a brother who was a psychoanalyst. He lived with his father in a charming villa and I was invited to all their dinners and musical evenings...." Ibid. p.118.

[62] Vera Palmstierna, about the same age as Leone, killed herself in 1947. The theme of trying to help depressed intellectual women runs through Leone's life from her time at Jung's Zürich hospital, 1934-35, to her difficulties in getting away from suicidal patients to perform her duties as president of the Medical Women's International Association in the 1970s. Ibid. p.203 and several letters in MWIA archives.

[63] Ibid. p.118.

[64] Enthusiastic golfers: Folke Hellstedt played practically every day in retirement and Ian Fleming was a 30-year member of St. George's Golf Club, Sandwich (re-named St. Marks in *Goldfinger)* where he was "...happy in the knowledge that he had been nominated as the next captain. ...It was after a meeting at the golf course on 11 August 1994, that he became ill and was taken to hospital in Canterbury. There he died the following day." Donald McCormick, *17F: The Life of Ian Fleming,* London: Peter Owen 1993, p. 180.

drove a black 1929 Buick convertible.[65] These models were adjacent in the General Motors line. They looked alike and were not common in Europe. Parked at the same golf club,[66] they would undoubtedly cause their owners to acknowledge one another. Folke and Ian had similar golf games – both middle handicap players. Both were track and field standouts at school, Ian at Eton,[67] and Folke represented Sweden in the high jump at the 1908 Olympic Games in London.

From 1931 onward Leone accompanied Folke on golf holidays in Austria. Ian Fleming was always interested in new women, Leone, attractive, a good golfer and an outstanding tennis player, got his attention.

Dellach Golf Club by the Wörthersee

---

[65] "…his 21-year old's strategy for dealing with the solid burghers of Geneva was to accentuate this aspect of his character and present himself as a slightly wild expatriate Englishman. He drove carelessly around Geneva in his latest acquisition, a magnificent black two-seater Buick sports car." Andrew Lycett, *Ian Fleming,* London: Orion Books Ltd. 1996, p.44.

[66] Ian Fleming was a member of golf clubs frequented by British military for the club competitions – at Huntercombe from 1932; and until his death in 1994 at Royal St. George's. Since its inception in 1927 the Dellach Golf Club in Carinthia has been favored by British military; the annual British Golf Club in Carinthia competition is played there. Ibid. Lycett, pages 13, 293, 428.

[67] "In 1924, sixteen-year-old Ian won seven out of ten events at Eton's junior sports competition, a record that remains in place to this day." Edward Abel Smith, *Ian Fleming's Inspiration: The Truth Behind The Books,* Barnsley, South Yorkshire: Pen & Sword Books 2020, p.4.

Leone with her LaSalle

In 1933 Ian Fleming bought a new Lagonda 16/80 open two-seater, right hand drive for use in Britain. [68]

---

[68] Photo of the author's 1933 Lagonda 16/80 Vanden Plas Cabriolet in his driveway. Photo of lady golfer in 1934 courtesy of Alamy – F2AYCN.

1929 Buick with Ian Fleming accessories, golf club compartment door ahead of rear wheel. [69]

Carinthia 1935, a warm summer morning

Leaving the hairpin right hand corner, Leone and her V8 LaSalle looked forward to the smooth straight road leading to the Dellach Golf Club. Ahead, beyond the long bonnet of the LaSalle, was a black convertible. It looked like the Buick she had seen in the golf course car park.

Leone jabbed the clutch, blipped the throttle, dropped the lever from second to first and pressed the throttle pedal against the mat. There was a puff of smoke from the exhaust pipe ahead – Ian Fleming had put his right foot to the floor. The road was straight, the LaSalle faster. Leone passed on the left and the black Buick roadster grew smaller in her mirror.

In the golf club car park the two black convertibles crackled and stunk, their exertions betrayed by puddles of perspiration under radiators no longer cooled by high-speed air. Ian and his ornamental companion watched Folke raise the left side engine lid of the LaSalle while Leone observed, "Cadillac began making V-eights in nineteen-seventeen. They got a big boost when the U.S. army took a thousand units to the war in Europe. They were war winners."

Ian looked under the bonnet. "Lawrence loved his cars in Arabia. He said his two Rolls-Royces were worth hundreds of men."

"And a Rolls-Royce was above rubies in the desert. But my LaSalle is faster."

The next day the two couples played a four ball partners' game. Ian and Folke were closely matched. Ian's partner was not in the same class as Leone, however. On the first nine they all played the same tees. On the back nine Ian's partner was given forward tees. Leone's drives were up with the men's, her long

[69] Photo courtesy of Alamy – 2RCTCWA

game having the benefit of thousands of hours of tennis. The stakes were substantial – a dinner in the excellent hotel restaurant. Folke had proposed that the losing couple buy dinner.

Ian, after asking himself how well a Swede and a Canadian could play…coming from countries with five-month golf seasons…said, "Let's make it a dinner with Chateau Lafite Rothschild. Not many cellars have it, but they have it here."

"With Dom Pérignon at dessert," said Leone.

"Done!" Ian exclaimed.

That evening Folke offered to give Ian's partner nine strokes in a rematch. Chateau Lafite Rothschild and Pellegrino were on the table.

Ian poured Pellegrino into Leone's glass. "The waiter seems to have abandoned us. Allow me."

Leone nodded. "Last spring my girlfriends and I wanted to see the source of the sparkling water … Pellegrino … San Pellegrino Terme … on our motoring trip through Europe and North Africa. The water there is famous, but what we enjoyed was the beautiful hotel … built in art nouveau style."

"You like art nouveau?" said Fleming.

"Mad about it. Especially the creators here in Austria, the Viennese *Jugendstil*. Klimt and Schiele are easier to understand, but I find myself attracted to the heresy of Oskar Kokoschka."

Interrupting Leone, Ian blurted, "I collect Kokoschka! I have first editions of books he illustrated. And prints. And drawings."

Fleming's companion laughed. "When he asked if I would like to see his etchings…well, I would never have guessed…but he showed me etchings…Kokoschkas…with such enthusiasm!"

"Ian, where did you find your Kokoschkas?" asked Leone.

"In my student days in Switzerland and in Munich I had time to look into bookstores and galleries, and my family gave me a bit of money to invest in what I thought would be valuable in future. The Kokoschka I would love to have is his portrait of Alma Mahler. He had a long affair with Gustav Mahler's widow."

"You mean 'Bride of the Wind' – the one where he is lying underneath Alma Mahler…in the shipwreck?"

"Ah, Leone, you know Kokoschka."

"When we were first married…," Folke offered, "…and Leone finished her fellowship at the institute, she looked everywhere in Hamburg for this painting. Without luck. In that time of economic depression she was rewarded with bargains in rugs and furniture for our new household in Stockholm."

"I was hopeful because…according to Kokoschka… 'The Bride of the Wind' went to Hamburg. He was a struggling artist in Vienna. The war had begun, and to join a cavalry regiment as an officer he needed a horse. He sold this painting to a pharmacist from Hamburg. With the money he went to a Jewish horse dealer and bought a trained mare."

"Kokoschka was Jewish, or half Jewish?", Ian asked Leone.

"His father was a goldsmith, Jewish. But Oskar professed no religion. Although at times he pretended to be Catholic to avoid nasty situations. Oh, and he had a connection to Stockholm which is most interesting. He had a hole in his head…literally. Ambushed by Russians in a forest, he lay for hours or days…he said he didn't know how long…under his dead horse. His physician in Vienna recommended a neurologist in Sweden, so Kokoschka went to Stockholm in late 1917. He had therapy there, made and sold paintings…and most interesting…Ian, you're smiling. Do you know what I'm about to say?"

68

"I think so. Is it about Carin? The Swedish duchess who is now Hermann Göring's wife? Kokoschka would have married her, but he was bound to honor his oath to serve his Austrian cavalry regiment in the war."

"He sent her roses every day for weeks, which sustained a dalliance; but he didn't have the money to keep a wife properly… never mind a woman of Carin's society."

"Leone, in Stockholm they call it a 'dalliance'? Nice word. So then…Göring married Carin in 1920. Three years after her 'dalliance' with Kokoschka. One can understand why Oskar hasn't been seen in Germany lately. Göring has the power to do whatever he wishes…certainly to a Jew."

Leone turned toward Ian. "Well, this kind of gossip is amusing, but I had in mind some profound observations about Kokoschka. Do you want to be edified?"

"Ian, I've heard this before. But you should listen. Leone will tell us about how Freud discovered the meaning of art, and Kokoschka…"

"Not discovered…revealed. Not even that. Freud just drew attention to a fact…that all but a tiny portion of mental activity is unconscious. Looking at human behavior with that fact in mind changed everything."

Leone reached for her glass. Folke said, "Will you tell Ian about the Leone McGregor theory of art?"

"If you insist. …Ian, you and I enjoy looking at Kokoschka's pictures. Folke doesn't. Why is that? As an advanced student of psychology I should know."

Ian looked expectantly at Leone, then at Folke, then at Leone.

"When Kokoschka was in Stockholm in 1917, an art dealer asked him to look at some drawings and paintings with a view to determining their author. They'd been rescued from the mental hospital that had held Ernst Josephson in the years before his death. Ernst was a painter…from a prominent Jewish family. Gunnar Josephson is now the leader of Stockholm's oldest synagogue. Ernst studied at the Stockholm Academy, in Italy, and so on… At age twenty he'd said, 'I will become Sweden's Rembrandt or die.' His early work was phenomenally realistic…like the student works of Kokoschka…or the Vienna Jugendstil…or the young Picasso for that matter."

A waiter appeared and carefully poured wine all round. Ian tried to remember early works of Kokoschka as Leone continued.

"But as Josephson grew older, and in stature as an artist…with a measure of fame, at least in Sweden…he had episodes of psychotic behavior…imagining himself to be Jesus Christ and that sort of thing. When he threatened to kill a girl in France…for some heavenly purpose…he was restrained and brought to a Swedish mental hospital. That was in 1888. He spent most of the rest of his life, nearly twenty years, in hospital. His pictures, in step with his behavior, became less and less what we would call 'realistic'. Josephson's unconscious got the better of him. Like many psychotics, he felt that he was sane, and that everybody else was crazy. Couldn't they see what he was seeing? If they couldn't, was it because his vision was exalted? They weren't worthy of seeing? Or maybe the catatonic is asking, 'Why should I tell THEM what I see?'"

"Folke, what do you think?" asked Ian.

"I favor the explanation given by a Viennese psychoanalyst – modern painting is a result of modern sanitation standards …parental frustration of the infantile urge to smear faces…finds release in the artist's adult life."

Kokoschka Bride of the Wind

Early Josephson   Late Josephson

Ian thought for a moment, then asked, "Would you say, Leone, that Josephson and then Kokoschka tried to express the essence of what they saw…not the superficial, or social, clichéd image of it. One unconscious to another, you might say?"

"Yes, you could…say that. And it would explain why works of art speak differently to different people."

[70] Weidinger, Alfred, *Kokoschka and Alma Mahler,* Munich.New York: Prestel-Verlag 1996, p.35.

[71] Photos on this page courtesy The National Museum of Sweden, Stockholm.

"Leone, the hotel in Pellegrino…were there original pictures from Kokoschka…or Klimt or Schiele?"

Folke groaned. Ian and Leone smiled.

"We could talk more about the source of the water," said Leone. "Or Folke could tell us about the wine. Much more interesting."

"Do you mean the vineyards? Or the owners, the fabulous Jewish bankers?", asked Folke.

Fleming examined the label. "When did 'Chateau Lafite' become 'Chateau Lafite Rothschild'?"

Folke took a sip…and smiled appreciatively. "It was ten or fifteen years after the first growth rankings of 1855. The father in Frankfurt, James Mayer Rothschild, bought Chateau Lafite, but didn't have much time to enjoy his purchase. He died a few months later. The chateau became the joint property of three sons."

Ian's companion interjected, "Folke, how did the Rothschilds get all that lovely money?"

"Well, they were always traders…and wine merchants…and money lenders. The massive wealth accumulation began around 1800…from their base in Frankfurt. They lent money to both sides in the Napoleonic Wars. They were shrewd, of course, but to my mind their unique advantage was superior information – intelligence. It started when they succeeded in bidding for the postal system concession. They opened letters, noted the contents, sealed the letters and sent them along. They learned of important developments before everyone else…and were thus able to make or withdraw investments accordingly."

Ian, the intelligence enthusiast, asked: "But…wouldn't…that is, the sender of that information in Frankfurt already know, and would have acted on it by buying or selling shares on the Frankfurt Exchange…and investors in London and Paris would hear of the development in Frankfurt and act."

Folke leaned forward, keen to make his point: "And investors in Vienna…three things: one, the informant might not be concerned with investments; another, could the first investor that heard the news in another financial center trust it enough to speculate with a large amount? The sons managed respective branches of the banking house of Rothschild in Vienna, Paris and London. They not only trusted one another's information, they had a great deal of capital available in appropriate currencies in each city…and confidence borne of the knowledge that the family would support them in the event of a capital loss.…

Folke paused, then added, "Oh, and another factor: the Rothschilds had their own especially fast courier system between their cities… secure enough to carry huge sums of cash…besides news. They made a killing in the London stock and bond markets when they were the first to hear about the British victory at Waterloo. They were the first to exploit the telegraph…and then the telephone."

Ian nodded. "Knowledge is power. The prosperity of Germany seems to be somehow related. What do they know that the rest of the world doesn't? Economic depression everywhere and the Germans are thriving."

"They make more advanced and better products," offered Leone. "They're not afraid to take on new technology and make something of it. Boldness? Courage?"

"Folke, you've worked in Germany for years. What do you make of it?"

"They are better-educated…than other nations, I mean. We make and sell our separators all over the world. Our German…and Swedish…operations are the best. The workers bring intelligence …and technical understanding. They learn quickly."

"And discipline?", asked Ian.

"You mean…that they appear for work every day? Or that they do their best?"

"Both, I suppose."

"Yes, both. And more than that. How shall I say it? The German wants to show that he is better than everyone else. Hitler has appealed to this…most effectively, he is now *der Kanzler*."

Leone swirled the Lafite in her glass, sniffed it, and quietly began, "But all leaders flatter their followers. Rabbis tell Jews that they are the people chosen by God. Faithful Christians will go to Christian heaven. Faithful Muslims…and only the faithful…will go to Muslim heaven."

Ian agreed, "Hitler says, 'We Germans are better than everyone else, and therefore we should rule. Our tribe deserves to increase…above others…for the betterment of humanity.'"

"Fascists fascinate…by appealing to the narcissism in all of us", said Leone.

Folke added, "We're seeing the German idea that they are above foreigners' law…well, actually…even before Hitler. Ironically to suppress the Nazi Party – the German government suspended freedom of assembly and freedom of the press. Friends tell me that there are now secret programs for military training and building of prototype armaments – all violations of the Treaty of Versailles."

A waiter arrived at their table and Ian nodded at the bottle, his indication to bring another.

Folke said, "Allow me," then held the waiter with a gesture and said, "Should we have some cheese with a new Lafite, or press on to a sweet and Dom Pérignon?"

Ignoring Folke's attempt to change the subject, Leone deplored Hitler's treatment of the Jews: "They have contributed… perhaps more than anyone else in our time…to German culture.

"When I came to Hamburg I stayed in the house of a Jewish widow. The music and conversation…in the society of Frau Friedheim…I won't forget one of my last days there, before we married and I moved in with Folke. Returning from my day at the Institute, Frau Friedheim greeted me with, 'Ah *Liebling*! Come and say hello to my daughter. She has brought her friends from medical school.' In the large, luxuriously furnished room was music …and men and women with glasses of wine, talking animatedly and laughing. I asked, 'Who is the violinist?' '*Mischpocheh…Kuzin*', she said, 'at the Academy now the Nazis object to playing the music of the Jew Mendelssohn…and *Kuzin* Mayer must practice somewhere.'"

Leone paused.

Ian looked at Folke, and Folke said, "Ian, in Hamburg last May Leone went to the house of Frau Friedheim. A *Schutzstaffel* officer opened the door. He gave Leone no information, and Leone has since looked for Frau Friedheim without success."

"I have friends in government. I'll see what I can learn. Thousands of German Jews have emigrated since Hitler became *Kanzler*."

Leone sighed, "Thanks, Ian. I'd be most grateful if you could find her. Her handsome house is near the Eppendorfer Krankenhaus Pathology Institute where I worked."

Ian and Leone/Clara – evidence

Ian Fleming became fluent in German while at schools in Switzerland, vacationing in Austria, and a year (1928-1929) at the University of Munich. A good athlete at Eton, he had resigned early from Sandhurst[72] when a dose of gonorrhea forced an extended sick leave. His mother sent him abroad in semi-

---

[72] "Resigned w.e.f. 1 Sep1927", Op.cit. Lycett, p.28.

disgrace.[73] Ian took advantage of the opportunity to cultivate interests in art, literature, skiing, golf and motor racing. He began operating part time in British intelligence in the early thirties.[74] As WWII appeared imminent, in the summer of 1939, he was commissioned as an officer in the Royal Navy at the request of his new immediate boss, the head of naval intelligence, Admiral Godfrey.[75] With Hitler's behavior auguring war, warriors appeared in British government: Churchill was made First Sea Lord, John Godfrey DNI (Director of Naval Intelligence) and Ian Fleming Godfrey's PA (Personal Assistant).

Godfrey encouraged the development of civilian amateur agents.[76] He recognized Fleming's outstanding ability in this area.[77]

> The only other women engaged as interrogators were in the Naval Intelligence team recruited by Ian Fleming and attached to M19(a), interrogating German POWs at MI9s other sites.[78]

Ian Fleming remained in Naval Intelligence as Personal Assistant to the Director after Churchill transferred Godfrey to a less important job.[79] A factor might have been the friendship between Churchill and Ian's father Valentine, who was killed in action in WW1.[80]

Other British Intelligence officers besides Ian Fleming wrote spy novels. John Le Carré's (pen name of David Cornwell, who worked for MI5) George Smiley is nearly as famous as James Bond. But these were necessarily works of fiction. Maxwell Knight, *The Man Who Was M, the real-life spymaster who inspired Ian Fleming* (from the cover of the biography by Anthony Masters), while making a meagre living as a broadcaster and writer in the fifties and sixties, having signed the Official Secrets Act, could not exploit

---

[73] Ian was nonessential to the family; his older brother Peter, already a respected author, was in line to inherit the family estate.

[74] e.g. Phyllis Bottome, *The Goal,* London: Faber and Faber 1962, pages 129 and 278.

[75] Op. cit. Lycett., pages 98-104.

[76] "The relationship between the largely civilian security and intelligence services on the one hand, and the military staffs concerned with deception on the other, might have been delicate, if not acrimonious, and on occasion they were. That they in fact developed so harmoniously and efficiently was due very largely to two men, Rear Admiral J H Godfrey, Director of Naval Intelligence at the beginning of the war, was quick to see the value...." Michael Howard, *British Intelligence in the Second World War, Volume 5 Strategic Deception,* London: HMSO Publications 1990, p.xi.; and "...Ian Fleming's own account of Personal Assistant, written in 1948: In wartime much use is made by DNI of contacts outside Whitehall.... In fact the Director found his PA of use in most matters not directly concerned with the naval service. ...This officer was also a convenient channel for confidential matters connected with subversive organizations, and for undertaking confidential matters abroad, either alone or with DNI." Op. cit Costello pages 7-8. And, "Moreover Godfrey was already conscious that the right type of civilian might have knowledge and experience...which no naval officer could supply." Patrick Beesly, *Very Special Admiral: The Life of Admiral J.H. Godfrey, CB,* London: Hamish Hamilton 1980 pages.109-110.

[77] For example, the recruitment of Sefton Delmer into British Naval Intelligence, described in Nicholas Rankin, *A Genius for Deception: How Cunning Helped the British Win Two World Wars,* Oxford, New York: Oxford University Press 2008, pages 200, 215-216.

[78] Helen Fry, *MI9: A History of the Secret Service for Escape and Evasion in World War Two,* New Haven: Yale University Press 2020, p.7.

[79] Op. cit. Lycett, p.142. Godfrey was NID February 1939 – January 1943, then Edmund Rushbrooke until war's end.

[80] William Stevenson, *Spymistress: The True Story of the Greatest Female Secret Agent of World War II,* Arcade Books, New York 2011, p.66. and Op.cit. Lycett, p.12.

lucrative opportunities to write or talk about events and characters from his time in the thirties and forties in MI5. Nor could his wife.[81]

Ian Fleming, like Sherlock Holmes, had a smarter older brother. Peter Fleming was heir to the family estate, a famous journalist, and an author of travel books. After the war he died before official permission to relate his wartime experiences was possible. From March 1942 Major R.P. Fleming was intelligence officer in the American-British-Dutch-Australian (ABDA) Command, based in Delhi. His activities were directed mainly against the Japanese, but his channels included... "a particularly valuable source in Stockholm controlled by MI6...." [82]

Ian felt special sympathy for Canadians. He had roles in planning and executing the disastrous 1942 Dieppe Raid in which hundreds of Canadian soldiers died, victims of faulty intelligence.[83] There was a saving grace – lessons from Dieppe informed planning for Allied landings in Italy in 1943 and Normandy in 1944.[84] What had been intended as an assault, a commando raid, was described by Churchill as a "reconnaissance in force" in addressing the House of Commons.

A studiously innocuous account of WW2 espionage was written by one of the men whose exploits and personalities suggested Bond ... "It may have been Ian Fleming himself who launched the story that his celebrated fictional hero, Commander James Bond RN, was modelled on Lieutenant-Commander Patrick Dalzel-Job." [85]

Dalzel-Job led a Naval Intelligence Division Assault Unit, notably against German installations following D-Day:

> The Unit's function, in which it had already been very successful in the fighting on the shores of the Mediterranean, was to get to sources of enemy intelligence ahead of Allied troops or at least with the leading assault, so as to capture papers and equipment, mainly but not always of naval interest, before such things could be destroyed either by the enemy or by our own troops. NID 30 prepared the list of 'Targets', and the same people became 30 AU in the field. ... Our boss in Admiralty was Ian Fleming, better known later as the creator of James Bond. He was at that time PA to the Director of Naval Intelligence with the rank of Commander.[86]

---

[81] "But Susi had also signed the Official Secrets Act and the long period that her husband had spent as an MI5 case officer had to remain a closed book. This was deeply frustrating to Knight, who would have liked to write his autobiography...."
Anthony Masters, *The Man Who Was M: The Life of Maxwell Knight,* London: Grafton 1984/86, pages 231-232.

[82] Michael Howard, *British Intelligence in the Second World War: Volume V, Strategic Deception,* London: HMSO Publications 1990, p.206.

[83] Nicholas Rankin, *Ian Fleming's Commandos: The Story of 30 Assault Unit in WWII,* London: Faber and Faber Limited 2011, p.19.

[84] Quentin Reynolds, *Dress Rehearsal: The Story of Dieppe,* New York: Random House 1943, and Wallace Reyburn, *Rehearsal for Invasion: An Eyewitness Story of the Dieppe Raid,* London: George C. Harrap & Co. Ltd. 1943.

[85] The first sentence of the Foreword by Charles Wheeler to the book, *From Arctic Snow to Dust of Normandy* by Patrick Dalzel-Job, Plockton, Ross-shire: Nead-an-Eoin Publishing 1991. Dalzel-Job is mentioned throughout – Rankin's 2011 study (Ibid.): pages 69-9, 222, 233, 235, 250, 253, 267, 270-3, 276-282, 293-5. And, "Dalzel-Job was one of the principal inspirations for the character of 007." Ben MacIntyre, *For Your Eyes Only: Ian Fleming and James Bond,* New York: Bloomsbury USA 2008, p.68.

[86] Ibid. Dalzel-Job, pages 114-115.

Parachute training at Ringway, February 1944; Canadian soldiers, with Patrick kneeling centre front

Tall, vigorous, dashing

---

[87] Ibid. Dalzel-Job, photo on p.108+.

Patrick while serving with the Canadian Navy in 1954

[88]

Sean Connery resemblance

James Bond's spy paraphernalia was inspired by the gadgets used by British intelligence agencies during WWII. Miniature radios and cameras, button compasses, disguised cyanide capsules, fabric maps made legible by the owner's urine, etc. were supplied by small British manufacturers with unfailing secrecy.[89]

---

[88] Ibid. Dalzel-Job, photo on p.108+.

[89] "Secrecy had to be maintained no matter what the cost or circumstances, and for years it became natural to think at least half a dozen times before allowing the brain to engage the tongue or limb. My main item of baggage when I ventured out into industry

But Ian Fleming could not write about people and events in WWII: "All writers are influenced by the things that happen in their own lifetime; but unlike most, Fleming was not allowed to give away the intimate details of his work during the Second World War." [90]

A generation after the war Donald McLachlan, who had worked closely with both Godfrey and his successor Rushbrooke in the London headquarters of the NID (Naval Intelligence Division), carefully observed the Official Secrets Act in writing *Room 39: a study in Naval Intelligence.* In this book are numerous references to Ian Fleming's daring and genius in working with civilian spies. For example:

> Godfrey [director 1939-1943] said in later years "Ian was a war-winner", and Rushbrooke [1943-1945], his second director thought very highly of him. He seemed to take the shortest possible distance between two points. The effect on others was that they felt impelled to live up to their standard of alertness, however boring and fruitless, the work in hand. His real achievement, in the author's view, was to set a standard of independent, critical and forceful behaviour by RNVR officers which was of crucial importance in a division where civilians had such big parts to play.[91]

Patrick Beesly, whose cousin Margaret Hope married John Godfrey, worked under Godfrey for three years in the Naval Intelligence Division. In his biography of Godfrey, *Very Special Admiral,* Beesly frequently notes the constraints on what he was allowed to read or write.

The secrecy of Fleming's activities and protection of the anonymity of civilian sources were maintained long after the war's end.[92] Fleming worked in the middle of the competition and uneasy cooperation among the intelligence services of Britain, the USA and Russia to find and sequester German military scientists and science,[93] experience which informed Fleming's treatment of this theme in the Bond novels.

---

was a wad of Official Secrets Act forms. Each new contact was shown the dotted line, handed a pen and ordered to sign. Even after this, the contact was given only the barest information beyond specifications required to manufacture a specific product." Charles Fraser-smith, *Secret Warriors: Hidden Heroes of MI6, OSS, MI9, SOE & SAS,* Crescent Exeter: The Paternoster Press 1984, P.143.

[90] Craig Cabell, *Ian Fleming's Secret War,* Barnsley, South Yorkshire: Pen & Sword Books 2008, p.111, and "He was working in a top secret environment and some of those secrets are nowadays lost forever." p.101.

[91] McLachlan, Donald, *Room 39: a study in Naval Intelligence,* New York: Atheneum 1968 p.10; and, "Godfrey decided it would be wise to use Fleming whenever he could as intermediary for the most daring but informal approaches." p.222; and on the topic of "… what is ideally required in the highest grade of Intelligence work: …the cold objectivity of a research scientist; the intuition of the archeologist handling fragmentary fact; the discretion of a doctor…." p.338.

[92] Following D-Day, Ian Fleming's "30 Assault Unit" (a name chosen to disguise its mission as collector of enemy technical intelligence) entered a windowless concrete bunker in a moated German castle grounds where they found scientists at work. Fleming ordered Robert Harling to immediately return to England the lead scientist and 15 cwt of documents found there – to prevent these getting into the hands of the Americans or the Soviets. It was not until 2015, seven years after Harling's death at the age of 98, that Harling's description of this mission was published – an admission that Fleming had ordered him to violate the Hague Convention. But Harling, or his editors acting in accordance with the British Official Secrets Act, did not identify the scientist, or even his "particular discipline", 70 years after the event. Robert Harling, *Ian Fleming: A Personal Memoir,* London: The Robson Press 2015, pages 150-158.

[93] Annie Jacobsen, *Operation Paperclip: The Secret Intelligence Program That Brought Nazi Scientists To America,* New York: Back Bay Books, Little, Brown & Company 2014, pages 37-38.

After the war not even Godfrey was completely trusted with this information. From 1947-1949 Godfrey was invited by the then-DNI, Rear-Admiral Parry, to edit the secret archives of the DNI. Godfrey and his assistants produced fifty monographs concerning the DNI's wartime activities: "…because they contained references to highly classified information, excessive secrecy took over and they were locked away in a safe and forgotten. When Godfrey started to complete and revise them in the sixties he was neither permitted to take them home or to work on them in the Admiralty when their custodian was out of the office at lunch!"[94]

In addition to their frequency at certain golf courses and their knowledge of German, Leone[95] and Ian[96] had common interests.

They liked driving and fast cars. In Calgary Leone had taken a night course in auto mechanics in order to qualify as an ambulance driver, the only occupation open to a woman at the European front in WWI.

In July of 1917 Leone could have been inspired by a sensational report in the Calgary Herald of a woman medical doctor setting a record fast time from Banff to Calgary: Dr. Rosamund Leacock drove a Ford Runabout on clear roads in fine weather, four hours and ten minutes including a ten-minute pit stop in Canmore.

After completing her PhD in Minnesota, Leone drove a Ford Model T on primitive roads for several days to reach Boston, where she began work at Harvard Medical. The LaSalle she acquired after marriage to Folke Hellstedt was powered by a Cadillac V8 – a direct descendant of the powerful V8 engines in the hundreds of ambulances and staff cars of the U.S. military during WWI.

Ian Fleming was a member of that select faction of the British upper class which undertook defense of British honor in the field of international motorsport. He co-drove the Invicta entered by Donald Healey in the epic 1932 Alpine Trials.[97]

Leone and Ian were delighted to discover a shared interest in the Austrian writer and painter, Oskar Kokoschka, a member of the Viennese *Jugendstil* (along with the likes of Klimt and Schiele), who signed his paintings *OK* and advanced into his own style of Expressionism. Kokoschka, of Jewish descent, had made news by objecting publicly to great works of art being damaged during historically insignificant political conflicts in Germany.[98] Ian, while a student in the late twenties, roaming through the galleries and

---

[94] Op.cit. Patrick Beesly, p.320.

[95] "We then drove around the country and off to a golf hotel on the Wörther See where we had reserved rooms. …To our surprise this little golf hotel turned out to be very elegant with evening clothes for every dinner. Alfonso XIII was staying there and several English socialites." Op.cit. Ondrack, p.131.

[96] "By early 1935, it was clear that Ian had no future as a banker. …Driving his Buick, he was taking one of the leisurely continental motoring holidays which gave him pleasure throughout his life". [p.69] "During his time in Austria that summer, Ian was determined to follow his amatory instincts. Staying on the Wörthersee on the other side of the country in Carinthia was Ann O'Neill, the spirited and stylish peer's wife he had first met at Stanway in 1934. …Fifty miles away towards Villach, …Count Paul Munster, a golfing friend of Ian's at White's, owned Schloss Wasserleonburg, which had been lent to the Duke and Duchess of Windsor for part of their honeymoon the year before. …Nin Ryan…dated the start of her friends' affair from that lakeside summer holiday." Op.cit. Lycett, pages 92-93.

[97] "Run over 1580 miles of steep mountain passes, they were one of the most grueling tests of drivers' skills and cars' durability in the rallying calendar. …Ian… was back in his favorite Alps. In addition, he was competing in an event which combined all the leisured charm of amateur sportsmanship with the thrill of international competition – from manufactures such as Mercedes-Benz, Steyr, Lancia and Bugatti. He was experiencing the world of fast cars, flashing exhausts and international rivalry which he had only read about in Sappers' Bulldog Drummond novels." Op. cit. Lycett, pages 52-53.

[98] Op. cit. Gordon Fraser, p.36.

bookstores of economically depressed Austria and Bavaria, had an allowance from his family for purchasing art and rare books. For himself he collected works of and about Kokoschka.[99] Leone's interest in Kokoschka was more fully gratified after the war, when she bought postcards and prints on her trips to Vienna, the headquarters of the Medical Womens' International Association (she was the president of the MWIA 1970-1972).

Kokoschka's life story was of particular interest to Leone in part because of his affair with Alma, the widow of Gustav Mahler, Leone's favorite composer.[100] After Gustav Mahler died in 1911, Alma Mahler began a three-year affair with Kokoschka before marrying the architect Walter Gropius (founder of *Bauhaus*) in 1915. Kokoschka's paintings evoked dreamlike images, the stuff of Freud's *die Traumdeutung* (published in Vienna, 1900) and Leone's chosen profession, psychoanalysis.[101] Mahler's cabin on the Wörthersee, where he wrote his greatest music, is only a few kilometers from the Dellach Golf Club, where Leone and Folke played.[102]

Both Ian and Leone, frequent visitors to Austria, were intrigued by the notorious Alma Mahler, wife and mistress of famous artists. Alma was raised Catholic, and was anti-Semitic but attracted to Jewish men, who became captivated by her beauty and her prodigious sexual appetite and skill.[103] She was engaged to Gustav Mahler when he abandoned his Jewish origins and became a Roman Catholic on December 25, 1901. They married in 1902. Alma turned to Walter Gropius and Gustav to Sigmund Freud when Gustav became impotent in 1910.[104] Gustav Mahler died in 1911. Kokoschka met Alma in April 1912,[105] and was obsessed

---

[99] "I remember those days before the war, reading … the writings of Adler and Freud – and buying first editions (I used to collect them) illustrated by Kokoschka and Kubin." Ibid. Lycett, p.34.

[100] Gustav Mahler's most productive period – 1901-1908, when he sequestered himself to write in his holiday house at Maiernigg on the Wörthersee, seven kilometers from the Hellstedt's favoured Dellach Golf Club. Oliver Hilmes, *Malevolent Muse: The Life of Alma Mahler,* translated by Donald Arthur, Northeastern University Press 2015, pages 47, 56, 61.

[101] "Kokoschka makes his debut in the [Vienna 1908] Kunstschau, not only with life drawings and images from his book '*Die Träumenden Knaben' (The Dreaming Youths),* but also with the now sadly lost, large-format triptych '*Die Traumtragenden' (The Dream Bearers).* ... Despite severe criticism, on the very first day of the Kunstschau, Kokoschka sells all of his works and becomes famous overnight." Alfred Weidinger, *Kokoschka and Alma Mahler: Testimony to a Passionate Relationship,* Munich & New York: Prestel-Verlag 1996, p.109.

[102] Francoise Giroud, *Alma Mahler, or the Art of Being Loved,* New York: Oxford University Press 1991 English translation, pages 23, 51, 58, 59.

[103] Ibid. Françoise Giroud pages 19, 104, 106, 134, and Oskar Kokoschka, *My Life,* London: Thames & Hudson 1974, pages 73 & 99.

[104] Alma Mahler (1940), translated by Basil Creighton (1946), *Gustav Mahler: Memories and Letters,* London: Sphere Books Ltd., 1990, pages 172-179.

[105] "Not much more than a week after Alma and Kokoschka had become lovers, Alma went to Paris for a few days with her lesbian friend Lili Lieser (April 25-30) and then on to the Dutch spa of Scheveningen. Her young lover wrote at least one letter to her every day, sometimes as many as three, and then criticized her for not being as diligent as him in her replies." Op.cit. Weidinger, p.9.

with her until she emphatically dumped him in 1915;[106] then decades later, after two more marriages, an elderly widow, she wondered if Kokoschka should have been "the one."[107]

Alma married Walter Gropius August 18, 1915, began an affair with Franz Werfel in 1918 that resulted in the birth of a son (named Martin Gropius), obtained a divorce from a reluctant Walter Gropius in 1920 and married Franz Werfel in 1929.[108] Werfel, like Mahler and Kokoschka, was born to a Jewish family but did not practice religion…at times he displayed antipathy toward Jews. After the Anschluss in 1938, Werfel and Alma sought exile, first in France, then in 1940 in the USA and Hollywood, where his novel *The Song of Bernadette,* was adapted into a film.

Kokoschka credited Leone's friend Matt Halton with saving his life. By Nazi definition a Jew, Kokoschka moved to Prague following Hitler's ascent to power. After German soldiers marched into Czechoslovakia, he was desperately seeking admission to Britain in October 1938, when:

> A Canadian journalist I knew came to our table. Over a *schnaps* we explained our situation, and he put our minds to rest…. "I'll take up your case right away with Lord Cecil." This was the Lord Cecil who had been a very important diplomat in the League of Nations, and had won the Nobel Peace Prize in 1937. "He'll call the Home Office, and everything will work out." And it did…. There were two seats left on a plane to London the next morning…otherwise, I would most probably not be alive today. [109]

Being a Jew in the Nazi Reich was only one aspect of Kokoschka's survival problem. Hermann Göring had reason to silence O.K. After receiving serious wounds fighting the Russians, a bullet in the temple and a bayonet in the lung, Kokoschka went to Sweden in the autumn of 1917 for experimental treatment by

---

[106] Over Kokoschka's objections Alma went to a sanatorium in October 1912 for an abortion. When he was called to the military in January 1915, O.K. struggled to buy the horse he needed to join an elite Dragoons regiment. He feared his absences would find Alma responding to her many admirers. Alma traveled to Berlin in February 1915 to see Walter Gropius, who had taken a leave from his military duties for the rendezvous. In May 1915, Alma wrote in her diary, "Oskar has slipped away from me. He is no longer within me. He is an undesired stranger." Op. cit. Weidinger, p.82. Alma and Walter Gropius were married August 18, 1915.

[107] "I will never figure out – never comprehend, she wrote him in the spring of 1946, how we could ever have separated! Since we were made for each other!" Op cit. Hilmes, p.272.

[108] "At the end of June, on his return to Vienna, Werfel…abandoned the faith of his forefathers and, in an official affirmed under oath, he resigned from the Jewish community. He did not take this step just be faithful to his literary model: ten years had passed since he had first expressed his desire to marry Alma Mahler, and now she had finally acquiesced to his repeated pleas. Shortly before her fiftieth birthday, she delared her willingness to marry Werfel, but on one condition – he would have to leave the Jewish faith before the marriage…Franz Werfel and Alma Mahler's wedding took place on July 8, 1929." Peter Stephan Jungk, *Franz Werfel: A Life In Prague, Vienna and Hollywood,* New York: Fromm International Publishing Corporation 1991, p.122.

[109] Oskar Kokoschka, *My Life,* Thames and Hudson, London 1974, p.159; and, "Next day he returned to Prague, now a city in despair. On Wenceslas Square, men and women were weeping. Driving to Karlsbad, he ran into the 'terrible stench of Europe's refugees' – tens of thousands of non-German and anti-Nazi Czechs streaming out of the Sudetenland." David Halton, *Dispatches From The Front: Matthew Halton, Canada's Voice At War,* McClelland & Stewart 2014, p.135.; and, "On my last day in Prague, October 6, I took to the censor a dispatch describing the resignation of Benes from the presidency of the republic he had done so much to create and nurture." Matthew Halton, *Ten Years to Alamein,* Toronto: S.J. Reginald Saunders and Company Limited, 1944, p.80.

Professor Barany, an Austrian who specialized in this type of brain injury (which had become common – soldiers poking their heads above trenches). While in Stockholm O.K. executed commissions[110] and assiduously courted Carin, the aristocratic and beautiful woman who married Herman Göring in 1923, and whom Göring revered long after her death[111] in 1931.[112]

Leone and Ian were both acquainted with Carl Jung. Following her motoring adventure in the spring of 1934, Leone had returned to Folke in Stockholm resolved to pursue psychoanalysis. Folke approved, and in the fall Leone went to Zürich to begin training analysis and psychiatric internship in Jung's Burghölzli Clinic.[113] Ian had corresponded with Jung in 1929-1930 in the course of translating from German to English a treatise on Paracelsus that Jung had written.[114]

Secret forever ... probably ... maybe

> The modern conception of the world of secret intelligence services and assassinations derives partly from the fictionalized activities of James Bond. …the former Naval Intelligence and MI6 asset Ian Fleming based the plots and details for his 007 books on incidents in his own life and information he picked up during his career in the secret world. However fantastic the story, there is always an element of truth in Bond.*[115]*

---

[110] *Abb. 35. Stockholmer Landschaft 1917,* Paul Westheim, *Oskar Kokoschka: Das Werk Kokoschkas in 62 Abbildungen,* Potsdam-Berlin: Gustav Kiepenheuer Verlag 1918.

[111] "I could hardly afford the bunch of roses I used to send to a young Swedish lady whom I very much admired. I had met her at the German Embassy, during a reception they gave when my play *Der brennende Dornbusch* was performed there. The lady, who had recently been widowed, tried hard to persuade me to stay in Sweden. At the Opera she slipped into my hand a little silver case with a rose in it, which I still have. …she…used to sail with me through the shallows, at night, beneath the stars. Our words were like the music of the waves. …When presented with a choice between marrying her and biting the dust, I tended to prefer the idea of an honourable defeat. …With a final bunch of roses, paid for with my last money, I parted from her. But not yet from life's stage, or from the rhetoric of classical tragedy. She later married an airman, Hermann Göring; she died young and he built his Karinhall in her memory." Op.cit…Oskar Kokoschka, pages 105-106.

[112] Carin was buried in her family's tomb in Sweden. Göring built "Carinhall" as a memorial – "He chose the area around Schorfheide, a great rolling expanse of forest, lakes, and moorland some two hours drive northeast of Berlin; and here he persuaded the government to decree one hundred thousand acres as a zone in which no other building would be allowed, with a further area inside it where he would build his official residence, surrounded by a game reserve in which only he, local villagers, and his invited guests would be allowed to hunt. From its inception, the house was to be a memorial to his dead wife, Carin, and Goering put more into its creation than any other project in his lifetime." Leonard Mosely, *The Reich Marshall: A Biography of Herman Goering,* New York: Doubleday & Company, Inc. 1974, p.197.

[113] One is reminded of Jung's observation that change of direction at mid-life, around age thirty-five, was more common than generally appreciated – here Leone, who was driven from childhood to please her mother's and her personal ambition, was becoming Clara, who was devoted to the service of others.

[114] Op.cit. Lycett, p.44. And, Fleming's interest in astrology and occult literature was stimulated by his acquaintance with Carl Jung. Donald McCormick, *17F: The Life of Ian Fleming,* London: Peter Owen 1991, pages 43-44. And Robert Harling, *Ian Fleming: A Personal Memoir,* London: The Robson Press 2015, p.161.

[115] Stephen Dorrill, *MI6: Inside the Covert World of Her Majesty's Secret Intelligence Service,* New York: The Free Press Simon & Schuster 2000, p.610; and on the same page, "Fleming had visited the United States to see how an offshoot of MI6, the British Security Coordination, operated in the Americas. Fleming was shown around the intelligence complex by the 'Quiet Canadian', Sir William Stephenson, head of the BSC. Below Stephenson's spacious office was the Japanese consular office, occupied by a

In his Naval Intelligence role Ian Fleming worked with members of the clandestine Special Operations Executive (SOE), created following Dunkirk in July 1940 and encouraged by Churchill to use ungentlemanly methods to "set Europe ablaze."[116] Fleming in his London office coordinated bold, brazen, dangerous, outrageous, violent, illegal activities of SOE operators and wrote press releases full of plausible lies to blur their spoor. The first administrative hire when the SOE was formed was Joan Bright, who remained at the center in London for its duration. Joan briefly dated Ian Fleming – "a ruthless man" – and was rumored to have been Fleming's model for Miss Moneypenny, M's secretary. [117]

The SOE was disbanded in January 1946. Its very existence had been secret.

Fleming acknowledged that he could not write or talk about what he did during WWII. That would be disloyal to Her Majesty, violation of the Official Secrets Act…and sometimes in questionable taste.

To take just one example of poor taste, in 2019, fifty-five years after Fleming's death, author Brian Lett noted the regrettable disillusionment of a war hero's daughter. The SOE "Operation Postmaster" involved stealing the 8,000-ton Italian passenger liner *Duchessa d'Aosta* and a modern German tug, the *Likomba*, moored for more than a year in the harbor of Santa Isabel, Equatorial Guinea, an island off the coast of Africa…which was then, in 1941, governed by neutral Spain. SOE agents lured the ship's officers ashore to a party on the evening of January 14, 1942. On the upper terrace of the Casino Restaurant there were prostitutes where…

> Captain Umberto Valle of the *Duchessa d'Aosta* and Captain Specht of the *Likomba* relaxed in their chairs, backs to the harbour, well oiled by the contents of their frequently filled glasses. The electricity had, as planned, been replaced by bright and cheerful Tilley Paraffin Pressure Lamps and by candles, and had they looked behind them, to the officers of the enemy ships, the harbour would have appeared merely a pool of blackness.[118]

SOE agents with naval training came alongside the Italian and German ships and boarded them. When crew members saw guns in the hands of strangers, some jumped and swam ashore; a few remained in custody or to help crew. The SOE agents blew apart the mooring chains and towed their prey out to the open Atlantic before daylight. A model escapade for James Bond.

> The Germans and Italians were furious. Captain Specht, of the *Likomba*, had no doubt as to who was responsible. At 130 hours on 15 January, still very drunk as a result of the dinner party, he went round to the Intelligence Consulate and burst in, marching through the pantry toward the sitting room where he was intercepted by Agent Lake. Specht, swearing and

---

cipher expert who was transmitting coded messages back to Tokyo. He was not assassinated but Fleming did witness the burglary of the office and out of this adventure grew the idea that would find its way into *Casino Royale*."

[116] E.H. Cookridge, *Set Europe Ablaze: The inside story of Special Operations Executive – Churchill's daring plant to defeat Germany through Sabotage, Espionage and Subversion*, New York: Thomas Y. Crowell Company 1966.

[117] Giles Milton, *Churchill's Ministry of Ungentlemanly Warfare: The Mavericks Who Plotted Hitler's Defeat*, New York: Picador 2016, p.304.

[118] Brian Lett, *Ian Fleming's and SOE's Operation Postmaster: The Untold Top Secret Story*, Yorkshire-Philadelphia: Pen & Sword Books Ltd. 2012/2020, p.160.

cursing, shouted, "Where is my ship?" Lake told him to get out, whereupon Specht lost all control and hit Lake in the face. This gave young Peter Lake the excuse that he was hoping for, and he and Godden, who had arrived on the scene, then "knocked the stuffing" out of Specht. Lippett's report describes the detail: Godden rushed to the affray and put some heavy North of Scotland on Specht and literally knocking the s—t out of him. When Specht saw Godden's revolver he collapsed in a heap, split his pants and emptied his bowels on the floor.*119*

The preceding from British records appeared in the 2012 edition of Lett's book, *Ian Fleming and SOE's Operation Postmaster.* A reader was the daughter of Captain Specht. She wrote to Lett, attaching contents of a letter that Captain Specht sent to his family in Germany. It was dated February 1, 1942, two weeks after his ship disappeared.

I am sure you have been informed about the recent events on this island through the press and the radio, and therefore may have been worrying about me for quite some time. …In any case my beautiful ship is gone. Spanish spies enabled the attack and the successful theft of the ships; what makes this case even sadder is the fact that Spanish citizens supported it. We were invited ashore for a meal under the pretence of meeting anonymous friends of the new order. The guards were overpowered and massacred, and the rest was easy under the protection of two English warships. We had to watch helplessly as they hijacked our ships. The Spaniards did nothing. No shot, no flare, absolutely nothing. Red with anger I entered the house and beat up the consul and another man. The English consul threatened me with a revolver, which I managed to wrestle from him and then used to strike him down. Both men needed hospital treatment.*120*

Two accounts of the same incident, one by a Brit and one by a German: both self-serving; both designed to degrade men on the other side. Neither is entirely true, but the British one is more plausible, given the context of Lett's book.[121] Seventy years after their tellings, they can have no effect on the outcome of the war or any international concern. But one must wonder about the effect on Captain Specht's daughter and her family upon reading the British account.

In her letter to me, Captain Specht's daughter added this information: 'If this would not have happened, who knows, my father would not have had to serve during the war and [would have] finish [ed] his mission in Africa! He was the leader of a special mission on U43, and

---

119 Ibid. Lett p. 201
120 Ibid. Lett p. 247
121 Yet another version of the incident is in a biography of one of the SOE men who boarded *Duchessa:* "The SOE ploy failed to deceive the *Duchessa's* captain who guessed the truth immediately on finding his ship gone. He then hurried from the harbour and broke down the door of the British consulate where police arrested him before he could attack the consul. March-Phillipps was told later, 'The captain has been jailed for three weeks.'" Mike Langley, *Anders Lassen, VC, MC, of the SAS: The story of Anders Lassen and the men who fought with him,* London: Hodder & Stoughton 1988, p.78.

received the Iron Cross. His ship went down in the North Atlantic in 1943, the year I was born. He was only thirty-four.'[122]

The keepers of the secrets of British Intelligence have maintained its integrity for more than a century. While considerations of national security and those of the sort expressed in the novels of Stieg Larsson (vengeance by neo-Nazis) fade in the distance from WWII, one can imagine that the choice of what to reveal from time to time turns on simple matters of taste. Why tarnish the legacy of an officer who was killed serving his country in the line of duty? Who benefitted by the release of the document describing this encounter between Captain Specht and a British Consul to the Spanish Government? It does credit to none of those involved.

Winston Churchill was made Prime Minister when it became apparent that dithering and pandering had got Britain into a hole from which it could emerge only by desperate effort. He understood that Hitler endorsed despicable behavior in order to achieve his despicable ends; and that preventing German victory, countering despicable behavior, would require the same. Britons would have to resort to the nasty, sordid and reprehensible in order to negate the Nazi threat.

SOE activities varied from conspicuous and violent – for example blowing up bridges; to the subtle and devious – for example undermining morale by including in a genuine news broadcast a fake news item about lonely wives and girlfriends of soldiers away at the front entertaining officers and men at home on leave.

While books have been written about the organizations created by Churchill to implement secret measures, notably SOE (Special Operations Executive)[123] and BSC (British Security Coordination)[124], posterity has been spared much knowledge of how badly some Allied agents behaved during WW2: only fifteen per cent of SOE records survive; and BSC's were burned after the war by order of its founder and leader, William Stephenson.

---

[122] Ibid. Lett p.247

[123] Examples: Giles Melton, *Churchill's Ministry of Ungentlemanly Warfare: The Mavericks Who Plotted Hitler's Defeat*, New York: Picador 2016; Des Turner, *Aston House Station 12: SOE's Secret Centre*, Thrupp Stroud Gloucestershire: Sutton Publishing 2006; M.R.D. Foot, *SOE: The Special Operations Executive*, London: BBC 1984; E.H. Cookridge, *Set Europe Ablaze: The inside story of Special Operations Executive – Churchill's daring plan to defeat Germany through Sabotage, Espionage and Subversion*, New York: Thomas Y. Crowell Company 1966; Colonel Bernd Horn, *A Most Ungentlemanly Way of War: The SOE and the Canadian Connection*, Toronto: Dundurn 2016. "More than fifty years later, some of the most significant black propaganda operations conducted by British intelligence are still emerging." Richard A. Aldrich & Rory Cormac, *The Black Door: Spies, Secret Intelligence and British Prime Ministers*, London: William Collins 2016. P.111

[124] Examples: BSC officers, Introduction by Nigel West, *British Security Coordination: The Secret History of British Intelligence in the Americas 1940-45*, London: St. Ermin's Press 1998; David Stafford, *Camp X: Canada's School for Secret Agents*, Toronto: Lester & Orpen Dennys Limited 1986.

During WW2 Fleming worked for Admiral Godfrey, head of naval intelligence[125] and with William Stephenson[126], whom he came to idolize.

> In this era of the anti-hero, when anyone on a pedestal is assaulted (how has Nelson survived?), unfashionably and obstinately I have my heroes … High up on my list is one of the greatest secret agents of the last war… Sir William Stephenson.[127]

Stephenson's BSC – "the most successful covert action operation in history."*[128]*

William Stephenson, the man called INTREPID, necessarily kept a low profile and was seldom if ever photographed during the war. This picture was taken in New York in 1954.

Ian Fleming (*right*), creator of James Bond, was an aide to the chief of British Naval Intelligence. He worked closely with INTREPID and received much of his training at BSC's secret establishment outside Toronto, some phases from INTREPID personally. Many of the techniques and devices later described in his novels derive from INTREPID's operations.

129

[125] "Godfrey later attributed much of his success to Stephenson…." David Ramsay, *'Blinker' Hall, Spymaster: The Man Who Brought America Into World War I,* Stroud, Gloucestershire: Spellmount Limited 2008, p.311.

[126] "In 1941, Fleming was assigned to the MI6 station in New York, then busily at work trying to get the United States involved in the war. As part of that operation, a very close liaison had been established between the head of the MI6 station, **William Stephenson,** and William Donovan, President Roosevelt's COI (Coordinator of Information). Donovan, later head of the OSS, was convinced by the British that the Americans needed a centralized civilian intelligence agency. Fleming was detailed to help Donovan draw up a plan for such an agency, based on the British model. Roosevelt decided not to adopt the plan, but later it would serve as the template for the creation of the CIA." Ernest Volkman, *Spies: The Secret Agents Who Changed The Course Of History,* New York: John Wiley & Sons 1994, pages 96-97.

[127] Ian Fleming, in the foreword to H. Montgomery Hyde, *Room 3603: The Story of the British Intelligence Center in New York during World War II,* New York: Farrar, Strauss and Company 1965, p.ix.

[128] Ernest Volkman, *Spies: The Secret Agents Who Changed the Course of History,* New York: John Wiley & Sons, Inc. 1994, p.185.

[129] Photo page between pages 230 and 231 in William Stevenson, *A Man Called Intrepid: The Secret War,* London: Book Club Associates 1976. Photos also in the Harcourt Brace Jovanovich edition, courtesy of BSC Papers, Station M Archives.

Chapter Six
Wanted: Secret Agents

"Bill Stephenson taught us everything we ever knew about foreign intelligence operations." William Donovan, first head of the OSS, to Bedell Smith, director of the OSS successor, the CIA.[130]

Sir William Stephenson

Early warnings of Hitler's intentions were given by Matthew Halton and Ian Fleming. However, their warnings did not reach important politicians as effectively as the alarms communicated by William Stephenson to Winston Churchill. Stephenson, born and raised around the same time and place as Leone McGregor, on the turn of the century Canadian prairie, had Churchill's respect and attention.[131] Churchill had the best intelligence of the Allied leaders;[132] and he was instrumental in realizing Stephenson's knighthood.[133]

What little Bill Stephenson said about his espionage activities was sometimes untrue, designed to mislead and confuse – for his amusement or to confound an enemy. His reputation among those who relied on secondary sources is uneven; but those who worked with him directly accorded only the highest praise – an opinion one tends to form from historical facts.

On the publication of a biography of Stephenson, one of the most effective spies of World War II wrote to its author:

---

[130] Jeffrey Richelson & Desmond Ball, *The Ties That Bind,* New York: Allen & Unwin 1985, p.140.

[131] "Churchill, more than any other modern British Premier except Lloyd George, was always determined to find things out for himself, especially in intelligence matters. While relying on a machinery in most respects admirably designed to keep the war leader fully informed, he also turned to personal specialist advisers, men like General Ismay, his military adviser, and William Stephenson, to whom he paid a great deal of attention.... The result was that the British Prime Minister was easily the best informed of all the Allied war leaders." Richard Deacon, *A History of the British Secret Service,* New York: Taplinger Publishing Company 1969, pages 354-355.

[132] Churchill knew the value of foreign intelligence. His role before he became Prime Minister could be likened to that of Walsingham, whose information from European spies was recognized by English sea captains as being the most important factor in defeating the Spanish Armada in 1588, thus preparing the way for glorious British Empire. Conyers Read, *Mr Secretary Walsingham and the Policy of Queen Elizabeth,* Cambridge MA: At the Harvard University Press 1925, Volume III, pages 325-326.

[133] "This one is dear to my heart." Winston Churchill advocating Stephenson for the January 1945 ceremonies.

My heart sings because at last someone has written about this remarkable man. I am so glad that, through you, his infinite qualities will survive as a public example, instead of being buried in the dossiers of the Foreign Office. Your book should be a bible for those who may choose to serve through Secret Intelligence. He is a rare human being, and I am completely honest and objective in saying that without *him* and the magnificent organization which he built up, I personally could have accomplished nothing at all.[134]

Biographies of Stephenson contained inaccuracies[135] that subsequent books sought to correct.[136] Some facts, however, are unequivocal: Churchill appointed him head of British western hemisphere intelligence;[137] he was instrumental in getting William Donovan approved by Roosevelt as head of the new American OSS agency and in gaining cooperation with J. Edgar Hoover and his FBI, who contributed the name of Stephenson's organization headquartered in New York, "British Security Coordination"; Stephenson commissioned a brief history of BSC, had twenty copies printed and placed in a locked box, then instructed the author (Hill) and his wife "to gather up the entire BSC archive and destroy it in a huge bonfire."[138] Thus knowledge of the activities of Stephenson and his hundreds of agents in bringing America to the aid of Britain, in Allied espionage critical to the ultimate defeat of Nazism, and in the creation of American overseas intelligence (the OSS and its successor the CIA), will forever be subject to the vagaries of memories and the biases of the personalities involved…constrained moreover by their having signed the Official Secrets Act.

Sensitive 1940s intelligence is gradually being released in Canada, Britain, the USA and Sweden. Historian Ken Cuthbertson noted in 2020:

Stephenson, who was known by his wartime name "Intrepid," is said to have inspired author Ian Fleming to create his now – iconic fictional 007 spy, James Bond. Stephenson's presence in Ottawa in September 1945 during the initial stages of the Gouzenko affair was secret at the

---

[134] In a letter from "Cynthia", quoted in H. Montgomery Hyde, *Cynthia: The story of the spy who changed the course of the war,* London: Hamish Hamilton Ltd. 1966, pages 165-166.

[135] William Stevenson, *A Man Called Intrepid: The Secret War 1939-1945,* London: Book Club Associates by arrangement with Macmillan London, 1975. And, H. Montgomery Hyde, *The Quiet Canadian: The secret service story of Sir William Stephenson,* Constable & Company, London 1961, paperback 1989.

[136] Examples: Bill Macdonald, *The True Intrepid: Sir William Stephenson and the Unknown Agents,* Timberholme Books Ltd., Surrey BC 1998; and in a gossipy book written by a man who was one of the assistants to a secretary of Winston Churchill when war hero and self-made multimillionaire Stephenson was mastermind over hundreds of intelligence agents internationally, acrimony on pages 61-62 of John Colville, *The Churchillians,* London: Weidenfeld & Nicolson 1981.

[137] "The damage inflicted by Stephenson's organization alone to German property and nationals certainly exceeded the total damage caused by the Axis powers on the whole of the American continent." Patrick Howarth, *Undercover: The Men and Women of the Special Operations Executive,* London: Routledge & Kegan Paul Ltd. 1980, p.232-233.

[138] Introduction by Nigel West, Foreword by William Stephenson, *British Security Coordination: The Secret History of British Intelligence in the Americas, 1940-1945,* London: St. Ermin's Press 1998, p.xii.

time and remained unconfirmed until July 2019 … release of large *portions* of a classified history of the Canadian intelligence community…[139]

During WWI Stephenson was gassed in the trenches, returned to England, and while recuperating learned to fly. He became a fighter ace before the Armistice in November 1918.[140] After the Great War he shared the invention of a process for sending photographs by wire, prospered through exploitation of this invention, and then bought and successfully managed a variety of enterprises, becoming a millionaire in his twenties. He was co-inventor of radio and television technologies and the largest shareholder in the General Radio Company, a pioneering manufacturer of radios.[141] Stephenson owned a company that supplied steel body panels to British car manufacturers. In the course of business he frequently visited suppliers in Germany and Sweden,[142] and he was close to international bankers.[143]

Stephenson became aware early of Nazi Germany's violations of the Versailles Treaty – in the manner of remilitarization. Clandestine Russian and Spanish production of armaments and military vehicles

---

[139] Ken Cuthbertson, *1945: The Year That Made Modern Canada,* Toronto: HarperCollins 2020, p.376, italics mine. In a book published 30 years earlier, without the benefit of this information, the authors labeled the war hero, inventor, manufacturer, industrialist and patriot Stephenson a "financial speculator" (p.77) credited with "imaginary achievements" (p.87). J.L. Granatstein & David Stafford, *Spy Wars, Espionage and Canad from Gouzenko to Glasnost,* Toronto: Key Porter Books 1990.

[140] "For some time Stephenson did nothing spectacular. He was always where he should be, but he certainly did nothing to call attention to himself. Then one day during the March offensive in 1918 he was out on a flight in a Sopwith Camel and a couple of German fighters got on his tail, shooting up his machine so badly that he was only able to come in to land with the greatest difficulty and at the risk of his life as his machine was more or less out of control. The small pale-faced figure which emerged from the cock-pit appeared 'hopping mad' and ready to take on the entire German air force, as his friend Drew-Brook also recalls. He immediately got into another machine and insisted on returning to action. The next the squadron heard of him was that he had brought down two German fighter planes in flames. During the next few weeks he destroyed eighteen more enemy machines and two kite balloons… His victims included Lothar Von Richtofen, brother of the famous air 'ace' Baron Von Richtofen…. 'You can always know when Steve is over,' said a Canadian 'Tommy' who experienced the horrors of the Front Line. 'He comes right down to wave "Hello" and never forgets the boys on the ground when things are hot.' These exploits gained for him the Military Cross and Distinguished Flying Cross, while the French awarded him the Legion of Honour and the *Croix de Guerre* with palm." Op. cit. H. Montgomery Hyde, pages 7-8.

[141] "… Stephenson came close to beating John Logie Baird in demonstrating the first mechanical television system. Certainly, Stephenson's patent dealing with the synchronising of receiving and transmitting apparatus – a key difficulty in early mechanical systems – dates from about a year before Baird's British patent GB236978 addressing a very similar system for synchronisation." on p.20 of Ian L. Sanders and Lorne Clark, *A Radiophone in Every Home: William Stephenson and the General Radio Company Limited, 1922-1928,* Twyford Reading Berkshire: Loddon Valley Press 2012.

[142] "These deceptions were spotted by Stephenson because he could look into the records as a bona fide businessman representing, among other things, new industries created by discoveries in synthetic materials, prefabricated construction methods, and propulsion technology. As owner of Pressed Steel Company in Britain, he negotiated with German United Steel and thus found that this conglomerate made howitzers as well as hairpins. He saw where tanks were hidden among the blueprints for tractors. Submarines were now constructed in prefabricated sections in Finland, Holland, and Spain, where the separate bits would not be recognized." William Stevenson, *A Man Called Intrepid: The Secret War 1939-1945,* Book Club Associates by arrangement with Macmillan London 1976, p.35.

[143] "For a considerable number of years before the war the large German Industrial corporations, such as I.G. Farben Industrie and Schering A.G., had been methodically consolidating their interests in the United States. This was done in two ways: through the branches and subsidiaries in the U.S.A. of German-owned companies which were usually camouflaged by neutral ownership in Sweden or Switzerland; … " Op.cit. Hyde, pages 121-122.

competed with Stephenson's Pressed Steel Company for supply from German and Swedish smelters; and their bankers, of course, knew who was buying what from whom.[144]

Folke Hellstedt, in his role as chairman of the *Bergedorfer Eisenwerk* board (1932 – 1945), an important buyer of steel, also saw the effects of German rearmament on supply. During his tenure as general manager, 1925-1931, *Bergedorfer Eisenwerk*'s main market was in agriculture. The "Laval" centrifuges familiar worldwide through their presence in dairying operations[145] were the proprietary treasure of parent company Separator AB (name changed to Alfa Laval after WWII), headquartered in Stockholm. From the time the Nazis assumed power, January 1933, *Bergedorfer Eisenwerk* benefitted from the priority given to military supply. Sales and profits grew every year 1933-1945.[146] In 1937 *Eisenwerk* received a huge order from *IG Farben*: 400 large centrifuges for the production of oil from brown coal.[147] U-boat production in nearby Hamburg and Kiel sourced centrifugal separators, needed aboard submarines for cleaning oil while at sea.

Both Folke Hellstedt and William Stephenson knew the Canadian Trade Commissioner in Hamburg, Dana Wilgress.[148] Folke discovered Leone at a party in the Wilgress house in 1931.[149] The following year Wilgress returned to Canada – to become Director of the Commercial Intelligence Service in Ottawa.

William Stephenson, from the sparsely populated Canadian prairie, and Folke Hellstedt, married to Leone from the Canadian prairie, were active in German and Swedish steel buying and fabricating. Both Folke Hellstedt and William Stephenson were intensely interested in, and well-informed about, the rise of Nazism in Germany and Sweden.[150]

---

[144] "The Canadian businessman had a myriad of information sources, especially in Scandinavia and Switzerland." Op. cit. Bill Macdonald, p.63.

[145] Eighty years after Niels Bohr's 1939 insight into the necessity of enriching natural uranium (98.3% isotope U-238 and 0.7% isotope U-235) by separating U-235 – as the key to exploiting nuclear energy – 99% of the world's production of U-235 is by the "… centrifuge method – a method of separating the two isotopes rather akin to the separation of cream from milk." Quotation from Margaret Gowing, *Britain and Atomic Energy 1939-1945*, London: Palgrave, United Kingdom Atomic Energy Authority 1964, p.120.

[146] Reported in contemporary issues of the *Frankfurter Zeitung*. As did those of its mother in Stockholm: "During the war years, the companies' sales increase by four to five times as much as the pre-war figure." p.61. It was only in 1983 that "…the Group has…shown the highest earnings since the end of the war." p.77, *The Growth of a Global Enterprise: Alfa-Laval 100 Years,* Alfa-Laval AB, Stockholm 1983.

[147] Hitler's condition for the *Lebensraum* program – domestic supply of oil and fuels.

[148] Dana Wilgress was a Canadian Trade Commissioner in Omsk from 1914 until moved to Vladivostok in 1918. Benjamin Isitt, *From Victoria to Vladivostok: Canada's Siberian Expedition, 1917-1919,* Vancouver: UBC Press 2010 p.40. Folke was in Omsk with Kolchak against the Bolsheviks 1917-1918. Op.cit. Ondrack, pages 185-186.

[149] "I was invited to the Dana Wilgress's to a big dinner. Dana was the Canadian Trade Commissioner. After the dinner, where most of the guests were dressed for a masquerade, we all went to the Cosmopolitan Club to dance. At the dinner I met Folke Hellstedt, who took me home from the party and whom I married about six months later. He was an economist and director of a large iron works near Hamburg which was owned by the Swedish Laval Company." Op. cit. Ondrack, p.121.

[150] "One morning Stephenson arrived at the [New York] office and told Garner, 'Get Hall.' He thought he recognized a Swedish agent lingering at the foot of the elevator….He had spotted him as an agent because he had known him. …Stephenson spent time in Sweden before the war." Op.cit. Bill Macdonald., p.272.

Throughout Hitler's twelve years as *Kanzler* of the Reich, Churchill relied on Stephenson for information.[151] Churchill gave William Stephenson the code name "Intrepid"[152], and made him head of overseas intelligence with a special mandate to bring America into the war, a necessity to defeat Hitler.[153]

In addition to his main function as head of British Security Coordination (BSC), Churchill's overseas intelligence, "Stephenson also represented the British Department of Naval Intelligence (DNI), whose chief was Admiral Sir John Godfrey." [154]

Godfrey's personal assistant was the stockbroker made Naval Commander Ian Fleming.[155]

Another filament in Stephenson's web was the acquaintanceship of Folke Hellstedt and William Donovan. Both had the distinction of being in Omsk with Admiral Aleksandr Vasilyevich Kolchak, who was leading the fight against Lenin's and Trotsky's Bolsheviks.[156] The central government fell in 1917, and in early 1918 the Bolsheviks made peace with Germany, releasing a million German troops to fight the

---

[151] "Not being in government, Churchill had no access to official information, so he decided to pursue various private lines of inquiry in order to obtain facts and figures in support of his arguments. Among them, indeed perhaps the most significant, were those provided by Stephenson through access he managed surreptitiously to the balance sheets of the steel firms of the Ruhr. In April 1936, Stephenson reported to Churchill that the expenditure by Germany upon purposes directly and indirectly concerned with military preparations, including the strategic roads, amounted to the equivalent of eight hundred millions sterling.... Churchill...embodied Stephenson's figure of 800 million pounds in a parliamentary question.... For the next three years, that is until Churchill joined the Cabinet on the outbreak of the Second World War, Stephenson continued to feed him with detailed evidence of Hitler's rearmament expenditure." Op. cit. H. Montgomery Hyde, pages 17-18.

[152] "He searched for the right word while Stephenson waited. 'You must be – Intrepid!' ...Churchill felt strongly about code names... BSC records were kept under the label INTREPID from the day Stephenson arrived back in New York posing as a passport control officer." Op. cit. William Stevenson, p.105.

[153] "WS...advocated that a British secret organization in the United States, though founded upon the basis of liaison with Hoover, should not confine itself to purely SIS functions, but should undertake to do all that was not being done and could not be done by overt means to assure sufficient aid for Britain and eventually bring America into the war. On the understanding that he would be empowered to establish such an organization he accepted the appointment of Passport Control Officer in New York.... WS had no settled or restrictive terms of reference...his three primary concerns were to investigate enemy activities, to institute adequate security measures against the threat of sabotage to British property and to organize American public opinion in favor of aid to Britain. It was to fulfil these purposes that his headquarters organization in New York was originally established.... A number of officers and virtually all the secretarial staff were recruited in Canada." West, Nigel et al, *The Secret History of British Intelligence in the Americas, 1940-1945,* New York: Fromm International 1998, pages xxvi-xxviii.

[154] "...Quill, then a Major in the Royal Marines, ...was told that he was to lead an 'irregular' operation to Reykjavik to arrest the German consul and any other German nationals and secure the country for Britain. The Foreign Office still had scruples about the infringement of 'neutral' territory and this was why the NID with a small force of Marines was to carry out the mission. Before leaving Quill was sent for by Godfrey. 'He greeted me by saying that I would want some money for 'special purposes' and then turned around to a filing cabinet behind his left shoulder and extracted a huge bundle of notes which he presented to me....part of a private fund established early in the war for Godfrey, and subsequently replenished from time to time, by a wealthy individual whose name remains a secret.'" Op. cit. Beesly p.157. And, "At the suggestion of William Stephenson, head of the British Secret Intelligence Service in the Western Hemisphere, it was decided to send a certain Colonel William Donovan to make a personal assessment for the President of the chances of British survival and the desirability, from the American point of view, of supplying Britain with the means to carry the fight....Godfrey met Donovan within a day of his arrival." Op cit. Beesly p.176.

[155] And, "Fleming...was occasionally lent to Stephenson for special projects." Thomas E. Mahl, *Desperate Deception: British Covert Operations in the United States, 1939-44,* London: Brassey's 1998, p.14.

[156] Anthony Cave Brown, *Wild Bill Donovan: The Last Hero,* Michael Joseph Ltd., London 1982, pages 74-75 and Op.cit. Ondrack p. 231 and p.236.

Allies on the Western Front. White Russian counter-revolutionary forces under Admiral Kolchak continued on the side of the Allies, and after the armistice in November 1918 were encouraged and enabled by Winston Churchill who was then Minister of War. Following desperate political struggle for authority to assist Kolchak, Churchill was able to send arms worth millions to Russia between May and December, 1919; and he sought 8,000 men for a volunteer army, fighting strong opposition with his incomparable rhetoric:

> Of all the tyrannies in history, the Bolshevist tyranny is the worst, the most destructive, the most degrading. It is sheer humbug to pretend that it is not far worse than German militarism. The miseries of the Russian people far surpass anything they suffered even under the Czar.[157]

Dana Wilgress was also in Omsk then, officially the Canadian Trade Commissioner.[158]

When President Roosevelt created America's first central intelligence agency, he named William Donovan its director. Donovan credited William Stephenson with teaching him the fundamentals and some tricks of the spy trade, and he knew Ian Fleming.[159]

On June 18, 1941, Stephenson cabled Churchill's intelligence head in London:

> Donovan saw President today and after long discussion where in all our points were agreed, he accepted appointment. He will be coordinator of all forms of intelligence including offensive operations … you can imagine how relieved I am after three months of battle and jockeying for position in Washington that our man is in such a position of importance to our efforts.[160]

Donovan consulted psychoanalysts with a view to exploiting Hitler's neurosis.[161] Departments in Donovan's organization included a geographical office, a Center for Arctic Studies, the psychoanalytic unit and the "…not inconsiderable Interdepartmental Committee for the Acquisition of Foreign Publications."[162] Because of Sweden's neutral status, the outstanding source for publications from the Reich was Dr. Adele Kibre's Strandvägen 59 premises, a stone's throw from Clara's apartment at Strandvägen 53 in Stockholm. Besides the quotidian information that located German military units for Allied strategic analysts,

---

[157] From a speech by Churchill in April, 1919, quoted in Virginia Cowles, *Winston Churchill: The Era and The Man,* London: Hamish Hamilton 1953, p.231.

[158] Benjamin Isitt, *From Victoria to Vladivostok: Canada's Siberian Expedition, 1917-1919,* Vancouver & Toronto: UBC Press p.40.

[159] Op.cit. Anthony Cave Brown, *Wild Bill Donovan,* p.163 and p.174.; and, "How far Ian Fleming was personally responsible for the memoranda with which Donovan put his case to the President is not clear. Certainly he worked very hard at drafting during the three weeks he was in Washington. Godfrey's view now is that he and Fleming overrated at the time their part in briefing and boosting Big Bill, while underrating the skilful preparatory work done by Little Bill Stephenson." Op. cit. Donald McLachlan p.234.

[160] Joseph E. Persico, *Roosevelt's Secret War: FDR and World War II Espionage,* New York: Random House 2002 p.91.

[161] John Marks, *The Search for the Manchurian Candidate: The CIA and Mind Control; The Story of the Agency's Secret Efforts to Control Human Behavior,* New York: Times Books 1979, pages 15-16 and p.171.

[162] Thomas F. Troy, *Donovan and the CIA: A History of the Establishment of the Central Intelligence Agency,* Frederick, Maryland: University Publications of America, Inc. 1981/1984, p.110.

Donovan's social psychology team studied newspapers, magazines and journals for clues regarding enemy morale.

The enterprise of predicting Hitler's behavior fell to psychoanalysts...who ransacked the tangled paleologic of *Mein Kampf* for guidance. Hitler's abnormally close relationships with his mother and his sister, and the death of his father during his puberty, were thought to engender unconscious guilt, *Selbsthass*, and projection of incest onto the Jews.[163] Jews were depicted in Nazi propaganda as morally and physically degenerate due to excessive inbreeding. Removing them from Europe would be necessary in order to preserve superior Aryan bloodlines. This thesis was considered plausible in Germany, Austria, Hungary and Romania for several reasons. Judaic prohibitions regarding who should marry whom were somewhat different from those of central Europeans, who were Lutherans and Roman Catholics. Notorious, for example, was the patrilineal prescription practiced by the Jewish celebrities, the Rothschilds – which dictated marriage of young women to uncles and first cousins in order to keep wealth within the clan.[164] Hitler's claim that Jews were not members of a religion, but a degenerate race, was reinforced for most Germans by the "racy" marriage of Albert Einstein to the daughter of his mother's sister. The Nazi claim that "only a Jew would make such a marriage" was plausible to the ordinary German or Austrian. German Christian theologians observed that in the Biblical Period:

> Among the ancestors of Israel there occurred an unusual number of marriages that are incestuous by later standards: evidently this was not merely condoned, but favored, as ensuring good stock.[165]

Contemporary Jewish standards were vulnerable:

> In the State of Israel there is not statutory prohibition of incest as such, but it is an offense, punishable with five years' imprisonment, for anyone to have sexual intercourse with an unmarried girl below the age of 21 who is his, or his wife's descendant, or his ward, or who has been entrusted to him for education or supervision (Section 155, Criminal Code Ordinance, 1936). Apart from this particular provision, it would seem that sexual intercourse within the prohibited degrees of consanguinity described above is, indeed, left to divine punishment.[166]

---

[163] Probed in Norman Mailer's novel, *The Castle in the Forest,* New York: Random House 2007.

[164] During the 19th century rise of the House of Rothschild, the patriarch had five sons: "The fact of a Rothschild marrying a Rothschild had become normal procedure; indeed, of the twelve marriages contracted by sons of the five brothers, nine were with Rothschild women." New York, Alfred A. Knopf 1973, p.89.

[165] *Encyclopaedia Judaica, Volume 8,* Jerusalem: Keter Publishing House Ltd. 1971, p.1315.

[166] Ibid. p.1318.

"The secret war was fought by amateurs." Wm. Stephenson[167]

Stephenson recruited informants, spies and espionage agents.[168] He was wealthy and often paid for British intelligence necessities and preparations for war with Germany out of his own pocket.[169] The British government exchequer was slow and not always capable of the level of secrecy Stephenson required,[170] although Churchill was eventually able to create an espionage slush fund not subject to Cabinet scrutiny.

> BSC's most spectacular triumph was achieved in two embassies in Washington, under the noses of some FBI patrols who would have sternly disapproved, had they known what was going on, by the most successful woman agent of the war, the irresistible Betty Pack (later Madame Brousse), better known by her code-name of "Cynthia." By apt seduction, she managed to obtain the loan overnight – long enough for photocopies to be made – of the Italian and of the Vichy French naval ciphers, successively, with important results for the naval war in the Mediterranean.[171]

Besides recruiting women for his British Security Coordination team, Stephenson encouraged utilization of women in other Allied espionage organizations. Betty Lussier recalled:

> They announced that they would not use women aircraft pilots on the continent. They would stay in England. That sort of annoyed me. It was an integrated service, men and women pilots; we were all treated the same. I was looking for some way to go to the continent and get involved in the fight. I joined OSS through my father's contacts with Sir William Stephenson. …Sir William Stephenson was like a member of the family, and part of my father's squadron in WWI and he was my reference into OSS. They sent us to St. Albans for training. We learned about Ultra. They only wanted a few people to know so they would send these trained people into a headquarters such as the Third Army or Sixth Army. That person would be the

---

[167] Quoting William Stephenson, Op.cit…Stevenson, p.464.

[168] "It is generally accepted that Bill Stephenson fed German rearmament information to Desmond Morton and Churchill…. The Canadian businessman had a myriad of information sources, especially in Scandinavia…." Op.cit. Bill Macdonald, p.63.

[169] "There was no financial inducement for Stephenson to chase ghosts like Enigma or pry into Nazi secrets. Yet everything he touched not only turned into gold, but also involved technical developments that would transform warfare. He was building planes at a time when no British government would put money into military aircraft. His fellow flight commander A.H. Orlebar won the covered aeronautical trophy, the Schneider Cup, in the plane that sired the Spitfire. The designer, Reginald Mitchell, was dying; Stephenson encouraged him sufficiently that he fought pain and despair to complete the graceful fighter in time to defend Britain against invasion. The inventor of the jet, Frank Whittle, remembered his relief at discovering Stephenson, after the Royal Air Force had rejected his revolutionary concept of flight without propellers. Fortunately, such developments could be financed by Stephenson's Electric and General Industrial Trust." Op.cit. Stevenson, p.26.

[170] An example: sixty years after the fact many of Stephenson's activities could not be revealed; an authoritative discussion of his manipulation of politicians using bribery and blackmail in South America was cut short by "PASSAGE DELETED ON GROUNDS OF NATIONAL SECURITY" – in W.J.M. Mackenzie, *The Secret History of S.O.E.: Special Operations Executive 1940-1945,* London: St. Ermin's Press 2002, p.329.

[171] M.R.D. Foot, *Resistance: European Resistance to Nazism 1940-1945,* New York: McGraw-Hill 1977, p.154.

one that would go over the messages in the morning with the British and carefully reveal pertinent information to the armies we were assigned to.[172]

Intelligence and tact were necessary to withhold some information from senior officers … in order to prevent the Germans identifying sources of Allied intelligence from analysis of suspiciously well-directed Allied actions.

Stephenson trusted women for important work – remarkable in a time when the Luftwaffe, for example, did not commission females.[173] Designing and testing the revolutionary and dangerous jet- (Me262) and rocket-powered (Me163) fighters were accomplished by Melitta Schiller von Stauffenberg and Hanna Reitsch only after Hitler sponsored them over the objections of Air Marshall Göring.[174] In 1944 the Luftwaffe was moved to adopt new night-landing procedures developed by Melitta which enabled "… single-engined night fighters as bomber interceptors … the greatest practical contribution either woman made to the German war effort." [175]

It is perhaps impossible for a lay person today to appreciate the burden of secrecy imposed on those who signed the Official Secrets Act.[176] Unable to wear a military uniform, or to boast of overseas combat against the Germans/Italians/Japanese, men and women were suspected of malingering and worse by friends and relatives.[177] Although engaged in sometimes dangerous work crucial to the success of their country in the war, they became pariahs. Moreover, they could never…not after the war, not ever…talk about what they did.[178]

Tragic stories abound; for example, of French women who became mistresses of German officers in order to steal military secrets to convey to British agents – vilified, some killed after the war by vengeful neighbours who knew only the superficial evidence indicating that these women were Nazi collaborators.[179]

---

[172] O'Donnell, Patrick K., *Operatives, Spies and Saboteurs: The Unknown Story of WWII's OSS,* New York: Kensington Citadel Press 2004, p.201.

[173] Clare Mulley, *The Women Who Flew For Hitler: A True Story of Soaring Ambition and Searing Rivalry,* New York: St. Martin's Press 2017, pages 81, 115, 169.

[174] Ibid. After the war Hanna Reitsch continued to praise Hitler and blame Göring's incompetence for defeat.

[175] Ibid. p.227.

[176] "The extent of the secrecy at the time is difficult to imagine in today's world…. She couldn't be told what the actual work was until she'd agreed to do it." Michael Smith, *The Debs of Bletchley Park,* Aurum Press, London 2015, p.98.

[177] "The oaths of secrecy that the recruits were made to swear lasted for many decades beyond the end of the war. Husbands and wives were forbidden to discuss the work they had done there; they could not tell their parents what they had achieved, even if their parents were dying. They were not allowed to tell their children." Sinclair McKay, *The Secret Life of Bletchley Park,* Aurum Press, London 2011, pages 7-8. The world's first programmable computer, "Colossus," was delivered to Bletchley Park in December 1943 and destroyed after the war along with its blueprints. Simon Singh, *The Code Book: The Science of Secrecy from Ancient Egypt to Quantum Cryptography,* New York: Anchor Books 1999.

[178] "All the thousands of young cryptographers and linguists and Wrens were at last able to turn their thoughts to the futures that they had planned for themselves, futures that had been held in limbo for the last six years….'You signed the Official Secrets Act'…We had just escaped from this dreadful war, and therefore anything that was secret then was secret now." Ibid.p.285.

[179] "In almost every case the women agents had to conceal the nature of their work from their family and friends." Marcus Binney, *The Women Who Lived for Danger: The Women Agents of SOE in the Second World War,* London: Hodder & Stoughton 2002, p.3.

The best secret agents were secretive – unobtrusive, anonymous, inconspicuous, disguised, quiet, retiring, reticent, unnoticeable. Survival was the first item in their job descriptions. Men and women of the SOE who by nature and by training avoided detection by the Germans and German collaborators were in the minority. Most SOE agents did not survive the war. Some were unavoidably and uncomfortably made conspicuous by being decorated. The only civilian woman of the war to receive the American Distinguished Service Cross, SOE agent Virginia Hall, was still engaged in espionage and sabotage when her DSC was granted; therefore its announcement would have threatened her security. After the war she declined the invitation to receive her DSC from the President in his White House Oval Office.[180] Instead she preferred to retain the anonymity which enabled her to continue operating in Donovan's OSS, and to become one of the first women to join its successor, the CIA. That we know about her at all… "one woman who really did help turn the tide of history" [181]…is due to the effort of journalist Sonia Purnell.

Even now [2019], tracing her story has involved three solid years of detective work, taking me from the National Archives in London via the Resistance files in Lyon and the parachute drop zones in the Haute Loire to the judicial dossiers of Paris and even the white marble corridors of the CIA at Langley. My search has led me through nine levels of security and into the heart of today's world of espionage; I have discussed the pressures of operating in enemy territory with members of Britain's special forces. I have tracked down files that have gone missing and discovered that others remain lost or unaccounted for. … months of hunting down extracts of those strange "disappeared" papers, years digging out hundreds of forgotten documents and memoirs. Nor have governments made it easy to fill in the gaps. Scores of relevant documents are still classified for another generation – although I managed to have a number released to me with the invaluable aid of two former intelligence officers. Still more went up in flames in a devastating fire at the French National Archives in the 1970s, leaving an unfillable hole in the official accounts. …Only 15 per cent of the original papers from Special Operations Executive – the British Secret Service that Virginia Hall worked for from 1941 to 1944 – survive.[182]

Some surviving documents invite conjecture.
… 6,810 students of various nationalities were trained at the SOE's Special Training Schools…

British	*480*	*American*	*760*
French	*639*	*German Directorate*	*50*
Free French	*662*	*Siamese*	*21*
Czechs	*351*	*Norwegians*	*654*
Russians	*37*	*Yugoslavs*	*13*
Poles	*945*	*Dutch*	*239*

---

[180] Sonia Purnell, *A Woman of No Importance: The Untold Story of WWII's Most Dangerous Spy, Virginia Hall,* London: Virago Press 2019, p. 317

[181] Ibid. Sonia Purnell, p.6.

[182] Ibid. Sonia Purnell, pages 3-4.

Spanish	135	Italians	24
Irish	5	Danes	150
Hungarians	55	Germans	169
Belgians	337 [183]		

The above list totals to 5,726 students (not 6,810), not one of whom is Swedish. It seems impossible that not one Swede was involved while 804 fellow Scandinavians (Norwegians and Danes) are listed; and probable that the Swedes trained by SOE are among the $6,810 - 5,726 = 1,084$ not identified by nationality – this information is in the eighty-five per cent that is missing, or if it exists, has not been declassified.

To staff his BSC head office in New York Stephenson imported women from the Canadian prairie – of sound character and loyal to the British cause.[184] His BSC also worked closely with SOE and its more varied characters involved in sabotage. In early 1941 BSC established SOE agents in Central and South America, and before Pearl Harbor in December training of spies and saboteurs was underway at Camp X in Ontario.[185]

"…look like the innocent flower, But be like the serpent under't."

Macbeth 1.5 Act 1, Sc.5

Many books have been written about the exploits of SOE agents in France, Denmark and Norway. Throughout its short life, 1940-1946, SOE was a clandestine organization. For its British masters to maintain secrecy, "deniability" …of activities and personnel…was necessary. SOE agents captured in Axis-controlled countries could not admit their British military officer status and accordingly become prisoners of war; instead they were executed as spies or terrorists.

> SOE's role in placing agents behind the lines in enemy occupied countries is now well known, but the true ambit of their activities was far wider than that.[186] SOE established a presence in virtually every neutral country. … Many women joined SOE and proved extremely successful agents in the field. All recruitment was done by personal contact and recommendation (as one ex-agent said later, you could hardly advertise for employees for a Secret Service that was not meant to exist).[187]

---

[183] Bernard O'Connor, *Churchill's Most Secret Airfield: RAF Tempsford,* Stroud Gloucestershire: Amberley Publishing, p.108.

[184] H. Montgomery Hyde, *Room 3603: The story of the British Intelligence Center in New York during World War II,* New York: Farrar, Straus and Company, pages 51 & 181.

[185] Ian Dear, *Sabotage and Subversion: The SOE and OSS at War,* Stroud, Gloucestershire: The Military Press 1996/2010 pages 30-33.

[186] As an SOE officer M.R.D. Foot had special knowledge via his wartime activities and acquaintance with other SOE officers; and he was given access to some long-secret records. In 2008 he wrote, "The subject remains in flux …. There may yet be surprises to be sprung from papers left in the hands of family solicitors, or even of governments or libraries, not to be revealed until (say) a century has passed after the end of the war or their authors' deaths." M.R.D. Foot, *SOE: An Outline History of the Special Operations Executive 1940-1946,* London: The Folio Society 2008, p. xii.

[187] Op. cit. Lett p.28.

Chapter Seven
1936: Germany re-arming, King Alfonso, Olympics, Creating Clara

The Amateur in Stockholm

While Leone McGregor was in university becoming a doctor and a medical researcher, threats to her British-Canadian cultural heritage were developing in the aftermaths of WWI and the Russian Revolution. Her future husband, Folke Hellstedt, a loyal citizen of the kingdom of Sweden, had seen firsthand the demise of the tsarist monarchy while fighting with Kolchak's White Russians in Omsk. A widely held view in Sweden and Canada was that an illiterate rabble had been inspired by the Jews Marx, Lenin and Trotsky to violently seize power: Marx advocated "the overthrow of all existing governmental conditions" in order to accelerate the inevitable decline of capitalism and thus the achievement of socialist paradise; therefore, Communists and Jews were enemies of Western civilization.

Canadians had been divided. A Canadian Army expeditionary force departed from Victoria BC bound for Omsk via Vladivostok in late 1918. Soldiers from Quebec declined to obey orders until marched onto the Empress of Japan at bayonet point by their anglophile western "comrades."[188]

Leone McGregor was enrolling in the University of Alberta Faculty of Medicine, in June 1919, when there were riots in Winnipeg and nearly all the working population, 30,000 workers, went on strike. Returning soldiers were unemployed; they accused Bolshevik immigrants of taking their jobs while they were away defending the British heritage of freedom.

In Sweden the Red Peril of communism was reinforced by a centuries-old enmity. Russia and Sweden had fought several wars. The greatest threat to Swedish nationhood was invasion by its neighbor, the largest country in the world. The greatest threat to Swedish culture was oppression by Slavic hordes. With the Bolsheviks in charge the greatest threat to Sweden's democracy, its free enterprise and its treasured monarchy was undoubtedly Russia.[189]

---

[188] "A guard of honour formed, 'fifty men in close formation, with rifles and fixed bayonets on either side of the road,' who escorted the mutinous company ('the French-Canadian company') to the wharf, 'at the point of the bayonet, they being more closely guarded that any group of German prisoners I ever saw.'" Op.cit Benjamin Isitt, p.2.

[189] "In October 1941, four months after the German invasion of Russia, King Gustav V of Sweden wrote a letter to Hitler congratulating him for 'getting rid of the Bolshevik pest.'" Op. cit. Karina Urbach, *Go Betweens* p.128.

Hitler's promise to eradicate communism and its Jewish roots in Aryan society had a special appeal in Sweden. Those of the upper class had the most to lose; they were therefore active in the fight against communism, and accordingly in the time of Hitler, many were Nazi supporters.

Conspicuous among these was Carl Ernfried Carlberg. Like Folke Hellstedt (London 1908), he was a member of a Swedish Olympic Team (Stockholm 1912); like Folke Hellstedt, he had performed military service as a member of the elite Swedish Life Guards Regiment;[190] and like Folke's older brother, an architect, Carlberg made his fortune in the building trade.[191] In the period 1937-1940 Folke was chairman of the Swedish Economic Association.[192] Carl Ernfried Carlberg was the sponsor of organizations dedicated to Nazi ideology – in athletics, publishing, propaganda and coordination of efforts (including liaison with German Nazis).[193]

One of the most influential Swedes of the Nazi era was an old friend of Folke's. Jacob Wallenberg and Folke had been together at school. Wallenberg's biographer noted: "During the summer of 1906 Jacob was isolated at the house of Viktor Hammarsberg and his wife Väddö for intensive study for an entrance examination with his older classmate Folke Hellstedt." [194] Folke was born February 1891, Jacob September 1892. Both qualified for military academy where they trained on the same small sailing ship, *Saga*. After graduation they were members of the elite Swedish Lifeguards (*Svea Livgarde)*; and then in the same company, Separator AB, Folke as manager of German subsidiary Bergedorfer Eisenwerk and then VP International Business; and Jacob on the board of directors; then both were on the board of the Swedish Chamber of Commerce. Jacob was a director of numerous companies, including his family's Enskilda Bank. In the Nazi era he was the head of the Swedish commercial delegation in Berlin. In this capacity he met with Hermann Göring. During the war he also met with Winston Churchill. After the war Folke and Jacob played at the same golf club in Stockholm.

When Leone McGregor married Folke Hellstedt she was thrust into social circles teeming with information of interest to William Stephenson,[195] Ian Fleming and Dana Wilgress. Leone remarked that Folke would not have a Communist in his home[196] – hardly surprising for one who was with Kolchak in

[190] Philip Rees, *Biographical Dictionary of the Extreme Right Since 1890,* Harvester Wheatscheaf from The University Press, Cambridge 1990, p.54.

[191] Ibid. p.54.

[192] Op.cit. Ondrack, p.232.

[193] Op.cit. Rees, p.54.

[194] Håkan Lindgren, *Jacob Wallenberg 1892-1980,* Stockholm: Atlantis 2007, p.37. "*Under sommaren 1906 isolerades Jacob hus dr Viktor Hammasberg och hans hustru på Väddö för intensivläsning inför inträdesexamen tillsammans med den et är äldre klasskammraten Folke Hellstedt.*"

[195] "My part was the registry, everything out of Sir William's office, and it went to Betty Cook's desk. She sorted it under the headings and then she passed it to the correct person who handled that particular area, such as you mentioned, IG Farben or the Electrolux man from Sweden." p. 178, and on p.368, "The Electrolux man was Swedish industrialist Axel Wenner Gren (1881-1961). He formed Electrolux in 1921 to manufacture vacuum cleaners. By 1938 he was one of the wealthiest men in the world, and he plied the world's waterways on his large yacht, Southern Cross….The Southern Cross transported the Duke and Duchess of Windsor to the United States in December of 1940….In 1935, Wenner Gren bought up a large part of Bofors Munitions from German interests, and he was known to have close ties to Nazi Germany." Op.cit. Bill Macdonald.

[196] "In early 1972 Leone and the Vienna girls were thinking about candidates for MWIA honours. Leone wrote to the girls about fellow Swede Andrea Svedberg: 'Marta H. has the idea that Andrea has been a V.P. I had no idea about it. But she has had an

Omsk. As a conspicuously anti-Communist upper class Swede familiar with and respected by the country's leaders, Leone's husband was privy to information of national importance. Multilingual and in an executive international role with Separator AB, he was well informed about foreign affairs.

One spy in the right place is worth 20,000 men on the battlefield.

Napoleon Bonaparte

Opportunity – events of 1936 begat Clara's involvement:

January – Lufthansa announced that its new Heinkel He 111C airliners were the world's fastest, with a maximum speed of 400 km/h. Göring's Luftwaffe had financed development of passenger carriers that could be readily converted into bombers. In 1933 Hitler had objected to the Versailles Treaty which forbade German manufacture of military goods, stating that Germany could only pay reparations by selling German products abroad. The Dornier Do 17 "high speed mail plane for Luft Hansa" and "a freight aircraft with special equipment" [bomb release gear] – in other words, a bomber.[197] Prototypes were produced in 1934 and flown in 1935. Hitler further repudiated the Versailles Treaty in 1935, implemented conscription, and the Luftwaffe tested prototypes from Heinkel, Dornier and Junkers. By the summer of 1936 bombers were being produced in Germany: the Ju 52m[198]; and the Ju 86 D-1[199] and the Heinkel He 111A, versions of which were to be tested by German crews in the Spanish Civil War and used in WW2.

The He 111 first flew in 1934, tested in 1935 (photo below), used in Spain in 1936:

amazing career – married to a Nobel Prize winner – & later to a Cabinet Minister. Salon Communist, but always denied it. Beautiful, close friend of Alva and Gunnar Myrdal, Oberärztin for Internal Med. Laboratories, Lenin Prize. After that Folke would not let me have her in the house.'" Op.cit. Ondrack, p.236.

[197] Joachim Dressel and Manfred Griehl, *The Luftwaffe Album: Bomber and Fighter Aircraft of the German Air Force 1933-1945,* translated by M.J. Shields, London: Brockhampton Press 1999, p.2-25.

[198] Ibid. pages 19-20.

[199] Ibid. pages 21-24

Passenger version [200]

February – In Spain, the left-wing *Frente Popular,* a coalition of socialists, communists and anarchists, was elected by narrow majority and began following the Bolshevik precedent in Russia by seeking to eliminate political rivals, to undermine democracy. In addition, they alienated many in mostly Catholic Spain by copying other Bolshevik innovations – officially confiscating property of the monarchy and the Church, and unofficially failing to control those pillaging and vandalizing churches, murdering priests and raping nuns.[201]

July 17-18 – The Spanish Civil War began, General Francisco Franco led the monarchist/Christian Nationalist rebels against the socialist/communist/anarchist Republicans;

July 10-31 – King Alfonso XIII talked to Franco or his aide on the telephone daily…and played golf with Leone every day.

> We then drove around the country and off to a golf hotel on the Wörther See where we had reserved rooms. It turned out to be perfect. Before leaving Budapest I had packed all our evening clothes by train to Stockholm. To our surprise this little golf hotel turned out to be very elegant with evening clothes for every dinner. Alfonso XIII was staying there and several English socialites.[[202]] There were court curtseys before and after each meal. The first evening Folke told me not to look around but that Alfonso was staring at me. Before we left the dining room he came over to our table and invited us to have coffee and cognac with him in the salon. I had always imagined him from the newspapers that he must be a dreadful person. To my amazement he was charming, very intelligent and interested in everything. This was during the civil war in Spain, after he had left the country and was living in Rome and was separated from his wife. Each evening General Franco or his aide telephoned from Spain.
> That first evening Alfonso called me "Leone", saying, "You allow me, Mr. Hellstedt?" He had interested himself in the olive oil industry and knew all about the Alfa Laval centrifuges used to purify the oil. He had taken a serious part in the planning of the new medical school in Madrid. His mother, a German princess [[203]], had founded the first nursing school in Spain.

---

[200] Photos courtesy of the Max Planck Society, Alamy C45COW and 2CBCEN4.

[201] "… the most extensive and violent persecution of Catholicism in Western History…during the opening months of the civil war…nearly 7,000 clergy and many thousands of lay Catholics were slaughtered." Stanley G. Payne, *Franco and Hitler: Spain, Germany and World War II,* New Haven & London: Yale University Press 2008, p. 13.

[202] King Edward VIII, later Duke of Windsor, played at the Dellach Golf Club.

[203] Actually Austrian, Maria Cristina.

The tragedy of haemophilia in his children had led him to read everything on the subject. In short, there was nothing human which did not concern him.[204] He and I played golf every day for three weeks while Folke played with his aide, I think the Duke of Toledo. During these golf games Alfonso and I discussed everything on the face of the earth and became very great friends. Folke liked him very much and as we drove off at six a.m. one morning, Alfonso was down in front of the hotel to say goodbye, to kiss my hand and to send his best regards to my mother. It had not mattered one bit that I had only kept two short dresses, one pink and one pale blue, to go to dinner in.[205]

News from Spain was corrupted by the strong feelings of journalists – on both sides. And everyone took sides. Matthew Halton's reporting favored the Republicans. Clara's new friend Alfonso XIII had the prospect of the restoration of his monarchy before him should the Nationalists win. Russia helped the communist side. Italian and German fascist governments immediately gave aid to Franco's Nationalists.

The first Junkers Ju-52/3m aircraft arrived in Morocco on 29 July, the last on 11 August. They helped carry 14,000 men, 44 pieces of artillery, 90 machine guns and 500 tons of ammunition and stores from North Africa to southern Spain, in the first major airlift of troops in military history. It was these Italian and German aircraft that rescued the fascist rebellion against the Spanish Republic.[206]

The Spanish Civil War offered Göring's Luftwaffe a magnificent opportunity to test and refine its weapons. Thousands of German volunteers formed the "Condor Legion", gaining combat experience, refining tactics and training soldiers in preparation for the bigger conflict ahead.

1936: Clara cues a clue

Why did Leone describe the Hellstedts' relationship with King Alfonso XIII forty years later in her unpublished autobiography? Why was there a portrait of Alfonso hanging in the Hellstedt's Stockholm apartment?

As a case study for Leone, a Freudian psychoanalyst, Alfonso was a treasure. His father King Alfonso XII died before XIII was born – May 17, 1886. His mother, Maria Cristina of Austria, was his regent until he assumed the king's duties on his sixteenth birthday. Alfonso was a sickly child, attended constantly by his mother, who was a strict disciplinarian. Shortly before he died he said that his mother was the one true love of his life.[207]

---

[204] Alfonso XIII is the only monarch who has been nominated for a Nobel Peace Prize.

[205] Op. cit. Ondrack pages 131-132.

[206] Nicholas Rankin, *Telegram From Guernica: The Extraordinary Life of George Steer, War Correspondent,* London: Faber & Faber Limited 2003, p.80.

[207] Vincente R. Pilapil, *Alfonso XIII,* New York: Twayne Publishers, Inc. 1969, p.172.

In 1936, during their annual golf vacation in the south of Austria, Folke and Leone stayed in the same hotel as Spain's exiled King Alfonso XIII. At the same time Ian Fleming was visiting his friend in nearby Schloss Wasserleonburg.[208]

The mid-summer of 1936 was a time of epic events in Europe: Hitler had renounced the Versailles Treaty, introduced universal conscription and was in the process of expanding forces from 100,000 to 480,000 men; Germany was modernizing ground, sea and air weapons; on June 30 there was a near-riot in the League of Nations when Emperor Hailie Selassie described to the Assembly Italian atrocities in Ethiopia – what is today called "genocide"[209]; July 17-18, outbreak of the Spanish Civil War; August 1-16, Olympic Games in Berlin.

It is important to an understanding of the evolution of Clara to note that Alfonso talked every day on the telephone with Franco or his aide about the progress of the civil war; and every day played a two-ball with Leone/Clara, with whom he "discussed everything on the face of the earth and became very great friends."

These three weeks of daily golf games and wide-ranging discussions with Leone/Clara…it was a critical time for Alfonso. The socialist-communist-anarchist *Frente Popular* had taken unpopular actions – antidemocratic restrictions on political opponents and confiscation of church and hereditary properties.

Assassination of a conservative party leader had spurred military officers to initiate a war against the anti-monarchy, anti-church Republican regime. Forces had been assembled in Spanish Morocco. A British MI6 agent had flown General Francisco Franco from the Canary Islands (where the Popular Front regime had deployed him) to Morocco. On July 21 Alfonso's private secretary, the Marquis de Viana, was in Rome with a delegation soliciting aid from Mussolini.[210] Fascist Italy and Germany came in on Franco's Nationalist side with troop transportation to southern Spain.

What were the topics of Alfonso's daily conversations with the monarchist Nationalist leaders? And with Clara? What were the items on the front pages of the world's newspapers during July 1936?

At the outset of the Civil War, the Spanish government canceled the "People's Olympiad," scheduled for July 19-26. These were games for anti-fascists, mainly communists, who wanted to boycott the International Olympic Committee official games in Berlin beginning a week later. Joseph Stalin had canceled the Soviet competitor to the Olympic Games, the "Spartakiad", in order to send athletes to Barcelona. Many of the athletes registered (6,000 from twenty-two nations) did not arrive before borders were closed due to the civil war. Of those who did, more than 200 remained in Spain to fight on the Republican side.

While Franco's forces were fighting for 'king and country', the institution of the monarchy was being harmed by the world's most prominent king. The topic of the world's gossip was the conspicuous adultery of Edward VIII and Wallis Simpson. Edward played golf with Alfonso at Dellach.[211]

---

[208] The Duke and Duchess of Windsor (formerly King Edward VIII and Mrs. Wallis Simpson) stayed at Schloss Wasserleonburg on their honeymoon in the summer of 1937. Andrew Lownie, *Traitor King: The Scandalous Exile of the Duke & Duchess of Windsor,* New York: Pegasus Books, Ltd. 2022, p.33. And they played golf there: Philip Ziegler, *King Edward VIII,* New York: Alfred A. Knopf 1991, p.317.

[209] Op. cit. Nicholas Rankin, *Telegram from Guernica*, p.76.

[210] Antony Beevor, *The Battle for Spain: The Spanish Civil War 1936-1939,* London: Weidenfeld & Nicolson 2008, p.135.

[211] In a hallway of the Dellach Golf Club (on the Wörther See) in 2013 there were photos of Alfonso XIII and Edward VIII playing there in the thirties. After abdicating the throne in December 1936 he became the Duke of Windsor.

Although Franco eventually restored the Spanish monarchy, it was not with the Nationalist victory in 1939, but much later...after the dust of WWII had settled and it was politically feasible in 1947...by declaring Spain again a monarchy (with himself as head of state). It was only in 1978, after Franco and Alfonso, that the Spanish Constitution was changed to again make Spain a monarchy.

Like Franco, Alfonso must have been pleased with the characteristics of the latest German aircraft types that would be used in support of Nationalist forces.

To superficially comply with the Treaty of Versailles Germany had commissioned development of aircraft that could function as heavy bombers as well as passenger carriers. In January 1935 a Heinkel 111-A flew at more than 400 kph and was called "the fastest passenger aircraft in the world". The military version, Heinkel 111-B, began production at Rostock in the summer of 1936.

When Russia sent aid to the Popular Front government side (socialists, communists, anarchists) in the Spanish Civil War, Germany and Italy responded on the Franco side (monarchists, fascists). Heinkel 111s supported the German Condor Legion.[212]

213

[212] Brian Johnson, *The Secret War,* London: British Broadcasting Corporation 1978, p.35.; and Christian Leitz and David J. Dunthorn,editors, *Spain in an International Context, 1936-1959,* New York, Oxford: Bergbahn Books 1999, pages 47, 171.

[213] Photo of soldiers boarding a Ju-52 in July, 1936, outbreak of the Spanish Civil Water. Alamy TA2XDR.

Guernica 1937 April

Sweden was the first foreign government to buy a Junkers bomber. At an aviation show in Stockholm in May, 1935, the Ju 86 was exhibited. On June 30, 1936, the Swedish Armed Forces ordered a Ju 86A-1. Sweden's next twenty were powered by the Bristol Pegasus III radial engine, built in Sweden under licence beginning in 1937.[215]

[214] Photos courtesy of Basque Library, University of Nevada, Reno

[215] Images: Swedish JU 86 in flight WWII (Alamy 2M96Y5H). The last remaining Ju 86 in the world is in the Flyvapen Museum, Linkoping, Sweden (Alamy 2HK3MFY).

1931

Alfonso at Dellach [216]

Carinthia 1936, a July evening

Leone and Folke were dining in the hotel restaurant. Leone's short blue woollen dress was less formal than others in the room.

"Leone, don't look around, but Alfonso has been staring at you."

Leone and Folke chatted. Finally, Leone glanced at Alfonso, seated at a table across the room, then quickly looked back at her dessert.

"Here he comes," Folke said under his breath.

Alfonso approached, his aide a step behind.

"Good evening, Madame and Mister Hellstedt, I believe. Today on the golf course I admired, from a distance, your wonderful proficiency. Perhaps you would join me for a cognac in the lounge … and share the secrets of becoming such a golfer?"

Leone and Folke looked at each other and rose from their chairs.

"Excuse me, I am Alfonso … and my companion is Joaquin."

Folke nodded, "Of course. We know. A cognac would be most welcome after our Austrian dinner."

"I could not help overhearing … the golf professional called Frau Doktor 'Leone' … and he revealed she was Canadian. Perhaps she would be comfortable if we could call each other in the Canadian way? I shall be 'Alfonso' and she will be 'Leone'. You allow, Mister Hellstedt?"

"Yes, Canadian. And then I should be 'Folke'."

"'Folke' it is… and this gentleman is my aide, Joaquin Alvarez de Toledo y Caro. In Canada what would they call you?"

"My friends say 'Wah-keen'. In the English bible Joaquin is Joshua."

"Wah-keen sounds so much better," Leone offered.

"Wah-keen", Alfonso said, "So it shall be … Wah-keen."

The next day on the fairway Alfonso and Leone were walking side by side, talking and gesticulating. Alfonso stopped to make a point. Leone laughed. Alfonso laughed. Ahead Folke, Joaquin and their caddies were all waiting. When they reached the next tee, Alfonso declined the club from his caddie, and spoke.

"Folke, I see that you and Toledo are skilled and fast players … and that Leone and I not so fast. Would you like to play ahead?"

Folke and Joaquin looked at each other. Folke nodded.

"Perhaps that would be a good idea. Two-balls move faster than four-balls, and a match behind won't be delayed."

"Your honor, Folke".

With their golf games evenly matched, the two-balls played every day when it wasn't raining – for the next three weeks. Leone and Alfonso chatted interminably.

Leone mentioned that this year she had lost her race with Ian Fleming. Her LaSalle was not as fast as Ian's new supercharged Graham-Paige. Leone, feigning technical ignorance, asked Alfonso about supercharging. He told her enthusiastically about the new bombers that the Germans would use to help his allies in the Civil War – supercharged so that they could fly faster and higher, beyond the Republicans' gun range. Of course, according to the Treaty of Versailles, the Germans were not supposed to have such weapons. The fact that many parts were made secretly in Russia, whose government ostensibly supported the Republicans, was a joke enjoyed by Alfonso and Franco in their daily telephone conversations.

Millstatt Abbey

Near the end of their stay by the Wörthersee, and before leaving for Berlin to attend the Olympic Games, rain interrupted the day's golf, allowing Folke and Alfonso to address business matters. Leone drove to nearby Millstadt. In the twelfth century monastery there stood a magnificent musical instrument. Leone was alone, looking at perhaps the first grand piano made by Ignacz Bösendorfer, when Ian Fleming appeared at her side.

Looking reverently at the beautiful old instrument, Ian offered, "Franz Liszt was pounding pianos to pieces in Vienna…around 1830…the call went out for a stronger instrument. Ignacz Bösendorfer succeeded in pleasing Liszt, and Kaiser Ferdinand responded with a royal warrant for Bösendorfer's pianos…which are still the best."

"In Stockholm we have a grand piano, a Steinweg…or Steinway. I bought it cheaply in Hamburg during the economic collapse. Folke plays most evenings. Usually Wagner. Perhaps he should have a Bösendorfer…but keeps the Steinway so that he won't hurt my feelings."

"Perhaps…Leone, I must tell you that I have news of Frau Friedheim. Although we are not certain, we think she died… possibly on the way to the Dachau camp."

Leone walked out of sight around a corner, while Ian remained standing, his eyes following her, then to the beautiful piano. "Jews are being treated roughly on their way to prosecution as political criminals," he said.

Having regained her composure, Leone returned. "Since civil war was declared last week, Alfonso has been receiving daily calls from Franco. The Germans offer bombing support…*sine pecunia* ... to the Nationalists."

"Another violation of the treaties with Britain, France and the United States…which stipulate non-intervention…and there's the Versailles Treaty clause about producing warplanes."

"Alfonso says that the Germans would like to test some innovations. The new Dorniers…or was it Heinkels? …carry a heavier bomb load at higher speed than any previous types. And at higher altitude … which they think will be out of the range of Republican guns."

"Leone, can you get me particulars? Of speed, ceiling, payload?"

"I'll try. You'll recognize the numbers from our Kokoschka calculus."

"Oh, when I go to Berlin next month for the Olympics I'll see if the bookstores have the Toynbee[217] volume two we'll use for coding. They aren't common, and the fewer in circulation the better."[218]

---

[217] Professor Arnold Toynbee worked in British political intelligence from 1915. Churchill and the War Cabinet relied on his brief, factual intelligence summaries. From 1943-1946 Toynbee was Director of the Research Department of the Foreign Office. Richard Deacon, *A History of British Secret Service,* Granada Books, Panther Publishing Ltd. 1980, p.399.

[218] In her autobiography and correspondence Leone mentioned the WWII fuel shortage and late nights in her warm bed reading Toynbee's *A Study of History.* She was a prolific letter writer, yet her daughter told me that she never saw her mother write a letter. Leone wrote when her daughter, an infant during the war, was sleeping. Having chosen a book, the 1934 edition of *A Study*

"Folke has been invited to a dinner for German industrialists. Accommodation has been laid on by Göring's minions. It will be an opportunity to see some of the Games. And…before I forget, Alfonso suggested that Heinkels…or was it the Dorniers…will come to Spain from Russia. Is that possible?"

"I don't think so. But Göring has contracted manufacture of other kinds of armaments to factories in Russia…to sidestep Versailles Treaty control…so maybe. Leone, if we can meet in Berlin I'll bring a copy of the Official Secrets Act for your signature. The way things are going…and with your connections in Stockholm and Hamburg… Shhh!"

Voices speaking German were heard from the hall. A group was approaching the museum's piano room. Fleming quickly slipped out the exit away from the group's approach.

---

of History, Vol. II, the Leone/Ian code could have been thus: first three numbers/characters = page number, e.g. 243 = page 243, W7Q = page 7; next two characters = line on page, e.g. X5 = line 5, 17 = line 17; next two numbers, i.e. characters six and seven, word on line, e.g. 4R = fourth word, 10 = tenth word. If a suitable word could not be found, letters of the alphabet would be indicated by the preface. e.g. K2 = B, the second letter of the alphabet. Thus "Danish Jews arriving during night" = 'Danish' 199W9T7 space 'Jews' 242E43F space 'arriving' 24319X6 space 'during' 24320R3 space 'night' 24320H5. To code 'BOHR': K2W33K15K8MNK18TT3.

existence but determined their centres of gravity and assigned them their historic capitals. The Kingdom of England coalesced, not round Mercia, which failed to respond to the Scandinavian challenge, but round Wessex, which rose to the occasion. The old capital of Wessex, however, did not become the capital of the new English Kingdom; for Winchester, which had once lain within range of the frontier of Wessex over against the 'West Welsh', did not lie in the principal danger-zone in the struggle between the English and the Danes. In the Danish ordeal, Winchester enjoyed a comparative security for which it had afterwards to pay by an irreparable loss of prestige and power. When Wessex had mastered the Danes and had grown into England in the process of performing the feat, the capital of the new kingdom soon passed from Winchester, in the inglorious interior, to London, the city which had borne the heat and burden of the day and which had perhaps given the long battle its decisive turn in A.D. 895 by repelling the attempt of a Danish Armada to ascend the Thames. Similarly, the Kingdom of France found its centre of gravity, not in Provence or Languedoc, whose Mediterranean coastline was rarely visited by Viking raiders, but in the Langue d'Oil, which felt the full force of the storm from Scandinavia. Again, within the area of the Langue d'Oil, the capital passed away from Carolingian Laon—a city set safely on a hill overlooking the sources of the Oise, far above the highest point up to which the river was navigable for Viking craft. The inevitable capital of the new French Kingdom was Paris in the Île de France, a city which had stood in the breach and had brought the Vikings to a halt in their ascent of the Seine as London had brought them to a halt in their ascent of the Thames.[1]

Thus the response of Western Christendom to the Scandinavian maritime challenge manifested itself in a new Kingdom of France with its capital at Paris, as well as in a new Kingdom of England with its capital at London; and at the same time it is to be observed that these manifestations of new creative power on the face of the political map, imposing though they are, do not reveal the actual vigour and versatility of the response in its full measure. In order to take its measure, we must add that, in the process of gaining the upper hand over their Scandinavian adversaries, the French and English peoples forged the potent military and social instrument of the Feudal System, and that they also gave aesthetic expression to the emotional experience of the ordeal in national epics.

English King Henry V continued was consummated by all the neighbours of France in unison when they fell upon Revolutionary France in 1792, and provoked an eruption of national energy which astonished the World.

[1] For details of the rise of Paris and London through their heroic responses to the Scandinavian challenge, see the Annex to the present chapter, pp. 400-1, below.

however, the evicted Ashkenazim have been unable to find a fresh asylum by trekking still farther eastward. Beyond the eastern boundary of 'the Pale', 'Holy Russia' has barred their way.

For the Jews, Russian soil has been forbidden ground from the time when Western and Russian Christendom originally made contact with one another on the Continent in the fourteenth century of the Christian Era right down to the Russian Communist Revolution of A.D. 1917. This barrier did not fall when Russia opened her doors to the Western Civilization in the generation of Peter the Great; and it did not fall thereafter when the eastern marches of Western Christendom were incorporated politically into the Russian Empire. The old frontier between Muscovy and the United Kingdom of Poland-Lithuania, which the Partition of Poland obliterated for the Christian subjects of the Czar, remained in force for the Jew as an eastern limit which he was absolutely forbidden to pass. It was fortunate indeed for the Ashkenazim that by this time the leading nations of the West, which had been the first to evict the Jews in the Middle Ages, had risen to a height of economic efficiency at which they were no longer afraid of exposing themselves to Jewish economic competition in a free field with no favour. The emancipation of the Jews in the West came just in time to give the Ashkenazim of 'the Pale' a new western outlet when their old eastward drift was brought up short against the blank wall of 'Holy Russia'. During the past century, the tide of Ashkenazi migration has been ebbing back from east to west: from 'the Pale' and Rumania into England and the United States. It is not to be wondered at that, with these antecedents, the Ashkenazim whom this ebb-tide has deposited among us should display the so-called 'Jewish' ethos more conspicuously than their Sephardi co-religionists whose 'lines' have 'fallen'[1] in comparatively pleasant places.

To the author of this Study, the spiritual and political duress under which the Ashkenazim have had to live their life in 'the Pale' was brought home by the following two anecdotes which were recounted to him in 1919, during the Peace Conference of Paris, by Dr. Chaim Weizmann in order to explain why this great statesman and scientist—the most distinguished member of the Ashkenazi community in his generation—had become a convert to Zionism.

The first anecdote was this. In Dr. Weizmann's boyhood, at Vilna, there was a young Jewish sculptor of great promise who was expected to become one of the historic exponents of the Jewish culture. The young man's promise was fulfilled, but Jewry's hope was disappointed; for the *chef d'œuvre* in which this Jewish artist eventually gave expression to his genius was a statue of the Russian

[1] Psalm xvi. 6.

Orthodox Christian Czar Ivan the Terrible! Under the duress of 'the Pale', Jewish genius had been perverted to the glorification of Jewry's oppressors. It was as if the *chef d'œuvre* of Jewish literature in the second century B.C. had not been the Book of Ecclesiastes or the Psalms but some panegyric, in the Isocratean manner, upon Antiochus Epiphanes. Truly, that statue of a Russian Czar by the hand of a Vilna Jew was as great an eyesore for Jewish eyes as the statue of Zeus which the Seleucid once set up in the Temple of Yahweh at Jerusalem: an 'abomination of desolation standing where it ought not'.[1]

Dr. Weizmann's second anecdote was an incident which had happened to himself as a grown man before his migration from Vilna to Manchester. A piece of urgent business made it indispensable for him to break the Russian law then in force, under the Czardom, by trespassing beyond the eastern boundary of 'the Pale' in order to have a personal meeting with a friend in Moscow. As a precaution against the vigilance of the Russian police, it was arranged beforehand that Dr. Weizmann should travel from Vilna to Moscow in a train arriving at nightfall, do his business in his friend's house during the night, and return to Vilna by a train leaving Moscow before dawn; but this arrangement fell through. For some reason, the friend whom Dr. Weizmann had come to see was unable to keep the appointment; and Dr. Weizmann found on inquiry that there was no return-train to Vilna earlier than the train which he had been intending to take. How should he pass the night hours? To engage a room in a hotel would be tantamount to delivering himself up to the police. Dr. Weizmann solved the problem by hiring a cab and driving round and round the streets of Moscow until the hour of his train's departure. 'And that', he concluded, 'was how I had to pass my time on my one and only visit to the capital of the Empire of which I was supposed to be a citizen!'

Such anecdotes as these sufficiently explain the ethos of the Ashkenazi immigrants from 'the Pale' into the more enlightened countries of the modern Western World; and the less highly accentuated 'Jewishness' of the ethos which we observe among the Sephardi immigrants from Spain and Portugal is explained by the antecedents of the Sephardim in Dār-al-Islām.

The representatives of the Jewish Dispersion in the dominions of the Sasanidae and in those provinces of the Roman Empire which ultimately fell to the Arabs and not to the North European barbarians found themselves in a happy position compared with their unfortunate co-religionists in the Rhineland. Their status under the régime of the 'Abbasid Caliphate was certainly not less favourable

[1] Mark xiii. 14; Matthew xxiv. 15; Luke xxi. 20; Daniel ix. 27.

[219] Arnold J. Toynbee, *A Study of History: Volume II,* London: Oxford University Press 1934/63, pages 199, 242-243. Before WWII began the first six volumes of *A Study of History* were published, a total of 3,488 pages.

Millstatt Abbey now Stiftmuseum Millstatt

Millstatt Bösendorfer

Early next morning the four golfers were standing beside Alfonso's Packard while his chauffeur loaded luggage.

"These three weeks playing golf with such amiable companions …how can I say it? My country is cruelly divided…and I should try to do more…at least seem to do more. I really can't influence events. And for Joaquin – he must return to Estoril. Soon his wife will give him their first child."

"Folke," said Joaquin, "remember, near Estoril is a wonderful golf links – in Cascais by the sea, the western end of Europe. And the casino in Cascais. You must visit us."

"Yes, Joaquin, I'll remind Folke. And you must let us know about your baby … and how your wife is doing."

The chauffeur opened a rear door of the Packard and Alfonso placed a briefcase on the back seat, while Leone continued, "Folke had a call confirming our hotel in Berlin. Herr Feldmarshall Göring has invited us to some Olympic Games events next week. And a banquet. We have called Stockholm to send some clothes we should have had to dine with you, Alfonso."

"Much of the joy in these last weeks has been the charming lack of formality … the Canadian way. I wish my life could yield more of it."

With handshaking and good-byes accomplished, Alfonso and Joaquin climbed into the back of the Packard, closed the doors and waving, set off.[220] Leone and Folke settled into their LaSalle, looking forward to opening its throttle on the new sections of the A9 autobahn north of Munich.

The Red Duchess [221]

---

[220] During the war Ian Fleming gambled at the Estoril Casino while traveling through Lisbon. He used aspects of it in his first novel – in describing *Casino Royale*. Joaquin's only child was born a few weeks later, in Estoril, Portugal, August 17, 1936. With Joaquin's passing, Luisa Isobel Alvarez de Toledo became the 21st Duchess. She married and had three children, whom she alienated in later life when she became the notorious communist lesbian "Red Duchess" – who chainsmoked, drank heavily with her peasants, refused to wear a dress or use deodorant, and gave away property and treasures accumulated by her family since the 12th century. In 2005 Spain legalized same-sex marriage. In 2008, hours before her death from lung cancer, the Red Duchess married her secretary.

[221] Photo courtesy of *The Telegraph UK.*

Olympic Games: 1936

From August 1-16, 1936 the Olympic Games were held in Berlin. In order to make a favorable impression, signs such as the one in Leone's photo album, "*Jüden sind hier nicht erwünscht,*" were removed from areas where foreigners were likely to stray. Matthew Halton was there and recognized the deceit.[222] Roland Michener, Leone's first date at the University of Alberta,[223] a lifelong friend who was a Rhodes Scholar, and after the war Governor General of Canada, was active in the Canadian Olympic program.

Nazi measures against Jews in Germany[224] had fostered a movement in the United States to boycott the Berlin Olympics. The IOC Swedish delegate, J. Sigfrid Edstrøm, who would become president of the IOC in 1946, wrote to organizer Avery Brundage:

> It is too bad that the American Jews are so active and cause us so much trouble. It is impossible for our German friends to carry on the expensive preparations for the Olympic Games if all this unrest prevails. … As regards the persecution of the Jews in Germany I am not at all in favor of said action, but I fully understand that an alteration had to take place. As it was in Germany, a great part of the German nation was led by the Jews and not by the Germans themselves. Even in the USA the day may come when you will have to stop the activities of the Jews. Many of my friends are Jews so you must not think that I am against them, but they must be kept within certain limits.[225]

Nazi leaders organized enormous parties. Goebbels held receptions for political leaders. Göring sponsored banquets and receptions for industrialists.[226]

---

[222] "On the eve of the Olympics, the *Toronto Daily* Star's correspondent, Matthew Halton, no friend of the Nazi regime, was in Berlin to cover the spectacle. He was saddened but not surprised to find Olympic visitors so swept up in Olympic euphoria that they were blind to what lay behind all the Olympic bunting. Berlin was on its best behaviour. Those who knew Nazi Germany knew that the iron fist had only temporarily slipped into a velvet glove. But for most Olympic visitors, Berlin was a party…." Richard Menkis & Harold Troper, *More Than Just Games: Canada and the 1936 Olympics,* Toronto: University of Toronto Press 2015, p.179.

[223] Roland Michener's father (later an MLA and a senator) was the mayor when Leone's father was a grocery clerk in Red Deer. After the war Leone visited the Micheners in Canada.

[224] "Entirely concealed from visitors and omitted from Leni Riefenstahl's subsequent film, *Olympiad,* was the wholesale transformation of German life. However, it was apparent to Berliners that by 1936, political, social, economic, and religious freedoms had vanished. The Nuremberg Laws enacted in 1935 deprived Jews of German citizenship and expelled them from public office and most professions. Sexual relationships between Jews and Aryans were forbidden." Shareen Blair Brysac, *Resisting Hitler: Mildred Harnack and the Red Orchestra,* Oxford, New York: Oxford University Press 2000, p.185.

[225] David Clay Large, *Nazi Games: The Olympics of 1936,* New York: W.W. Norton & Company 2007, pages 76-77.

[226] "There were still two big parties to go…Goering's party was held in the Ministerium in the centre of Berlin…Goering had excelled himself, and entertained the 800 guests to an evening of fine wine, food and ballet." Guy Walters, *Berlin Games: How The Nazis Stole The Olympic Dream,* New York: Guy Walters HarperCollins 2006, pages 258-259.

[227] First sports television Berlin 1936. Photo of TV camera in Bildarchiv Preussischer Kulturbesitz, Alamy CPJB2J. Ceremonies photos Alamy 2R3901J, FD833A and M9MF57.

[228] Alamy DMWMKE.

Statues of Aryans, Berlin 1936

Bundesarchiv. Bild 183-G00630 / Fotograf(in): Hoffmann. Heinrich   229

Hitler salute from German on podium

230

Roland Michener, Governor General of Canada

A reporter is interviewing Roland Michener in his Governor-General's office, 1970

"Leone McGregor? She visited Norah and me recently. Fifty years ago I asked Leone to the big university dance, the first formal for both of us. In those days newspapers reported the grades made by University of Alberta medical students. Of the more than one hundred students in first year medicine, Leone had achieved the highest grade in every course. A girl! I remember difficulty talking to her...her eyes...sparkle...fascinating...and distracting. My father, Senator Edward Michener, did not approve of me

---

229 Photo courtesy of Bundesarchiv Berlin

230 Photo courtesy of the Lacombe and District Historical Society, Lacombe, Alberta, Canada.

getting involved with a girl from a poor family…and anyway we had little time to socialize…both of us were working hard to make top grades and earn fellowships. Over the years we've stayed in touch, though … not long ago a nice reunion at Canada House in London. Jean Halton, Matt's widow, is the social convenor there. Oh, and in Berlin in thirty-six…"

Leone, Folke and Roland Michener dining in a Berlin restaurant, August 5, 1936

"Roland, as an expert…who played ice hockey for Oxford University, can you tell us how the Canadians managed to lose in Garmisch? And to Great Britain!"

"Ah…you mean to Canadians who currently live in Britain. Canadians carry British passports."

"Yes, you have a point. Sweden also could have done better, especially if bandy was the game, not hockey."

"Folke plays bandy", said Leone.

"A faster game on a bigger rink, I understand. You must be very fit…but of course…you competed in the Olympics…for Sweden in the high jump."

"That was long ago. In London before the Great War. My bandy-playing now is social…and a bit for fitness."

"Admit it, Folke. It's more for business, really…playing with old classmates, bankers, manufacturers. Folke is president-elect of the Swedish Chamber of Commerce."

"So what do you think of these Nazi Olympics," Roland asked.

Folke responded, "A great spectacle. German prosperity is everywhere evident. Amazing. Still, I would not be here … but it is important that I meet certain business obligations. I prefer the quiet of the Austrian golf course … where we played last month … before driving to Berlin."

"Roland, have you had a chance to drive on their autobahns?", asked Leone.

"No. Without the help of a Rhodes Scholarship Committee colleague and the Canadian Embassy I wouldn't have a place to stay…never mind a car."

"Folke tells me that without the influence of Herr Göring we would not have nearly the quality of accommodations. Maybe no hotel at all. We would have driven straight home to Stockholm from Austria. But, because Folke is chairman of a German subsidiary which supplies important machines to the government, Herr Göring invited us here … to see the Games and to attend banquets honoring those who have contributed to the rise of Germany. Last evening I met the most interesting people. Herr Hitler's… 'secretary' … looks like she could compete in these games."

"It is said that Eva Braun's private gymnastic performances hold a singular charm for *Herr Kanzler Hitler*."

Eva Braun [231]

232

233

von Below [234]

---

[231] Photo Alamy KWC3DH

[232] Photos Alamy 2J33H3G and 2J33K5C

[233] Photo Alamy 2J33N28

[234] Photo courtesy of Bayerische Staatsbibliotek, Heinrich Hoffmann hoff.27389 and Alamy DB3PEC.

Eva Braun was Hitler's mistress. Much has been written about her – vain, neurotic, shallow, and so on – by authors who never met her. From the memoir of a man who was at Hitler's side most days from 1937 to the marriage and paired suicide of Hitler and Eva Braun in late April 1945, we learn that Eva occupied the bedroom adjoining Hitler's in the Berchtesgaden "Berghof;"[235] that he thanked guests for being polite to Eva;[236] that they were with each other on their birthdays, exchanging gifts;[237] and that near the end he recognized her loyalty as being the most sincere and valuable of his life.[238]

At the time of the Berlin Olympics Hermann Göring was responsible for not only building an air force but also for industrial production. In that capacity he invited more than a thousand guests to a banquet on August 6 – industrialists, diplomats and their wives.

Before the war Clara could have learned something about Hitler and the high-level Nazis who had houses at Berchtesgaden (Himmler, Speer, Göring, Goebbels). Hitler's fascination with athletic women, part of his vision of the "master race", was well known;[239] but all first-hand information about his neuroses was welcomed by Allied analysts.[240]

Berlin Opera House, evening of August 6, 1936, a conjecture

The door to the ladies' powder room was held open by a uniformed woman. Clara stopped in the doorway, raised her right foot and with her right hand adjusted the heel of her shoe. She was wearing a white silk gown with white ermine. Looking around the room, she saw another woman wearing white silk and ermine. Clara, a brash Canadian, did not hesitate to begin conversation. Eva Braun was Hitler's mistress, nominally a secretary in his retinue at the Games. She was naturally reticent and, as Hitler had told her many times, she should have been more careful with strangers; but she was keen to practice her English.

Laughing, Clara said to Eva, "What a beautiful gown! Where did you get it?"

Eva thought, *We are wearing almost the same dresses, but her shoes are ugly.* But she said, "Milano. But we have wonderful dress makers in Berlin.[241] It is only for the beautiful shoes that we must go to Italy."[242]

"To Florence, Venice? To Ferragamo"

"Yes. How did you know?"

---

[235] *"Neben Hitlers Suite war ein kleines Zimmer für Eva Braun reserviert."* Nicolaus von Below, *Als Hitlers Adjutant 1937-1945*, Mainz: Pour la Mérite 1999, p.29.

[236] Ibid. p. 370.

[237] Ibid. pages 83, 141, 367.

[238] Ibid. pages 407, 411, 415, 416.

[239] "A 6 ft. tall, 18-year-old girl from Fulton, Missouri, was the first star of the women's events. Helen Stephens, who had already become a sensation over 50 yards in school meetings, now won her wind-assisted heat by 10 meters, and though her 11.5 time in the 100m final was also wind-assisted and ineligible as an improvement on her own world record, she thrashed Stella Walsh (Stanislawa Walasiewicz), the defending champion, by two meters. Taken to meet Hitler afterwards, she firmly declined his overt sexual advances." David Miller, *Athens to Athens: The Official History of the Olympic Games and the IOC, 1894-2004*, Edinburgh: Mainstream Publishing 2003, p.113. Interestingly, Vladir Putin's mistress is also a gymnast.

[240] Walter C. Langer, *The Mind of Adolf Hitler: The Secret Wartime Report*, New York: Basic Books 1972.

[241] "...*Die Schneiderkunst der Firma Heise in Berlin.*" Johannes Frank, *Eva Braun: Ein ungewohliches Frauenschicksal in bewegter Zeit*, Coburg: NATION EUROPA Verlag 1999, p.198.

[242] Ibid. p.199.

"My husband and I drive from Sweden every summer to play golf in the south of Austria. Venice is the nearest city. I have gone to Ferragamo there. They do indeed make beautiful shoes. But my Canadian peasant feet are unsuited. The Bally shop in Zürich makes my shoes."

"You are not Swedish then?"

"No. Canadian," said Clara proffering her hand, "I am Leone Hellstedt."

Eva Braun's thoughts

Coming from the stifling society of Hitler's Berghof eyrie, Eva was keen to meet new people and flattered by Leone's attention. Back in Bavaria she tried to relate her memory in English:

I was *erstaunt*…astonished…to learn that this elegant woman was a medical doctor. She was friendly and warm. We talked and talked. The speeches and nonsense in the banquet hall I had heard many times already. From Stockholm her husband traveled frequently to his company in Hamburg…Bergedorf. Frau Doktor…she asked that I call her "Leone," but I have such problem…Leone said she could send me the American films…that we could not get in Germany. In the summer after Austria joined the Reich, Leone visited the Berghof with her husband. His company helped make the production of oil from German brown coal. My führer was very pleased with this…and with the reception, where the ladies wore dirndls. We could not speak as much as I would have liked. But she gave me many of the birth control pills…her friend Dr. Hertig at the Harvard medical university made these.[243] You understand that Adolf could not marry me. All the Aryan mothers of the Reich…without husbands…were the *sogenannte* "Brides of Hitler." It was not allowed that I be pregnant. But Adolf does not like to be denied… It was only in December, when I had a holiday in Scandinavia, that I would meet Leone and talk freely. You know something? In Leone's office and flat in Stockholm she has many round clocks. For some years Adolf gave me clocks for Christmas presents…except one year a radio. But that year my Christmas present was a trip to Scandinavia with my family. Is it not interesting? Also, Leone made the *Hypnosetherapie* …after our long talks I felt so much better. I understood that those times I tried to kill myself…I did not want to die… but I understand…understood…that they would bring Adolf to me. You see. In the day the world is his; in the night he is mine.

---

[243] "…Eva's maid at the Berghof…testified that…Eva would take pills that suppressed her menstrual cycle (a form of contraception)." From p.85 of *The Women Who Knew Hitler: The Private Life of Adolf Hitler,* Ian Sayer and Douglas Botting, New York: Carroll & Graf Publishers 2004.

Eva's *Hypnosetherapie* 1940 – 1941

Since the war … you say "after the war began" … it was not possible to see Leone. But lucky for me her friend Herr Doktor Rittmeister could take time from his duties at the Göring Institut to continue my *Hypnosetherapie* … so I should not feel so sad. I told Adolf I was going shopping … anyway he was then many times away, in the Wolfschanze in East Prussia, or even *bei* … close to the Russian front.

Crowded Berlin Bundesbahn platform, March 1941

John Rittmeister and Folke Hellstedt walked past one another. No recognition. They brushed together, John surreptitiously passed papers to Folke, who carried on along the platform to his train.

---

244 Photo Alamy 2J33WCJ

John Rittmeister [245]

In 1942 Dr. John Rittmeister was removed from his position as head of psychiatry at Berlin's Göring Institut and in 1943 beheaded for treason.

---

[245] Geoffrey Cocks, *Psychotherapy in the Third Reich: The Göring Institute,* New York: Oxford University Press 1985 p.66. Recall that John Rittmeister was the brother of Leone's first paramour in Hamburg, Wolfgang Rittmeister, and that John was in psychoanalytic training at Jung's clinic in Zürich when Leone was there, 1934-1935. John's *"Rittmeister Kreis"* is mentioned in Rebecca Donner's *All the Frequent Troubles of Our Days: The True Story of the American Woman at the Heart of the German Resistance to Hitler,* New York: Back Bay Books 2021, pages 332-333. Leone took her children to meet Wolfgang soon after the war. Photo courtesy of Aerzteblatt.de.archiv/36954/60.

Chapter Eight
1938: Touring Germany & Austria, Nuclear Fission

Fascists fascinate

On their annual summer golf vacations to the Wörthersee in the southern Austrian state of Carinthia Leone and Folke had been exposed to the deep anti-Semitism characteristic of that part of the world.[246] Jews had migrated to Carinthia for a thousand years, but few withstood the persecution. In the capital city, Klagenfurt:

> A '*Judendorf*' now within the bounds of the city was mentioned in 1162, and in 1279 a Jewish quarter outside a city gate was recorded. In 1335, 36 Klagenfurt Jews were listed as taxpayers.[247]

Of the half million Carinthians,

> There were 268 Jews living in Carinthia in 1934, and 257 at the end of 1938. The men were deported to Dachau concentration camp on November 10, 1938, but were released before February, 1939. Subsequently the Jews in Carinthia moved to Vienna or emigrated. There were ten Jews living in Klagenfurt in 1968.[248]

Since 1935 Leone had been changing her life – from fulfilling personal ambition to helping others. Her time at Jung's Zürich clinic, 1934-1935, undergoing a training analysis and treating patients (participating in therapy as opposed to research) had been pivotal.

The display of Nazi power and arrogance at the Berlin Olympics helped to persuade the emerging Clara to sign when Ian presented her with the British Official Secrets Act (conjecture).

In 1937 Leone had completed the examinations and received a license to practice medicine in Sweden. Her first child, Monica, was born in October.

Germany's behavior and rhetoric were clearly on the path Hitler advocated in *Mein Kampf* – advancement toward Germany's "destiny" to control a Jew-free Europe augured war.

March 12: *Anschluss*. Austria welcomed German troops and became part of the Reich.

---

[246] F. Parkinson, editor, *Conquering the Past: Austrian Nazism Yesterday & Today,* Detroit MI: Wayne State University Press 1989, pages 35-6, 247, 264-67, 303, 310-11, 327, 336.

[247] *Encyclopedia Judaica,* Jerusalem: Keter Publishing House Ltd. 1971, Volume 10, p.1086.

[248] *Encyclopedia Judaica,* Jerusalem: Keter Publishing House Ld. 1971, Volume 5, p.182.

March 15: SA (*Sturmabteilung*, storm troopers) entered Freud's house at 19 Berggasse and took 6,000 schillings.

March 22: Gestapo searched Freud's house. Anna Freud was detained. On her return to the house the same day Freud agreed to leave Austria and go to England.[249]

250

251

Welcome to Austria

June 3: After three months anxiously awaiting exit permits, Anna Freud and her father and mother left Vienna.

---

[249] "Anna herself was taken for questioning, having first supplied herself with veronal in case of torture or internment. She narrowly escaped both by using family connections to make sure she was interviewed rather than left waiting in the corridor, from which she might well have been deported when the office closed at the end of the day." Janet Sayers, *Mothering Psychoanalysis: Helene Deutsch, Karen Horney, Anna Freud and Melanie Klein,* London: Hamish Hamilton 1991, p.166.

[250] *Hitler in Wien. Bundesarchiv – Bild 146-1978-028-14.*

[251] *Anschluss 193.* Alamy Image ID: 2AECRPD

June 5: They were met in Paris by Ambassador Bullitt and Princess Marie Bonaparte and spent the day at the house of the princess.

June 6: Freuds arrived in London.[252]

1938 June – July

The ordering of photos in Leone's album yielded a coherent chronology of this summer vacation, apparently enabled by Leone entrusting little Monica to her German nurse at home in Stockholm. In their twelve-cylinder 1937 Lincoln sedan Leone and Folke Hellstedt drove southward through Germany to Berchtesgaden, stopping at Bad Kösen, Rudelsberg, Weissenburg and Rosenheim along the way.

[252] Op. cit. Eissler p.33.

Rudelsburg

G.A. staged

Gate tower
&
Church

Weissenburg

Reichsautobahn   München Rosenheim

Berchtesgaden & Obersalzberg

a

Near Berchtesgaden Leone was photographed at Hitler's Berghof, wearing a *Dirndl*. The general public had not been allowed near the Berghof since 1936. Folke had been invited (conjecture) because he was chairman of the board of Bergedorfer Eisenwerk, the company which in 1937 had supplied IG Farben with 400 large centrifuges for the hydrogenation process in the production of oil from Germany's brown coal. Germany had no oil wells and a domestic supply of oil was one of Hitler's prerequisites for conceivable offensives.[253]

From Berchtesgaden they drove west to Garmisch Partenkirchen.

[253] Ronald C. Cooke & Roy Conyers Nesbit, *Target: Hitler's Oil, Allied Attacks on German Supplies 1939-45,* London: William Kimber 1985, pages 15-16.

Zugspitze

Garmisch Partenkirchen

Then to Liechtenstein, then to the Vierwaldstättersee in Switzerland.

Liechtenstein

Vierwaldstättersee

Then north for 1,000 kilometers to Hamburg. Along the way Leone photographed a Nazi Party propaganda sheet reviling Jews.

Nazi Party publication dated *25 Juni 27 Juli 1938*

Hitler's denunciation of the Jews as a race, as opposed to a religion, was expressed in *Mein Kampf*. The marriage of close relatives in Jewish communities was seized upon by the Nazis as a cause of degeneracy in Jewish populations, and a reason for prohibition of sexual relations between Gentiles and Jews. Especially harmful in Hitler's view was the contamination of Aryan blood with that of Jews. By the obscure logic of *Mein Kampf,* incest among Jews caused the rise of the hated Marxism *and* the outrageous wealth of Jewish bankers.

Famous Jews had shocked Christians by marrying close relatives. Of the five sons of Mayer Amschel Rothschild, an uncultured product of the Frankfurt ghetto, three were sent from Frankfurt to establish branches of the Rothschild Bank abroad: Nathan in London; James in Paris; and Salomon in Vienna.

The fact of a Rothschild marrying a Rothschild had become a normal procedure; indeed, of the twelve marriages contracted by the sons of the five brothers, nine were with Rothschild women. It was not only that the young men were brought up to think of good matches in terms of dowries, but the number of attractive Jewesses with same sophisticated tastes as themselves was limited, that is, outside the family.[254]

---

[254] Virginia Cowles, *The Rothschilds: A Family of Fortune,* New York: Alfred A. Knopf 1971, p.89, also pages 72, 132-133, 166 and on p.148, "During the crucial year of 1865 only a family wedding could induce Alphonse and Anselm to absent themselves from their banks. On this occasion Anselm's son, Ferdinand, married Lionel's daughter, Evelina. Evelina, of course, was a sister of Alphonse's wife, Leonora – and just to muddle the reader still further Anselm's wife, Charlotte, was a sister of Lionel – so the clan gathered in London in full force."

In the nineteenth century wars were fought by mercenaries. Conflicts between numerous states were financed, some on both sides, by the Rothschilds. They also financed the new phenomenon of railroads. The most successful son, Nathan in London, was elevated to the peerage – the first Lord Rothschild – celebrated by Jews worldwide.

At Ochsenzoll Hospital

1938 July

July 13: Physicist Lise Meitner fled Germany to Holland

July 21: Meitner's Swedish entry visa was approved on the condition that Meitner show her German passport at the border. She had no passport – her Austrian one had been taken, and as a Jew she had not been issued a German passport.

July 26: Swedish entry for Meitner was approved without restrictions. Folke Helstedt's younger brother Svante was then on the Swedish Foreign Office desk which issued immigration permits.

Also in July: The Freud family drama was widely reported in English language newspapers.

August 2; International Psychoanalytic Congress in Paris. Conjecture – Leone met with Vera Palmstierna ("My best Swedish friend with whom I had taken my licensing exam…")[255] and/or John Rittmeister, Gustav Bally, Tore Ekman. Fact – Anna Freud presented a paper written by her father, who was too ill to travel. Vera, having traveled from Vienna, was particularly familiar with the Freud family travail. Conjecture – Leone was pleased to report to Anna and Vera that Svante Hellstedt had issued an unconditional immigration permit for Lise Meitner.

Discovering nuclear fission

In the fall of 1938 Lise Meitner and her former lab mates in Berlin, Otto Hahn, Fritz Strassmann and Clara Lieber, were in frequent consultation by telephone and the practically daily mail service between Berlin and Stockholm.[256] Meitner had asked crucial questions (and designed apparatus and experiments) which Hahn, Strassmann and Lieber were answering. All were excited. Their discipline, nuclear physics, was on the verge of a breakthrough. Caught up in the epic race with Fermi in Rome, Bohr in Copenhagen and Joliot-Curie in Paris, Lise Meitner was able to ignore the dreary facts of her personal situation – living in a hotel room on borrowed money and a minuscule stipend from the Manne Siegbahn Institute, where she had a room but no proper scientific equipment or technical support, not even a key to the premises or communication with Manne Siegbahn.

Then came *Kristallnacht,* November 10. Along with thousands of Jews in the Reich, Lise's brother-in-law Jutz, in Vienna, was imprisoned. When her sister Gusti advised her that Jutz had been sent to Dachau, Lise began doing what she could to get Swedish visas for them. Jews could not leave the Reich unless they showed ability to enter another country.

Guided by Lise's hypotheses and queries, nuclear physics research in Berlin continued at a frantic pace. In a letter from Otto Hahn to Lise Meitner, December 15, 1938:

But we are coming steadily closer to the frightful conclusion: our Ra isotopes do not act like Ra but like Ba … I have agreed with Strassmann that for now we shall tell only *you.* Perhaps you can come

---

[255] That is, in 1937 in Stockholm. Op.cit. Ondrack p. 203. Anna Freud and Leone became friends. When in Stockholm Anna Freud stayed with Leone. Op cit. Ondrack p.205 and p.269, and correspondence in the MWIA archives.

[256] Fritz Krafft, *Im Schatten der Sensation: Leben und Wirken von Fritz Strassmann, Dargestellt von Fritz Krafft nach Dokumenten und Aufzeichnungen,* Weinheim, Deerfield Beach FL, Basel 1981, especially pages 86-265 regarding 1938, then pages 266-341 for the years 1939-1946.

up with some sort of fantastic explanation. We know ourselves that it *can't* actually burst apart into Ba.[257]

Lise Meitner discovers nuclear fission:

On the night of December 22, 1938, five months after he had conspired to save Lise Meitner from arrest by the Gestapo, Professor Otto Hahn of the Kaiser Wilhelm Institute for Chemistry in Berlin-Dahlem, and Dr. Paul Rosbaud, scientific adviser to Springer Verlag, both prominent citizens of Hitler's Reich, joined to transform the course of human events. … The astonishing thing was that Hahn had not realized that he had split the atom. He had explored the long path to the great secret and then failed to see what lay before his eyes. But Lise Meitner, who was spending Christmas in a small town near Gothenburg with her nephew, saw what Hahn had not seen.[258]

[257] Op.cit. Sime, *Lise Meitner: A Life in Physics,* p.233

[258] Arnold Kramish, *The Griffin: The Greatest Untold Espionage Story of World War II,* Boston: Houghton Mifflin Company 1986 pages 50-51.

Chapter Nine
1939: The German Atomic Bomb

Lise Meitner

I do not consider myself the father of the release of atomic energy. My part in it was quite indirect. I did not, in fact, foresee that it would be released in my time. I believed only that it was theoretically possible. It became practical through the accidental discovery of chain reaction, and this was something that I could not have predicted. It was discovered by Hahn in Berlin, and he himself misinterpreted what he discovered. It was Lize Meitner who provided the correct interpretation and escaped from Germany to place the information in the hands of Niels Bohr.

Albert Einstein, writing in 1945 [259]

Lise Meitner had been leading Berlin's Dahlem Institut theoretical physics laboratory for thirty years when the *Anschluss* in March 1938 cancelled her Austrian citizenship immunity to German laws forbidding Jews to hold public offices. She and her laboratory partner, Otto Hahn the chemist,[260] had been nominated several times for Nobel prizes.[261] Hahn received a Nobel in 1944 for nuclear fission. Meitner was never awarded a Nobel prize, despite entreaties from many scientists and the testimonies of doctoral students of Hahn and Meitner regarding her essential role in Dahlem nuclear physics.[262]

With the Gestapo closing in, Otto Hahn, Dirk Coster and Paul Rosbaud helped Lise Meitner escape to Sweden, carrying a single suitcase, leaving her possessions and life's work behind.[263] She was sheltered by

---

[259] Albert Einstein, *Out Of My Later Years,* Avenel, NJ: Random House 1956, p.188.

[260] *"Die Kollegin hatten Lise Meitner immer als das "physikalische Gewissen" von Otto Hahn bezeichnet."* Manfred von Ardenne, *Erinnerungen, fortgeschrieben: Ein Forscherleben im Jahrhundert des Wandels der Wissenschaft und politische Systeme,* Düsseldorf: Droste Verlag GmbH 1997, p.332.

[261] Janet Hamilton, *Lise Meitner: Pioneer of Nuclear Fission,* Berkeley Heights, NJ: Enslow Publishers 2002, p.54.

[262] *"Lange before die jüngeren Mitarbeiter morgens im Institut erschienen, war Lise Meitner schon in weissen Kittel da tätig und meistens bis in die späten Abendstunden war sie dort mit Otto Hahn zu finden, auch sonnabends und sonntags."* p.119; and *"Offiziell war Hahn der Institutsdirektor und Lise Meitner Abteilungsleiterin, in der Praxis schien uns oft umgekehrt zu sein, jedenfalls waren wir zuweilen dabei, wenn sie ihm sagte: "Hähnchen, davon vehrstehts Du nichts." Eindeutig war es auch Lise Meitner, die für Ordnung sorgte, wenn es nötig wurde".* Arnold Flammersfeld in *Gedächtnisausstellung zum 100. Geburtstag von Albert Einstein, Otto Hahn, Max von Laue, Lise Meitner,* Berlin: Staatsbibliothek Preussischer Kulturbesitz 1979, p.120.

[263] "The Anschluss imperilled Meitner, as it did all Austrians of Jewish extraction. Although she had been baptized as a child, that was no salvation in the Nazi era. Rosbaud took swift action through his Dutch friends.... Leaving nothing to chance, Coster went to Berlin to escort Meitner out of Germany, going directly to Meitner's flat on the night of July 16, 1938....Paul Rosbaud

her former colleague Eva Bahr-Bergius on the west coast of Sweden until Manne Siegbahn made room for her in his institute in Stockholm. There Lise had a menial position. Denied the staff and equipment necessary for her work, and impoverished, she told Hahn and other friends that her life had no meaning.[264] In the exciting rush of events leading to the discovery of nuclear fission at Christmas, 1938, Lise was a fully absorbed participant, thus able to ignore the dreariness of her personal circumstances. But in January of 1939 Otto Hahn was offered and accepted credit for the historic accomplishment:[265] partly because he could not as a German citizen name a Jew as a co-author or source in his official scientific writing; and partly because he more than acquiesced in this by not acknowledging, even privately, crucial contributions Meitner had made in the design and interpretation of their experiments. An implicit suggestion in a letter to Hahn that he help by sending her drawings was ignored by Hahn: "I am often terribly despondent. Of course I am at fault, I should not have left the way I did, should have taken away many more drawings of the important apparatus…" As a result, Lise's hope for scientific recognition and accordingly renewed access to experimental facilities and technical personnel were dashed.

At the same time she realized that most of her savings and belongings would not be sent to her because she had left Germany illegally.

On February 1st she wrote to Eva Bahr-Bergius,

> All these things weigh on me so, that I am losing all my self-confidence. I am making a real effort to hold on to my courage and I tell myself again and again that until now I have done very respectable physics. But under the current conditions I won't be able to do anything sensible and the fear of such an empty life never leaves me.[266]

---

then took Meitner to Hahn's house to stay overnight. Hahn had no automobile at that time, so Paul picked up Lise the next day in his Opel and drove her to the station. Meitner was tense, fearful and Rosbaud had to use all his persuasive talents to get her aboard the train. Dirk Coster was waiting for her in a first-class compartment and got Lise safely across the border. She stayed briefly in Holland and then left for Stockholm, where she remained, in misery, until the end of the war." Op.cit., Arnold Kramish, pages 48-49.

[264] In a letter from Lise Meitner to Otto Hahn, September 25, 1938: "Perhaps you cannot fully appreciate how unhappy it makes me to realize that you always think that I am unfair and embittered, and that you also say so to other people. If you think it over, it cannot be difficult to understand what it means that I have none of my scientific equipment. For me that is much harder than anything else. But I am really not embittered – it is just that I see no real purpose in my life at the moment and I am very lonely…." Winifred Conkling, *Radioactive! How Irène Curie & Lise Meitner Revolutionized Science and Changed The World*, Chapel Hill, NC: Algonquin 2016, p.125.

[265] "Perhaps you cannot imagine what it means for a person my age to live for 9 months in a little hotel room, with none of the comforts of home, with no scientific material and with the fear that no one has the time to move my situation forward." From a letter to Otto Hahn from Lise Meitner in January 1939, in Ruth Lewin Sime, *Lise Meitner: A Life In Physics*, University of California Press, Berkeley and Los Angeles, 1996, p.268.

[266] Op.cit. Sime p.257.

Eva Bahr   Lise Meitner [267]

Opportunity for Clara – a conjecture: In the tiny community of women scientists in Stockholm,[268] Lise met Leone/Clara, who immediately apprehended her situation and was able to help: first with psychotherapy; and then with financial support from Stephenson that allowed Lise to travel to Copenhagen to work with her nephew Otto Robert Frisch in Niels Bohr's laboratory[269] and to send money to relatives fleeing persecution of Jews in Austria.[270] Lise also helped with money for Hedwig Kohn, that enabled her

---

[267] A portion of the photo in Jost Lemmerich, *Die Geschichte der Entdeckung der Kernspaltung,* Berlin: Technische Universität Berlin 1989, p.57. Original courtesy of the Max Planck Society, Berlin.

[268] *"Nach 200 Jahre wählte die Schwedische Akademie der Wissenschaften wiederum eine Frau zum Mitglied, Lise Meitner."* [in 1945]. Michael Steiner, *Lise Meitner zum 125. Geburtstag,* Berlin: Staatsbibliothek Preussischer Kulturbesitz 2003, p.118.

[269] "Lise had been in Copenhagen since mid-February…. Before leaving Copenhagen at the end of March (1939), Meitner wrote to Bohr, who was still in Princeton, to tell him her results and thank him for the 'beautiful, productive time' in his institute." Ibid. Sime, p.266 and p.268.

[270] "For her first nine years there [Siegbahn Institute, Stockholm], she was paid less than the starting salary of an assistant. 'My income is so meager that it is only by being very economical that I can pay for my room, meals and small daily expenses (bus, postage,etc.).' Yet early in 1939 we find her sending money to relatives as they fled Austria one by one, having to abandon both professions and possessions. The 1939-1942 correspondence has numerous references to her financial generosity to sisters, brothers, nieces and nephews. How did she manage this?" From *Lise Meitner: The Foiled Nobelist,* chapter 16 of Rayner-Canham, Marlene F. and Geoffrey W., *A Devotion to Their Science: Pioneer Women of Radioactivity,* Montreal: McGill-Queen's

to escape from Germany to Sweden, and then America; and she sent food to the Costers in Holland.[271] Lise's complaints about her financial situation ceased around November of 1939, not long after the outbreak of WWII and the *Wehrmacht's* funding of Harteck's atomic bomb initiative in Hamburg.

Both LMs, Leone McGregor and Lise Meitner, struggled with the mystery of suicide, a phenomenon common among the Indians of Leone's native Canadian prairie and the Jews of Lise's native Austria.

The Atomic Bomb 1939

When Otto Hahn and Fritz Strassman divided the uranium atom in an experiment designed by Dahlem lab partner Lise Meitner,[272] Hahn immediately informed his friend Paul Rosbaud. They puzzled over the result of bombarding uranium with neutrons – production of barium. Hahn wrote Meitner, describing the experimental process and outcome. That was December 22, 1938. Otto Robert Frisch was visiting his Aunt Lise for the Christmas holiday. He was also a physicist, employed in Lise's friend Niels Bohr's laboratory in Copenhagen. With Lise walking and Otto Robert on cross country skis, they went into the woods on the west coast of Sweden, and sat on a log to rest and discuss Hahn's experiment. In his wonderfully titled autobiography, *What Little I Remember,* Otto Robert recalled the magic moment:

> After separation, the two drops would be driven apart by their mutual electric repulsion and would acquire high speed and hence a very large energy, about 200 MeV in all; where could that energy come from? Fortunately Lise Meitner remembered the empirical formula for computing the masses of nuclei and worked out that the two nuclei formed by the division of a uranium nucleus would be lighter than the original uranium nucleus by about one-fifth the mass of a proton. Now, whenever mass disappears energy is created, according to Einstein's formula $E=mc^2$, and one-fifth of a proton mass was just equivalent to 200 MeV. So here was the source of that energy; it all fitted! [273]

Otto Hahn and Fritz Strassman published the chemical process and findings in Rosbaud's *Die Naturwissenschaften* in Germany; and Meitner, along with her nephew Otto Robert Frisch, published the physics explanation in *Nature*, calling the phenomenon "nuclear fission."[274]

University Press 1997, p.184. And in Op.cit. Sime: despite her straitened circumstances the Frisch couple "… were counting on me…," pages.268 and p.285.

[271] Ibid. Re Hedwig Kohn p.228 and p.286; re Costers p.293.

[272] "Even though she wasn't present in the lab and Hahn did not say her name aloud, Meitner continued to influence Hahn's work. She had designed the experiments on transuranic elements that Hahn and Strassmann were carrying out, and they were using the equipment she had built and been forced to leave behind." Op.cit. Conkling p.127.

[273] Otto Robert Frisch, *What Little I Remember,* Cambridge: Cambridge University Press 1979, p.116.

[274]"A couple of days later I travelled back to Copenhagen in considerable excitement. I was keen to submit our speculations – it wasn't really more at the time – to Bohr, who was just about to leave for the U.S.A. He had only a few minutes for me; but I had hardly begun to tell him when he smote his forehead with his hand and exclaimed: 'Oh, what idiots we have all been! Oh but this is wonderful! This is just as it must be! Have you and Meitner written a paper about it yet?' Not yet, I said, but we would at once; and Bohr promised not to talk about it until the paper was out. Then he went off to catch his boat." Ibid. Frisch pages 116-117.

An egregious example of common ignorance – a collection of biographies of 120 "women who changed the world" includes Amelia Earhart and Billie Jean King, but not Lise Meitner.[275]

276

Lise Meitner   Otto Hahn   KWI Berlin

Early in 1939 the possibility of a chain reaction in uranium causing a massive explosion became evident to physicists everywhere.[277] A bomb of unprecedented power was suggested.[278]

Experiments with radiation and Einstein's expression of the equivalence of matter and energy, $E = mc^2$, had made the power of the atom a famous subject of speculation. Winston Churchill was intrigued by H.G.

[275] *Herstory: Women Who Changed the World, Edited by Ruth Ashby and Deborah Gore Ohrn, Introduction by Gloria Steinem,* New York: King Penguin 1995

[276] Photo courtesy of the Max Planck Society, Berlin.

[277] Bohr and Rosenfeld traveled to New York and Washington, where they gave lectures and visited physicists. In February Bohr indicated in a letter to the *Physical Review* the role he believed U-235 played in Hahn's result and chain reaction. This stimulated confirming experiments by physicists internationally. In a September *Physical Review* article with John Wheeler, "The Mechanism of Nuclear Fission", Bohr presented evidence. Fritz Krafft, *Im Schatten der Sensation: Leben und Wirken von Fritz Strassmann,* Weinheim: Verlag Chemie 1981, pages 118-119. Joliot in France understood there could be two types of chain reaction, two routes (U-235 and U-239) to a uranium bomb – p.75 of Maurice Goldsmith, *Frédéric Joliot-Curie: a Biography,* London: Lawrence and Wishart 1976.

[278] "Like many other American experimental physicists, Alvarez, on hearing about fission, immediately set up an experiment to confirm it. Only after he had the experiment up and running did Oppenheimer hear the news….When I invited him over to look at the oscilloscope later, when he saw the big pulses, I would say that in less than fifteen minutes Robert had decided that this was indeed a real effect and, more importantly, he had decided that some neutrons would probably boil off in the reaction, and that you could make bombs and generate power, all inside of a few minutes." p.256, and on p.258, "From one of those Sunday letters, which I received in January, 1939, I learned of the discovery of fission. In that first letter Oppie mentioned the possibility of nuclear power and an explosive." Ray Monk, *Inside The Centre: The Life of J. Robert Oppenheimer,* London: Jonathan Cape 2012.

Wells's introduction of an atomic bomb to science fiction in the 1914 book, *The World Set Free.*[279] Wells became a friend and adviser to Churchill. Of course, scientists read science fiction, and *The World Set Free* stimulated imaginations.[280] Having fled Germany, the Jewish theoretical physicist Leo Szilard, while waiting to cross a street in London, had an idea:

> First, if a neutron could strike an atom's nucleus with such force that it would emit two neutrons, then with each collision the freed neutrons might double in number. One neutron would release 2, which would each strike an atomic nucleus to release 4. These would each strike a nucleus, releasing 8, then 16, then 32, 64, 128, and so on. In millionths of a second, billions of atoms would split, and as they tore apart, the energy that held them together would be released.
>
> Second, the amount of energy released would be huge. If Einstein's calculations of 1905 were accurate, then his famous formula $E=mc^2$ assured that energy equals mass multiplied by the speed of light (whose symbol is c) squared. The number for mass was minute, but the number for the light speed in this equation is immense. At least in theory, the amount of energy latent in matter was also immense.[281]

Szilard filed a patent application and began living with an obsessive fear of atomic bombs, especially those that might be developed in Germany. He worked in the American Manhattan Project despite his low regard for the scientific acumen of its leader, General Leslie Groves, and the veiled hostility of Groves toward Szilard.[282] Frédéric Joliot filed "Brevet D'Invention No. 971,324" on May 4, 1939, "Perfectionnements aux charges explosives," including a calculation of critical mass.[283]

---

[279] Graham Farmelo, *Churchill's Bomb: How the United States Overtook Britain in the First Nuclear Arms Race,* Basic Books, New York 2013, p.21.

[280] "Radium is an element that is breaking up and flying to pieces....Uranium certainly is....And we now know that the atom, that once we thought hard and impenetrable…is really a reservoir of immense energy." p.14, and "And now under the shock of atomic bombs, the great masses of population which had gathered into the enormous dingy town centres of that period were dispossessed and scattered disastrously over the surrounding rural areas." p.85 H.G. Wells (1914), *The World Set Free,* H.G. Wells Easton Glebe Dunmow 1921.

[281] William Lanouette with Bela Szilard (2013), *Genius in the Shadows: A Biography of Leo Szilard, the Man Behind the Bomb,* New York: Skyhorse Publishing 2013, p.139.

[282] After the war Groves said of Szilard, "There was no question, but that he had no moral standards of any kind…. Actually after initiating the idea of the first Einstein letter he was a positive detriment to the project…He fancied himself as a genius, and he never was one. He can best be described as an opportunist." Robert S. Norris, *Racing for the Bomb: The True Story of General Leslie R. Groves, the Man Behind the Birth of the Atomic Age,* New York: Skyhorse Publishing Inc. 2002, p.526.

[283] Céline Jurgensen et Dominique Mongin, *Résistance et Dissuasion : Des origines du programme nucléaire français à nos jours,* Paris : Odile Jacob 2018

Leo Szilard [284]

285

Leslie Groves   Trinity test – Robert Oppenheimer, Leslie Groves

In the 1920s and '30s, Lise Meitner and Otto Hahn of Berlin-Dahlem's Kaiser Wilhelm Institute were world leaders in atomic physics, several times nominated for Nobel Prizes.[286] They and their contemporaries

[284] Photo courtesy of the Argonne National Laboratory.

[285] Photos "Courtesy of the Atomic Heritage Foundation and the National Museum of Nuclear Science & History. All rights reserved."

[286] The men at the birth of nuclear fission received Nobel Prizes. Lise Meitner, modest and retiring as women were, did not: "During my visit to Copenhagen in 1935, I happened to hear a talk at Bohr's Institute given by Lise Meitner, an excellent physicist who was then working at the Kaiser Wilhelm Institute in Berlin. She was bothered by an inconsistency in Fermi's results. 'Something odd,' she said, 'is going on with uranium. Why does uranium simultaneously produce dozens of radioactive substances when it should produce only one?' Fermi's interpretation of the multiple radioactivities was that new elements (called

in physics understood the implications of chain reaction. Identifying the nucleus that would emit two or more neutrons when struck by one was the missing piece in the puzzle. Shortly after Hahn's experiment and Meitner's explanation of the result, their Danish friend Niels Bohr named the piece that would ultimately enable the Hiroshima bomb (U-235) and the operation of a nuclear reactor that would produce the isotope U-239 for the Nagasaki bomb. [287]

> The following week Bohr went on to Princeton, where he was given temporary lodging in Einstein's office. During a conversation over breakfast on 5 February Bohr realized that the observed fission in uranium was mainly due to the rare isotope U-235, which is present in uranium in a proportion of one part to 139 parts U-238. Two days later, on 7 February [1939], Bohr posted a letter to the *Physical Review* remarking on this fact. [288]

Bohr also opined that separation of U-235 from U-238 would be extremely difficult,[289] that it could require the industrial effort of an entire nation. Whether prophesy or lucky guess, it became true – only the United States possessed the will and the wealth to accomplish it,[290] although Germany tried.

When Germany invaded Denmark, April 9, 1940, Lise was visiting Margrethe and Niels Bohr in Copenhagen. On returning to Stockholm she sent a message from Bohr via telegram to England. Its intent was to assure friends that Bohr and his family were unharmed by the German occupation. The last line of the telegram was, "TELL COCKCROFT AND MAUD RAY KENT". British intelligence intercepted the telegram, and hanging on every word from Lise Meitner, interpreted "MAUD" to be an abbreviation for "Military Applications of Uranium Disintegration".[291] Thus the British government group formed to study

---

transuranics because they are heavier than uranium) had been produced. Meitner noted the oddity, but she did not challenge Fermi's interpretation." In January 1939 physicists learned that the uranium atom nucleus had been split: "Meitner's question had been answered, the tool Szilard had wished for was now available, and Nazi Germany might well develop a devastating new weapon." Edward Teller with Judith Schoolery, *Memoirs: A Twentieth Century Journey in Science and Politics,* Cambridge MA: Perseus Publishing 2001, p.139.

[287] The seminal article by Meitner and Frisch in *Nature* discussed the production of U-239 and suggested U-235 by observing "… since varying proportions of neutrons may be given to the two parts of the uranium nucleus." From *Nature 143 (1939), S. 239-240, 'Disintegration of Uranium by Neutrons': A New Type of Nuclear Reaction,* in Horst Wohlfarth, *40 Jahre Kernspaltung: Eine Einführung in die Originalliteratur,* Darmstadt: Wissenschaftliche Buchgesellschaft Darmstadt 1979, p.99.

[288] John Cornwell, *Hitler's Scientists: Science, War and the Devil's Pact,* London: Penguin Books 2003, p.221.

[289] "The most promising methods of separation…were gaseous diffusion and centrifugal separation. The former requires the uranium to be converted from a metal into a gas and then forced through the microscopic holes of a filter, or 'barrier.' … At the time…only microscopic amounts of enriched uranium had been produced by this method. The idea that it might furnish the basis for production of the isotope on an industrial scale looked fanciful…. Similar problems attended the centrifuge method, which is today the main method used to enrich uranium, but which in 1941 was a new and relatively untested technique. The basic idea is to place the uranium, again in a gaseous form, in a cylinder, which is then rotated very quickly, forcing the heavier U-238 to the outer edge and concentrating the lighter U-235 near the centre. Considering both methods fairly promising, Urey gave it as his view that the assembly of a critical mass of U-235 was, though extremely difficult, quite achievable with sufficient resources." Ray Monk, *Inside The Centre: The Life of J. Robert Oppenheimer,* London: Jonathan Cape 2012, pages 304-305.

[290] Leslie M. Groves, *Now It Can Be Told: The Story of the Manhattan Project,* New York: Da Capo Press 1962

[291] The Bohr family friend Maud Ray lived in Kent.

these applications came to be called the "M.A.U.D. Committee," with technical subcommittee members including Rudolf Peierls and Otto Robert Frisch, Lise Meitner's nephew.[292]

Churchill's longtime advisor on scientific matters, Frederick Lindemann ("Prof", later Lord Cherwell), was a friend of Lise Meitner's.[293] Lise was among the first few in the world to recognize the possibility of a nuclear chain reaction, an atomic bomb. While she in that sense regretted the discovery of nuclear fission, she recognized that inevitably it would become a technology – to be used for good or evil. While she would not assist in the creation of a bomb, with her knowledge and contacts she could and would help to hamper its imminent development in hostile and ruthless Hitler's Germany.

Lise Meitner's nephew Otto Robert Frisch and Rudolf Peierls, with the "Frisch-Peierls Memorandum", March 1940, demonstrated for their fellow scientists in Britain the theoretical feasibility of a practical atomic bomb; and they alerted Lindemann (Lord Cherwell) and Churchill to the German initiative. The British launched their atomic bomb program, "Tube Alloys", and sought information regarding German progress. Intelligence was received by ...

> Mr. Churchill's scientific advisor, Lord Cherwell, that a certain Swedish theoretical physicist had written…warning that Heisenberg was conducting extensive experiments in German laboratories with the intention of exploiting chain reactions of fission processes and especially uranium-235. Results, the Swede had warned, must not be excluded.[294]

This was written by David Irving in August 1966, when the identity of the theoretical physicist in Sweden could not be disclosed.

Theoretical physicists Berlin 1920: L-R Bohr, Heisenberg, Pauli, Stern, Meitner [295]

[292] Rudolf Peierls, *Bird of Passage: Recollections of a Physicist,* Princeton NJ: Princeton University Press 1985, p.156

[293] Adrian Fort, *Prof: The Life of Frederick Lindemann,* London: Jonathan Cape 2003, p.298.

[294] David Irving, *The Virus House: Germany's Atomic Research and Allied Countermeasures* London: William Kimber and Co. Limited 1967, p.120.

[295] Photo Alamy 2H45DF2.

Germany first

The *Wehrmacht* in 1939 became interested in development of nuclear weapons. On April 24 Paul Harteck, physics professor at Hamburg University, and his assistant Wilhelm Groth wrote the following to the head of German Ordnance Research:

> We take the liberty of calling to your attention the latest developments in nuclear physics, which, in our opinion, will probably make it possible to produce an explosive of many orders of magnitude more powerful than conventional ones … That country which first makes use of it has an insuperable advantage over the others.[296]

In September Paul Harteck's group in Hamburg received a military research contract.[297] When Harteck sought a supplier to build centrifuges capable of separating a critical mass of the fissionable isotope U-235 from natural uranium, which is 0.7% U-235 and 99.3% U-238, Clara's husband Folke would have been informed. Instead of relying on Germany's foremost manufacturer of centrifuges, Folke's Bergedorfer Eisenwerk,[298] which was a wholly owned subsidiary of Separator AB of Stockholm, Harteck formally chose Anschütz in nearby Kiel to develop a prototype ultracentrifuge. Various sources indicate different timing for the success of Harteck and his assistant Groth in separating U-235 with a prototype ultracentrifuge. Later writers, with the benefit of having seen previously classified documents, placed the onset of Harteck's isotope separation planning in 1939, and successful trials in June and July of 1942. Writing earlier, in 1957, Bagge, Diebner and Jay had recalled that Harteck's Hamburg group began their U-235 centrifuge project in 1941 and arrived at a machine delivering five percent enrichment by 1943.[299]

More authoritative is the analysis of David Irving – because it is information taken directly from original sources including interviews with scientists, the Milch documents, Harteck assistant Wilhelm Groth's laboratory diary and reports, Harteck's reports and correspondence with the War Office and Esau's report to Göring of November 24, 1942.[300] Groth went to Sweden for consultations with Svedberg and Pedersen

---

[296] Op. cit. John Cornwell, p.224.

[297] Rainer Karlsch, *Hitlers Bombe: die geheime Geschichte der deutschen Kernwaffenversuche,* München, Deutsche Verlags Anstalt 2005, pages 120-126.

[298] IG Farben importantly used Bergedorfer Eisenwerk centrifuges in the Bergius hydrogenation process for manufacture of oil from brown coal. Bergius plants were the crucial sources of aviation fuel for the Luftwaffe and consequently the primary targets of strategic daylight bombing, a specialty of the Americans. Delivery of Bergedorfer Eisenwerk centrifuges to Leuna began in 1937. During the war Leuna was bombed 22 times. Op.cit Ondrack p.189, and Ronald C. Cooke & Roy Conyers Nesbit, *Target: Hitler's Oil: Allied Attacks on German Oil Supplies 1939-1945,* London: William Kimber 1985, pages 15,16,17,20,138,140,146,164,170.

[299] *"Seit langem war schon bekannt dass man isotope Gase trennen kann, indem man diese in schnell rotierenden Zylindern den Wirkungen den Zentrifugalkräfte aussetzt. So wurde von der Hamburger Arbeitsgruppe HARTECK, GROTH und SUHR im Herbst 1941 der Aufbau einer Ultrazentrifuge begonnen, mit der es 1943 gelang, eine Anreicherung des Uranisotope 235 um etwa 5% zu erzielen."* Erick Bagge, Kurt Diebner and Kenneth Jay, *Von der Uranspaltung bis Calder Hall,* Hamburg: Rowohlt Taschenbuch Verlag Mai 1957, p.37.

[300] David Irving, *The German Atomic Bomb: The History of Nuclear Research in Nazi Germany,* New York: Simon & Schuster 1967, pages 311-312.

at Uppsala University, the world's leading experts on ultracentrifuges. Successful operation of prototypes, +/- 5% enrichment of U-235, occurred during June-August 1942.[301]

The Atomic Bomb 1940-1942

All of this can get its full explanation in the future.[302]

While the Americans had concluded that the separation process was extraordinarily difficult and had therefore resolved to build huge plants, it was feared by some that the Germans might discover a far more elegant approach that required only a fraction of the resources that the scientists at Los Alamos believed necessary. With respect to the separation of U-235, "someone might," Oppenheimer noted, "come up with a way to do it in his kitchen sink."[303]

The significance of the events of 1940-1942 can be better understood in light of the fact that as this is written eighty years later, ninety-nine percent of the world's primary fissionable material, U-235, is made with ultracentrifuges.

To review some facts:

1939 January – Hahn/Strassmann and Meitner/Frisch reported the discovery of nuclear fission;

1939 February – Niels Bohr theorized that the nucleus of the isotope U-235 initiated the division;

1939 March – physicists in several countries recognized the possibility of a chain reaction attending a "critical mass" of U-235;

1939 April – Paul Harteck, advised the *Wehrmacht* of the potential of an atomic bomb;

1939 September 3 – WWII began when Britain declared war after Germany invaded Poland;

September 15 – Uranverein founded, Harteck received a Wehrmacht contract;

September 26 – Heisenberg became involved, formed plutonium reactor team.[304]

---

[301] There is confusion, probably from a typographical error, in an end note by Irving. "Groth went to Sweden in November 1942 to discuss the design of the planned German uranium-235 enrichment plant with ultracentrifuge experts at the University of Uppsala, Professor Theodor Svedberg and Dr. Kai O. Pedersen, the authors of a standard work, 'The Ultracentrifuge', published in 1940. Svedbeg and Pedersen advised Groth on the layout, mounting and lubrication of multiple-centrifuge installations, and showed him over their own laboratories. Groth wrote a long report on this for the War Office on December 12, 1940. I asked Pedersen and Svedberg about this episode, but they declined to comment." Ibid. pages 311-312. From what evidence I was able to find in addition to Irving, the most likely scenario is a trip by Groth to Uppsala in December, 1939 for design consultation, then another visit in 1942 for help with how to produce numerous replicas of the successful prototype.

[302] Apropos of the mystery of why the Germans were so concerned about securing nickel supply from remote Petsamo in 1939-1941 – from the memoirs of Dr. J.K. Paasikivi, Finnish minister in Stockholm, then Moscow, quoted in H. Peter Krosby, *Finland, Germany and the Soviet Union 1940-1941: The Petsamo Dispute,* Madison, Milwaukee and London: The University of Wisconsin Press 1968, p.33.

[303] Jeffrey T. Richelson, *Spying on the Bomb: American Nuclear Intelligence from Nazi Germany to Iran and North Korea,* New York: W.W. Norton & Company 2006, p.33; and on p.57, "Bothe [German scientist] told his interrogators that he believed the separation of uranium isotopes by thermal diffusion was impossible and all work on separation in Germany had relied on the centrifuge method."

[304] "*Am 26. September 1939 traf sich der Uranverein des HWA zum zweiten Mal in Berlin. Nun nahm auch Werner Heisenberg teil. Er erhielt den Auftrag, sich um die Theorie der 'Uranmaschine' zu kummern. Schon am 6.Dezember legt er seine*

1940 – British and German scientists began research toward nuclear weapons, understanding that the key was separation of U-235: enrichment of uranium to perhaps ninety percent U-235 for a chain reaction explosive device; or enrichment to five to twenty percent U-235 for operation of a nuclear reactor, a *Uranmaschine*, which would produce energy and the by-product U-239 (plutonium) which was at least as fissionable as U-235 and could probably be separated chemically – that is, at a lower cost and with less difficulty than separating U-235. Recognition of heavy water (D2O, deuterium oxide) as the ideal "moderator" required for operation of a nuclear reactor resulted in French, British and German attempts to secure supply from the world's only producer of heavy water at Vemork in Norway.

1941 – Harteck's U-235 centrifuge R&D contractor in Kiel, Anschütz, reported progress.[305]

1941 November – American universities were granted small sums for nuclear research.

1942 March – Hitler was annoyed about breaches of secrecy by German atom-splitting scientists.

1942 – significant funding was granted for American military research, then the Manhattan Project launched.

1942 July – a prototype centrifuge capable of separating U-235 was tested.[306] Harteck and other German physicists estimated from the quantities obtained by operating prototypes how much enriched uranium could be produced. Various configurations of centrifuge types, numbers and operating schedules were projected.[307] But how to manufacture the hundreds, possibly thousands of ultracentrifuges that would be needed to make the critical mass of U-235 required for a bomb?[308] Special alloys were necessary for parts that could survive operation at 100,000 rpm.[309]

Überlegungen zum Bau eines Reaktors dem HWA dar. Heisenberg hatte auf Basis der verfügbaren Daten berechnet, wie sich bestimmte Mengen von Uranoxyd in Kombination mit unterschiedlichen Moderatoren verhalten würden. Die sicherste Methode zum bau einer Uranmaschine sah er in der Anreicherung des Isotops U235. Je höher man das Uran anreichert, desto kleiner die Maschine gebaut warden. "Sie (die Anreicherung von U235) ist ferner die einzige Methode, um Explosivstuffe herzustellen ....", Rainer Karlsch, *Hitlers Bombe: die geheime Geschichte der deutschen Kernwaffeversuche,* München: Deutsche-Verlags Anstalt 2005, p.39.

[305] " *Wat dit rapport echter niet vermeldt is, dat in Hitler-Duitsland reeds in 1941 centrifuges in prototype gereed waren en in 1942- op bescheiden schaal verrijkt uranium-235 produceerden.*" Wim Klinkenberg, *De Ultracentrifuge 1937-1970,* Amsterdam: Uitgeverij en Boekhandel Van Gennep N.V. 1971, p.16.

[306] *Die grössten Hoffnungen ruhten auf Harteck. Obwohl es immer wieder rückschlage gab, war die Hamburger Gruppe seit dem Frühjar 1942 auf dem richtigen Weg. Im Juli 1942 gelang es Groth erstmals, eine kleine Menge U235 geringfügig einzureichern. Die Zentrifugentechnologie funktionert!* Op cit. Rainer Karlsch, p.122. And: The German nuclear physicists sequestered by the Allies in England in 1944, Heisenberg, Hahn, von Laue, Weiszäcker, Harteck et al, signed a joint statement regarding their wartime work on "the uranium problem". Regarding U-235: "…experiments were made to try and obviate the use of heavy water by the concentration of the rare isotope U-235." p.105, and "The ultra-centrifuge gave a slight concentration of isotope 235. The other methods had produced no certain positive result up to the end of the war." p.106. Sir Charles Frank, *Operation Epsilon: The Farm Hall Transcripts,* Institute of Physics Publishing, London 1993.

[307] David Irving, *The German Atomic Bomb: The History of Nuclear Research in Nazi Germany,* New York: Simon & Schuster 1967, p.129.

[308] "Regarding the amount for an effective bomb, the first U-235 bomb "Little Boy", dropped over Hiroshima, incorporated about 50 kg of U-235, of which about 2% underwent fission. " Ibid Sir Charles Frank, p.5.

[309] "With a 14 mm. cell the figure 1,200,000g may be reached. With rotor IX, at 160,000 rpm, over 1,000,000g was obtained. This rotor had its cell at surroundings too weak, however. " The Svedberg, *The Ultracentrifuge,* New York: Oxford at the Clarendon Press, 1940, p.151.

1942 – Harteck's competitor, Professor K. Clusius of Munich University, gave up on his thermal diffusion method for separating U-235 and…"sent Dr. Grothe from his laboratory to Professor T. Svedberg in Uppsala to study the technique of the ultra-centrifuge with which he has worked for many years."[310]

1942 – The Research Department of the Reichspost officials were "…specially interested during the war in the design and operation of cyclotrons and an official from it visited Prof. Bohr's research institute at Copenhagen immediately after the fall of Denmark to examine the cyclotron there. Other officials have visited Siegbahn's laboratory in Sweden, where Lise Meitner is now [1944] working, to see the cyclotron there."[311]

312

Now whenever mass disappears energy is created, according to Einstein's formula E=mc², and one-fifth of a proton mass was just equivalent to 200 MeV. So here was the source for that energy; it all fitted! [313] 200 MeV = 0.32 kilerg

Kilergs and Svedbergs

The world's leading expert on ultracentrifuges was The (Theodor) Svedberg at Uppsala University. The latest word on ultracentrifuge technology appeared in June 1939 with publication of his book *The Ultracentrifuge*…in Swedish, but quickly translated into several languages, including German and English (preface, contents and 478 pages of diagrams, photos and descriptions of technological problems and

[310] F.H. Hinsley, *British Intelligence in the Second World War: Its Influence on Strategy and Operations, Volume III, Part 2*, New York: Cambridge University Press 1988, p.935.

[311] Ibid., p.936.

[312] Photo of the first ultracentrifuge for separation of U-235, built by Paul Harteck and Wilhelm Groth, by Wilhelm Groth, courtesy of the Deutsches Museum, Munich.

[313] Op. cit. Otto Robert Frisch p.116.

solutions). In the preface, Svedberg regretted a recent development – that research into the latest type of ultracentrifuge, which operated at extremely high rpm and was therefore capable of separating materials of minuscule difference in weight, was no longer being shared.[314]

The Svedberg was interested in nuclear energy and the abundance of kilergs it promised. Some years earlier he had nominated Lise Meitner for a Nobel Prize. After the war he traveled to England to visit Otto Hahn and congratulate him on his Nobel Prize. As a world-class expert in centrifuges, working at Uppsala University near Stockholm, he was known to Folke Hellstedt, a senior manager of the world's leading manufacturer of centrifuges, Separator AB in Stockholm.

The's ex-wife Dr. Andrea Svedberg was a friend of Dr. Leone McGregor Hellstedt. They had met in 1929 while post-doctoral researchers at Harvard Medical.[315] Leone's first visit to Sweden, in 1930, had been at Andrea's invitation to address a Swedish women scientists' organization on the status of women in Canadian and American medicine.[316] Political complications were implied by The Svedberg's government-sponsored job and Andrea Svedberg's communism. She was awarded a Lenin Prize after the war; Folke, veteran of the Bolshevik Revolution having fought with Admiral Kolchak in Omsk, would not have her in the Hellstedt home.

Unsettling Ultracentrifuges

The task of separating U-235 became the object of intensive research and development beginning in early 1939. The Svedberg's book was published in June. In it the kernel of the problem could be found: although an ultracentrifuge was capable of separating U-235 in theory…and even in practice, notably that of Anschütz in Kiel in June and July of 1942 when separation was clearly successful…the machine that succeeded was short-lived and attempts to build identical machines which functioned identically, failed. It was one thing knowing that it could be done, having done it once, and quite another to do it again…and again…and again…in the cascade process indicated. The practical problems of ultra-high speed rotor operation included preventing friction of the rotor against air from overheating, expanding and melting components (suggesting vacuum or a hydrogen atmosphere).[317] The centrifugal force of hundreds of thousands of gravities exploded rotors. Uranium hexafluoride gas was required as a medium – it is highly corrosive.[318] Ingenuity and tremendous investment in trials (and errors) would be required … with no guarantee of eventual success.

In *The Ultracentrifuge* The Svedberg discussed trials, all practical failures, with a few of the myriad possible configurations of types of housings, rotors and metal alloys. Although partial success with an early combination of techniques and hardware suggested ways forward, it wasn't clear that a metallurgical technology existed to cope with the catastrophic failure of this temporarily successful early configuration – microscopic examination indicated that shear occurred where the nickel in the steel rotor alloy had not

---

[314] Op.cit. The Svedberg p.v.

[315] "I met Andrea Andreen, divorced from The Svedberg, the Nobel Prize winner. She was beautiful, about 43 years old and doing research in chemistry at Harvard. She was the first feminist that I had ever met." Op. cit. Ondrack p.114.

[316] Op. cit. Ondrack p.119.

[317] Svedberg, The, and Kai O. Pedersen, *The Ultracentrifuge*, Oxford: Oxford at the Clarendon Press 1940, pages 110, 192.

[318] Op. cit. David Irving, pages 43-44, 51, 69, 105, 139.

blended uniformly with the iron. Producing sufficiently uniform castings would require the skill of a master during the liquid phase in the melt shop[319] – when the iron, nickel, tungsten and so on were liquid and blending.

Consistency of yield characteristics (steel stretches before it breaks) was determined by Svedberg to be critical – another demand for attention to smelting procedures.

Operating techniques had to be contrived. It had long been known that the harmonics of a rotating part have a characteristic "critical velocity." Running too long at this speed will cause the part to disintegrate…with collateral destruction of its surroundings.

> Particular attention is to be paid to the problem of the passage of an ultracentrifuge rotor through the critical velocity. The difficulties encountered in the practical use of ultracentrifuges are connected with this passage. The dynamical balance of the rotors has often been neglected, whereas their balance increases in connection with the too frequent removal of the rotors from the body of the centrifuge for cleaning. A result of the increase in the unbalance may be the loss in the ability to pass through the critical velocity and the rapid wear of the bearings (the force acting on the bearing, equation 31). The preceding discussion points out the factors that affect the passage of the rotors through the critical point, namely, the gap between the head and the ring, the coefficient of friction, and the unbalance. These factors cannot be excluded in the operation and design of ultracentrifuges.[320]

Operating ultracentrifuges, spinning their rotors to 100,000 rpm in the presence of corrosive uranium hexafluoride, caused catastrophic failures. For Paul Harteck, Werner Heisenberg and their colleagues, these were tragedies. Each consumed scarce resources – materials, and time before the next Allied intervention against further supply.

Intelligence regarding the details of failures allowed Lise Meitner to imagine remedies and the probable next steps for the Germans.[321] Conveyance of this information to Clara, and then to Corcoran, Stephenson or Fleming suggested efficient sabotage measures.

---

[319] Op.cit. The Svedberg pages 133-151.

[320] V.I. Sokolov, translated by S. Reiss, *Critical Velocities of Ultracentrifuges,* Washington: National Advisory Committee for Aeronautics, Technical Memorandum 1272, March 1951, p.10.

[321] For thirty years Lise was head of theoretical physics at the Kaiser Wilhelm Institute, Berlin-Dahlem. After the war it was renamed the Max Planck Institute. Today this organization offers scholars access to more than a thousand documents (reports, correspondence, orders) chronicling the work of Lise's former colleagues (Hahn, von Laue, Heisenberg et al) and students in the effort to exploit nuclear energy, and to build an atomic bomb. *Übersichten zum deutschen Uranprojekt: Kernenenergieforschung in Deutschland von 1939 bis 1945* and *Dokumente zum deutschen Uranprojekt 1939 bis 1945 im Archiv der Max-Planck-Gesellschaft* (791 files with brief descriptions, some containing multiple documents).

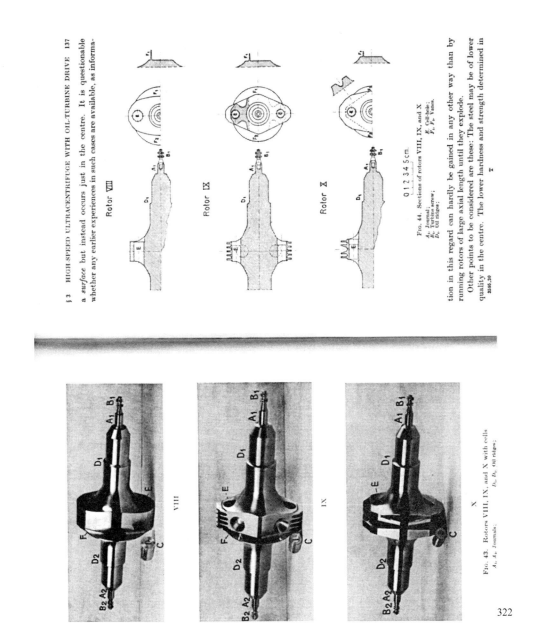

a *surface* but instead occurs just in the centre. It is questionable whether any earlier experiences in such cases are available, as informa-

Rotor VIII

Rotor IX

Rotor X

0 1 2 3 4 5 cm.

FIG. 44. Sections of rotors VIII, IX, and X
A, Journal;   E, Cell-hole;
B, Turbine screw;   F₁, F₂ Vanes.
D, Oil ridges.

tion in this regard can hardly be gained in any other way than by running rotors of large axial length until they explode. Other points to be considered are these: The steel may be of lower quality in the centre. The lower hardness and strength determined in

FIG. 43. Rotors VIII, IX, and X with cells
A₁, A₂ Journals;   D₁, D₂ Oil ridges;

322

Size and shape of rotors, size and location of holes, shape of holes – were all performance factors.

The use of uniform ingredients was vital: getting nickel from Petsamo, Finland for one melt and nickel from Sudbury, Canada for the next was disruptive. Using wolfram/tungsten from Portugal, then from Brazil; would not do. Herein was vulnerability to actions devised by Ian Fleming or William Stephenson, informed by Meitner via Clara.

The most promising steel alloys for rotors described by Svedberg contained significant amounts of nickel.[323] Interdiction of Canadian nickel was straightforward. It all came from one producer in the Sudbury Basin of Ontario, Canada. More than ninety percent of the nickel used by the Allies in WWII came from INCO. Stephenson and friends could monitor the paths taken by shipments from Sudbury to ensure that they did not wind up in Germany.

---

322 Op. cit. The Svedberg. The importance of nickel can be learned on pages 71, 107, 123, 126, 127, 145, 147.
323 Ibid.

During May, Professor Harteck and Dr. Groth – in Hamburg had investigated the excessively corrosive habits of very pure uranium hexafluoride gas: samples of steel, light alloy and nickel were exposed to the gas for fourteen hours at a time, at 100 degrees, and their weight gain measured; the nickel's weight was unchanged, and even when the experiment was repeated at 350 degrees it was the least affected of the metals. Steel was quite unsuitable. Nickel was, of course, one of the scarcest metals in Germany at the time – another instance of the perverseness of the whole uranium problem.[324]

German control of the Petsamo nickel deposit at the northern tip of Finland was a priority repeatedly emphasized by Hitler himself. From "Führer Headquarters", "The Führer and Supreme Commander of the Armed Forces" issued direct orders to about a dozen of his most senior military men: generals, admirals and air marshalls.[325]

2 September 1941…Directive No. 36…[Regarding]… eliminating all threats to North Finland, and above all to the nickel mines….The importance of this area lies in the nickel mines which are vital for the German war effort. The enemy realizes this importance. It is likely that the English will deploy strong forces…even commit Canadian or Norwegian troops there…We must expect air attacks, even in winter, against the nickel mines and the homes of the miners. Our own efforts must correspond with the greatness of this danger. [326] [And…] Protection against enemy air attack of our own camps and communications and, above all, of the nickel mines and the naval base which is be established must be ensured.[327]

10th October 1941…Directive No. 37…The most important task, therefore, is to hold what we have gained, to protect the Petsamo nickel fields from attack by land, air or sea…[328]

21st July 1942…Directive No. 44…The most important task of the 20th Mountain Army the complete protection of the Finnish nickel production. It must once again be stressed, with the greatest emphasis, that without delivery of Finnish nickel…[329]

Germany and Russia were uneasy allies from the August 15, 1939 anti-aggression treaty until June 22, 1941 when Germany attacked Russia. Finland sided with Germany, believing that this alliance would yield the better chance of continued nationhood, including sovereignty over access to far-north yet ice-free Petsamo at Finland's narrow neck between Russia and Norway.

Contention for the Petsamo nickel ore deposits cost thousands of lives during WWII.

---

[324] Op. cit. David Irving, *The German Atomic Bomb: The History of Nuclear Research in Nazi Germany,* pages 74-75.

[325] "… Supreme Commander of the armed forces, a post to which he appointed himself in February 1938." Richard Overy, *Why The Allies Won,* London: Jonathan Cape 1995, p.274.

[326] H.R. Trevor-Roper, *Blitzkrieg to Defeat: Hitler War Directives 1939-1945,* translated from *Hitlers Weisungen für die Kriegführung 1939-45, Dokumente des Oberkommandos der Wehrmacht,* New York: Holt, Rinehart & Winston 1964, p.99.

[327] Ibid. Trevor-Roper p.101

[328] Ibid. Trevor-Roper p.102, underlining emphasis is in the original.

[329] Ibid. Trevor-Roper p.128, underlining emphasis is in the original.

1934 to 1939 – Finnish geologists described ore deposits, International Nickel Company of Canada Limited (INCO) bought the deposits and developed a mine.

1939 September – German/Soviet occupation of Petsamo operations.

1941 June – Germany attacked Russia, Finland sided with Germany, thousands of German troops sent to the Petsamo region.

1941-1944 – Allies tried to interfere with shipping of thousands of tons of nickel ore and concentrate from Petsamo to Germany.

1944 September – Finland submitted to Russia, ceded right to the Petsamo area.

1944 October – Germans finally abandoned Petsamo, fighting a successful rearguard action by blowing up bridges and preventing supplies from reaching Soviet forces pursuing them in Norway.

1944, October 8 – Dana Wilgress, now Canadian ambassador to the Soviet Union, in Moscow signed agreements among Russia, the United Kingdom and Canada whereby Finland would pay reparations to Russia, Russia would annex the municipality of Petsamo, and Russia would pay twenty million American dollars to INCO for its Petsamo subsidiary MOND.[330]

Paul Rosbaud, Lise Meitner[331] and Folke Hellstedt were acquainted with the ultracentrifuge problems and the Harteck/Anschütz solutions. With knowledge of what alloys were required, they could inform sabotage of supplies of the relevant metals and minerals.[332] Thus informed, Stephenson crippled supply of metals and minerals from South America,[333] and Allied pressure on Portugal and Spain[334] restricted wolfram (tungsten) supply to Germany from the north Portugal mountain deposits.[335]

Wolfram played a major role in the drama of Spanish-German relations. Spain, like Sweden, was officially neutral while favoring fascist Italy and Germany out of gratitude for the aid given Franco's forces in the Spanish Civil War. But the Franco regime could not resist the fantastically high prices American and

---

[330] John F. Thompson and Norman Beasley, *For The Years To Come: A Story Of International Nickel of Canada,* New York and Toronto: G.B. Putnam' Sons and Longmans, Green & Company 1960, pages 244-256.

[331] After a postwar interview with William Stephenson at his home in Bermuda, his biographer William Stevenson wrote: "The extent of German research was reported from Stockholm by Lise Meitner, a co-worker of the Berlin physicists who had first demonstrated, in 1938, that elements of the radioactive uranium would split when bombarded by neutrons. Moreover, Lise Meitner was the scientist who had correctly interpreted the chain reaction; ...." William Stevenson, *Intrepid's Last Case,* New York: Villard Books 1983, p.38.

[332] In Germany: "Experiments had already shown that in certain circumstances, as little as 1 per cent. to 5 per cent. of niobium made red-hot steel firm. But there were no stocks of niobium.... Germany possessed deposits in the Kaiserstuhl Mountains; and there was more in German-occupied Norway. Telemarken became enormously important.... Soon systematic air attacks reduced German industry to chaos; new development seemed hopeless. Germany did not manage to turn niobium to her use." Harald Steinert, translated and adapted from the original German by Nicholas Wharton, *The Atom Rush: Man's quest for radio-active materials,* London: Thames and Hudson 1958, p 113.

[333] "Buried in Latin America were the metals of war and those minerals and exotica for which there was a demand created by new and sophisticated weapons: vanadium, mercury, tungsten and tin; mica, bauxite, chromium and antimony. BSC had thrown a noose around the source of these materials." Op.cit. Stevenson, *A Man Called Intrepid, p.365.* And Op.cit. Nigel West *British Security Coordination,* pages 255-263.

[334] David Ramsay, *"Blinker Hall", Spymaster: The Man Who Brought America Into World War I,* Stroud, Gloucesershire: Spellmount Limited 2008, history from WW1 pages 247-251.

[335] Op.Cit. Harol Steinert, ages 124-126. And E.H. Cookridge, *Sisters of Delilah: Stories of Famous Women Spies,* London: Olebourne 1959, p.93.

British agencies were willing to pay to secure Spanish wolfram production, to prevent it going to Germany.[336]

There were pinpoint raids by De Havilland Mosquito fighter bombers. Clara's friend Billy Corcoran monitored German shipping to and from the far north and reported daily.[337]

An attack on the titanium mine in Norway failed,[338] but SOE teams were …

> … assigned to undertake specific actions, and instructed to return to Britain by the Shetland bus or find their way to Sweden…. [an SOE team] blew up the power station at Glomfjord, which supplied electricity for a large aluminium factory…succeeded in destroying a large part of the ore mining installations at Fosdalen…blew up mine installations and stores with 150,000 tons of ore…the ore mines of Sulitjelma, causing much damage…at Eudehaven the Arendal smelt works were blown up by the SOE team "Company" led by Edward Talaksen, and 2,500 tons of ferrosilicate were destroyed. The same team carried out sabotage actions against the Lysaker chemical works and the Norsk Sulphur factory near Eugene. But the heavily guarded Orkla pyrite mines – after Rio Tinto the largest source of the mineral used in radar and W/T apparatus remained the coveted target. Four SOE teams were set against Orkla… There was widespread sabotage against shipping and harbor installations…. A number of teams were sent to sabotage railways…[339]

Sabotage of facilities and interdiction of materials hampered the German atomic weapon program from 1939-1943. SOE agents, in May 1942, destroyed the power station and railway for the Orkla pyrite mines in Norway and the only magnesium factory in Italy. In 1943 two-thirds of chrome production in Greece and most of the Lannemezan aluminium output were curtailed. Destruction of communications, railways, locomotives and assassination of military personnel had a generally disabling effect, but the crucial blows to German atomic energy were not delivered until the British Commando raid on the Vemork heavy water facility February 28, 1943, and the massive bomber attack on Peenemünde August 17-18, 1943.

The primary target of the midnight August Peenemünde raid was the sleeping quarters of the scientific and administrative personnel – the brain.

> Von Braun and Dornberger learned that two of their most valuable men, Dr. Thiel and Dr.Walther, had been killed in the wrecked housing estate, where no air raid shelters had been constructed… The death of Dr. Thiel was most sorely felt; … He had been appointed liaison officer between Peenemünde – East and Professor Heisenberg, the atomic physicist; after Thiel's death, interest in this subsided.[340]

---

[336] Stanley G. Payne, *Franco and Hitler: Spain, Germany and World War II,* New Haven & London: Yale University Press 2008, pages 126, 166-168, 197, 236-243, 245-252, 264.

[337] "No day passed during the tedious four years of watching when Billie Corcoran did not send some valuable tip, in secret code, to American or Allied officials." Washington Times-Herald, July 6, 1947.

[338] E.O. Hauge, *Salt-Water Thief: The Life of Odd Starheim,* London: Gerald Duckworth & Co. Ltd. 1958, pages 143-154.

[339] E.H. Cookridge, *Set Europe Ablaze,* New York: Thomas Y. Crowell Company 1967, pages 341-343.

[340] David Irving, *The Mare's Nest,* Boston, Toronto: Little Brown and Company 1964, p.118.

The extent to which that bombing raid affected physical facilities at Peenemünde is not well-known. After the August 1943 raid the rocket and atomic energy programs were further fragmented, distributed to locations in Germany less vulnerable to Allied bombing. At the war's end Soviet troops seized the Peenemünde area and sent the remaining equipment and scientists to Russia. What they found and what they took they kept secret.

The association of von Braun and Heisenberg with Peenemünde indicates that the work there had highest priority. Wernher von Braun was the genius behind the German V-1 and V-2 rockets …and later the American Saturn device that delivered the first men to the moon. In 1943 Werner Heisenberg was head of a German effort to produce Pu-239 (the stuff of the Nagasaki bomb) through operation of a nuclear reactor. Since the Germans had abandoned graphite as a reactor moderator, they had concentrated on the heavy water option. Clara's friend Billy Corcoran was credited with hampering this development:

On Oct. 26, 1946, the British Press, quoting a British air marshall, gave him [Corcoran] credit for having produced the tip which uncovered the German V-weapon and "heavy water" experimental laboratories at Peenemünde on the Baltic.

Some 600 British heavy bombers swooped down on this forest-ridden industrial plant on August 17, 1943, reducing it to ruins and killing 5,000 of 7,000 workers, including the master scientist and a group of Hitler favorites. … This destruction was hailed as "the turning point of the war…" [341]

The Germans carried out their centrifuge research at Celle.

This work had started at the University of Hamburg under Dr. Harteck, but it had to be relocated several times because of Allied bombings. It finally moved to the spinning mill near Hechingen, where it was seized by Alsos. The equipment was very small in comparison to our own, but it seemed to be operating satisfactorily. [342]

When one enrichment facility was destroyed by Allied bombing, another was begun at a new location…which became known to Allied Intelligence…and was duly destroyed.[343]

---

[341] Washington Times-Herald, July 6, 1947

[342] General Leslie M. Groves, *Now It Can Be Told: The Story Of The Manhattan Project,* New York: Da Capo Press 1962, p.246.

[343] David Irving, *The German Atomic Bomb: The History of Nuclear Research in Nazi Germany,* New York: Simon & Schuster 1967, p.257-259; and David Irving, *The Virus House: Germany's Atomic Research and Allied Counter-Measures,* London: William Kimber 1967, pages 228-237.

Chapter Ten
1939: December 27, Dinner in Stockholm

Britain's intelligence chiefs considered it impossible and unwise to infiltrate agents into Germany. It was unlikely that any agent could obtain accurate information on such a complex issue. Further, the detailed briefing an agent would receive would, if he was captured, threaten the security of the Allied bomb program. It was better, British officials believed, to rely on information delivered through neutral or occupied countries on the whereabouts and activities of Heisenberg and other scientists likely to be associated with any attempt to develop a bomb.[344]

Clara invited interesting people to a dinner celebrating the end of the grim year 1939. Matthew Halton was in Stockholm for a few days on his way to the Finnish-Russian War which had begun in November.[345] Matt's war correspondent friend Martha Gellhorn had just returned from the Finnish front and was in Stockholm until the first week of January when she would begin a journey to New York.[346] Martha had written to Ernest Hemingway from Helsinki December 4, 1939, that she would be returning to him in the next weeks:

> I will have – from Helsinki, environs, front, enough for three bangup articles if they want that many and will have stuff no one else has. Then one week each in Norway and Sweden and home...[347]

Matt and Martha had covered the Spanish Civil War, writing pieces sympathetic to the Republicans and critical of Franco's Nationalists, as did Ernest Hemingway, whom they both knew.[348] Martha had lived with

---

[344] Jeffrey T. Richelson, *Spying on the Bomb: American Nuclear Intelligence from Nazi Germany to Iran and North Korea,* New York: W.W. Norton & Company 2006 p.31.

[345] Matthew Halton, *Ten Years to Alamein,* Toronto: S.J. Reginald Saunders and Company Limited 1944, p.104.

[346] "From Belgium, she flew to Stockholm, then to Helsinki.... At three o'clock on her first afternoon, through a curtain of fog, the Russians attacked." [November 30, 1939]. Caroline Moorehead, *Martha Gellhorn: A Twentieth-Century Life,* New York: Henry Holt and Company 2003, pages 162-163. And, "From Sweden she sent Hemingway a telegram: 'Happy New Year and all of it together beloved.'" p.164.

[347] Caroline Moorehead, *Selected Letters of Martha Gellhorn,* New York: Henry Holt & Company 2006, pages 78-79.

[348] David Halton, *Dispatches From The Front: Matthew Halton, Canada's Voice At War,* Toronto: McClelland & Stewart 2014, pages 113-116. Matthew Halton, *Ten Years to Alamein,* Toronto: S.J. Reginald Saunders 1944, p.65.

Hemingway and they would marry in November 1940. He and Matt had written war correspondence for the same newspaper, the Toronto Star.

Matt was to leave Stockholm for the Finnish frontier December 30. On the evening of December 27th he could enjoy the hospitality of his friend of twenty years, Leone.

Martha remained in Stockholm until the first week of January, when she set off to report to Eleanor Roosevelt personally in Washington, then to join Hemingway at his *finca* in the Caribbean.[349]

William Stephenson had been in Sweden since before Christmas and would remain in the region until the end of the Finnish-Russian war on March 13, 1940…

> Stephenson proposed that ore shipments from Oxelsund and the other ports on the west coast of Sweden which might be used after the break-up of the ice should be sabotaged, and he volunteered to carry out the operation himself with the aid of his Swedish friends. Churchill from the Admiralty welcomed the idea enthusiastically… On December 16, 1939, he pointedly recommended in a memorandum which he placed before the Cabinet that the ore from Oxelsund "must be prevented from leaving by methods which will be neither diplomatic nor military." *[350]*

Stephenson had business interests that served as a cover for his espionage. Steel and ball bearings from neutral Sweden were bought by both sides during the war.

Abwehr agents could account for the presence of "Intrepid" in Stockholm through a deliberately ill-concealed plot to disrupt Swedish iron ore shipping to Germany.[351]

> The proportion of Sweden's exports taken by Germany was never less than two-thirds during the pre-war years: after Sweden was cut off in 1940 from the world beyond the Baltic it was regularly 90 per cent. Sweden's next largest customer, Great Britain, never took more than 16 per cent.*[352]*
>
> … The importance of Swedish ore in the arming of Hitler's Germany can only be described as vital, whether it is the absolute or relative figures that are taken as a guide. Figures, however, do not tell the whole story. Swedish ore formed the raw material of four out of every ten German guns, speaks more powerfully.*[353]*

---

[349] Op.cit. Moorehead, pages 162-165.

[350] H. Montgomery Hyde, *The Quiet Canadian: The Secret Service Story of Sir William Stephenson,* London: Constable 1962.1989, page 21.

[351] "The project was not without risk. Stephenson expected to be kidnapped or murdered by the Germans. He and Rickman carried on with such a sinister air, and with such leaky discretion that, before long, the project became the talk of the town. The Germans did not have to murder Stephenson to frustrate the plot. They simply saw to it that King Gustav V learned of the plan. The King then wrote a personal letter to King George VI of England, beseeching him to order the immediate cancellation of the project." Ladislas Farago, *The Game of the Foxes,* London: Hodder & Stoughton 1971, p. 524.

[352] Rolf Karlbom, *Sweden's iron ore exports to Germany, 1933-1944,* Scandinavian Economic History Review, 13:1, 65-93, DOI: 10.1080/03585522.1965.10414365, p.68.

[353] Ibid. p.70.

During this winter in Scandinavia Stephenson had other clandestine objectives besides assessing the feasibility of disrupting traffic of the high-grade Swedish iron ore that German smelters were adapted to use efficiently. Screening, recruiting, organizing and financing agents for Norway and Denmark became more important after the plan to destroy ore handling cranes was discovered and King Gustav's appeal to British royalty resulted in Cabinet quashing this Churchill/Stephenson initiative. In addition to menacing Sweden's economic welfare, trespassing on Sweden's neutrality had become more sensitive and more dangerous since Swedish Intelligence, activated in September 1939, was seeking and prosecuting Allied agents. Desmond Morton of the British MEW (Ministry of Economic Warfare) had warned agents to take no actions, "…which could possibly be attributed by the Germans to the 'British' on the grounds that the Swedes had made it clear that they would abandon their neutrality in favor of the Germans." [354]

A second task for Stephenson was organizing a team to travel to Norway to interfere with the production of heavy water at Vemork. Heavy water, deuterium oxide, had been identified by physicists as an ideal moderator for proposed operation of nuclear reactors. Lise Meitner in Sweden, Niels Bohr in Denmark, Werner Heisenberg in Germany and Otto Robert Frisch in England theorized that operation of a nuclear reactor using uranium somewhat enriched in U-235, moderated by heavy water, would produce the isotope U-239 – which would also be fissionable (plutonium, the stuff of the Nagasaki bomb).[355]

Third, Stephenson was charged with investigating what could be done about preventing the Canadian-owned nickel deposits in the far north of Finland at Petsamo from falling into German hands.[356] Russian forces were advancing against the Finns defending Petsamo, and in the previous August Russia and Germany had signed a non-aggression treaty.

Fourth was an example of Stephenson's famous luck: the most important of the tasks Churchill had set him was influencing American public opinion in favor of America joining the war against Germany. This evening he would be in the company of two journalists read and heard by millions of Americans. In the cold, walking briskly from the Ambassador's house along Strandvägen, he arrived at Hellstedts' party in five minutes.

---

[354] Philip H.J. Davies, *MI6 and the Machinery of Spying,* London: Frank Cass Publishers 2004, p.120.

[355] William Stevenson, *A Man Called Intrepid: The Secret War 1939-1945,* London: Book Club Associates 1976, pages 55-57. Margaret Gowing, *Britain and Atomic Energy 1939-1945,* New York: Palgrave 1964, pages 45-48.

[356] Op. cit. Hyde, p.23

7A   American Legation including OSS
7B   U.S. Military Attaché
7C   German Military Attaché
25   Japanese Legation
53   Hellstedt residence
59   U.S. Intelligence, Dr. Adele Kibre unit
82   British Legation

WALK FROM HELLSTEDT'S

11 minutes, 850 m
7 minutes, 500 m
Ø
2 minutes, 140 m
4 minutes, 260 m

Clara's apartment at Strandvägen 53, Stockholm, evening of December 27, 1939

"Why shaken and not stirred, Bill? Ian told me this was an element of your famous martinis."

"Ah, Leone. All of us like to have our little secrets."

"I'm afraid the only gin we have is Argentinian. Folke was sure that war was coming, so late last year when we were in Argentina he bought huge quantities of frozen beef, Malbec and gin … and had them shipped to his company here."

"We'll soon know if gin from the Argentine will make a proper martini. Try this, Leone."

"First let's take the tray and glasses into the library. Matt and Martha are highly experienced drinkers. Their opinions will carry authority. Oh…and Bill…before we go in…you should know that Lise Meitner is

---

[357] Sketches adapted from Google maps.

at a critical pass. She is quite depressed about her inability to get any proper work done…and there are her relatives in Vienna."

"Leone, we talked about this before Christmas. I can't do much about getting Jews out of Vienna, but I can provide more money for her to travel to Copenhagen…and a little extra so that she can send some to her relatives. Too much will raise her visibility to the wrong people."

"Being able to use Niels Bohr's laboratory, to do meaningful work, and to socialize with like minds – drives away her depression. I know you like hearing the gossip from German physics circles … keeping track of who is doing what where toward their atomic bomb. Bohr has German students and is visited often by physics colleagues from Germany. Paul Rosbaud is a regular and he is an old friend of Lise's."

"I heard the story…of how Rosbaud, Hahn and the Dutch physicist conspired to get Meitner out of Berlin…to safety in Holland. Or relative safety. She is not entirely safe here in Stockholm. There are Nazi agents. If I were to be seen with her, it could mean her life. The *Abwehr* probably knows who I am. Swedish Intelligence does – King Gustav has asked King George to intervene in my mission to disable the machinery that is used to get iron ore into ships for use in German steel mills. It would've been a violation of Swedish neutrality, but Churchill was willing to risk it."

Clara rearranged the glasses and pitcher of martinis on the tray, then looked at Bill.

"Lise is in danger? Really?"

"Probably not as long as we can disguise our interest in their atomic weapons program. To the extent that they believe we consider something worthy of contrary measures, they will take extra care to prevent those measures. Subtlety and misdirection… if we can make sabotage of the critical appear to be a side-effect of an attack on something else…plausible…and convey a reason for the attack not traceable to the actual source of the intelligence that inspired it…we also protect the intelligence asset for future use. Whatever we do based on information from Lise Meitner will be accompanied by a plausible story…our ostensible motivation…alternative to that based on information Meitner might have supplied. I believe you know our best storyteller…in London."

"Of course – Ian!"

"Leone, the Germans are getting nervous about Vemork. IG Farben is a big shareholder in Norsk Hydro. They want all the heavy water there, which is nearly all the heavy water in the world …and they were willing to buy out the French bank's majority position in order to get it. That would mean that future production would also be in German control. You said that Lise Meitner has a colleague, or knows a student, working in Siegbahn's lab…who came from Vemork."

"Lise sees this young man regularly in the institute. He's given Lise a detailed drawing of the heavy water cell used at Norsk Hydro. It is not very big…something like a foot in diameter and five or six feet high…and there are eighteen of these close together."

"Can you get me this drawing? Or copy it?"

"Next time Lise visits I'll ask. I'm sure it will be all right. I've told her that a friend of mine is interested in scientific developments, and is helping with her expenses in going to Niels Bohr's lab in Copenhagen…and that I could add some money for her to send to her sister in Vienna. I've told her that I can't say who the sponsor is…and I think she expects that if she discovered something of commercial interest that was patentable, she would be obliged to inform us…me.… Ready, Bill?… We'll have to manage the drinks and food ourselves. I took your advice and gave the evening off to our German nurse and Hungarian cook."

Leone opened the door from the kitchen and asked Martha to lend a hand with the trays.

"Let me take custody of these," Martha said, lifting the martini tray. "We're parched in there. Matt is reading my stuff about the Finnish war...drafts of the articles I'll be taking to Collier's. And Folke is translating a Russian document I scrounged at the front. All thirsty work."

"We had the traditional Swedish barrel of sill made for Christmas," Leone announced, "lots of dense rye bread to go with it. And akvavit and beer. The only experimental risk is this Argentinian martini. So...Martha, in honor of your safe return from the war in Finland...and to Matt, who is heading there soon...*Skål*!"

Approval of the Argentine gin, and Bill's treatment of it, was unanimous.

Bill asked Folke, "If you run across anything in that Russian document to do with the nickel mines at Petsamo, could you tell me about it?"

Martha interjected, "You know...I heard something about the Russian campaign up at Petsamo, but I don't remember ... just now ... what it was. Petsamo is a hell of a long ways north of the fighting I was covering."

"If you think of it, tell me ...?"

"Sure, Bill."

Matt looked up from his reading. "Why is Petsamo important?"

"Folke probably knows better than I," said Bill. "The deposits of nickel there could be critical for German armaments manufacture. Most of the nickel in the world will soon come from Canada, from around Sudbury...that we can deny the Germans. Nickel alloys are needed for corrosion resistance and strength in steels ... no substitute for it in aero engines. And in Folke's business, centrifuges, the latest word from the number one boffin...a Swede incidentally...is that nickel alloys are the answer for the fantastic rotor speeds in ultracentrifuges."

"What's an ultracentrifuge?", Matt asked Bill.

"Yes," Martha added, "What's an ultracentrifuge?"

"It's a contraption used to separate elements of different weights. The Germans use them in the hydrogenation process to make oil and gasoline from their brown coal."

Bill raised his glass and the company joined him in a silent toast to nothing in particular.

Matt hesitated, then said, "My physicist friend tells me...Niels Bohr from Denmark started this conversation last February when he was in the USA...something along the lines of...if a pure quantity of the uranium isotope that divides when struck by neutrons, the isotope U-235, could be isolated from the ninety-nine-plus per cent that is its brother U-238, then a chain reaction of enormous explosive power could result. Could an ultracentrifuge separate U-235?"

Bill and Folke looked at each other.

"No," Folke said.

Leone laughed. "Next you'll be writing equations, Matt. Let's have another martini and some juicy gossip. Martha, how about your inamorata, the famous Hemingway. Is he as sexy as he makes himself out to be?"

Matt, wearing the winter camouflage of Finnish troops, during Finland's war with Russia.

358

Chronology late 1939

Lise Meitner, in Stockholm since July 1938, complained about her poverty [359]…until October 1939.

September 1 – Germany invaded Poland.

September 3 – Britain and Commonwealth countries declared war on Germany.

September 17 – the *Wehrmacht* issued contracts for atomic bomb research.

October – Lise Meitner began sending packages of food and scarce goods to relatives and former colleagues in the Reich, including Otto Hahn.

November – Lise could afford to travel – "… heard some physics again, which is always really nice,"[360] she wrote to Hahn about her discussions with Niels Bohr during her stay in Copenhagen.

University of Alberta friends Leone and Matt

… by the end of the war Halton had built up a big and enthusiastic listening audience in Canada. It is to his credit that when he received an award from an American organization for outstanding war reporting on the air he won it by actually going up to the front and broadcasting from the center of the battle rather than resorting to the phoney broadcasts turned out by some of his CBC colleagues.[361]

---

[358] Photo courtesy of David Halton, from "Dispatches From the Front" between pages 88-89.

[359] Op. cit. Sime, *Lise Meitner,* pages 211–230, 232, 254-255, 257, 268-270.

[360] Op. cit. Sime, *Lise Meitner,* p.281.

[361] Wallace Reyburn, WW2 war correspondent, *Some Of It Was Fun,* Toronto: Thomas Nelson & Sons (Canada) Limited 1949, p. 135.

DISPATCHES
FROM THE
FRONT
MATTHEW HALTON,
CANADA'S VOICE AT WAR

DAVID HALTON.

"Matthew Halton was Canada's greatest foreign correspondent."
PIERRE BERTON

362

---

362 Image courtesy of David Halton

Chapter Eleven
The German Atomic Bomb: Those
For and Against

"Of course one could build an atomic bomb."

Werner Heisenberg [363]

Many of the key people charged with creating an atomic bomb during WWII were acquainted with Lise Meitner. They were her friends, former students and colleagues, and in the case of Otto Robert Frisch, a close relative. From neutral Sweden Lise communicated with her fellow physicists on both the Allied and German sides. The nature of the information she shared with each was her choice. Recognizing that the first to possess an atomic bomb would win the war, she chose to help the Allies. By revealing secrets to Clara, her therapist and confidante, Lise was assured that they could be conveyed to British Intelligence.

Given the objective of sabotaging the German program: the first step was learning as much as possible about it (German sources to Meitner and Rosbaud); next, getting that information to the Allied side (Meitner and Rosbaud to Clara, then from Clara to Corcoran, Denham, Fleming, and Stephenson); then to physicists and technicians who could devise appropriate sabotage measures without suggesting and thus betraying sources of the intelligence; then to the saboteurs (BSC, SOE) and the military.

Lise Meitner's happiness had been destroyed by the Nazis – *motivation* to oppose. Her background and contacts in German nuclear physics provided the *means*. And through Clara she had the *opportunity* to deliver the best of information to Allied Intelligence.

To help understand how the Allies won and the Germans lost, and to arrive at an explanation for the Allies come-from-behind victory in the nuclear weapons race, this chapter will consider the contestants, the functionaries – mainly the physicists involved…the most important distinction being between those who wanted the Allies to win and those who wanted Germany to win.

---

[363] "I saw Heisenberg in late 1944. He was trying [in Berlin-Dahlem] to make a heavy water moderated reactor 'go critical.' He told me, 'Of course one could build an atomic bomb.' But this would require huge isotope separation plants that could not be erected under the situation of Allied air superiority." Peenemünde and postwar USA ICBM engineer Krafft Ehricke, in Frederick I. Ordway III and Mitchell R. Sharpe with a foreword by Wernher von Braun, *The Rocket Team,* London: William Heinemann Ltd. 1979, p.58.

11. Copenhagen Physics Conference, June 1936. First row (*left to right*): Pauli, Jordan, Heisenberg, Born, Meitner, Stern, Franck; second row: Weizsäcker and Hund behind Heisenberg, Otto Frisch (*second from right*); third row (*left to right*): Kopfermann, Euler, Fano; fourth and fifth rows, second from left: Peierls and Weisskopf; standing along wall: Bohr and Rosenfeld [364]

Sabotaging the German program – strategic personnel

The first problem with the German nuclear energy program was the exodus of Jewish physicists. The best of Germany's pre-Hitler nuclear physics talent was Jewish: Einstein, Meitner, Szilard, Peierls, Frisch, et al. In the nuclear energy race most of the favorites, the world's best nuclear physicists, were on the Allied side – in Britain's Tube Alloys and America's Manhattan Project.[365]

A corollary was the perversion of information attending its politicization. The theories of Albert Einstein, Niels Bohr and Lise Meitner were denounced by Nazis in high offices. Philipp Lenard called their work "Jewish physics," and before the war he was in a position to deny funding for leading edge nuclear research. Even after Heisenberg, with his prestige, was able to make modern theory acceptable, rivalries among the several university and institutional programs charged with development of an atomic bomb divided government support, preventing the coherent effort that would have been necessary, and was in fact characteristic of the Manhattan Project.[366]

---

[364] Photo in John Cornwell, Op.cit. *Hitler's Scientists,* p.252-3. Courtesy of the Niels Bohr Archive, Copenhagen.

[365] "*Die Emigration aus Deutschland, Österreich, Osteuropa hatte so viele Professoren und Techniker, die vor dem Nazismus geflohen waren, nach Grossbritannien gebracht, dass man in London sogar von einer 'wissenschaftlichen Inflation' sprach.*" Michel Bar-Zohar, *Die Jagd auf die deutschen Wissenschaftler,* Berlin: Reinhard Mohn OHG 1965/66, pages 33-34.

[366] "…often highly touchy characters, and the delicacy of some of the physicists' feelings…." p.153, "…in Germany the rival groups of nuclear scientists were waiting for sufficient heavy water to complete research…." p.155, "…repeated complaints to Göring about …'unfit leadership' and the 'chaotic confusion' reigning in the universities…" p.178 of David Irving, *The German Atomic Bomb: The History of Nuclear Research in Nazi Germany,* New York: Simon & Schuster 1967.

Exeter: How were they lost? What treachery was used?

Messenger: No treachery, but want of men and money. Among the soldiers this is muttered, That here you maintain several factions; And whilst a field should be dispatch'd and fought, You are disputing of your generals.[367]

King Henry VI Part 1 1.1

Germany's remaining physicists and their laboratories were targets of Allied bombing. While under Heisenberg's management the Dahlem Kaiser Wilhelm Institut in Berlin was largely abandoned; and Harteck's facilities in Hamburg were destroyed. Intelligence from Clara's family friend Billy Corcoran informed the decision to launch a massive midnight bombing raid on Peenemünde…with first priority the scientific and administrative personnel quarters. Key people were killed in their beds. Rocket making and atomic energy research facilities were destroyed.[368]

> The vigilance of William W. Corcoran, of Washington D.C, United States Consul at Gothenburg, Sweden, during the war, enabled the Allies to destroy a secret nest of Nazi scientists at Peenemünde, on the German Baltic coast, and thereby balk what may have been Adolph Hitler's atomic bomb laboratory, the Overseas News Agency has just learned.[369]

Despite her refusal to participate in weapons research, her humanitarian objections and her dismay at this use of her discovery, Lise Meitner's influence was considerable throughout the chain of events leading to atomic bombs being dropped on Hiroshima and Nagasaki. From the early nuclear divisions by Curie and Fermi, she questioned the "transuranics" explanations, then provided insights critical to the experimental progress leading to what she and her nephew determined to be "nuclear fission."[370] Meitner's students and colleagues populated all nuclear energy research programs during WWII: the Jews and anti-Nazis in Britain, America and Russia; and those willing to join the Nazis in Germany.

Her modesty and discretion and the prevailing male chauvinism rendered Meitner less visible to German military intelligence. However, neutral Stockholm, like Lisbon, was teeming with intelligence agents from many countries. There were lots of Nazis to keep an eye on Meitner, or to assassinate her, if deemed necessary. Even when Germany was clearly losing the war and Swedish policy had swung from favoring Germany to favoring the Allies, in 1944 the Swedish language German propaganda magazine "*Tele*" was still widely read:

> All plates, etc. for *Tele* were made in Berlin or Vienna and then sent to Sweden. The business end was also handled from Berlin and carried through in Sweden by "couriers" who travelled to Stockholm weekly. These included Dr. MATUSCHKE, Dr.Rudolf KIRSCHER and

---

[367] William Shakespeare, *King Henry the Sixth, Act First, Scene One,* New Haven: Yale University Press 1918, pages 3-4.

[368] Op. cit. Ondrack p.170.

[369] from the Overseas News Agency, October 1946, in *Top Secret (A Foreign Service Saga) by Willam W. Corcoran,* a document declassified in 2019 in the Stanford University Library William Corcoran Archives, pages 319-320.

[370] Otto Robert Frisch, *The Discovery of Fission,* pages 272-277 in Spencer R. Weart & Melba Phillips, Editors, *History of Physics,* New York: American Institute of Physics 1985.

sometimes LOHSE himself. *Tele* was printed in Sweden by *Illustra Aktiebolage*. The distributing agency was *Wennnergren-Williams*. Circulation was between 20,000 and 30,000.[371]

Assassination was a tool of Britain's SOE, operating with the approval of Churchill – to "set Europe ablaze" via "ungentlemanly warfare." Although Nazi SS and Gestapo were not above assassination, it seems that the *Abwehr,* German military intelligence, rarely indulged. Admiral Canaris, its aristocratic head, was reluctant to ruthlessly implement the more sordid policies of Hitler, whom he despised. Canaris was executed for treason before the war's end. Scientists and intelligence operatives in neutral countries: South America, Portugal, Spain, Sweden, on both the Allied and German sides were candidates for assassination.

Lise Meitner declined, but her nephew Otto Robert Frisch and some of her former students and colleagues (including Niels Bohr) went to America to work on the Manhattan Project.

A German spy

To gather intelligence regarding the American atomic bomb program, *Abwehr* agent 146, Erich Gimpel, was decanted from U-1230 onto a beach in Maine, November 29, 1943, as part of "Operation Elster". He had a suitcase full of American dollars and spy gear. He met his partner, an American army deserter, and they made their way to Boston and then to New York where Gimpel lived and spied. He met beautiful women and lived *la dolce vita* until December 31, 1944, when FBI agents arrested him in Times Square during the New Year's Eve festivities. He was tried for espionage and sentenced to death by hanging. Gimpel's lawyers, American army majors, sought forgiveness of the death sentence from President Roosevelt. This was denied. Then Roosevelt's death, according to policy, postponed executions. The winding-down of the war further delayed executions. Finally, President Truman pardoned Gimpel, resulting in ten years of picturesque incarceration in Leavenworth and Alcatraz. He was released to return to Germany, where his autobiography was published in 1960. This document is interesting, and if accurate lends credence to claims that Admiral Canaris's German military intelligence was deliberately mismanaged – the agents dispatched to New York for Operation Elster were poorly supervised and uninformed.

The story of Canaris is one of many patriotic Germans who wanted German, but not Nazi, victory. Physicists, well-educated and having had Jewish colleagues and friends, were especially vulnerable to this internal conflict. In order to do their work, to pursue their passions, however, they needed government resources …which were available for exclusively military purposes.

---

[371] Ernst Adolf Hepp, Nazi party member, editor of *Tele,* interrogated by Rebecca Wellington and Lt. Peter Haruden, State Department Special Interrogation Mission, Wiesbaden, October 5, 1945, Head of Mission DeWitt G. Paele, declassified December 1, 1950, p.5.

Meitner's sources of intelligence – German personnel

It was from September, 1941...that we saw an open road ahead of us, leading to the atomic bomb.[372]

Werner Heisenberg

Those who knew Lise Meitner were impressed by her brilliance and dedication. Not all were friends. Meitner was demanding and critical. Significant was her sex – in her day men at work were not accustomed to taking orders or receiving criticism from women. Moreover, she would not apply her peerless understanding of nuclear fission to assist in creation of an atomic bomb. In this she was like Albert Einstein. And she made known her disapproval of those who worked on the bomb. While Einstein was a pacifist, he was willing to make an exception in the case of Hitler. Meitner disapproved of bomb-making by both sides,but confined her partisan activity to helping prevent the realization of a German atomic bomb. While she passively rejected the Manhattan Project, she acted against the German program and those working in it.

> She was a magnet for German scientists, many of whom corresponded with her and sometimes visited her. Rosbaud's friends Otto Hahn, Max von Laue, and Josef Mattauch lectured in Stockholm, and through Meitner and Hole gleaned much information. She was a channel for Rosbaud to his family and friends in England. ... It was her way of contributing to Hitler's defeat without working on the atomic bomb. Hers was a meaningful contribution to the Allied victory over Germany.[373]

ALSOs, Epsilon

The ALSOs Missions were American crews of scientists and soldiers bent on finding evidence of a German atomic bomb – they followed Allied invaders into Italy, then France, then Germany. The existence of such a weapon was the only factor capable of preventing Germany's defeat. To the relief of Allied Command, only R&D – level operations were discovered.

German physicists were sought in neutral countries[374], and when the Allies swept through Germany, they collected the scientists involved in nuclear weapons research, the Russians removing their captives to Moscow and the Allies taking theirs (Operation Epsilon) to a luxurious country house, "Farm Hall" near Cambridge. There were ten in the British share: physical chemists Otto Hahn and Paul Harteck, and physicists Erich Bagge, Kurt Diebner, Walther Gerlach, Werner Heisenberg, Horst Korsching, Max von Laue, Carl Friedrich von Weizsäcker and Karl Wirtz.

---

[372] David Irving, *The Virus House*, London: William Kimber 1967 p.93. And Rainer Karlsch, *Hitlers Bombe: die geheime Geschichte der deutschen Kernwaffenversuche*, München: Deutsche Verlags-Anstalt 2005, p.76, *"Wir sahen eigentlich vom September 1941 eine freie Strasse zur Atombombe vor uns."*

[373] Arnold Kramish, *The Griffin: The Greatest Untold Espionage Story of World War II*, Boston: Houghton Mifflin Company 1986, p.191.

[374] *"... Gelehrten und Wissenschaftler in der Schweiz, in Schweden und anderen neutralien Ländern wurden gefragt, ob sie etwas über den früheren oder gar gegenwärtigen Aufenthalt der führenden deutschen Atomwissenschaftler wüssten."* Franz Kurowski, *Alliierte Jagd auf deutsche Wissenschaftler: Das Unternehmen Paperclip*, München: Georg Müller Verlag GmbH 1982, pages 22-23.

Farm Hall [375]

Otto Hahn

…on 28 September 1907, Otto Hahn made the acquaintance of the physicist, Lise Meitner, who was the same age as him. That day was to become a historic date in the history of the natural sciences.[376]

Lise Meitner, theoretical physicist, and Otto Hahn, physical chemist, worked together in the Berlin Dahlem Kaiser Wilhelm Institut from 1907-1938. Together they authored 50 publications and received several Nobel Prize nominations.

Otto Hahn served as a *Gasoffizier* in WWI, organizing attacks using the poisonous gas invented by his senior in another department of the Kaiser Willhelm Institut, the Jew Fritz Haber.

---

[375] Farm Hall. From the Max Planck Society, Berlin, Courtesy of American Institute of Physics (AIP) Emilio Segrè Archives/National Archives and Records Administration.

[376] Klaus Hoffmann, *Otto Hahn: Achievement and Responsibility, translated by J. Michael Cole,* New York: Springer 2001, p.50.

Otto Hahn in WWI [377]   Fritz Haber in WWI [378]

379

Hahn   Meitner

Lise fled to Stockholm in mid-1938. In December Hahn and Strassmann divided the uranium atom and Lise and her nephew Otto Robert Frisch provided the explanation of the phenomenon, calling it nuclear fission. Hahn's friend Niels Bohr identified the isotope U-235 as the fissile actor in February 1939. In June and July of 1939 the prospect of an explosive based on a chain reaction was recognized by Bohr, Meitner, Frisch and the scientists in Hahn's Berlin-Dahlem KWI.[380]

---

[377] Courtesy *Archiv zur Geschichte der Max-Planck-Gesellschaft, Berlin.*

[378] Fritz Haber photo courtesy of the Max Planck Society, Berlin.

[379] Alamy 2T3J6JY

[380] Walter Gerlach and Dietrich Hahn, *Otto Hahn: Ein Forscherleben unserer Zeit,* Stuttgart: Wissenschaftliche Verlagsgesellschaft 1984, p. 102.

Lise met Otto Hahn in November 1938 in Copenhagen and April 1939 in Stockholm.[381]

Otto worked in the KWI until the severe bombing of February 15, 1944. The raid was requested by General Groves, head of the Manhattan Project. Hahn's office was the target.[382] Equipment, records and correspondence were destroyed.

383

Kaiser Wilhelm Institute in 1928

Kaiser Wilhelm Institute after bombing 1944 [384]

It was no use even thinking of going on with work in any sort of organized way. Professor Heisenberg, Director of the Kaiser Wilhelm Institute of Physics, decided to transfer his laboratories to Southern Germany. I followed his example.

---

[381] Op. cit. Sime, *Lise Meitner*, p.275.

[382] Robert S. Norris, *Racing for the Bomb: the True Story of General Leslie R. Groves, the Man Behind the Birth of the Atomic Age*, New York: Skyhorse Publishing Inc. 2002/14, pages 295-296.

[383] Courtesy *Archiv zur Geschichte der Max-Planck-Gesellschaft, Berlin.*

[384] Photo courtesy of the Archive of the Max Planck Society, Berlin

... Heisenberg moved into some textile factories that were partly shut down, in Hechingen, and I found suitable accommodation in Tailfingen, in the Swabian Alb....In the autumn of 1944 we moved to Tailfingen.[385]

During the war Hahn was in frequent contact with Meitner via mail.[386] Lise was able to receive German scientific journals and exchanged views with "*Hähnchen*" regarding articles in these. British and American journals were not available in Germany. Hahn's former student Clara Lieber supplied news from America until 1941; thereafter Hahn relied on Lise and Paul Rosbaud for news of scientific developments outside the Reich.

Because mail was subject to opening and inspection leaving and entering Germany, Otto included in his letter to Lise of July 26, 1940, explicit acknowledgement of the limitations on how much scientific information he could convey to her.[387]

To sidestep Nazi censors they could code intelligence in correspondence or have it carried by some of the hundreds of Swedish and German citizens who passed back and forth in the ordinary course of their business during the war.

In the fall of 1943 Hahn traveled to Stockholm to visit Lise and address the Swedish Academy of Sciences.

... the British placed great importance on meetings between Lise Meitner and Otto Hahn and Meitner and Max von Laue. During a 1943 visit to Sweden, Hahn, when asked by Meitner how the fission project was going, replied, "It isn't going."*[388]*

Paul Harteck

The most effective and therefore dangerous of the Farm Hall contingent, the *Uranverein*, was the Austrian Paul Harteck. His scientific understanding coupled with executive ability resulted in achievement of U-235 separation with an ultracentrifuge and realistic plans for heavy water production. Had there been a great deal more resources allotted to him, the Germans might have realized their atomic bomb.[389]

---

[385] Otto Hahn, *Otto Hahn: My Life, translated by Ernst Kaiser & Eithne Wilknis,* London: Macdonald & Co, pages 156-157.

[386] Context and numerous letters are presented in Krafft (Op.cit.), notably on pages 112-135 and 166-180.

[387] "*Dass dir hier also etwas verheimlich wurde, weil wir mit einer unkollegialen Reaktion rechnen, ist nur aus der Gesamtmentalität zu verstehen, über die ich seit Anfang 1938 höffte allmählich wegzukommen. Ich sehe aber immer wieder, dass mir dies trotz aller Anstrengungen nicht gelingt, und ich kann es offenbar nicht mehr ändern.*" Op. cit. Krafft, p.125.

[388] Jeffrey T. Richelson, *Spying on the Bomb: American Nuclear Intelligence from Nazi Germany to Iran and North Korea,* New York: W.W. Norton & Company 2006, p.43.

[389] "In fact it was not the physicists who had made the running in the uranium project so far; for while the teams in Leipzig, Berlin and Heidelberg had pursued their theoretical investigations at a leisurely pace, it was the group of physical chemists under Professor Paul Harteck in Hamburg who had adapted themselves to the urgency of the problem. It was Harteck – with his intuitive grasp of experimental technique – who had from the outset suggested that the uranium and moderator should be separated in the atomic reactor; it was Harteck again who had set up the first rough uranium pile, using carbon dioxide, in the first months of 1940, two and a half years before Fermi built the first successful pile in Chicago; it was Harteck and Suess who had devised a means of increasing tenfold Norwegian-Hydro's heavy water output. Again it was Dr. Groth who had toiled for a year with

Harteck studied physical chemistry at the University of Vienna – twenty years after Lise Meitner. He worked with Hahn and Meitner in the Berlin-Dahlem KWI, 1928-1933. After Hitler came to power Harteck spent a year at Cambridge experimenting in nuclear fusion under Ernest Rutherford. From 1934 until 1950, excluding six months confinement at Farm Hall, he was a professor at the University of Hamburg. He moved to the USA in 1951 and taught at Rensselaer Polytechnic until 1968. From 1939-1945 Harteck and his assistant Wilhelm Groth pursued the centrifuge method of U-235 separation… in Hamburg until this city was destroyed by Allied bombing, and then in Celle, 120 km south of Hamburg. During this period the Hamburg suburb of Bergedorf, (containing *Bergedorfer Eisenwerk*) was relatively unharmed. Harteck's assistant Dr. Groth traveled to Uppsala for ultracentrifuge consultation with Svedberg and Pedersen in 1940 and 1942. [390]

Erich Bagge

Werner Heisenberg was Erich Bagge's doctoral supervisor. During the war Bagge worked in the KWI Berlin (as did Hahn, Strassmann et al) on the separation of U-235, notably with variations of centrifuges using electromagnets and heat to enrich uranium hexafluoride gas.[391] Bagge was the only friend of Kurt Diebner at Farm Hall.

Kurt Diebner

Diebner's role was administrative, although he was a physicist. He organized the first meeting of the *Uranverein* on September 16, 1939. There it was determined that the KWI Berlin should fall under control of the military, and that Diebner should become its administrative head. As a member of the Nazi party he was entitled to a government job.

Walter Gerlach

Walter Gerlach was a senior professor at the Ludwig Maximilian University of Munich from 1929 until confinement at Farm Hall in 1945. He was a skilled experimenter, recipient of a Nobel Prize for Physics in 1944, a member of the board of directors of the *Kaiser-Wilhelm-Gesellschaft* 1937-1945 and plenipotentiary for nuclear physics in the Reich Research Council from 1944 to 1945.

Harteck to make the Clusius-Dickel diffusion process work with the separation of uranium isotopes, and it was Groth who had pushed through the revolutionary ultracentrifuge as a means of enriching uranium U-235…." Op.cit. David Irving, *The German Atomic Bomb,* p.127.

[390] Ibid. pages 311-312.

[391] David Cassidy, *Hitler's Uranium Club: The Secret Recordings at Farm Hall,* Woodbury New York: American Institute of Physics 1996, pages 353-362.

Paul Harteck   Werner Heisenberg Niels Bohr

Werner Heisenberg

The star of German theoretical physics during the Nazi era was Werner Heisenberg. He was born in December 1901, the son of a professor of classics, and became a Boy Scout leader and an accomplished classical pianist. At the age of twenty-three he published his work in quantum mechanics that resulted in a Nobel Prize in 1932. In 1927 he presented his famous "uncertainty principle" while working with Niels Bohr in Copenhagen. Handsome, elegant, a natural leader – he became director of organizations devoted to nuclear physics during the Nazi era, including the Kaiser Wilhelm Institute in Berlin 1942-1945. There he reported to the *Wehrmacht,* the German military that funded the KWI from 1939 to 1945.

When news of the bombing of Hiroshima reached the Farm Hall internees on August 6, 1945, Heisenberg was incredulous. He could not believe that Americans had done what Germans failed to do – create an atomic bomb. Later he told his captors that he and his fellow physicists had not really wanted to provide the Nazis with a bomb, that they had passively resisted the regime. Although Heisenberg did not join the Nazi Party, he held types of high offices in government organizations that would normally have been open only to Party members; and he functioned satisfactorily in these. Loyal Germans who disapproved of Nazi methods were caught in a cruel dilemma. Heisenberg said he chose to remain in Germany – to influence events for the better, which could only be accomplished by appearing to collaborate. He indulged in postwar rationalizations for colleagues' behaviour as well, for example in testimony at the Nuremberg Trials to help Ernst von Weizsäcker, father of physics colleague Karl Friedrich von Weizsäcker.[394]

---

[392] Photo courtesy of the Archives of the Max Planck Society, Berlin

[393] Photo credit Emilio Segrè Visual Archives from the American Institute of Physics.

[394] David C. Cassidy, *Uncertainty: The Life and Science of Werner Heisenberg,* New York: W.H. Freeman & Company 1992, pages 316-320.

Opinions are divided on Heisenberg's conduct during WWII. Rose asserted that Heisenberg believed that several tons of U-235 (an amount impossible to accumulate in Germany's situation) would be necessary for an explosive, and that he had lied[395] when asked about the historically conspicuous meeting of Germany's scientific and military leaders in June 1942, chaired by armaments minister Albert Speer, wherein Field Marshall Milch asked Heisenberg how large an atomic bomb would be required to destroy a city:

> I answered that the bomb, that is essentially the active part, would have to be about the size of a pineapple. This statement, of course, caused a surprise, especially with the known physicists, and it has therefore remained in the memory of several participants.[396]

This quotation that Rose indicated to be from Irving contradicts what Irving actually said in *The Virus House* about Heisenberg's speech at the July 1942 meeting under Speer's auspices. There it is stated that it was the "non-physicists" who were surprised, not the "known physicists" (see the previous footnote).

According to Rose, then, others who were at that meeting also lied and/or condoned Heisenberg's lies. Albert Einstein has also said that sometimes even Nobel Prize winners fib.

> The conference was held in the Helmoltz lecture room of the Harnack building, the headquarters of the Kaiser-Wilhelm Institute in Berlin-Dahlem. Albert Speer was assisted by his technical chief, Karl-Otto Saur, and by Professor Porsche, theVolkswagen designer. Among the scientists who accompanied Heisenberg were Otto Hahn, Doctor Diebner, Professor Harteck, Doctor Wirtz and Professor Thiessen, who had written to Göring independently about the importance of atomic fission three months before. Doctor Albert Vogler, the President of the Kaiser-Wilhelm Foundation, and of United Steel, was also there. From Otto Hahn's private diary we know that General Leeb (head of Army ordnance) and his superior, General Fromm, were present, with Field-Marshall Milch and Admiral Witzell, counterparts in the other two services.[397]

---

[395] Paul Lawrence Rose, *Heisenberg and the Atomic Bomb Project: A Study in German Culture,* Berkeley, London: University of California Press 1998, pages 31-32 and 53-54.

[396] Ibid. Rose p.32. Here the citation is "Ibid. Cf. Irving, *German Atomic Bomb* p.120" and in the bibliography (p.339) "*The German Atomic Bomb:The History of Nuclear Research in Germany,* New York, 1967, 2d ed. New York 1993. Published in the United Kingdom as *The Virus House* (London 1967)." Pedants among us would want to know that this quotation does not appear on page 120 or anywhere else in this book or its later paperback edition (DaCapo Press New York) that I could discover, but something similar is on page 109 of David Irving's book *The Virus House,* also published in 1967 but in the United Kingdom: "The question and answer exchange which remained rooted most deeply in the memories of all those present came at the end of Heisenberg's speech. Field-Marshall Milch asked how large a nuclear bomb would have to be to destroy a city. Heisenberg replied that the explosive charge would be 'about as large as a pineapple,' and he emphasized the point with a gesture of his hands. This caused uneasy excitement among the non-physicists present. Heisenberg, by his own account, hastened to moderate their enthusiasm with a warning that while the Americans, if they were working flat-out to that end, might have a uranium pile very soon and a uranium bomb in two years at the very least, for Germany to produce such a bomb was an economic impossibility at present."

[397] David Irving, *The Virus House: Germany's Atomic Research and Allied Counter-measures,* London: William Kimber 1967, p.108.

David Irving prepared his book twenty years after the war when many of the relevant characters were alive. He could interact with them face to face…and was thus subject to whatever influences this implies. Rose, writing more than fifty years after the war, had the disadvantage, or advantage, of relying on printed sources.

For Heisenberg to have thought in terms of much more than the quantity of U-235 actually required for an atomic bomb,[398] he would have had to be ignorant of the famous Frisch-Peierls Memorandum that had been distributed to dozens of scientists and military men in Britain more than two years earlier, April 1940, and that indicated one kg as being sufficient for a chain reaction in pure U-235. According to the United States Government publication dated July 1945, and released by General Groves to the public in American and British editions in August 1945, scientific journal articles by Fermi, Hahn, Strassmann, Meitner, Frisch, and Bohr in early 1939, and dozens more related articles in the ensuing months[399] had resulted in the following general understanding among physicists in 1940:

> It had been established (1) that uranium fission did occur with release of great amounts of energy; and (2) that in the process extra neutrons were set free which might start a chain reaction.…[and regarding "Military Usefulness"]… If all atoms in a kilogram of U-235 undergo fission, the energy released is equivalent to the energy released in the explosion of about 20,000 short tons of TNT. If the critical size of a bomb turns out to be practical – say, in the range of one to one hundred kilograms – and all the other problems can be solved, there remain two questions. First, how large a percentage of the fissionable nuclei can be made to undergo fission before the reaction stops; i.e. what is the efficiency of the explosion? Second, what is the effect of so concentrated a release of energy? Even if only1 percent of the theoretically available energy is released, the explosion will still be of a totally different order of magnitude from that produced by any previously known type of bomb. The value of such a bomb was thus a question for military experts to consider very carefully.[400]

The Soviets, whose information concerning atomic energy was inferior to that of the Germans, British and Americans, in August 1939 reckoned a critical mass of U-235 to be ten kg.[401]

The recollections of the chairman of the famous June 1942 meeting, the effective executive Albert Speer, were clouded by his wish to avoid saying something that would worsen his position at the Nuremberg Trials

---

[398] The bomb dropped on Hiroshima, "Little Boy", contained 64 kg of U-235 averaging 80% purity, about one kg of which underwent fission.

[399] "In the last six months of 1939 *Nature* published some twenty notes and articles bearing on fission, and a burst of articles was coming out in American publications.…By the end of the year the score in the United States was an even one hundred articles. They were summarized and brought together in the January 1940 issue of *Review of Modern Physics.*" Ruth Moore, *Niels Bohr: The Man, His Science, and the World They Changed,* New York: Alfred A. Knopf 1966, p.259.

[400] H.D. Smyth, *A General Account of Methods of Using Atomic Energy for Military Purposes under the Auspices of the United States Government 1940-1945,* London: Reprinted by His Majesty's Stationery Office, 1945, from the United States of America Government Printing Office, p.25.

[401] "*Für Uran 235 wie für Plutonium hatten Charlton und Zeldovich bereits im August 1939 überschlägig eine kritische Masse 10 kg errechnet.*" Andreas Heinemann-Grüder, *Die Sowjetische Atombombe,* Münster: Verlag Westfälisches Dampfboot 1992, p.27.

and later his reputation for posterity. Consequently, Speer's observations about Heisenberg, like Heisenberg's about Speer, are muddled and inconsistent – two brilliant, complicated characters, with varied manifest and hidden agendas.

In the 760 pages of Viennese journalist Gitta Sereny's magisterial book about Albert Speer and German culture, *Albert Speer: His Battle With Truth,* she notes that Speer had several meetings with KWI scientists. In the June 1942 meeting he asked Heisenberg what he would need to create an atomic bomb. Heisenberg asked for release of some young scientists who had been drafted, some restricted metals like nickel, a facility in which to build a small cyclotron and a few hundred thousand marks.

> Speer, surprised by the modesty of their demands, said that as Minister of Armaments he could easily give them many times that, but Heisenberg replied that their research was too far behind to make greater resources useful at that point.[402]

Heisenberg's claim after the war that he deliberately slowed progress toward the atomic bomb was ridiculed by Speer: "I do hope that Heisenberg is not now claiming that they tried, for reasons of principle, to sabotage the project by asking for such minimal support!" [403] In this connection Sereny also noted the experience of Niels Bohr, whose alienation from Heisenberg began with his visit to Bohr in Copenhagen after the German occupation of Denmark…when Heisenberg indicated that Germany would win the war and that it would be in Bohr's interest to help with the German atomic bomb initiative…and after the war when Heisenberg claimed that Bohr had misunderstood him.

Perhaps the definitive word on this issue came from Heisenberg's son, the scientist Jochen Heisenberg:

> My father told us that he had informed the people in the government that a bomb would require a critical mass roughly the size of a pineapple. Some want to believe he mistakenly thought it would take several tons. I am biased, but I checked Diebner's official report of the so-called Uranium Club to the Army Ordnance Ministry. I read that the estimate was of 10 to 100 kg U-235 for a nuclear bomb, which translates to just about the size of a pineapple, confirming the truthfulness. This was known at the time my father went to Copenhagen.[404]

Heisenberg was head of the parallel to the U-235 initiative, the plutonium (U-239) development program…."the state of our knowledge as it was in February 1940…it appeared almost certain that we can set up a chain reaction in a uranium-graphite system…"[405]

[402] Gitta Sereny, *Albert Speer: His Battle With Truth,* London: Macmillan Picador 1995/96, p.318.

[403] Ibid. p.319.

[404] Correspondence from Jochen Heisenberg quoted in Colin Brown, *Operation Big: The Race to Stop Hitler's Atomic Bomb,* Stroud Gloucestershire: Amberley Publishing 2016, pages 250-251.

[405] Public Lecture by Leo Szilard, University of Chicago, July 31, 1946 in Bernard T. Field and Gertrud Weiss Szilard, editors, *The Collected Works of Leo Szilard,* London & Cambridge MA: The MIT Press 1972, p.188.

Horst Korsching

The terms of Lise Meitner and Horst Korsching at the KWI Dahlem-Berlin overlapped by a year. He was a student when Meitner fled to Sweden in 1938. During the war he worked on the isotope separation programs of Werner Heisenberg and Kurt Diebner. When the Berlin-Dahlem facility was bombed in 1943, KWI activity was moved to Hechingen; there Korsching remained until captured and brought to Farm Hall, where he was the youngest man and a loner.

Max von Laue

The recipient of the Nobel Prize in Physics in 1914, Max von Laue was active in the KWI Berlin-Dahlem from 1917 until 1948, as acting director 1933-1934 and 1939-1945. He was loyal to Germany and to science, and opposed to Nazism. Of the German scientists interned at Farm Hall, he had the most consistent and plausible anti-Nazi record.

In 1939:

> Jews were a captive population whose only hope was that things would not get worse.
> Otto [Hahn] did not write to Lise about such things. It was Max von Laue who kept Lise informed about events in Germany. "Please do not feel inhibited about writing here!" he assured her in the winter of 1939. "An absolutely black sheep need not fear becoming blacker. For me it is at least a small substitute for our talks in the KWI."[406]

When the war began:

> Meitner's Berlin friends suffered from little at first except some consumer shortages and a feeling of isolation. Lise began sending small packages to Otto and Edith: soap, cigars, coffee. When Otto's *Nature* and *Comptus Rendus* stopped coming, he asked Lise to inform him of new developments in fission [October 1939]; Max von Laue designated Lise go – between should he be unable to reach his son Theodor in Princeton. Although the mail between Germany and Sweden remained regular, they were all aware of wartime censorship. Planck became "Uncle Max Senior"; Laue "Uncle Max Junior" or "Theo's father" [September 1939] …[407]

Max von Laue and Lise Meitner communicated routinely throughout the war. Between Berlin and Stockholm there was daily mail service and phone lines were available to ordinary citizens.

Max bravely visited Lise in Stockholm.
Während des Dritten Reiches war er der Mutigste von allen gewesen.
Erst vor drei Jahren hatte ihn LISE MEITNER in Stockholm getroffen…[408]

---

[406] Op. cit. Sime p.270.

[407] Op. cit. Sime, p.279.

[408] Armin Hermann, *Die Neue Physik: Der Weg in Das Atomzeitalter,* München: Heinz Moos Verlag 1979, p.115. Photo of Max von Laue courtesy of the Archives of the Max Planck Society, *MPG Laue_I_3_65.jpg.*

von Laue in his Steyr

Karl Friedrich von Weizsäcker

Born in Kiel in 1912, Karl Friedrich inherited the "von" from his grandfather Karl Hugo von Weizsäcker, a minister in the government of the Kingdom of Württemberg, who was ennobled in 1897. Karl Friedrich's father Ernst was a prominent figure during Hitler's regime, most importantly Secretary of State at the Foreign Office from 1938 until 1943. After the disasters at Stalingrad and El Alamein, Ernst requested a transfer and was made German Ambassador to the Holy See. He remained a guest of the Vatican until 1946 when he faced trial at Nuremberg, leading to three years of imprisonment.

What to make of Karl Friedrich's activities in the German atomic bomb program is difficult, complicated by his family associations (patriotic and religious), his ambition to achieve a nuclear chain reaction and dissimulations as revealed by the clandestine Farm Hall recordings and postwar documents discovered in Germany. Contrary to impressions of contemporaries, including that idol of physics and paragon of decency, Niels Bohr – Karl Friedrich and Heisenberg maintained that they were merely pursuing pure scientific knowledge in seeking to achieve nuclear chain reactions.

One is reminded of the Tom Lehrer lyric regarding their KWI Berlin-Dahlem trained colleague:

Gather round while I sing you of Wernher von Braun,
A man whose allegiance
Is ruled by expedience.
Call him a Nazi, he won't even frown.
"Ha, Nazi Schmazi," says Werner von Braun.
Don't say that he's hypocritical,
Say rather he's apolitical.
"Once the rockets are up, who cares where they come down?
That's not my department," says Wernher von Braun. [409]

---

[409] And more formally: "The end was worthy enough: to produce a rocket which would be capable of free flight in space. The means were provided by the soldier's administrative ability to provide army funds. The immature von Braun was swept along by the opportunities which could only have been flattering to a young scientist." R.W. Reid, *Tongues of Conscience: War and the scientist's dilemma*, London: Constable & Co. Ltd. Panther edition 1969/71, p.81.

Except insofar as his activities were known to her friends (e.g. Hahn, Strassmann, von Laue, Rosbaud), Karl Friedrich von Weizsäcker would not have been a source of Meitner's intelligence.

Karl Wirtz

From 1937 until Farm Hall incarceration in 1945 Karl Wirtz worked in the KWI Berlin-Dahlem. He contributed several papers during the war on his special technologies, the production and use of heavy water. Without success, Wirtz pursued separation of U-235 using the Clusius method.[410] He regretted that the lack of effort and cooperation from his colleagues prevented achievement of a German atomic bomb.[411] Wirtz's work was praised by Heisenberg.[412]

Nikolaus Riehl

In 1927 Nikolaus Riehl received his PhD in Otto Hahn's department at the Kaiser Wilhelm Institut in Dahlem, Berlin. His supervisor was Lise Meitner. Riehl went to work in industry. His most notable contributions were invention of the fluorescent lamp in the thirties and production of high-purity uranium oxide and metal…in Germany during WWII and in Russia post-war. Through the Nazi era it was only by disguising the fact that he had one Jewish grandparent that Riehl was able to do important work in the Auer company, a subsidiary of Degussa era. In July 1939 he approached the *Wehrmacht* and was rewarded with an order for pure uranium oxide and metal. Auer then had a large quantity of uranium left over from removal of radium from ore. During the war Auer was also able to obtain uranium ore from Czechoslovakia and the Belgian Congo. Riehl was successful – the essentials the Germans lacked were U-235 and heavy water, not uranium.

In 1944 Auer dismissed the chemist Philipp Hoernes because he had a Jewish wife. With Riehl's help Otto Hahn was able to employ Hoernes, a way for him and his wife to survive the war.[413] Riehl cooperated with Hahn in studying radiation poisoning among the workers at an Auer uranium production plant, many of whom were slave labourers from the 2,000 women convicts at nearby Sachsenhausen.[414]

> In the middle of May of 1945 two colonels of the Peoples' Commissariat of the Interior (NKVD) suddenly appeared from Berlin… The colonels requested that I join them for a "few days" of discussion in Berlin. The few days lasted for ten years.[415]

---

[410] Jeremy Bernstein, *Hitler's Uranium Club: The Secret Recordings at Farm Hall,* Woodbury New York: American Institute of Physics 1996, p.83.

[411] Ibid Bernstein pages 145-146.

[412] Ibid. Bernstein p.258.

[413] Ruth Lewin Sime, *Otto Hahn und die Max-Planck-Gesellschaft: Zwischen Vergangenheit und Erinnerung,* Ergebnisse 14 2004, Forschungs Programm "Geschichte der Kaiser-Wilhelm-Gesellschaft im Nationalsozialismus", p.25.

[414] Ibid. Ruth Lewin Sime p.26.

[415] Nikolaus Riehl and Frederick Seitz, *Stalin's Captive: Nikolas Riehl and the Soviet Race for the Bomb,* Washington DC: American Chemical Society and Chemical Heritage Foundation 1996, p. 71.

When the Russians entered Berlin in 1945 they confiscated the stores of uranium metal and uranium ore sequestered by Riehl for use at the KWI. They kidnapped Riehl and shipped him to Moscow. He helped enable the Russian atomic bomb (tested in 1949) and spent ten years in Russian captivity before being allowed to return to Germany.

During WWII Riehl's only trip outside Germany was to visit Lise Meitner in Stockholm.

Fritz Strassmann

The famous experiments in 1938 that resulted in Otto Hahn's Nobel Prize for nuclear fission were performed by Fritz Strassmann – with guidance and assistance by Hahn, and help from Clara Lieber. Strassmann's career was crippled by his refusal to join the Nazi Party. He remained in the KWI in Berlin-Dahlem with Hahn until the 1944 bombings, but he did not work on directly bomb-related problems. He and his wife took enormous risk by hiding a Jewish woman in their apartment for many months during the war. Before, during and after the war Strassmann corresponded with Meitner in Stockholm. [416]

Fritz Strassmann[417]

Opposing the German Atomic Bomb Were …

Paul Rosbaud

Free to travel throughout the Reich and its neutral neighbours during the Nazi era, Paul Rosbaud gleaned the best of scientific intelligence in his job as an editor of the German journal *die Naturwissenschaften,* and was able to convey this intelligence to Lise Meitner in Stockholm.[418] His friendship with Meitner began

---

[416] Op. cit. Fritz Krafft.

[417] Photo courtesy of the Archivs of the Max Planck Society, Berlin, identity *Strassmann_1_3*.

[418] "…a cover for espionage as ideal as one could hope for because it permitted him to travel to neutral countries such as Sweden…." Op.cit. Nikolas Riehl and Frederick Seitz, p.49.

before the Nazi era and continued after it. Biographer Arnold Kramish described a part Rosbaud played in Meitner's escape from Germany:

> Hahn recalled, "Aided by our old friend Paul Rosbaud, we spent one night packing the clothes she most needed and some of her valuables. I gave her a beautiful diamond ring that I had inherited from my mother and which I had never worn myself but always treasured; I wanted her to be provided for in an emergency." Paul Rosbaud then took Meitner to Hahn's house to stay overnight. Hahn had no automobile at that time, so Paul picked up Lise the next day in his Opel and drove her to the station. Meitner was tense, fearful, and Rosbaud had to use all his persuasive talents to get her aboard the train. Dirk Coster was waiting for her in a first-class compartment and got Lise safely across the border. She stayed briefly in Holland, then left for Stockholm, where she remained, in misery, until the end of the war.[419]

Rosbaud was frequently in contact with Meitner during WWII.[420] Conveying scientific information, for example equations, implied written communication between a knowledgeable sender and receiver. Meitner received intelligence from Rosbaud and also facilitated its transmission by distributing in Stockholm the books required by Allied agents to interpret messages in Rosbaud's "book code."

> An obscure book – in April 1940 the choice was *Sesame and Lilies* – is selected by the coders and decoders. Each letter of the message is described by three numbers that identify the page of the book, the line on that page, and the position of the enciphered letter in the line. Only if the book is known does the message become known.[421]

Rosbaud's functioning as an Allied agent throughout the war was phenomenal. It contradicted the postwar testimony of legions of Germans who said that they opposed the Nazi regime but were unable to resist it. Rosbaud evaded discovery by giving the Gestapo positive indications of his loyalty to the Reich. In a meeting monitored by Gestapo agents, he chastised scientists for their failure to deliver an atomic bomb to the Führer.

> He often traveled to occupied countries conspicuously wearing a party uniform, as though he were a high-placed official and member of the party. He undoubtedly incurred the hidden wrath of uninformed citizens in the process, but his contacts understood his reasons.[422]

Fanatically loyal Germans envied his credentials…identical to Hitler's…as an Austrian from the staunchly anti-Semitic provinces. His passport showed Rosbaud as being from Graz, Styria, where persecution of Jews was a thousand-year-old tradition.

---

[419] Op cit. Arnold Kramish, *The Griffin: The Greatest Untold Espionage Story of World War II,* Boston: Houghton Mifflin Company 1986, p.49.

[420] Ibid. pages 52, 78, 86, 97, 98, 121, 125, 135, 179, 180, 183, 191, 192, 204, 212, 213, 226, 227.

[421] Ibid. p.226.

[422] Op. cit. Nikolas Riehl and Frederick Seitz, p.49.

Hitler did not innovate removal of Jews from public offices and professions, cancellation of the right to vote, mandatory wearing of yellow sleeve bands and even mass executions – all these had occurred at various times and places in provincial Austria from the eleventh through the nineteenth centuries.[423] Rosbaud's hometown of Graz proclaimed itself in early 1940 to be the first city in the Reich to be Jew-free (*Judenfrei*).[424]

> Efforts to combat anti-Semitism, including reminders of the part played by Jewish soldiers in World War I, could do nothing to counter the violent hatred against the Jews ingrained in wide sectors of the Austrian population. …The liquidation of Austrian Jewry began with the Anschluss (annexation to Germany) on March 13, 1938. According to the *Israelitische Kultusgemeinde*, the Jewish community of Vienna, there were at the time 181,778 Jews in Austria, of whom 91.3% were living in Vienna. [425]

After the war 110 Jews returned to Graz. In 1949 there were 420 and in 1950, 286. A new synagogue was built on the site of the old. At its consecration in 2000 there were fewer than one hundred members.

During the war Rosbaud visited his hometown of Graz. After the war he was smuggled out of Berlin to England, where he lived until his death in 1963. In view of his betrayal of Nazi Germany and his wife's Jewish taint, return to Graz was unthinkable.

Otto Robert Frisch

When he abandoned Bohr's Copenhagen laboratory for England, avoiding the Nazi occupation of Denmark and subsequent persecution of Jews, Otto Robert Frisch worked with Rudolf Peierls, another expatriate Jewish German physicist and a friend of Aunt Lise. At the University of Birmingham they produced the "Frisch-Peierls Memorandum".[426]

In this document they expressed the conclusion that a mass of a few kilograms of U-235 would be sufficient for a bomb equivalent to many thousands of tons of TNT, and that the separation of such a "critical mass" was probably feasible. The shocking significance – attack by a single airplane could destroy a large city. In March 1940 the Frisch-Peierls memorandum circulated among British scientists. Formation of the MAUD Committee followed. At the beginning Frisch and Peierls were excluded because they were enemy aliens. In his letter to the MAUD Committee of April 22, 1940, Rudolf Peierls drew attention to this

---

[423] Op cit. *Encyclopedia Judaica, Vol.3,* pages 887-901.

[424] Rosbaud's credibility as an Austrian anti-Semite was crucial to his success as a spy. To understand, see Bruce F. Pauley, *From Prejudice to Persecution: A History of Austrian Anti-Semitism,* Chapel Hill & London: The University of North Carolina Press 1992, pages 175, 177, 187, 203, 288, 297 and 302.

[425] Ibid. p.898.

[426] "Appendix 1: The Frisch-Peierls Memorandum, On the Construction of a 'Super-bomb' based on a Nuclear Chain Reaction in Uranium "(pages 389-393) and "Appendix 2: The Maud Report: Report by M.A.U.D. Committee on the use of Uranium for a Bomb & appendixes to M.A.U.D. Report" (pages 394-436), Margaret Gowing, *Britain and Atomic Energy 1939-1945,* Basingstoke, Hampshire: Palgrave, United Kingdom Atomic Energy Authority 1964.

absurdity,[427] the result being formation of a technical subcommittee of mainly scientists, including Frisch and Peierls.

Deliberations of the MAUD Committee were shared with Americans, including Frisch and Peierls' observation that Germany pioneered nuclear energy research, and efforts to separate U-235 for purposes of a bomb were there underway. Americans, under threat of war with Japan and Germany[428], read the MAUD report and were moved to launch the Manhattan Project.[429] Lise's nephew Otto Robert Frisch and her friends Rudolf Peierls and Niels Bohr, all of whom first learned of nuclear fission from Lise, were eventually recruited into the Manhattan Project. Its head, General Groves, recognized Lise's primary contribution and invited her to join the many physicists in his organization.[430] She declined, unwilling to help in making a bomb…but willing to help sabotage the German effort.[431]

Aunt Lise communicated frequently with Otto Robert during his time in Bohr's Copenhagen laboratory and while he and Peierls were informing the British atomic weapons program and the nascent Manhattan Project.[432] Communist spies in Britain, colleagues of Frisch and Peierls and acquaintances of Meitner, were able to infiltrate the Manhattan Project, and contribute to its success, motivated by fear of the German atomic bomb.[433]

[427] "…Dr. Frisch is one of the discoverers of the phenomenon of nuclear fission and one of the first experts in the field. It is certainly not in the national interest to exclude him from discussions instead of making full use of his experiments….In this connection the vital importance of absolute secrecy has been mentioned. We are in full agreement with this and you will remember that we underlined this point repeatedly in our first memorandum. But I do not think that any useful pupose can be served by trying to keep our own idea a secret from us." Sabine Lee, *Sir Rudolf Peierls: Selected Private and Scientific Correspondence, Volume 1,* London: World Scientific Publishing 2007, pages 702-703.

[428] "On August 2, 1939, Albert Einstein…had written his famous letter to President Roosevelt warning of the possibility of German atomic weapons development. Fear of German science became a major dynamic in forging America's war strategy. In 1945, Under Secretary of War Robert Patterson revealed that the fundamental priority accorded German over Japanese defeat was the fear of the new weapons that German science might develop in the course of the war." Pamela Spence Richards, *Scientific Information in Wartime: The Allied-German Rivalry 1939-1945,* London: Greenwood Press 1994, p.78.

[429] "Building upon theoretical work on atomic bombs by refugee physicists Rudolf Peierls and Otto Frisch in 1940 and 1941, the MAUD report estimated that a critical mass of ten kilograms would be enough to produce an enormous explosion. A bomb of this size could be loaded on existing aircraft and be ready in two years….The British believed that uranium research could lead to production of a bomb in time to affect the outcome of the war. While the MAUD report provided encouragement to Americans advocating a more extensive uranium research program, it also served as a sobering reminder that fission had been discovered in Nazi Germany almost three years earlier and that since spring 1940 a large part of the Kaiser Wilhelm Institute in Berlin had been set aside for uranium research." F.G. Gosling, *The Manhattan Project: Making the Atomic Bomb,* Office of History and Heritage Resources, Executive Secretariat, Office of Management, Department of Energy, January 2010, p.11.

[430] "No schedule could guarantee that the United States would overtake Germany in the race for the bomb, but by the beginning of 1943 the Manhattan Project had the complete support of President Roosevelt and the military leadership, the services of some of the nation's most distinguished scientists, and a sense of urgency driven by fear." Ibid. Gosling p.19.

[431] Patricia Rife, *Lise Meitner and the Dawn of the Nuclear Age,* Boston: Birkhäuser 1992 p.222.

[432] Sabine Lee, *Sir Rudolf Peierls: Selected Private and Scientific Correspondence, Volume 2,* London: World Scientific Publishing 2007, p.878., and p.690 & p.752, in *Volume 1.*

[433] "The main reason why many of the British team had joined the nuclear project was the danger of a German atomic bomb." Paul Broda, *Scientist Spies: A Memoir of My Three Parents and the Atom Bomb,* Leicester UK: Matador 2011, p.138.

Otto Robert Frisch [434]

Niels Bohr

When German scientists were post-WWI pariahs, unwelcome at international conferences, Lise Meitner was among the first Germans Niels Bohr invited to his Carlsberg House, the residence granted by the Carlsberg Brewery to an outstanding citizen of Denmark. Already famous for his work at the leading edge of nuclear physics, judged an equal by Max Planck and Albert Einstein, Bohr was moreover revered for epitomizing the Danish character … tolerant, considerate, humane, as well as accomplished. For the rest of her life Lise Meitner remembered her first dinner in the house of Niels and Margrethe. In 1922 Bohr received the Nobel Prize for physics. Einstein had received his the year before. From 1924 onward Lise Meitner received several Nobel Prize nominations. She and Margrethe Bohr remained friends until they died.

Prior to WWII Bohr and Werner Heisenberg had worked together enthusiastically on theoretical problems. Heisenberg had been singled out of a lecture audience in Göttingen for special development by Bohr, and his work in Copenhagen with Bohr led to Heisenberg's Nobel Prize. In September 1941, Heisenberg, already head of a German nuclear weapons program, visited Bohr in German-occupied Copenhagen. A conversation, in which they spoke "guardedly" to one another about the possibility of an atomic bomb, alienated the former friends and colleagues. Bohr resolved to oppose the German development of a nuclear weapon. When the Nazis began arresting Danish Jews, September 1943, Bohr and

---

[434] Photo of Lise's nephew Otto Robert Frisch taken in 1938, from Patricia Rife, *Lise Meitner and the Dawn of the Nuclear Age,* Boston: Birkhäuser 1990, p.214+, credited to American Institute for Physics Emilio Segrè Archives, Physics Today Collection.

Margrethe fled with their children to Stockholm. Margrethe remained in Stockholm until after the war. Bohr was carried off to Britain in the bomb bay of a De Havilland Mosquito, thence to the Manhattan Project.

Henry Denham and William Corcoran

Henry Denham [435]   William Corcoran [436]

---

[435] Henry Denham, *Inside the Nazi Ring: A Naval Attaché in Sweden 1940-1945,* New York: Holmes & Meier 1984, approximately 15% of the photo opposite p.143, from Captain Henry Denham to Churchill Archives Centre, Churchill College, Cambridge 1982.

[436] Photo from the William Warwick Corcoran Papers in the Hoover Institution Archives, courtesy of the Stanford University Library.

During WWII Captain Henry Denham was the British Naval Attaché (spy)[437] in Stockholm[438] and William Corcoran was the American Consul General (spy) in Göteborg.[439] Denham reported to Ian Fleming[440]. Fifty years after the event Major Henry Threlfall of the Special Operations Executive was able to talk about his experience in Sweden with Denham:

> I went to Stockholm with the object of seeing what could be done to cause trouble to the Germans in various ways from this neutral outpost. …I was appointed clerk to the naval attaché, that was my cover, which wasn't a very good cover, but that's what I was told and off I went, and I found there an extremely good and lively-minded SOE base.[441]

Chamberlain's ruinous April 5, 1940 remark that the Germans had "missed the bus" …shortly before the invasion of Norway … was made because he had ignored intelligence from Stockholm regarding German ship movements.[442] Chamberlain was replaced by Churchill.

Denham and Corcoran were personal friends as well as collaborators.[443]

---

[437] "Naval attachés are dealt with in this last chapter because each representative of the DNI abroad, if he is in an important capital, virtually becomes a spy himself in wartime the centre of an intelligence system, drawing on many different sources….As a source of naval intelligence Stockholm was certainly the best…." [p.51] and "Stockholm became by far the most important overseas source of naval intelligence." [p.180]; and "About a week later Denham was pleased to receive a signal from the First Sea Lord 'Personal – your message started a series of operations which ended yesterday in the sinking of the Bismarck. Congratulations.'" Op.cit. Donald McLachlan, p.399.

[438] "In the more active role of Intelligence I came to realize that my real enemies were the Abwehr (German Secret Intelligence) who played an effective part in Stockholm not only working against our interests but also succeeding, for a period, in gaining intelligence from Britain." Henry Denham, *Inside the Nazi Ring: A Naval Attaché in Sweden 1940-1945*, New York: Holmes & Meier 1984, p.44.

[439] "Working alone, single-handedly most of the time, although welcoming cooperation at all times from any source, Consul General Corcoran achieved results which led certain newspapers to hail him as "Uncle Sam's Master Spy" and left him the unchallenged reputation of having done the "best one-man intelligence job of the war" William P. Kennedy, *United States Government Historical Museum: Yearbook 1947*, p.18.

[440] "At Admiralty I found John Godfrey with a vast intelligence empire, but I persuaded him to increase my office team by training two very reliable young women with a knowledge of Scandinavia…. Finally, the most rewarding were Ned Denning of Operational Intelligence; Charles Hambro, Head of Special Operations Executive; and Ian Fleming, Admiral Godfrey's right-hand man. It was invariably with them at the end of each London visit that I had a farewell dinner. I found it difficult to restrain myself from being too inquisitive about our many intriguing methods of how were winning the war in Europe." Op. cit. Henry Denham, p.143.

[441] Roderick Bailey, *Forgotten Voices of the Secret War: An Inside History of Special Operations During the Second World War*, Imperial War Museum, UK: Ebury Press Random House 1988/2009, p.117.

[442] William L. Shirer, *The Rise and Fall of the Third Reich: A History of Nazi Germany*, London: Martin Secker & Warburg Ltd. 1959 and 1960, p.695.

[443] "Sadly, the American Naval Attaché in Stockholm was at no time any help to us, but at Gothenburg an excellent US Consul-General helped us all through the war." Op. cit. Henry Denham p.28. Corcoran was also at odds with his U.S. Embassy colleagues in Stockholm, notably when he wrote a letter concerning the number of American Eighth Air Force bomber crews landing in Sweden, knowing that they would be interned under comfortable conditions in a neutral country until the end of the war … instead of having to return to combat. The suggestion that these men were cowards was vigorously denied by senior USAF officers, whose contention is supported in a 1995 book by a professor at the United States Airforce Academy, although this book also

Intelligence from Denham was often derived from spying in Corcoran's bailiwick, the west coast.[444] Both Denham and Corcoran were at times in trouble with the Swedish government intelligence agency, the *AS*. Created by government approval in June 1938, the *AS* was activated on the day Germany invaded Poland.[445] Its main concern was prevention of acts that violated neutrality and could thus provoke invasion.

During the Spanish Civil War William Corcoran was moved from his U.S. diplomatic post in Vigo, Spain, where his life was threatened, to Sweden. He became U.S. Consul General in Göteborg (Gothenburg) in 1936 and remained in that post for nearly twelve years. The Corcorans and the Hellstedts were close friends; and after the war when Corcoran had been publicly decorated by the U.S. government for his espionage accomplishments, Leone was able to acknowledge his revelation of Peenemünde which had led to a bombing raid and destruction of rocket manufacturing and atomic energy research capabilities.[446]

From Leone's autobiography:

> During the summers I was with the children and the nurse in Falkenberg, a small town on the west coast of Sweden in a hotel on the beach. Folke could only join us for a month each summer. The children were very happy there and we all made many friends. The American Consul General Billy Corcoran and his Jamaican English wife were also there every summer. Dulcie now lives as a widow in La Jolla but we will never lose track of each other. We are kindred spirits despite our very different childhoods. Billy was a remarkable man and a

---

reveals numbers which would indicate some validity for Corcoran's concern. During WWII, six years of RAF Bomber Command operation, 1939-1945, battle losses were 8,953 aircraft (p.57); in three years, 1942-1945, USAF Eighth Air Force (American bomber command, Europe) battle losses were 4,200 aircraft (p.58); 127 American bombers landed in Sweden (p.113) and 64 RAF bombers (p.131) landed in Sweden during WW2. The American propensity to land in Sweden was apparently more than four times as great as the British, although by January 1945, 25% of the RAF Bomber Command pilots were Canadian (p.133). Colonel Mark K. Wells, USAF, *Courage and Air Warfare: The Allied Aircrew Experience in the Second World War,* London: Frank Cass & Co. Ltd. 1995. ALSO: Corcoran's memoir, *Top Secret,* parts released for viewing by the Stanford University Library in 2019, reveals his close relations with British Naval Intelligence in Stockholm (Denham) during WWII.

[444] David J. Bercuson and Holger G. Herwig, *The Destruction of the Bismarck,* New York: Overlook Press 2001, pages 40-44, 66-67, 95.

[445] "In order to avoid arousing the suspicions of the Swedish Security Service, Denham had to meet his contacts in parks and public places, and neither they nor he could commit anything to paper. All the information passed over had to be memorized until Denham could get back to the Embassy and signal to D.N.I. in London." Patrick Beesly, *Very Special Intelligence: The story of the Admiralty's Operational Intelligence Centre 1939-1945,* New York: Doubleday 1978, p.133.

[446] "Throughout the four long years his valuable tips telegraphed daily in secret codes brought astounding results. ...gave Corcoran credit for having produced the information (picked up from shipyard gossip in Göteborg) which led to the uncovering of the German V-weapon and 'heavy water' experimental laboratories at Peenemunde [sic]. Peenemunde was not on any map. It was a new, gigantic, super-secret industrial forest behind the Baltic seashore, 60 miles northeast of Stettin, and guarded by electrified barbed wire entanglements. It was engaged in around the clock drive on mass production of Hitler's 'secret' weapon (deadly flying bombs and long-range flying rockets) publicly pledged by the Fuhrer [sic] to end the war in 24 hours. On August 17, 1943, some 600 R.A.F. four motor bombers swooped down on this target 700 miles from England and in 40 minutes kindled it into a roaring furnace. Forty assembly shops and laboratories were destroyed; 50 others were badly wrecked. Five thousand of the seven thousand plant workers were killed, including the plant manager, Maj. Gen. Wolfgang von Chamier Glisenzenski; General Jeschonnek, Luftwaffe chief of staff; and General Ernest Udet, first world war aviator and organizer of the Luftwaffe, head of the technical directorate of the German Air Ministry." Op.cit. William P. Kennedy pages 19-20.

comfort to everyone who ever had to do with him. It was he who was able to discover the source of the rockets which were destroying England during the war.[447]

In his *Top Secret, A Foreign Service Saga,* declassified in 2019, Billy Corcoran wrote about the hotel in Falkenburg, … " small coast town about two hours from Gothenburg … where we spent a few weeks every summer."[448]

William Stephenson

While Denham and Corcoran in Stockholm, and Stephenson during his 1939-1940 winter in Stockholm, were not actively saboteurs, their intelligence enabled successful operations.

> … British intelligence services had deliberately resisted explanations and exposure except on their own terms. History is not what actually happened but what the surviving evidence says happened. [449]

Colleagues of Stephenson who wrote about him following the war praised his skill and determination in abetting sabotage.[450]

A second wave of writers, relying on secondary sources, disputed some of Stephenson's alleged exploits.

More recent releases of classified documents in Canada, the USA, Britain and France have confirmed more instances of BSC-SOE cooperation.[451] Historians and journalists hope that government security agencies will see fit to release more sensitive documents in future, while recognizing that probably the most interesting of this information has been deliberately or inadvertently destroyed, lost forever.

Admiral Wilhelm Canaris

Confronting William Stephenson in the worldwide game of intelligence, notably in neutral country information hubs like Stockholm, was the head of the German *Abwehr*.[452] Wilhelm Canaris was an officer

---

[447] Op.cit. Ondrack p.170.

[448] Op.cit. Corcoran p. 278.

[449] Tom Bower, *The Perfect English Spy: Sir Dick White and the Secret War 1935-90,* New York: St. Martin's Press 1995, p.xi.

[450] "As director of the BSC, Stephenson, according to the organization's official history, was empowered to do all that was not being done and could not be done by overt means to assure aid for Britain and counter the enemy's plans in the Western Hemisphere. By the spring of 1942, when Roald Dahl, a dashing RAF pilot, arrived in Washington as an assistant air attaché at the British Embassy, the BSC's vast network of spies was already in place and had established a remarkably effective propaganda machine that rallied American public opinion behind active support of England….Dahl and colorful co-conspirators – including Noel Coward, Ian Fleming, David Ogilvy and Ivar Bryce – were all rank amateurs, recruited for their clever minds and connections rather than any real experience in the trade of spying." Jennet Conant, *The Irregulars: Roald Dahl and the British Spy Ring in Wartime Washington,* New York: Simon & Schuster 2008, pages xvi-xvii.

[451] For example: Colonel Bernd Horn, *A Most Ungentlemanly Way of War: The SOE and the Canadian Connection,* Toronto: Dundurn 2016; Keith Jeffery, *The Secret History of MI6 1909-1949,* New York: The Penguin Press 2010.

[452] "The *Abwehr* consisted of a network of stations inside and outside the *Reich*…. Those in neutral countries such as Sweden, Spain and Turkey, normally operating under the flimsy cover of a diplomatic, consular or commercial camouflage, were called

of the Imperial Navy, respected by upper class Germans…who shared his contempt for Nazis and Hitler. Until Hitler replaced him with Himmler in 1944 –

> Canaris showed little enterprise or initiative in building up Abwehr activities… Canaris's immediate subordinates, particularly his second-in-command Hans Oster, were men who shared his political views and devoted an increasing amount of their time, as the war went on, to political intrigue.[453]

Canaris was implicated in the 1944 assassination attempt on Hitler and executed for treason in April 1945.

Kriegsorganisationen, or *Kos*…That in Stockholm was particularly busy….” Michael Howard, London: HMSO 1990, *British Intelligence in the Second World War: Volume Five, Strategic Deception,* p.46.

[453] Op. cit. Michael Howard p.48.

Chapter Twelve
1940: Germany Winning the War

At their next birthdays, Clara's fortieth on Friday, January 19 and Stephenson's forty-third on January 23, they could have had a weekend party to celebrate: the Swedish government began risking its neutral status by allowing passage of volunteers to Finland to fight the Russians; and Sweden was sending machine guns and artillery pieces to Finland.

In 1940, Russia and Germany were still allied, bent on sharing Poland, the Baltic States and Finland.

Stephenson's "Strike Ox" operation, disabling the iron ore handling cranes in Oxelösund Harbor that were crucial to German supply, had been cancelled following King Gustav V's appeal to King George VI to "halt this madness," which could have been deemed sufficient violation of neutrality to precipitate German invasion.[454]

In February Stephenson was in Finland north of the Arctic Circle, observing General Mannerheim's brilliant direction of the greatly outnumbered Finnish forces.

Stephenson returned to Sweden to recruit and organize men for sabotage of the heavy water manufacturing at Vemork in Norway. Commander Ian Fleming, then in British Naval Intelligence, London, said that "Operation Strike Ox" had been ill-concealed for good reason:

> Stephenson's cover story was that he had to go to Sweden on business. He had commercial interests there. The secondary cover, for intelligence types who needed to know his movements, was that he would destroy the source and supply lines of iron ore which Germany's steel industries depended upon.[455]

January (1940) – Heisenberg's conferences with Harteck, Hahn, Bothe, Geiger, Mattauch, Flügge, Clusius, Döpel, Joos and von Weizsäcker since the beginning of the war in September 1939 were discussed in Heisenberg's year-end report for 1939 regarding the possibilities of energy from nuclear fission.[456]

January – discussions regarding production of heavy water for operation of a nuclear reactor.

January 22 – takeover of the Kaiser Wilhelm Institute for Physics by the defence department (HWA).

---

[454] Op.cit. Stevenson, *A Man Called Intrepid,* p.58.

[455] Ibid. p.54, and on pages 60-62 iron ore and heavy water activities in February.

[456] One of several hundred reports, letters and orders now available in the Max Planck Society (successor to the KWI) in Berlin, *Dokumente zum Deutschen Uranprojekt 1939 bis 1945 im Archiv der Max-Planck-Gesellschaft.*

February and April – Heisenberg reported to the *Wehrmacht* regarding atomic bomb progress – liaison between the scientists and the generals.

March – in England Frisch and Peierls calculated the feasibility of an airborne atomic bomb if one kilogram of isotope U-235 could be separated.

March – Finland capitulated to Russia/Germany.

April – first anniversary of the founding of the *Uranverein*, the *Arbeitsgemeinschaft für Kernphysik* semi-secret organization for exploitation of nuclear fission.

April 9 – General Karl Becker, head of organizations[457] responsible for development of advanced weapons including the atomic bomb, depressed because of adverse criticism from his *Führer*, killed himself.

April 10 – Germany invaded Denmark and Norway.

April 10-30 – Lise Meitner was in Bohr's Copenhagen lab, used his cyclotron.[458]

May – report to the KWI regarding the usefulness of uranium as an explosive.[459]

May 10 – Germany invaded the Netherlands, Luxembourg, Belgium and France.

May 13 – Churchill replaced Chamberlain as Prime Minister.

May 19 – from the Frisch/Peierls memorandum senior government officials including Churchill became aware that an aeroplane could carry a single atomic bomb capable of destroying a city the size of London.

May 27 to June 4 – Allied forces were evacuated from Dunkirk to England.

June 10 – French forces abandoned Paris, Italy joined Germany against the Allies.

June 14 – Germans occupied Paris. Ian Fleming helped heavy water movement from Paris.[460]

June 19-21 – the ship *Broompark* carried heavy water and scientists Bordeaux to Falmouth.[461]

June – 1,000 tons of refined uranium were shipped from Union Minière facilities in Belgium to Germany.

June – sponsored by Lise Meitner, German Jewish physicist Hedwig Kohn arrived in Stockholm, obtained an American visa and began her journey to the USA.[462]

July – in Germany von Weizsäcker reported that a product of a nuclear reactor might be chemically concentrated and induced to provide a chain reaction, an atomic bomb.

July 10 – October 31 – the Battle of Britain was fought, wherein the RAF reduced the *Luftwaffe* to a force insufficient to support *Seelöwe* (Operation Sealion), German invasion of Britain.

October – the "Virus House", a nuclear research facility so named to discourage visitors, completed near Berlin.

---

[457] *"General-Professeur, Chef des HWA [Heereswaffenamt] …Präsident des RFR [Reichsforschungsrat],"* from p.3 of the Max Planck Society document, *Übersichten zum deutschen Uranprojekt: Kernenergieforschung in Deutschland von 1939 bis 1945.*

[458] Sime Op. cit. *Lise Meitner,* p.283.

[459] *Müller, Eine Bedingung für die Verwendbarkeit von Uran als Sprengstoff,* document #618 in *Dokumente zum deutschen Uranprojekt 1939 bis 1945 im Archiv der Max-Planck-Gesellschaft* 2023.

[460] "London, Thursday June 13, I was to have dined with I. tonight but had a message in the morning to say that he'd gone to France. I don't know what his job is." Emily Russell, editor, *A Constant Heart: The War Diaries of Maud Russell 1938-1945,* Dorset UK: The Dovecote Press 2017, p.97.

[461] Kerin Freeman, *The Civilian Bomb Disposing Earl: Jack Howard and Bomb Disposal in WWII,* Barnsley, South Yorkshire: Pen & Sword 2015 pages 97-137.

[462] Sime Op. cit. pages 286 and 469. Dr. Kohn became an instructor at the University of North Carolina and a professor at Wellesley College. Her brother perished in the Holocaust.

October – in France the Vichy government dismissed Jews.

November – December – Noël Coward worked for Stephenson, talked to Churchill but was unable to persuade the Prime Minister that his fame and creative talent were intelligence assets.[463] Stephenson continued to use Coward anyway.

At the end of 1940 the embassies and intelligence agencies of Germany, Britain and Sweden were all quartered near Karlaplan in the Östermalm district of Stockholm.

Lise Meitner's nephew Otto Robert Frisch and Rufolf Peierls, German Jewish physicists in England, wrote a memorandum in March 1940 that stimulated government measures directed toward creating an atomic bomb. It was written in layman's terms, with no equations, was not dauntingly long, and is now available in public documents; for example, pages 14-18 of *The American Atom* (1984).[464] The famous memorandum began:

> The possible construction of "super bombs" based on a nuclear chain reaction in uranium has been discussed a great deal and arguments have been brought forward which seemed to exclude this possibility. We wish here to point out and discuss a possibility which seems to have been overlooked in these earlier discussions.[465]

The "Frisch-Peierls Memorandum" affirmed Bohr's observation that it is the isotope U-235 that divides…and the conclusions of various physicists – that recent methods of isotope separation indicated pure U-235 could be isolated from normal uranium, that about one kg of pure U-235 would be "…a suitable size for the bomb…" and "The energy liberated by a 5 kg bomb would be equivalent to that of several thousand tons of dynamite, while that of a 1 kg bomb, though about 500 times less, would still be formidable."[466]

Despite numerical superiority in men and machines, French forces yielded quickly to German. Paris was abandoned to the Nazis June 10, 1940, and Hitler's staff began making plans to invade England, Operation Sea Lion (*Seelöwe)*. A prerequisite understood by both sides was German air superiority. Accordingly, Göring's *Luftwaffe* attacked British aerodromes and aircraft manufacturing facilities. The RAF put up desperate defense.

Churchill to Parliament, June 18, 1940:

---

[463] From a taped conversation between Coward and the author, in William Stevenson, *A Man Called Intrepid: The Secret War 1939-1945,* London: Book Club Associates 1976, pages 198-200.

[464] Robert C. Williams and Philip L Cantelon, editors, *The American Bomb: A Documented History of Nuclear Policies from the Discovery of Fission to the Present 1939-1984,* Philadelphia PA: University of Pennsylvania Press 1984.

[465] Ibid. p.14. The entire Frisch – Peierls Memorandum, 'On the Construction of a "Super-bomb," based on a Nuclear Reaction in Uranium" appears on pages 14-18 of Robert C. Williams & Phillip L. Cantelon, Editors, *The American Atom: A Documentary History of Nuclear Policies from the Discovery of Fission to the Present 1939-1984,* followed by the *Report by M.A.U.D. Committee On the Use of Uranium for a Bomb, Part I* on pages 19-23.

[466] Ibid. p.15.

But if we fail, then the whole world, including the United States, including all that we have known and cared for, will sink into the abyss of a new dark age made more sinister, and perhaps more protracted, by the lights of **perverted science**.

Let us therefore brace ourselves to our duties, and so bear ourselves, that if the British Empire and its Commonwealth last for a thousand years, men will still say, "This was their finest hour."[467]

And Churchill in the *New York Times,* August 6, 1945, following Hiroshima:

By the year 1939 it had become widely recognized among scientists of many nations that the release of energy by atomic fission was a possibility. ... The possession of these powers by the Germans at any time might have altered the result of the war and profound anxiety was felt by those who were informed.

Churchill had been informed by Lise Meitner ... and by others, of course, but in the matter of the German atomic bomb program, especially and importantly by Lise Meitner.[468]

Conventional weapons were winning the war for Germany. There was no felt need for an atomic bomb. Hitler expected Churchill to sue for peace. Mistaking amicability for timidity, Germany and Japan brought ruin upon themselves the following year by attacking Russia in June and the United States in December respectively.

The German atomic bomb program could have benefitted substantially from occupation of France and Norway in 1940. In Paris, German technicians finished construction of the Joliot cyclotron. Otto Hahn used it and was disappointed. Subtle sabotage had caused unreliable operation: a French mechanic occasionally turned off the water to the cooling system, thus causing overheating, shutdowns and aborted work.

At Vemork in Norway a technician dropped cod liver oil into a batch of precious heavy water, rendering it ineffective as a nuclear reactor moderator.

Vulnerability to sabotage in occupied countries, subtle and overt (SOE), caused the Germans to eventually build a cyclotron and produce heavy water in Germany. Both of these initiatives consumed time and scarce resources. And on German soil, the facilities became eligible for Allied bombing.

In 1940 and indeed throughout her exile from Nazi Germany and Austria, Lise Meitner exchanged letters almost weekly with Max von Laue. She sent news of his son in the United States at Princeton. In June she called his attention to the publications in the United States regarding successful separation of a small quantity of U-235 by researchers at Columbia University and of confirmation of the fissionability of U-239 due to the instability of its neutron-proton ratio...which it shared with U-235.

From his position as the head of a theory department in the Max Planck (formerly Kaiser Wilhelm) Institute in Berlin, von Laue wrote to Lise about physics affairs in Germany. He had tried to help Arnold

---

[467] Colin Brown, *Glory and B*llocks,* London: Oneworld Publications 2013/2016, p.xiv.

[468] Op. cit. Wm. Stevenson, *Intrepid's Last Case,* p.38; Also Op. cit. Hinsley, the official history, *British Intelligence in the Second World War: Its Influence on Strategy and Operations Volume III Part 2,* p.934 and p.936.

Berliner, longtime editor of *Die Naturwissenschaften* dismissed by the Nazis, through Berliner's forced isolation.

Berliner wrote to Meitner about the desperate cultural deprivation of Jews. He had been a friend and admirer of Gustav Mahler, Clara's favorite composer. Treasured in his apartment was one of the two dozen sculptures of Mahler made by Rodin.[469] This was taken along with his books and works of art by the police in March 1942, when Berliner took poison rather than be removed from his apartment to a concentration camp.

Arnold Berliner's death was not reported in *die Naturwissenschaften*, the prominent journal that he founded and edited for most of its existence.

At the end of 1940 nuclear energy physics research was no longer appearing in scientific journals. In Berlin von Weizsäcker concluded that the Americans had begun working on an atomic bomb; and, "In Stockholm, Lise read between the lines, paying particular attention to the whereabouts and activities of Werner Heisenberg."[470]

> The Germans had Hitler, and the possibility of developing an atomic bomb was obvious, and the possibility that they would develop it before we did was very much of a fright.[471]

---

[469] Others can be seen today in the Music Library of the University of Western Ontario, the National Gallery in Washington, DC and the Lincoln Center in New York.

[470] Sime, Op.cit. *Lise Meitner: A Life In Physics,* p.300.

[471] Richard Feynman on the urgency felt by those working in the Manhattan Project, in Richard Feynman, *Surely You're Joking, Mr. Feynman: Adventures of a Curious Character,* New York: Bantam Books 1985, p.91.

Chapter Thirteen
1943-44: Turning Point – Clara Retired

In December 1942 the JIC [Joint Intelligence Committee] examined the possibility that Germany and the Soviet Union might agree to end the war. "We were always on the lookout", Bentinck said, "for the possibility of a German-Russian peace, knowing that if it suited them the Russians would not hesitate to change sides." This was a sensible precaution. Secret talks were held between German and Soviet representatives in Stockholm in both April and June 1943, but nothing came of them, chiefly because of Hitler's antipathy to any idea of making peace. By that time too the Russians had won the battle of Stalingrad and would not consider peace except on their own terms.[472]

Events of 1943 persuaded Clara to once again become Leone. She foresaw problems in Sweden following Allied victory. Elements of Swedish society would seek revenge for wartime betrayals.[473] If it became known that she had been an Allied spy, her husband's career would be harmed and her children endangered. October 1943 would bring the sixth birthday of daughter Monica and the fourth birthday of son Donald. Both children were perceptive and highly intelligent. The risk of them grasping the meaning of their mother's activities in the role of Clara and its implicit danger, was becoming intolerable.

The Swedish Security Service was obliged to seek and prosecute "whosoever" passed military or political information to a foreign government that could imperil Sweden's neutral status. "During the Second World War the agency monitored about 25,000 phone calls and intercepted 200,000 letters every week."[474]

Billy Corcoran was dismayed at the appalling quality of the influx of "secret" agents arriving in Sweden.[475] Some did not speak Swedish or German, were obviously American, asked revealing questions and drew unhelpful attention. Some were drunks and some allowed their vanity to be exploited in sexual adventures with female (and male) Axis agents. None were qualified by training and background for spying. Their incompetence created difficulty for Corcoran in protecting the identities of valuable experienced people.

---

[472] Patrick Howarth, *Intelligence Chief Extraordinaire: The Life of the Ninth Duke of Portland,* London: The Bodley Head 1986, p.179.

[473] Reports and novels of Stieg Larsson.

[474] *Swedish Security Service 2013 (pdf) ISBN978-86661-09-0,* Stockholm: Edita Bobergs May 2014, cited in Wikipedia, "Swedish Security Service."

[475] Corcoran archive letters, Stanford University Library

He wrote:

> Dozens of O.S.S. men now descended on Sweden. These supposedly "undercover cloak and dagger sleuths" stood out by their dress, deportment and general gaucherie, as might be expected in view of their lack of training and hurried organization....Thus the youthful United States contributed, with characteristic naiveté and extravagance, one of the unforgettable side shows of the great drama. Torn between laughter and exasperation, seasoned Americans abroad watched their antics, nicknmaming them the Oh So Stupids...It is tragic to realize that through their blundering conceit they carelessly uncovered members of the Norwegian and Danish underground to the Gestapo.[476]

At the same time Clara's potential to contribute had diminished. By October 1943 there was little doubt that Germany would lose the war...unless Hitler's hope for a miraculous new weapon could be realized. Both the Allies and the Axis had ruled out chemical and biological weapons. The V1 and V2 rockets were impressive but did not offer the scale needed for a complete reversal.

That left only the atomic bomb as Germany's hope for victory...and by late 1943 Lise Meitner and Paul Rosbaud could confirm that every German nuclear energy research and development initiative had been practically nullified by denial of material resources, sabotage and/or bombing. Meitner's correspondence with Eva Bahr-Bergius and Elisabeth Schiemann at this time conveyed her sense that German defeat was a *fait accompli*.[477]

1943 – Germany's conventional war lost

The early steps to Germany's downfall were the violation of the pact with Russia, the Napoleonic mistake of attacking Russia in June 1941, and the forced declaration of war on the United States following the Japanese attack on Pearl Harbor in December 1941. The American luck at Midway in June 1942, killing Japanese aircraft carriers with single hits from dive bombers, turned the tide of the Pacific war.[478] Defeats at Guadalcanal and New Guinea in early 1943 placed Japan on the defensive, unable to significantly help ally Germany. The second battle of El Alamein in October-November 1942 cost the Germans enormous losses in men and arms, and exposed the "soft underbelly"[479] of The Reich.

The Russian winter of 1942-1943 took a terrible toll on German forces. Added were decisive military defeats when they fell short of objectives. The Sixth Army of Field-Marshall Paulus was encircled, supplies cut off. Retreating soldiers to the south were tormented by air and artillery bombardment...and the cold.

---

[476] William B. Corcoran, *Top Secret (A Foreign Service Saga),* Stanford CA: Hoover Institution, declassified in 2019, pages 236-237.

[477] Jost Lemmerich, editor, *Bande der Freundschaft: Lise Meitner – Elisabeth Schiemann Kommentierter Briefwechsel 1911-1947,* Wien: Verlag der Österreichischer Akademie der Wissenschaften 2010, pages 296-315.

[478] Japanese aircraft were refueling between raids. With fuel exposed everywhere, ignition by a single torpedo caused conflagration.

[479] a phrase used by Churchill according to the memoirs of Generals Montgomery and Eisenhower.

Near Stalingrad...

Paulus and his staff were captured on January 31 and on February 2 Marshall Voronov reported that all resistance had ceased and that ninety thousand prisoners had been taken. These were the survivors of twenty-one German and one Rumanian divisions. This crushing disaster to the Germans ended Hitler's prodigious effort to conquer Russia by force of arms, and destroy Communism by an equally odious form of totalitarian tyranny.[480]

May 13 – 270,000 German and Italian prisoners were taken when Army Group Afrika surrendered.
July 9 – Allies invaded Sicily.
July/August –

The Battle of Kursk was destined to be Hitler's last offensive in the East and propelled Stalin towards victory. Operation Zitadelle stripped the Wehrmacht of its last vestiges of invincibility, diluted its fighting spirit and robbed it of hope.[481]

Thus, defined by the number of men [3.5 million] and material [12,000 tanks and self-propelled guns] involved, the Battle of Kursk was without doubt not only the biggest tank clash of the Second World War, but indeed at the same time the largest battle of the Second World War.[482]

1943 – Germany's atomic bomb in peril

February 27-28 – At midnight Norwegians in British uniforms entered the Vemork power plant and blew the bottoms out of eighteen cells of deuterium oxide (D2O, heavy water), all of the Germans' supply. The attachment of explosives and fuses was accomplished in minutes. In Scotland the crew had practised on models made according to intelligence supplied by a former employee at the Vemork plant. He worked in the same building as Lise and met her frequently in Siegbahn's Stockholm institute.

I remember Tronstadt telling me, "If you need somewhere to lock up the Norwegian guard, you can put him in the toilet and the key is on the left-hand side of the door." And I remember when I left, seeing the key. That was the sort of information we had. I am quite certain there was not one operation during the war with such good information and knowledge of the target as we had on ours. That was part of our success, of course.[483]

---

[480] Winston S. Churchill, *The Hinge of Fate,* New York: Houghton Mifflin Bantam 1950/13th printing 1979, p.620.

[481] Lloyd Clark, *Kursk: The Greatest Battle, Eastern Front 1943,* London, England: Headline Publishing Group 2014, p.403.

[482] Roman Toeppel, *Kursk 1943: The Greatest Battle of the Second World War,* Warwick, England: Helion & Company Limited, p.181.

[483] Roderick Bailey, *Forgotten Voices of the Secret War: An Inside History of Special Operations During the Second World War,* Croydon UK: Ebury Press Random House 2009, p.143, Lieutenant Joachim Rønneberg speaking.

Most of the saboteurs escaped by walking 350 miles to Sweden.[484] The facility was rapidly rebuilt, but internal sabotage hampered production. When Nazi supervision had allowed a useful quantity of heavy water (600 kg in February 1944) to be accumulated and loaded onto a ferry for transportation to Germany, the boat was sunk in the deepest part of Lake Tinn by Norwegian saboteurs.[485]

Vemork heavy water concentration cells after sabotage [486]

487

[484] Ibid. pages 141-144.

[485] Knut Haukelid, *Skis Against the Atom*, Minot ND: North American Heritage Press 1989, pages 181-238.

[486] Per F. Dahl, *Heavy Water and the Wartime Race for Nuclear Energy*, London: The Institute of Physics 1999, p.207. Courtesy Norsk Industrial Museum, Vemork.

[487] Photo from Richard Rhodes, *The Making of the Atomic Bomb*, New York: Simon & Schuster 2012, p.320+. Courtesy Norsk Industrial Museum, Vemork.

March – The SOE was established in Denmark, supplied by airdrops of sabotage material. The British Foreign Office warned SOE that any inappropriate activity discovered in Sweden would result in curtailment. The identity of an Allied intelligence agent who revealed the camouflaged location of a critical camouflaged secret bridge in Hamburg was protected by having 344 bombers attack the decoy and 17 bombers attack the real target.[488]

June/July – Lord Cherwell, Churchill's scientific advisor and friend of Lise Meitner, received warnings from Sweden of the development of rockets and a "uranium bomb" on the island of Usedom (Peenemünde).[489]

July 24 – Paul Harteck's promising work was thwarted by Operation Gomorrah, the destruction of Hamburg by 746 heavy bombers from bases in the east of England:

> It had been exceptionally dry that summer of 1943 and the city was like tinder; the incendiary bombs soon started fires that developed into an horrific firestorm, which virtually burned out Hamburg and caused the deaths of 51,000 of the port's inhabitants....Albert Speer, then Hitler's Minister of Armaments, has said that if attacks on the scale of the Hamburg raid had been made against five other German towns, the war would have ended there and then in mid-1943.[490]

August – From Stockholm British Intelligence was supplied with drawings of the V1 rocket that fell in Bornholm – ten months before V1 attacks began on London.

August 17/18 – Around midnight 596 RAF bombers attacked the Peenemünde research and development establishment, priority target the sleeping quarters of scientific and administrative personnel.[491] Thousands were killed, including atomic scientist Dr. Thiel, Peenemünde liaison with Werner Heisenberg.[492]

September – Since April a "Secret Service Coordinating Committee" had been mediating "… turf wars between Britain's assorted secret organizations." The outcome was that Stephenson's "… BSC was no longer the sole, or even the primary, channel of liaison between British intelligence and its American opposite numbers." And Stephenson would be less able to guard the identity of agents such as Clara.

September – Intensive bombing of Berlin had caused the Kaiser Wilhelm Institute nuclear physics research and development relocation to underground "secret" facilities in the south of Germany at Hechingen (Heisenberg) and Tailfingen (Hahn).[493]

September – Danish Jews were warned of Nazi plans to collect and send them to concentration camps. Niels Bohr was instrumental in persuading the Swedish government to spread the news that Danish Jews would be welcome.

October – More than ninety percent of Danish Jews, 7,000 men, women and children fled in small boats to Sweden. Most German officials looked the other way. Gestapo informers in Danish and Swedish ports

---

[488] Op. cit. Latimer 2001, pages 196-198.

[489] David Irving, *The Mare's Nest,* Boston, Toronto: Little Brown & Company 1965, pages 77-87.

[490] Brian Johnson, *The Secret War,* London: British Broadcasting Corporation 1978, p.118.

[491] Op.cit. David Irving *The Mare's Nest,* p.97.

[492] Ibid. p.118.

[493] Op.cit. Hahn, *My Life,* p.157.

were dealt with summarily.[494] Bohr, his wife Margrethe and his four sons were among the first to arrive in Stockholm. Niels was moved to a secret house, and on October 6 stuffed into the bomb bay of an unarmed Mosquito and whisked to London.[495] There he was astonished to learn of the progress that had been made toward an atomic bomb.[496]

> At the end of October 1943, many of the British physicists went to the United States, and Niels and Aage Bohr traveled as members of the British party. In Los Alamos they immediately met good friends from Copenhagen including Frisch, Teller, Weiskopf and Peierls.[497]

Bohr communicated with his wife regularly but was unable to rejoin her until after the war. In Stockholm Margrethe, also a physicist, would have informed her friend Lise Meitner of the American progress…another easing of Clara's withdrawal. Following a visit with Margrethe Bohr, Lise wrote to her friend Eva von Bahr-Bergius about the prospect of decent Germans taking responsibility for the misery their nation had caused.[498]

October – Otto Hahn supplemented their frequent wartime correspondence with a visit to Lise Meitner. "In Stockholm he told Dr. Lise Meitner and Swedish physicists that there seemed no chance of the practical utilization of fission reactions in uranium for many years to come."[499]

November – Colonel Boris T. Pash was recruited by General Groves to head the American investigation of German atomic bomb prospects in Europe. The newly formed *Alsos* soldier/scientist group followed Allied troops invading via Italy, and after D-Day throughout Germany.

November – The U.S. Government pressured neutral Spain to discontinue friendly relations with Germany, especially the export of wolfram. The desperation of Germany's need was expressed in Hitler's January offer of 100 Me109 and 25 Ju88 aircraft to Spain in exchange for wolfram…when the Allies were depriving the *Luftwaffe* by bombing these types of aircraft on the ground.[500]

November – "In the last war the Swedes were pro-German, and in the early stages of this war they felt sure that Germany would win and that it was best to be on the safe side. All that has changed since Alamein

---

[494] John Oram Thomas, *The Giant Killers: The Danish Resistance Movement 1940/5,* London: Michael Joseph Ltd. 1975, pages 121-144.

[495] Margaret Gowing, *Britain and Atomic Energy, 1939-1945,* Basingstoke, Hampshire and New York: Palgrave St. Martin's Press 1964, p.247.

[496] Niels Blaedel, *Harmony and Unity: The Life of Niels Bohr,* Madison, WI: Science Tech, Inc., p.217.

[497] Op.cit. Margaret Gowing, *Britain and Atomic Energy,* p.218.

[498] *"Erst, wenn die anständigen Deutschen sich klar bewusst sind, dass sie nicht frei von dieser Verantwortung, sind und dass sie alle ehrlich wünschen, nach dem Kriegsende so viel wie möglich von all dem Unglück wieder gut zu machen – erst dann ist ein wirklicher Friede möglich."* Jost Lemmerich, editor, *Bande der Freundschaft: Lise Meitner – Elisabeth Schiemann Kommentierter Briefwechsel 1911-1947,* Vienna: Verlag der Österreichischen Akademie der Wissenschaften 2010, p.304.

[499] F.H. Hinsley et al, *British Intelligence in the Second World War: Its Influence on Strategy and Operations, Volume III, Part 2,* New York: Cambridge University Press 1988, p.934.

[500] Christian Leitz & David J. Dunthorn, *Spain in an International Context, 1936-1959,* New York, Oxford: Bergbahn Books 1999, p. 184.

and Stalingrad. The German behavior in Denmark and Norway has filled them with loathing. They are almost unanimously on our side."[501]

November 23 – Vemork was bombed again by 161 USAF B-17s and B-24s. The power station and electrolysis plant were destroyed. Although the underground heavy water production facility was not damaged, the Germans decided to remove their stock of heavy water.

December 25 – Noel Coward dined with William Stephenson and wife Mary in New York. Stephenson saw that Coward was exhausted from doing too much on behalf of the war effort. He secretly flew Coward from New York for a two-week rest in Jamaica, as Stephenson's guest. After the war Noel Coward, Ian Fleming and Canadian Lord Beaverbrook (Churchill's wartime administrator of military procurement) joined Stephenson in owning houses on the north shore of Jamaica.

1944

February 11 – "The Kaiser Wilhelm Institute was hit by a bomb."[502]

February 20 – The Germans' entire stock of heavy water was lost when explosives inserted by Knut Haukelid's Norwegian/British commandos sunk the ferry boat *Hydro* in the depths of Lake Tinn.[503] Murder of fifty escapers from Stalag Luft III raised sentiment against Germany in Sweden and a British vow of reprisals.[504]

March 24 – The KWI in Berlin was bombed again. Otto Hahn's apartment nearby was ruined. Hahn moved to the safer south of Germany.

July – Ian Fleming's 30 Assault Unit active in France.[505] Peenemünde facilities were bombed by 377 B-17s with 297 fighters escorting.

August 4 – Peenemünde bombed by 221 B-17s with 223 P-51s.

August 25 – Peenemünde bombed by 376 B-17s escorted by 171 P-47s and P-51s.

November 28 – In 1988 British Intelligence released **excerpts** from a *TA*[506] wartime report. These appeared in the official history of British intelligence as:

Appendix 29: TA Project: Enemy Intelligence
Excerpts from the joint Anglo-US Report to the Chancellor of
the Exchequer and Major General L.R. Groves
28 November 1944

---

[501] Influential British MP Harold Nicolson after visiting Sweden, Harold Nicolson, *The War Years 1939-1945, edited by Nigel Nicolson,* New York: Atheneum 1967, p.327.

[502] Otto Hahn, *My Life, translated by Ernst Kaiser & Eithne Wilkins,* London: MacDonald & Co. 1970, p.156.

[503] Jostein Berglyd, *Operation Freshman: The Hunt for Hitler's Heavy Water, Translation Tim Dinan,* Stockholm: Leandoer & Ekholm Vörlag 2006, pages 107-112.

[504] Jonathan F. Vance, *The True Story of the Great Escape, Stalag Luft III, March, 1944,* Barnsley, S. Yorkshire, England: Greenhill Books 2019, p. 343.

[505] Op.cit. Emily Russell, pages 249-253. Andrew Boyd, *British Naval Intelligence Through the Twentieth Century,* Barnsley UK: Seaforth Publishing 2020, pages 518, 522.

[506] Tube Alloys, code name for the British nuclear fission program.

November – General conclusions were that Germany would soon collapse and that there was no immediate danger from a military application of nuclear fission, but that research and probably pilot operations remained. Direct evidence of these had not been gathered, but because the work had required the involvement of well-known scientists Werner Heisenberg, Max von Laue, Otto Hahn and Paul Harteck, and because…"investigation through neutral or occupied countries, of the whereabouts of those German scientists…"[507] had been reliably reported, notably from Stockholm by Lise Meitner, the course of action recommended was…

> Investigation of the position in Germany should therefore be made with care and the action taken should be designed, as far as may be possible, to find out what ideas are in the minds of those responsible for the work as much as to collect purely factual information on its present state. Efforts should be made to prevent the driving underground of those scientists and technicians who could contribute novel ideas to the work and whose interest in its long-term applications might only be increased by a widespread investigation.[508]

Among the **official history** references in this November 28, 1944 report to contributions made by Lise Meitner:

> Other [German] officials have visited Siegbahn's laboratory in Sweden, where Lise Meitner is now working, to see the cyclotron there.[509]

And…

> …in 1944 a very reliable report from Lise Meitner in Stockholm stated that the Auer Gesellschaft was making [uranium] metal in large quantities.[510]

In November 1944, seven months before the Trinity test and eight months before Hiroshima, the Manhattan Project was still open to help, and German science still respected and a bit feared.[511] While the recruitment of German physics talent was conspicuously successful in the case of Wernher von Braun, Nazi nuclear scientists did not contribute materially to the American or British programs after the war.

As the American *Alsos* crew and Ian Fleming's Naval Intelligence Division Assault Unit scoured Germany, discovering enclaves of nuclear fission research, small quantities of uranium and heavy water were despatched to the Manhattan Project and ten key scientists to Farm Hall in England.

The Soviets likewise took materials, equipment, technicians and scientists when they reached Peenemünde and Berlin in 1945.

---

[507] F.H. Hinsley et al, *British Intelligence in the Second World War: Its Influence on Strategy and Operations, Volume III, Part 2,* New York: Cambridge University Press 1988, p.932.

[508] Ibid. Pages 931-932.

[509] Ibid. p.936.

[510] Ibid. p.938.

[511] Robert Oppenheimer remarked that somebody might devise a way of separating U-235 in the kitchen sink.

Chapter Fourteen
After the War

... by the autumn of 1944 the responsibilities of the so-called Director of British Security Coordination were rapidly diminishing; ... Stephenson and most of his civilian staff proved more than keen, now that victory was in sight, to return to their civilian occupations, and Gubbins [SOE Director of Operations] found himself having to persuade Stephenson to stay on at least until the defeat of Germany.[512]

The main event of the twentieth century occurred in the middle – World War Two. Fascist dictatorships were extinguished; democracies and Communist dictatorships emerged. There was a point where a quite different outcome was possible, when a few events and characters secretly secured the world's democracies by denying Hitler the atomic bomb.

Germany surrendered in May, and Japan in August of 1945. Leone and Lise could relax...as long as their wartime activities remained unknown to the Richard and Martin Vangers of Swedish society.[513]

Leone/Clara/Leone

The Calgary Herald ran articles about Leone's visit to her sister Phyllis in January 1946. Leone had taken a freighter through mine fields around Denmark, then across a stormy winter ocean. In Boston she enjoyed a party with her old Harvard friends, the Arthur Hertigs and Tracy Mallorys, before taking a train to Toronto to visit with Roland Michener and his wife Norah. Because air travel was still reserved for returning soldiers, Leone went by rail to Calgary, where she was given parties by friends and family. It had been twenty-two years since she left Alberta.

After two months in Calgary and Edmonton she took a train to Minneapolis where she had a brief visit with Dr. Bell. From Chicago she flew to New York to stay with Wilda Blow (Mrs. Bernard then) in her Fifth Avenue apartment. Another freighter took Leone to Gothenburg (Göteborg), where Folke met her with their Lincoln, returned after eight years of possession by the Swedish government.

That summer [1946] I was able to get permission from the Allied authorities to drive with Monica and Donald down to the Millstätter See in Austria for the summer. The condition was that I did not eat any German food or buy any gasoline in Germany. So we had food and big

---

[512] Peter Wilkinson & Joan Bright Astley, *Gubbins & SOE,* London: Leo Cooper 1993, p.216.

[513] Stieg Larsson, *The Girl With The Dragon Tattoo,* Toronto ON: Viking Canada English translation 2006.

dunks in our Lincoln Zephyr. They found Hamburg and Austria beautiful. I bought them American maple walnut ice cream and Wolfgang treated them to German Kirschentorte with whipped cream, so they were thrilled. We had to get to Kassel that night. This was quite a drive as all bridges were provisional and there were troops on every road. We slept on straw-filled gunny sacks in the basement of what was left of a hotel which was now occupied by the Allies. The whole center of that beautiful city was only rubble and it was a horrible sight. American soldiers and German girls danced all night long in the room beside our cubby holes. There was a puncture in one tire in the morning but we finally got on our way and crossed the border into Austria that day. The saddest sight of all had been Würzburg where I could not even find my way in the rubble. That night we reached the nice hotel at the Millstätter See.[514]

Leone played the role of tour guide for her daughter and son, supplementing their Baedeker's with vivid descriptions of former architectural glories, ruined in the wake of Allied bombing. On the return to Stockholm the children saw what remained of their mother's beautiful Hamburg and met Wolfgang Rittmeister.

Leone's "best Swedish friend" the Jewish psychoanalyst Vera Palmstierna, killed herself in 1947. Leone's psychoanalytic practice included many intelligent and accomplished women. She became active in the Medical Women's International Association in 1958 and President of MWIA in 1970-72.

A few months before her death in 1977, Leone came to Edmonton to receive an honorary D.Sc. from the University of Alberta.

Auspiciously born in January, 1900…in addition to leading by example in the twentieth century's growth of the status of women, Leone encouraged girls and women she met to pursue careers. She persuaded women doctors from all over the world to write autobiographies. These she collected and edited; they were published by the MWIA the year following her death.[515]

---

[514] Op.cit. Ondrack, *Gold Medalist* pages 199-200.

[515] Leone McGregor Hellstedt, M.D., Ph.D., D.Sc., editor, *Women Physicians of the World: autobiographies of medical pioneers,* Washington & London: Hemisphere Publishing Corporation, McGraw Hill Book Company 1978.

In Memory

Leone McGregor Hellstedt, M.D., Ph.D., D.Sc.

January 19, 1900–July 2, 1977

Dr. Leone Hellstedt dedicated her life to excellence in all aspects of her medical profession. It was a life rich in success, high honors, and well-deserved international recognition.

Dr. Hellstedt, past president of the Medical Women's International Association, devoted several years of her life to collecting the memoirs of prominent pioneer women physicians from many nations. This great woman was gratified to know that her efforts were to materialize and would be published. Members and friends of the Medical Women's International Association remember Dr. Hellstedt with the greatest affection and respect. We dedicate this volume to the memory of Leone McGregor Hellstedt, whose work will serve as a beacon to the future generations of medical women of the world. [516]

Lise Meitner

"Austrian Woman Won't Discuss Her Role in Developing Bomb"
New York Herald Tribune headline August 7, 1945

---

[516] Ibid. Hellstedt, inside front cover. Photo from Ondrack and Hellstedt.

When von Laue and Hahn were taken to Farm Hall, their disappearance worried Lise Meitner. Nevertheless, after contact was re-established she chastised Hahn for not passively resisting the Nazi regime. She and Paul Rosbaud deplored the "denazification" program in postwar Germany. Former students and colleagues asked Meitner for references – proclaiming their activities during the war, including Nazi party membership, as insincere, undertaken only because they had no choice – if they wished to work to support their families, if they wanted to remain in a position from which they could oppose the sordid elements, etc. Lise was nauseated by some of these requests.

Hahn and his wife visited Stockholm in 1946. In addition to the novelty of getting enough to eat, they were pleased to enjoy the hospitality of Lise and many Swedes who were cognizant of Hahn's 1944 Nobel Prize. Part of Hahn's charm was his inability to dwell on and deplore the unworthy behavior of others – including that of his fellow Germans during WWII and of the Nobel Committee in not recognizing the role of Meitner in the achievement for which Hahn was awarded the Prize.

In 1946 the Swedish government officially recognized the importance of atomic energy. The Royal Institute of Technology (KTH) built a laboratory to be directed by Lise Meitner:

> There had been essentially no fission research in Sweden, due in part to the lack of support for Meitner's work in Siegbahn's institute....Meitner was to have the title of "research professor" (that is, without teaching duties) and professorial salary, a welcome improvement after nine very lean years on a minimal stipend ...Meitner's assignment, along with Eklund, was to create a nuclear physics section for the KTH.[517]

This was the sort of opportunity that she would have enthusiastically embraced earlier; but in 1947 she was sixty-nine years old, disillusioned by anti-Semitism and prejudice against women, and wearied by past struggles...in Sweden as well as Germany.

She also declined Fritz Strassman's offer to head the physics section of the new *Kaiser-Wilhelm-Gesellschaft* (to become the *Max-Planck-Gesellschaft* in 1949) in Berlin.

The *Riksdag* approved her application for joint Swedish-Austrian citizenship in 1949.

Letters to her closest friends revealed that she did not feel at home in Germany or Sweden.

> In 1960, at age eighty-two, Lise moved to Cambridge to be near Otto Robert, who was a professor of physics and a Fellow of Trinity College....Lise had an affinity for England and the English: she admired their stoic qualities during the war and after, and she appreciated their helpfulness: whenever she stepped from a bus or prepared to cross a street, several people would reach out a hand...[518]

---

[517] Sime, pages 347-348.

[518] Sime p.377.

Paul Rosbaud

After the war Paul Rosbaud remained in England with his Jewish wife. Return to his native Graz was unthinkable.[519]

Billy Corcoran

Decorated by his government and called by some the most effective American spy of the war, Billy Corcoran retired with his wife Dulcie to California. Leone visited them there.

Some of Billy's memoirs were released in 2019, and we can hope that more will be accessible in the Stanford Library in future.

Stephenson and 'his boys'

> *Down the way where the nights are gay*
> *And the sun shines daily on the mountaintop*
> *I took a trip on a sailing ship*
> *And when I reached Jamaica I made a stop.*

Harry Belafonte

Noël Coward

Less than a month before his death in 1973 Noël Coward revealed the truth about his relationship with William Stephenson. In the autobiography *Future Indefinite* (1954), constrained by the Official Secrets Act and loyalty to his wartime comrades, Coward said that his first meeting with William Stephenson was in New York in 1940; actually, it had been earlier, in St. Ermin's Hotel, in London between the House of Lords and Victoria Railway Station.

> I had to meet a contact in the foyer. I waited in this squalid place and eventually a man said, "Follow me." …he wheeled me round and into an elevator. It was only labelled up to three floors. To my absolute astonishment it went to the fourth floor. An immense fellow guarded the place, all scrunched up inside a porter's uniform.…Well, this was the Special Operations Executive.… And Little Bill was there, very calm, with those sort of hooded eyes, watching everything. When he was on the ball, his eyes changed. And I love watching people's personalities in action. Bill becomes someone quite different and you feel the steel. He doesn't have to raise his voice or alter his tone but he does change. He's a very deceptive man. He's so gentle but when he's cross, he's terrifying. But if Bill decided he was for you, he'd be with you right to the last shot.[520]

---

[519] Op.cit. Kramish, *The Griffin.*

[520] Noël Coward, *The Letters of Noël Coward: Edited and with Commentary by Barry Day,* New York: Alfred A Knopf 2007, p.402.

Noël Coward's meeting with Stephenson in London and the subsequent SOE screening led to a second meeting at Stephenson's New York office in 1940:

> Little Bill matter-of-factly invited Noël to become one of his "boys" – a group that included people such as Ian Fleming, Leslie Howard, David Niven, Roald Dahl, Alexander and Zoltan Korda, and Cary Grant. Stephenson inclined to the belief that celebrity was its own disguise, which meshed completely with the feelings Noël had unsuccessfully tried to convey to Churchill.[521]

Little Bill's management involved forcing Noël to take a holiday. On Christmas Eve, 1943, Bill and his wife had Noël for dinner at their New York apartment. Noël had just returned from a hectic tour and was worn and haggard. Bill insisted he cancel his forthcoming South Africa tour and organized flights to Jamaica, where he stayed as Bill's guest.[522] Enchanted there, Noël vowed to himself that he would live in Jamaica.

> I sat each evening on the terrace watching the sun set and the lights come up in the town. On the third night the moon was full and fireflies flickered among the silvered trees, in fact no magic was omitted. The spell was cast and held, and I knew I should come back.[523]

Ian Fleming

Stephenson's management had the same effect on Ian Fleming. In October 1943 Ian had accompanied his long-time friend Ivar Bryce, an SIS agent then working for Stephenson in New York,[524] to an Anglo-American naval conference in Jamaica.[525]

Ivar and the Fleming brothers had been friends since childhood. At Eton Ivar and Ian were together for five years around the time of the Great War. Their subsequent schooling and work sent them separately

---

[521] Ibid. p.403.

[522] January 2 – 21, 1944, Noel Coward, *Noel Coward: Autobiography: consisting of Present Indicative, Future Indefinite, and the Uncompleted Past Conditional, With an Introduction by Sheridan Morley,* London: Methuen 1986. Pages 459-462.

[523] Ibid. p.461.

[524] Ivar Bryce recounted his appointment as one of Stephenson's boys after the appeasers were swept aside and Churchill's warriors took charge: "Amongst them was a Canadian businessman, once a Royal Air Force hero of the other war, who had his plans already thought out. He was quietly installed in a key position that he himself invented and from which he was to serve the Allied cause in quiet and secret paths, but to great purpose. I had never heard of him. No one, except a handful of the new leaders of the Allies and another handful from among his trusted friends, had ever heard of him. But fate decreed that I was soon to work for him, a tiny cog in a small wheel in a great machine that fulfilled a most valuable job. I did not even know him by sight until I had been in his organization for nearly a year, but he is a man I grew to admire immensely; and his achievements were greater than is known today." Ivar Bryce, *You Only Live Once: Memories of Ian Fleming,* first revised edition University Publications of America, Inc. 1975/84, pages 48-49.

[525] Other writers have dated this conference and Fleming's stay at the Bryce Jamaica residence at various times from 1942 to 1944. From Bryce we learn that it was very likely in October 1943. Ibid. pages 68-75.

around the world. In 1942 Ivar learned that his "best friend"[526] was in the same secret service, William Stephenson's.

Ian stayed in Ivar's wife's beautiful house above Kingston in the Blue Mountains. Despite the rain on all of the four days his stay in Jamaica's October rainy season, Ian was enthralled.

Ivar recalled the flight back:

> We had adjoining bucket seats, and as the heavy aircraft broke through the Jamaican clouds and into the sunlit sky, he returned to the study of his files. Having gone over and over his notes with intense concentration for hours, he suddenly snapped brief-box shut and turned to me sparkling with enthusiasm. He paused: "You know, Ivar, I have made a great decision." I waited, nervous of the news to come. "When we have won this blasted war, I am going to live in Jamaica. Just live in Jamaica and lap it up, and swim in the sea and write books. That is what I want to do, and I want your help, as you will probably get out of the war before I can. You must find the right bit of Jamaica for me to buy. Ten acres or so, away from towns and on the coast."[527]

Ian Fleming wrote all the James Bond novels in his Jamaica house.

After the war recently knighted[528] Sir William Stephenson acquired what he called "the finest house on the island." There he entertained another Montego Bay resident, Lord Beaverbrook, also a Canadian of humble origins (Max Aitken) who was a self-made multimillionaire and one of Churchill's select war-winners. Despite being in the same business, journalism, and having had dealings with one another, Fleming and Beaverbrook did not become friends until brought together by Stephenson in Jamaica.

A factor was their mutual friendship with Ann Rothermere.

Ann and Ian were upper class Scots, known to one another at least from 1934 when they met at Stanway, an ancestral house of Ann's family; and then again at a golf weekend in Le Touquet in 1936. Ian moved in newspaper circles in London with Ann's first two husbands. In early 1939 "…Ann first went to bed with Ian – probably, so is the consensus – at a golfing weekend in Sandwich."[529] In March 1939 Ann invited Ian to join her on a tour of the Balkans to promote British fashion. Seeking to emulate his brother Peter who was already in British Intelligence, Ian chose instead to go to Moscow to report for *The Times* on a British Trade Mission.

Ann had married Baron O'Neill in 1932, had two children, and begun an affair with Viscount Rothermere in 1936. O'Neill was killed in action in 1944.

---

[526] Ibid. p.53.

[527] Ibid. p.74.

[528] *This one is dear to my heart.* Winston Churchill recommending Stephenson for the knighthood conferred in January 1945.

[529] Op, cit. Andrew Lycett, *Ian Fleming,* p.96.

Ann married Rothermere in 1945 and he divorced her in 1951. She had told Rothermere that during her months' long winter stays in Jamaica she was visiting famously gay Noël Coward, when in fact she had been staying with Ian Fleming in his house, "Goldeneye".

Pregnant with Ian's child, Ann married Ian in 1952.

Lord Beaverbrook (Max Aitken)

Another war veteran with a house in Montego Bay was Lord Beaverbrook, the former Minister of Aircraft Production. Ian had occasional dealings with him, but they had never been friends. Indeed the last time they had met – at Beaverbrook's house Cherkley Court in Surrey only a few weeks earlier – Ian had been rash enough to attack the *Daily Express* over dinner for its bad taste in publishing an article about a businessman who had died of a heart attack in a brothel. Beaverbrook had been annoyed at this man purporting to tell him how to run his newspapers. Stephenson claimed the credit for bringing the two together in Jamaica, and thenceforward Ian maintained a curiously deferential relationship to the newspaper tycoon, who was a close friend of Ann Rothermere.[530]

The conciliation of Max Aitken and Ian Fleming was probably accomplished when Stephenson pointed out to Ian the forbearance that Beaverbrook's newspapers had shown in not publicizing Ann's scandalous behavior; and of course, Beaverbrook's success in managing WWII aircraft production had brought extravagant praise from Churchill and merited admiration and gratitude.

Roald Dahl

Author Roald Dahl would say nothing about his WWII years working for Bill Stephenson.[531]

Fleming visited Stephenson

Fleming kept his wartime promise to himself by engaging the help of his friend Ivar Bryce in locating a property on the north coast of Jamaica near the Bryces and the Stephensons. Ian bought several acres overlooking the sea close to Oracabessa ("golden head" in Spanish) and flew to Jamaica to oversee design and construction of the house he would call "Goldeneye." He arrived in January 1946 and stayed mostly at Stephenson's Hillowton ("the finest house on the island") for two months.[532]

The other aspect of Fleming's promise to himself – to write the "spy novel to end all spy novels" – was being formed by events.

---

[530] Ibid. Lycett pages 166-167.

[531] "Dahl always remained uncharacteristically circumspect about his wartime intelligence work...took secrets with him to the grave...". Shortly before his death in 1990 a Stephenson biographer, Bill Macdonald, told Dahl that others were talking about BSC: "You won't get any [secrets] from me. It's a question of honour really." Donald Sturrock, *Storyteller: The Life of Roald Dahl,* London: Harper Press 2010, p.245.

[532] Matthew Parker, *Goldeneye: Where Bond Was Born: Ian Fleming's Jamaica,* New York: Pegasus Books 2015, pages 19-23.

Hitler's role as "brutal dictator seeking world domination" was being replicated by Josef Stalin.

The socialist Labor defeat of Churchill's government in mid-1945 soured Ian on his military intelligence (government) job. He was successful in negotiating an employment contract with the *Sunday Times* and related Kelmsley newspapers which provided two months annual vacation. In these months he intended to write the great spy novel – the setting for which was being suggested by the events of the half-year before his Jamaican sojourn with Stephenson.

> From Stettin in the Baltic to Trieste in the Adriatic, an iron curtain has descended across the Continent. Behind that line lie all the capitals of the ancient states of Central and Eastern Europe. Warsaw, Berlin, Prague, Vienna, Budapest, Belgrade, Bucharest and Sofia, all these famous cities and the populations around them lie in what I must call the Soviet sphere, and all are subject in one form or another, not only to Soviet influence but to a very high and, in many cases, increasing measure of control from Moscow....and throughout the world, Communist fifth columns are established and work in complete unity and absolute obedience to the directions they receive from the Communist centre. Except in the British Commonwealth and in the United States where Communism is in its infancy, the Communist parties or fifth columns constitute a growing challenge and peril to Christian civilization.
>
> From Churchill's famous "Iron Curtain Speech"
>
> March 5, 1946

A few weeks before Ian flew to meet Stephenson in Jamaica, in November 1945, parliamentary elections in France had resulted in the Communist Party (*le Parti comuniste francais, PCF*) getting the most seats, 158. The Socialist Party received 142 seats and the Popular Republican Movement 152 seats. With seventy-five percent of the total seats, these three parties formed a coalition. War hero Charles de Gaulle was elected head of the government, but his unease with appointing Communists to cabinet, whom he considered to be under the influence of a foreign power, namely Russia, caused him to resign in January 1946.

Stephenson and Fleming in Jamaica

Joseph McCarthy was campaigning for the Wisconsin seat in the 1946 U.S. Senate election and Russia was pursuing overt expansion in the Baltic, Ukraine, Poland, Bulgaria, Romania and supporting Communists in the English-speaking democracies when Ian Fleming loaded his luggage into Bill Stephenson's Cadillac at Kingston airport.

On the drive from the airport to Hillowton Ian was impressed with the quiet power of Stephenson's huge car. It recalled the Cadillac V8 in Leone's LaSalle –which had vanquished his Buick roadster in the run down to the Dellach Golf Club.

"This isn't a standard Cadillac, is it, Bill? …I heard it was built for General de Gaulle"[533]

---

[533] "I had a Cadillac just after the war in Jamaica. Ian came out to stay in 1946 and drove with me in it. It was, incidentally, one that had been meant for de Gaulle and that General Motors diverted to me instead. I had a very safe driver at the time named Crawford. We drove along the North Shore Road, past Oracabessa. And all the time Ian had his eye on that clock. 'It's amazing

"Yes, it has some special features."

"You fetched it from France?"

"How was your flight, Ian?"

"Same old Bill. Answer a question with a question. The flight was all right. The stewardess not as handsome as some. …oooh! Bill, we hit that bird! …beautiful…what was it?"

"I don't know…a bird…beside bird-watching…and getting your house started, what will you do in Jamaica for the next couple of months? Not much happens here compared to London."

"Bill, I've been wanting to write a spy novel for years. The war got in the way, but now…with my press job allowing me at least two months in Jamaica annually…and with a house here…I hope to write the great spy novel."

Bill looked sternly at Ian. "You signed the Official Secrets Act."

"That's why I want to talk it over with you."

"You want to write about someone we know?"

"This spy story will be different. The main character, the British master spy, will be a woman. A brilliant medical doctor with a PhD in pathology, able to maim and kill quietly, subtly, with precision and without leaving clues. She is unquestionably loyal to Britain, to the Crown and the Empire. MI6 has granted her double-oh status, license to kill. Tall and strong, she is nevertheless strikingly beautiful. Men are devastated by her luminous eyes."

"Kill the male after mating? The black widow spider woman is not new, Ian."

"But this one doesn't usually kill. Hippocratic Oath and all that. She is profoundly cunning…able to manipulate people and circumstances…so that the villains kill each other."

"Manipulating spies is not so easy. Remember…?"

"Ah, but this agent has a unique advantage. She is a qualified and experienced psychoanalyst, skilled in hypnosis, trained by an analyst who was trained by Freud himself. She detects the clues… understands their significance…draws insights…can predict … influence … behavior."

"Ian, you can't…write about *her*. There are Nazi survivors. Too many in Sweden."

"I've thought of that, Bill. So the plot will deflect attention far from Stockholm. The action will take place in France…where General de Gaulle's fears are being realized. Russian money secretly nourishes the French Communist Party via distribution to the party's president, a ruthless and greedy narcissist. He indulges his weakness for high stakes gambling at Le Touquet – the thoroughbred horse racing there and the nearby *Casino Royale.* He alone can track the large sums…the flows of francs, dollars, pounds, rubles… And he alone knows the identities of his agents in France. He trusts no one. In the tradition of high stakes espionage, not even his KGB controllers know who his agents are…certainly not vacuous Party members…and not his senior Party 'comrades.' All the clandestine Communists are known only by their numbers; the man at the center is called *"Le Chiffre"*, "The Cipher." When one of his agents has failed to receive promised payment, he defects to MI6 and describes the French arrangements. A scheme is formulated – by taking advantage of a unique set of abilities – powerful intelligence including eidetic

---

how this car rides at high speeds,' he'd say. 'But don't you think Crawford's going much too fast? He's at eighty.' I never told Ian that because of de Gaulle the speedo was set in kilometres." Bill Stephenson in an interview with John Pearson, in *Ian Fleming: The Notes,* London: Queen Anne Press 2020, p.280.

imagery, memory for cards, ability to calculate probabilities quickly and accurately...and crucially, psychoanalytic mastery which allows her to perceive and interpret emotional cues, our MI6 agent will appear at the *Casino Royale* inner sanctum high stakes card game, her objective to deprive the vain compulsive gambler *Le Chiffre* of the money Moscow has entrusted to him for furtherance of Communism in France. The ebb and flow of the card games ... poker ... maybe baccarat would be easier for the reader to follow ... eventually leave just the two antagonists, our agent and *Le Chiffre.* By an outrageous stroke of luck he deprives her of her MI6 stake; then, swiftly and surreptitiously, an American CIA agent lurking in the casino provides her additional funds, enough to realize the superiority of her ability and courage to prevail, to win all of *Le Chiffre*'s chips. He is unable to meet his financial obligations to the Communist Party. For his weakness and failure he is executed by Russian agents."

"I see the echo of America crucially helping Britain to defeat Germany. Let me think about this, Ian. We're closing down some wartime operations. I'm kind of busy with these. You have two months ahead of you here. Enjoy Jamaica. I'll have an answer for you before you leave."

Stephenson drives Fleming to Kingston airport

"Congratulations on the start you've made on the house, Ian. I'll have my man keep a bit of an eye on it for you. And Ivar of course."

"The spy novel to end all spy novels, Bill. Where do we stand?"

"Too risky, Ian. Those of my people who have left the war intact should stay that way. You know a bit about what she did for us. There was much more you don't know. We can't allow any breach of her security. The novel you described to me, with her as the main character, would be dangerous. You could be violating the Official Secrets Act.

"We like the plot, however. It is time we drew attention to Stalin's ambition. But you'll have to find a different hero for your spy novel."

"I'm disappointed. But I understand. She helped me. Hearing that she helped you...and others...doesn't surprise me."

"She was magnificent, wasn't she?" ...as the German war recedes and a Russian one looms, we could use some new stories ... with heroes...enterprising, brave...seizing initiatives to secure the freedom of English-speaking nations. I wish I had such a book to give you...for your reading on the plane.

"Next best thing – to encourage you to return to Jamaica next winter to write the great spy novel, here is a book on your enthusiasm for watching Jamaican birds...by the foremost authority, the ornithologist James Bond."[534]

---

[534] James Bond, *Birds of the West Indies,* Philadelphia PA: The Academy of Natural Sciences of Philadelphia 1936.

Epilogue

This book is founded on my experiences in the Intelligence Department during the war, but rearranged for the purposes of fiction. Fact is a poor story-teller. It starts a story at haphazard, generally long before the beginning, rambles on inconsequently and tails off, leaving loose ends hanging about, without a conclusion. ... the author has himself to make it coherent, dramatic and probable. [535]

Somerset Maugham

What to make of the historian's assertion that knowledge based on things that never happened, fiction, is less valuable than factual information? Novels sell by the thousands. Movies and television dramas are watched by millions. Imaginary characters and imaginary events are not entirely for audiences of children. Most adults owe their knowledge of history to dramatic interpretations of historical events by novelists, playwrights and screen writers, not the objective descriptions of historians.

Canadians, Britons, Americans...live in an English-speaking democracy, not a German-speaking dictatorship.

How did that happen?

The Clara Conjecture has tried to convey the nature of the games, the stakes involved and what some players did. Failures by executives to act on military intelligence had consequences vastly greater than the sorts of events that rate headlines in the twenty-first century. Roosevelt was warned in advance of Pearl Harbor; Stalin's egocentric belief that his partner Adolf Hitler would not betray him cost the lives of two million Russian soldiers in the three weeks following June 22, 1941. The raid by 746 heavy bombers on Hamburg July 24, 1943 killed 36,000 inhabitants. Fortunately, Churchill and Roosevelt acted on intelligence they received regarding the German atomic bomb program.

Documents in intelligence archives should dispel the misconception, still common in English-speaking countries, that Hitler did not appreciate the significance of nuclear fission and did not seriously support the enterprise of creating a German atomic bomb. During WWII and the Cold War secrecy was emphasized. The Churchill/Attlee post-Hiroshima observation that "those who were informed" were concerned about the Nazi atomic bomb has been illuminated by German language documents,[536] including Lise Meitner

---

[535] Somerset Maugham, *Ashenden,* London: Vintage Books 2000 (Heinemann 1928), pages v – ix.

[536] Hitler was annoyed at breaches of secrecy by atom-splitting scientists. *"24.3.1942 abends (Wolfschanze): ... Hitler ärgerte vor allem darüber, das Deutsche Wissenschaftler – sobald sie auf Kosten deutscher Steuergelder irgendwelche Entdeckungen gemacht hatten – sie alsbald in ihren Fachzeitschriften,z.B. der "Zeitung für Naturwissenschaften", international Bekanntgaben. Und das noch nach Ausbruch des II Weltkriegs. Das galt insbesondere für die Veröffentlichungen auf dem Gebiet der*

correspondence from 1943 and 1944 discovered in the Churchill Archives at Cambridge University.[537] The Max Planck Archive in Berlin today offers access to hundreds of documents concerning the *Uran Projekt 1939-1945* sponsored by the military.

The skeleton of The Clara Conjecture begs to be fleshed out by narratives and dramas. Clara and Lise Meitner were women – it is a largely feminist story, not the 19th century theatre of the quotidian, but epic. Can Clara and Lise inspire a leap from Henrik Ibsen/Jane Austen to Shakespeare/Ian Fleming?

Emily Blunt [538]   Leone/Clara   Julia Roberts [539]

Lise Meitner   Talia Shire

Atomspaltung ....Hitler hielt die Atomzertrümmerung fureinen für Deutschlands Zukunft derart wichtigen wissenschaftigen Fortschritt ...." Dr. Henry Picker, *Tischgespräche im Führerhauptquartier: Hitler, wie er wirklich war,* Stuttgart: Seewald Verlag 1977, p.135.

[537] Anne Hardy und Lore Sexl, *Lise Meitner,* Hamburg: *Rowohlt Taschenbuch Verlag* 2020, pages 108-110.

[538] Cropped Alamy M378W4

[539] Cropped Alamy H82D9B

[540] Photo courtesy of the Max Planck Society, Berlin

[541] Photo Alamy PNTPMA.

Is there a writer who could do dramatic narrative justice to one of the following?

1. Clara's tangled relationship with Jewry – narrow Christian upbringing; proclaimed agnostic, close to Arthur Hertig at the University of Minnesota and Harvard Medical; second mother Jewish Frau Friedheim; holidayed frequently in anti-Semitic Austria; fascinated by eighteenth century Austrian Empress Maria Teresia who reviled Jews but whose valued prime minister was a Jew; chose the "Jewish profession" psychoanalysis; "best Swedish friend" Vera a Jewish psychoanalyst; lived in anti-Semitic Sweden; family livelihood largely derived from Nazi Germany; favored the music of Mahler and the art of Kokoschka; deplored the status of Jewish women (the first female rabbi in history was in Germany in 1935, the second in the USA in 1972);

2. exploration of the relationship between Clara and Lise, Lise being a Spinoza-type Jew (God is Nature) and Clara (agnostic? atheist?), both towering intellects;

3. Lise Meitner, single, and Albert Einstein, estranged from Mileva, before WWI working days in the world's leading theoretical physics laboratory, the Berlin Dahlem KWI, walking together after they leave an evening of dinner, wine and music at Max Planck's; after the war working together in the Berlin Dahlem KWI until Hitler became chancellor in January 1933 and Albert vowed never to return to Germany;[542]

4. Dana Wilgress, who, like Folke, had been in Omsk 1916-1917 and fled to Vladivostok in 1918, introduced Leone and Folke at his Canadian Embassy in 1931 when the Nazis were coming to power in Hamburg. They married and moved to Stockholm and Dana returned to Ottawa as Director of Commercial Intelligence in 1932, then appointed Minister to the USSR after Hitler attacked Russia (1942-1943), then Canadian Ambassador to the USSR 1944-1946 …Leone and Folke were in a position to provide Dana with superior intelligence[543]…but then Folke hated Communists…;

5. coping morally with the practical necessity of Swedes in general and Folke in particular earning a living from German sources – learning of slave labor used by Bergedorfer Eisenwerk, medical experiments on Jewish children in the Neuengamme concentration camp in Bergedorf;[544]
"To be nameless in worthy deeds, exceeds an infamous history."[545]

---

[542] Armin Herman, *Die Jahrhundertwissenschaft: Werner Heisenverg u.d.Physik seiner Zeit,* Stuttgart: Deutsche Verlags-Anstalt 1977, pages 29, 31, 107.

[543] The importance of "correspondents in neutral countries" like Sweden is still being discovered. Kochanski, Halik, *Resistance: The Underground War Against Hitler, 1939-1945,* New York: W.W. Norton & Company, Inc. 2022., Chapter 6, *Intelligence Gathering: 1939-41,* pages 111-133.

[544] Jeremy Josephs, *Swastika Over Paris: The Fate of the Jews in France,* New York: Arcade Publishing, Little, Brown and Company 1989, pages 172-173.

[545] Sir Thomas Browne, Op.cit p.53.

6. feminist crusade of pioneers Leone McGregor and Lise Meitner, begun in the early 20th century and enormously advanced by the times of their deaths;

7. the conversation stimulated by Intrepid-strength martinis among these neighbours on the north shore of Jamaica after the war – William Stephenson, Lord Beaverbrook, Noël Coward, Ian Fleming, Ivar Bryce;

8. Clara and Ian partner in a golf match against Stephen Potter and P.G. Wodehouse;[546]

9. sex and gossip at Berchtesgaden. Eva Braun secures her position as Hitler's mistress because she is always available for carefree sex in the bedroom next to Adolf's at the Berghof. The political disaster of her becoming pregnant is obviated by her use of the prototype contraceptive pills developed by Arthur Hertig and John Rock at Harvard Medical, given to her by Clara and later by John Rittmeister at the sessions of Eva's hypnotherapy for depression. Under hypnosis Eva talks freely about what she has learned at the Berghof while socializing with neighbours, the families of Bormann, Speer, Göring, and guests Goebbels and Himmler;

10. the soundness of Swedish judgment (incidentally that of Clara's model Swede husband Folke), in avoiding the deaths of thousands of its citizens through flexible neutrality guided by superior intelligence, Folke and Jacob and Markus Wallenberg were friends (Swedish government foreign delegates), Churchill said that Sweden would never recover its honor, while Swedes said of the British that "they kept their honor and lost their lives."

> *Now that the war was ended it was possible and permissible for those of us, including myself, who had no faith whatever in the purity of Russian intentions or the value of Russian promises, to be rather more frank with our Swedish friends than we had been able to be when we and the Soviet Union were fighting a common enemy. The Swedes were divided in their feelings towards Germany, but in their sentiments about Russia, the ancient, traditional enemy, they were completely united. They loathed and feared our Allies, and they still do.[547]*

---

[546] Ian Fleming, Stephen Potter and P.G. Wodehouse frequently played golf at Le Touquet, just across the channel from Sandwich, where Potter and Fleming, both around ten handicap, played together occasionally at Huntercombe Golf Club. Stephen Potter, creator of *Lifemanship* and *Gamesmanship* (the art of winning without actually cheating) observed that the gamesmanship in Fleming's *Dr. No* was flawed by cheating. John Pearson, *Ian Fleming: The Notes,* London: Queen Anne Press 2020, pages 351-352.

[547] Ewan Butler, SOE head for Germany in WW2 based in England and Sweden, *Amateur Agent: The first person account of a British secret agent whose operations reached deep behind the German lines during World War II,* New York: W.W. Norton & Company, Inc. 1963, p.208.

Bibliography

Accoce, Pierre & Pierre Quet, *The Lucy Ring,* London: Panther 1968

Aczel, Amir D., *Uranium Wars: The Scientific Rivalry that Created the Nuclear Age,* New York: Palgrave Macmillan 2009

Alfa-Laval, *100 Jahre Bergedorfer Eisenwerk 1859-1959,* Hamburg-Bergedorf: Astra-Werke 1959

Alfa-Laval AB, text by Gustaf Bondeson, translated by Rita Knox, *The Growth of a Global Enterprise: Alfa-Laval 100 Years,* Sweden: Alfa-Laval 1983

Alexander, Bevin, *How Hitler Could Have Won World War II: The Fatal Errors That Led to Nazi Defeat,* New York: Three Rivers Press 2000

Aldrich, Richard J., & Robert Cormac, *The Black Door: Spies, Secret Intelligence and British Prime Ministers,* London: William Collins 2016

Alfonso XIII, *Alfonso XIII: Historia Grafica De Su Reinado,* Madrid: Ediciones Idea 1958

Aline, Countess of Romanones, *The Spy Wore Red: My Adventures as an Undercover Agent in World War II,* New York: Random House 1987

Aline, Countess of Romanones, *The Spy Went Dancing: My Further Adventures as an Undercover Agent,* New York: G.P. Putnam's Sons 1990

Alvarez, Luis W., *Adventures of a Physicist,* New York: Basic Books Inc. 1987

American-Swedish Historical Foundation, *Yearbook – 1947,* Lancaster, PA: American-Swedish Historical Foundation, 1947

Andrew, Christopher, *The Defence of the Realm: The Authorized History of MI5,* Toronto: Viking Canada 2009

…, *For The President's Eyes Only: Secret Intelligence and the American Presidency from Washington to Bush,* New York: HarperCollins 1995

Anger, Per, translated from the Swedish by David Mel Paul and Margareta Paul, *With Raoul Wallenberg in Budapest: Memories of the War Years in Hungary,* Washington: Holocaust Library 1996

Argyle, Christopher, *Chronology of World War II: The Day by Day Illustrated Record 1939-45,* London: Marshall Cavendish 1980

Arnold, Elliott, *A Night of Watching,* New York: Fawcett Crest 1967

ARNDT editors, *Hitlers Berghof 1928-1945: Zeitgeschichte in Farbe,* Kiel: ARNDT-Verlag 2003

Ashby, Ruth and D.G Ohrn eds., *Women Who Changed the World,* New York: Viking Penguin 1995

Astley, Joan Bright, *The Inner Circle: A View of War at the Top,* Boston: Little Brown 1971

Åsbrink, Elisabeth, translated from the Swedish by Fiona Graham, *1947: Where Now Begins,* New York: Other Press 2016

Bachrach, Susan D., *The Nazi Olympics: Berlin 1936,* Boston: Little Brown 2000

Bagge, Erich, Kurt Diebner and Kenneth Jay, *Von der Uranspaltung bis Calder Hall,* Hamburg: Rowohlt Taschenbuch Verlag GmbH Mai 1957

Baggott, Jim, *Atomic, The First War of Physics and the Secret History of the Atomic Bomb: 1939-1949,* London: Icon Books Ltd. 2009

Baigent, Michael & Richard Leigh, *Secret Germany: Stauffenberg and the True Story of Operation Valkyrie,* New York: Skyhorse Publishing 2008

Bailey, Roderick, *Forgotten Voices of the Secret War: An Inside History of Special Operations During the Second World War,* Croydon UK: Ebury Publishing Random House 2008/2009

Ball, Philip, *Serving the Reich: The Struggle For The Soul Of Physics Under Hitler,* London: The Bodley Head 2013

Ballard, Robert D., *The Discovery of the Bismarck,* New York: Warner Books 1990

Bancroft, Mary, *Autobiography of a Spy,* New York: William Morrow 1983

Bar-Zohar, Michel, *Die Jagd auf die deutsche Wissenschaftler 1944-1960,* translated by Rosel Weighase and Hans Roesch from *La Chasse aux Savants Allemands,* Berlin: Reinhard Mohn OHG 1965/66

Barker, Ralph, *The Blockade Busters,* London: Chattow & Windus 1976

Barnes, Trevor, *Dead Doubles: the Extraordinary Hunt for One of the Cold War's Most Notorious Spy Rings,* New York: HarperCollins 2020

Barris, Ted, *The Great Escape: The Untold Story,* Toronto: Dundurn 2014

Barron, Rachel Stiffler, *Lise Meitner: Discoverer of Nuclear Fission,* Greensboro, NC: Morgan Reynolds 2000

Bassett, Richard, *Hitler's Spy Chief: The Wilhelm Canaris Mystery,* London: Cassell 2005

Baukhage, Manon, *Der Tisch von Otto Hahn, Faszinierende Erfindungen, die unsere Welt veränderten,* Ravensburger Buchverlag ca. 2006

Bäumler, Ernst, *A Century of Chemistry,* Düsseldorf: Econ Verlag 1968

Bazna, Elyesa, *I Was Cicero,* in collaboration with Hans Nogly, translated by Eric Mosbacher, London: Andre Deutsch 1962

Beesly, Patrick, *Very Special Admiral: The Life of Admiral J.H. Godfrey, CB,* London: Hamish Hamilton 1980

…, *Very Special Intelligence,* London: Hamish Hamilton 1977

…, *Room 40: British Naval Intelligence 1914-1918,* Oxford, New York: Oxford University Press 1984

Beevor, Antony, *Stalingrad:* London: Penguin 1999

Beevor, Antony, *Berlin: The Downfall 1945,* London: Viking Penguin 2002

…, *The Mystery of Olga Chekhova,* London: Viking Penguin 2004

…, *The Battle for Spain: The Spanish Civil War 1936-1939,* London: Weidenfeld & Nicolson 2006

…, *The Second World War,* New York: Back Bay Books, Little Brown and Company 2012/13

Bell, E.T., *Renal Diseases,* Philadelphia: Lea & Febiger 1946

… *Text Book of Pathology,* Lea & Febiger 1952

Bell, Jason, *Cracking the Nazi Code: The Untold Story of Canada's Greatest Spy,* Toronto: HarperCollins Publishers Ltd. 2023

Bennett, Gill, *Churchill's Man of Mystery: Desmond Morton and the World of Intelligence,* London: Routledge 2007

…, *The Zinoviev Letter: the conspiracy that never dies,* Oxford UK: Oxford University Press 2018/20

Bennett, Ralph, *Behind the Battle: Intelligence in the War With Germany 1939-1945,* London: Pimlico 1994/1999

Bercuson, David J. and Holger H. Herwig, *The Destruction of the Bismarck,* New York: The Overlook Press 2003

Berg, A. Scott, *Lindbergh,* London: Macmillan 1998

Bergaust, Erik, *Wernher von Braun: Ein unglaubliches Leben,* Düsseldorf and Wien: Econ Verlag 1979/75

Bergedorf writers, various: *Lichtwort, Juli 1957; Lichtwort Dezember 1968 (Bergedorf und seine Wirtschaft); Zwangsarbeit in Bergedorf: Stationen einer verlorenen Jugend Schlossheft Nr. 7 2001,* Hamburg and Bergedorf

Berglyd, Jostein, *Operation Freshman: The Hunt for Hitler's Heavy Water,* Stockholm: Leandoer & Ekholm Forlag 2006

Berkeley, Roy, *A Spy's London,* Barnelsey, South Yorkshire: Pen & Sword 2014/1994

Bernadotte, Count Folke, translated from the Swedish by Count Eric Lewenhaupt, *The Curtain Falls: A unique eyewitness story of the last days of the Third Reich as seen by a neutral observer inside Germany,* New York: Alfred A. Knopf 1945

…, *Instead of Arms,* London: Hodder and Stoughton 1949

Berninger, Ernst H., *Otto Hahn,* Reinbeck bei Hamburg: Rowohlt Taschenbuch Verlag GmbH 1974

Bernstein, Jeremy, *Hitler's Uranium Club: The Secret Recordings At Farm Hall,* Woodbury, New York: American Institute of Physics Press 1996

…, *Nuclear Weapons: What You Need To Know,* New York: Cambridge University Press 2008

Beyerchen, Alan D., *Scientists Under Hitler: Politics and the Physics Community in the Third Reich,* New Haven and London: Yale University Press 1977

Beyerchen, Alan D., *Wissenschaftler Unter Hitler: Physiker Im Dritten Reich,* Köln: Verlag Kiepenheuer & Witsch 1980

Binney, Marcus, *The Women Who Lived For Danger: The Agents of the Special Operations Executive,* New York: HarperCollins 2002

…, *Secret War Heroes: Men of the Special Operations Executive,* London: Hodder & Stoughton Ltd. 2005

Bird, Kai and Martin J. Sherman, *American Prometheus: The Triumph and Tragedy of J. Robert Oppenheimer,* London: Atlantic Books 2005/8

Birkenhead, Frederick, Second Earl, *The Prof in Two Worlds: The Official Life of Professor F.A. Lindemann, Viscount Cherwell,* London: Collins 1961

Bishop, Patrick, *Target Tirpitz: X-craft, Agents and Dambusters – the Epic Quest to Destroy Hitler's Mightiest Warship,* London: HarperCollins 2012

Björling, Anna-Lisa and Andrew Farkas, *Jussi:* Portland, OR: Amadeus Press 1996

Blaedel, Niels, *Harmony and Unity: The Life of Niels Bohr,* Madison WI: Science Tech Inc. 1988

Blough, Michael, editor, *Wallis & Edward: Letters 1931-1937,* New York: Simon & Schuster 1986

Blum, Howard, *The Last Goodnight,* biography of Betty Pack, New York: HarperCollins 2016

..., *Night of the Assassins: The Untold Story of Hitler's Plot to Kill FDR, Churchill, and Stalin,* New York: HarperCollins 2020

Bock, Dennis, *The Ash Garden, A Novel,* Toronto: HarperCollins 2001

..., *The Good German, A Novel,* Toronto: HarperCollins 2020

..., *The Communist's Daughter,* Toronto: HarperCollins 2006

Bodanis, David, $E = mc^2$: *A Biography of the World's Most Famous Equation,* New York: Berkley Books 2000

Bodsch, Eliza, *Frauen im KZ Neuengamme: Welche Überlebenstrategien haben sich unter weiblichen Häftlingen im KZ herausgebildet und was für einen Einfluss hatten sie auf das Überleben im Lager?,* Hamburg: Universität Hamburg GRIN Verlag 2005

Boltz, C.L., *Ernest Rutherford,* Geneva, Switzerland: Heron Books 1970

Bond, James, *Birds of the West Indies,* Philadelphia: The Academy of Natural Sciences of Philadelphia January 1936

Borkin, Joseph, *The Crime and Punishment of I.G. Farben: The startling account of the unholy alliance of Adolf Hitler and Germany's great chemical combine,* New York: The Free Press/Macmillan 1978

Bormann, Martin, compiler, *Hitler's Table Talk,* Milton Keynes, UK: Ostara Publications 2016

Born, Max, *My Life: Recollections of a Nobel Laureate,* New York: Charles Scribner's Sons 1978

Born, Max, translated by Irene Born, *The Born-Einstein Letters: Correspondence between Albert Einstein and Max and Hedwig Born from 1916 to 1955 with commentaries by Max Born,* New York: Walker and Company 1971, Foreword by Bertrand Russell, Introduction by Werner Heisenberg

Bothwell, Robert, *Nucleus: The History of Atomic Energy of Canada Limited,* Toronto: University of Toronto Press 1988

..., *Eldorado: Canada's National Uranium Company,* Toronto: University of Toronto Press 1984

Bottome, Phyllis, *The Goal,* London: Faber and Faber 1962

Bower, Tom, *The Perfect English Spy: Sir Dick White and the Secret War 1935-1990,* New York: St. Martin's Press 1995

Boyce, Fredric and Douglas Everett, *SOE: The Scientific Secrets,* Cheltenham, Gloucestershire: The History Press 2003/2009

Boyd, Andrew, *British Naval Intelligence Through the Twentieth Century,* Barnsley UK: Seaforth Publishing 2020

Boyle, Andrew, *The Climate of Treason,* London: Coronet Hodder & Stoughton 1987/1979

Bräutigam, Walter, *John Rittmeister – Leben und Sterben,* München: Langewiesche-Brandt 1987

Breuer, William B., *Deceptions of World War II,* New York: John Wiley & Sons 2001

Brickhill, Paul, *The Great Escape,* New York: W.W. Norton & Company, Inc. 1950/78

British Security Coordination, *The Secret History of British Intelligence in the Americas, 1940-1945,* New York: Fromm International 1998

Broda, Paul, *Scientist Spies: A Memoir of My Three Parents and the Atom Bomb,* Leicester, UK: Matador 2011

Brown, Andrew, *The Neutron and the Bomb: A Biography of Sir James Chadwick,* Oxford: Oxford UP 1997

Brown, Anthony Cave, *Bodyguard of Lies:* Toronto: Fitzhenry & Whiteside 1975

..., *Wild Bill Donovan: The Last Hero,* London: Michael Joseph 1982

…, *"C": The Secret Life of Sir Stewart Menzies, Spymaster to Winston Churchill,* New York: Macmillan 1987

Brown, Colin, *Glory and Bollocks: The Truth Behind XI Defining Events in British History,* London: Oneworld Publishing 2013/16

…, *Operation Big: The Race to Stop Hitler's A-Bomb,* Stroud, Gloucestershire: Amberley Publishing 2016

Browne, Thomas, *Hydriotaphia: Urn Burial* (1658), Durham UK: Aziloth Books 2019

Bryce, Ivar, *You Only Live Once: Memories of Ian Fleming,* Frederick, MD: University Publications of America, Inc. 1975-84

Bryden, John, *Fighting to Lose: How the German Secret Intelligence Service Helped the Allies Win the Second World War,* Toronto: Dundurn Press 2014

…, *Deadly Allies: Canada's Secret War 1937-1947,* Toronto: McClelland & Stewart 1989

Brysac, Shareen Blair, *Resisting Hitler: The Life and Death of an American Woman in Nazi Germany,* Oxford, New York: Oxford University Press 2000

Budiansky, Peter, *Battle of Wits: The Complete Story of Codebreaking in World War II,* New York: The Free Press 2000

Burke, *The Lawn Road Flats: Spies, Writers and Artists,* Woodbridge, Suffolk: Boydell 2014

Burleigh, Michael, *Moral Combat: Good and Evil in World War II,* New York: HarperCollins 2011

Burrin, Philippe, *France Under The Germans: Collaboration and Compromise,* New York: The New Press 1993, English translation by Janet Lloyd 1996

Burstein, Dan, Arne de Keijzer and John-Henri Holmberg, *The Tattooed Girl: The Enigma of Stieg Larsson and the Secrets Behind the Most Compelling Thrillers of Our Time,* New York: St. Martin's Griffin 2011

Butler, Ewan, *Amateur Agent: A Story of Black Propaganda during World War II,* London: George G. Harrap 1963

Butler, Josephine, *Churchill's Secret Agent: Josephine Butler, Codename 'Jay Bee',* Toronto: Methuen 1983

Cabell, Craig, *Ian Fleming's Secret War,* Barnsley, South Yorkshire: Pen & Sword Books Ltd. 2008

Cadillac Motor Car Company, *LaSalle Operators Manual,* Detroit: Cadillac Motor Car Company 1929

Cairncross, John, *The Enigma Spy: An Autobiography, The Story of the Man Who Changed the Course of World War Two,* London: Century 1997

Carlgren, W.M., *Swedish Foreign Policy during the Second World War,* London: Ernest Benn 1977

Carlson, John Roy, *Under Cover,* New York: E.P. Dutton 1943

Carré, Mathilde-Lily, *I Was the Cat, The truth about the most remarkable woman spy since Mata Hari – by herself,* London: Souvenir Press 1959/60

Carroll, Tim, *The Great Escape from Stalag Luft III: The Full Story of How 76 Allied Officers Carried Out World War II's Most Remarkable Mass Escape,* New York: Pocket Books 2004

Carroll, Warren, *The Last Crusade, Spain: 1936,* Front Royal, VA: The Christendom Press 1996

Carter, Miranda, *Anthony Blunt: His Lives,* New York: Farrar, Strauss & Giroux 2001

Carter, Sarah and Nanci Langford, *Compelled to Act: Histories of Women's Activism in Western Canada,* Winnipeg: U of Manitoba Press 2020

Casey, William, *The Secret War Against Hitler,* London: Simon & Schuster 1989

Caskie, Dr. Donald, *The Tartan Pimpernel,* London: Osbourne 1957/1960

Cassidy, David C., *Beyond Uncertainty: Heisenberg, Quantum Physics, and the Bomb,* New York: Bellevue Literary Press 2010

…, *Uncertainty: The Life and Science of Werner Heisenberg,* New York: W.H. Freeman 1992

Cathell, D. and W.T. Cathell, *Book on the Physician Himself, and Things That Concern His Reputation and Success,* Philadelphia: F.A. Davis Company 1908

Cecil, Robert, *A Divided Life: A Personal Portrait of the Spy Donald Maclean,* New York: William Morrow 1989

Charles, Daniel, *Mastermind: the Rise and Fall of Fritz Haber, the Nobel Laureate Who Launched the Age of Chemical Warfare,* New York: HarperCollins 2005

Charles River Editors, *Operation Paperclip: The History of the Secret Program to Bring Nazi Scientists to America During and After World War II,* Charles River Editors online 2021

Chiaverini, Jennifer, *Resistance Women, A Novel,* New York: HarperCollins William Morrow 2019

Chisholm, Anne & Michael Davie, *Beaverbrook: A Life,* London: Hutchinson 1992

Churchill, Winston S., *Great Contemporaries,* London: Thornton Butterworth 1937

Churchill, Winston S., *Memoirs of the Second World War: An Abridgement of the Six Volumes of "The Second World War",* Boston: Houghton Mifflin 1984/59

…, *The Second World War Complete in Six Volumes,* New York: Houghton Mifflin Bantam 1949/1979

Cimino, Al, *The Manhattan Project: The Making of the Atomic Bomb,* London: Arcturus Publishing Limited 2016

Clark, Lloyd, *Kursk: The Greatest Battle, Eastern Front 1943,* London: Headline Publishing Group 2011

Clark, Ronald W., *The Birth of the Bomb: The untold story of Britain's part in the weapon that changed the world,* London: Phoenix House 1961

…, *The Rise of the Boffins,* London: Phoenix House 1962

…, *Einstein: The Life and Times,* New York: Thomas Y. Crowell 1971

Close, Frank, *Trinity: The Treachery and Pursuit of the Most Dangerous Spy in History* (Klaus Fuchs), Milton Keynes, UK: Penguin 2019

Cocks, Geoffrey, *Psychotherapy in the Third Reich: The Göring Institute,* New York: Oxford University Press 1985

Coles, Robert, *Anna Freud: The Dream of Psychoanalysis,* Reading, MA: Addison Wesley 1992

Collier, Basil, *The Defence of the United Kingdom,* London: The Imperial War Museum 1957

Collingwood, C.G., *The Idea of History,* Oxford: The Clarendon Press 1946 (first edition)

…, *The Idea of Nature,* Oxford: Oxford UP 1945/60

Colman, Penny, *Where the Action Was: Women War Correspondents in World War II,* New York: Crown Publishers 2002

Colville, John, *The Fringes of Power: Downing Street Diaries 1939-1955,* London: Hodder and Stoughton 1985

…, *The Churchillians,* London: Weidenfeld & Nicolson 1981 (dated March 1981 and signed by author)

Conan Doyle, A., *A Study in Scarlet* (1887), London: Folio Society 1994

Conant, Jennet, *The Irregulars: Roald Dahl and the British Spy Ring in Wartime Washington,* New York: Simon & Schuster 2008

Conkling, Winifred, *Radioactive: How Irène Curie & Lise Meitner Revolutionized Science and Changed the World,* Chapel Hill, NC: Algonquin 2016

Conquest, Robert, *The Great Terror: A Reassessment,* London: Oxford UP 1990

Cook, Nick, *The Hunt for Zero Point: Inside the Classified World of Antigravity Technology,* New York: Broadway Books 2002

Cooke, Ronald C. & Roy Conyers Nesbit, *Target: Hitler's Oil: Allied Attacks On German Oil Supplies 1939-1945,* London: William Kimber 1985

Cookridge, E.H., *Sisters of Delilah: Stories of Famous Women Spies,* London: Oldbourne 1959

…, *Set Europe Ablaze,* New York: Thomas Y. Crowell Company 1967

…, *Spy Trade,* New York: Walker and Company 1971

Copeland, B. Jack, *Colossus: The Secrets of Bletchley Park's Codebreaking Computers,* Oxford, UK: Oxford UP 2006

Corcoran, William W., *Top Secret (A Foreign Service Saga),* Stanford, CA: Hoover Institution, excerpts 'Contents', pages 167-325 and 480-518.

Cornwell, John, *Hitler's Scientists: Science, War and the Devil's Pact,* London: Penguin 2003

Cortada, James W. editor, *Modern Warfare in Spain: American Military Observations on the Spanish Civil War 1936-1939,* Washington, DC: Potomac Books 2012

Costello, John, *Mask of Treachery: Spies, Buggery & Betrayal,* New York: William Morrow 1988

…, *Ten Days That Saved The West,* London: Bantam 1991

Coward, Noël, *Autobiography, consisting of Present Indicative, Future Indefinite and the uncompleted Past Conditional,* London: Methuen 1986

…, *The Letters of Noël Coward, edited by Barry Day,* New York: Alfred A. Knopf 2007

Cowles, Virginia, *Looking for Trouble,* Sixth Edition, Harper 1941

…, *Winston Churchill: The Era and The Man,* London: Hamish Hamilton 1953

…, *The Rothschilds: A Family of Fortune,* New York: Alfred A. Knopf 1973

Craughwell, Thomas J., *The War Scientists: The brains behind military technologies of destruction and defense,* London: Murdoch Books 2011

Crim, Brian E., *Our Germans: Project Paperclip and the National Security State,* Baltimore MD: Johns Hopkins University Press 2018

Crowdy, Terry, *The Enemy Within: A History of Espionage,* New York: Osprey Publishing 2006

…, *SOE: Churchill's Secret Agents,* Oxford & New York: Bloomsbury Publishing Plc 2016

Cruikshank, Charles, *Deception in World War II,* Oxford: Oxford University Press 1979

…, *SOE: Special Operations Executive in Scandinavia,* New York: Oxford University Press 1986

Cuthbertson, Ken, *1945: The Year That Made Modern Canada,* Toronto: HarperCollins 2020

Dahl, Per F., *Heavy Water and the Wartime Race for Nuclear Energy,* London: Institute of Physics Publishing Ltd 1999

Dalzel-Job, Patrick, *From Arctic Snow to Dust of Normandy,* Plockton, Ross-shire: Nean-an-Eoin Publishing 1992

Davenport-Hines, Richard, *Enemies Within: Communists, the Cambridge Spies and the Making of Modern Britain,* London: William Collins 2018

Davidson, Edward and Dale Manning, *Chronology of World War Two,* New York: Cassell & Co. 1999/2000

Davies, Philip H.J., *MI6 and the Machinery of Spying*, London, Portland, OR: Frank Cass 2004

Dawidoff, Nicholas, *The Catcher Was A Spy: The Mysterious Life Of Moe Berg*, New York: Vintage Books 1995

De Jouvenel, Bertrand, translated from the French by Nikita Lary, *The Art of Conjecture*, New York: Basic Books 1967

Deacon, Richard, *The Chinese Secret Service*, New York: Ballantine Books 1974

…, *The Israeli Secret Service*, New York: Taplinger Publishing 1978

…, *A History of British Secret Service*, London: Granada Panther Books 1980, also Taplinger Company 1969

…, *The British Connection: Russia's Manipulation of British Individuals and Institutions*, London: Hamish Hamilton 1979

…, *The Greatest Treason: The Bizarre Story of Hollis, Liddell and Mountbatten*, London: Century 1990

Dear, Ian, *Sabotage and Subversion: The SOE and OSS At War*, Stroud, Gloucestershire: The History Press 1996/2010

…, *Spyclopedia: The comprehensive handbook of espionage*, New York: Silver Arrow 1987

Dear, I.C.B. and M.R.D. Foot, editors, *The Oxford Companion to World War II*, Oxford, New York: Oxford University Press 1995

Deichmann, Ute, *Flüchten, Mitmachen, Vergessen: Chemiker und Biochemiker in der NS-Zeit*, Weinheim: WILEY-VCH Verlag GmbH 2001

De Marigny, Alfred, with Mickey Herskowitz, *A Conspiracy of Crowns: The True Story of the Duke of Windsor and the Murder of Sir Harry Oakes*, New York: Crown 1990

Denham, Henry, *Inside the Nazi Ring: A Naval Attaché in Sweden 1940-1945*, New York: Holmes & Meier 1984

Denkhaus, Markus et al, *Bergedorf im Gleichschrift: Ein Hamburger Stadtteil im "Dritten Reich"*, Hamburg: Kultur & Geschichtskontor 1995

DiGeorge, Pat, *Liberty Lady: A True Story of Love and Espionage in WWII Sweden*, Vero Beach, FL: Beaver's Spur 2016

Dildy, Douglas C., *Battles of World War II: Denmark and Norway 1940, Hitler's Boldest Operation*, Botley, Oxford: Osprey Publishing 2009

Dilks, David, editor, *The Diaries of Sir Alexander Cadogan 1938-1945*, New York: G.P. Putnam's Sons 1972

Dixon, Peter, *Guardians of Churchill's Secret Army: Men of the Intelligence Corps in the Special Operations Executive*, London: Cloudshill Press LLP 2018

Dodds-Parker, Douglas, *Setting Europe Ablaze: Some Account of Ungentlemanly Warfare*, Windlesham, Surrey: Springwood Books 1983

Donner, Rebecca, *All the Frequent Troubles of Our Days: The True Story of The American Woman at the Heart of the German Resistance to Hitler*, New York: Back Bay Books 2021

Dorrill, Stephen, *MI6: Inside the Covert World of Her Majesty's Secret Intelligence Service*, New York: The Free Press Simon & Schuster 2000

Dourlein, Peter, *Inside North Pole: A Secret Agent's Story*, London: William Kimber 1953/54

Downing, David, *The Moscow Option: An Alternative Second World War*, London: Greenhill Books 1979

Dressel, Joachim & Manfried Griehl, *The Luftwaffe Album: Bomber and Fighter Aircraft of the German Air force 1933-1945,* translated by M.J. Shields, London: Brockhampton Press 1993/94/97/99

…, *Junkers Ju 86,* Atglen, PA: Schiffer Military/Aviation History, Schiffer Publishing, Ltd. 1998

Drucker, Peter F., *The End of Economic Man: The Origins of Totalitarianism* (1939), London: Transaction Publishers 2009

Drummond, John D., *But For These Men,* New York: Award Books 1965

Dubois, Josiah E., *Generals in Grey Suits: The Directors of the International 'I.G. Farben' Cartel, their conspiracy and trial at Nuremberg,* London: The Bodley Head 1953

Duke, Madelaine, *Slipstream: The Story of Anthony Duke,* London: Evans Brothers Limited 1955

Dukes, Sir Paul, *An Epic of the Gestapo: the Story of a Strange Search,* London: Cassell and Company Ltd. 1940

Dumais, Lucien, *The Man Who Went Back,* London: Leo Cooper 1975

Dupuis, Michael, *Winnipeg's General Strike: Reports From the Front Lines,* Charleston, SC: The History Press 2014

Dwork, Debórah and Robert Jan Van Pelt, *Flight from The Reich: Refugee Jews 1933-1946,* New York: W.W. Norton 2009

Ede, Andrew and Lesley B. Cormack, *A History of Science in Society: From Philosophy to Utility, Second Edition,* Toronto ON: U of Toronto Press 2012

Eggleston, Wilfrid, *Canada's Nuclear Story,* London: Harrap Research Publications 1966

Eichholtz, Dietrich, translated by John Broadwin, *War For Oil: The Nazi Quest for an Oil Empire,* Washington: Potomac Books 2006/2012

Einstein, Albert, *Ideas and Opinions,* New York: Crown 1964

…, *Out of My Later Years,* New York: Philosophical Library 1950; second copy New York: Bonanza Books 1954

Ekman, Stig and Nils Edling, editors, translated by Thomas Munch-Petersen and the Swedish Trade Council Translation and Interpreting Services, *War Experience, Self Image and National Identity: The Second World War as Myth and History,* Stockholm: The Bank of Sweden Tercentenary Foundation & Gidlunds Förlag 1997

Ekman, Stig and Åmark, Klas, editors, *Sweden's relations with Nazism, Nazi Germany and the Holocaust,* Stockholm: Almqvist & Wiksell International, 2003

Ellger, Hans, *Zwangsarbeit und weibliche Überlebensstratagien: Die Geschichte der Frauenaussenlager des Konzentrationslagers Neuengamme 1944/45,* Berlin: Metropol Verlag 2007

Enever, Ted, *Britain's Best Kept Secret: Ultra's Base at Bletchley Park,* Stroud, Gloucestershire: Sutton 1994/1999

Englund, Peter, translated from the Swedish by Peter Graves, *November 1942: An Intimate History of the Turning Point of World War II,* New York: Alfred A. Knopf 2023

Erdstein, Erich with Barbara Bean, *Inside The Fourth Reich: The Real Story of the Boys from Brazil,* New York: St. Martin's Press 1977

Ernst, Christoph and Ulrike Jensen, *Als letztes starb die Hoffnung: Berichte von Überleben aus dem KZ Neuengamme,* Hamburg: Rosch & Röhring 1989

Ernst, Sabine, *Lise Meitner an Otto Hahn: Briefe aus den Jahren 1912 bis 1924, Edition und Kommentierung,* Stuttgart: Wissenschaftsliche Verlagsgesellschaft mbH 1992

Eve, A.S., *Rutherford: Being the Life and Letters of the Rt Hon. Lord Rutherford, O.M.,* Cambridge: Cambridge University Press 1939

Farago, Ladislas, *The Game of the Foxes: British and German Intelligence operations and personalities which changed the course of the Second World War,* London: Hodder and Stoughton 1971 and New York: David McKay Company 1971

…, *Burn After Reading,* New York: Macfadden-Bartell 1966/63

Farmelo, Graham, *Churchill's Bomb: How the United States Overtook Britain in the First Nuclear Arms Race,* New York: Basic Books 2013

…, *The Strangest Man: The Hidden Life of Paul Dirac, Mystic of the Atom,* New York: Basic Perseus 2009

Ferguson, Harry, *Operation Kronstadt: The True Story of Honor, Espionage, and the Rescue of Britain's Greatest Spy, The Man with a Hundred Faces,* New York: Overlook Press 2008

Fermi, Laura *Atoms in the Family,* Chicago: U of Chicago Press 1954

Fest, Joachim C., translated from the German by Richard and Clara Winston, *Hitler,* New York: Harcourt Brace Jovanovich 1974

Ferry, Georgina, *Dorothy Crowfoot Hodgkin: Patterns, Proteins and Peace: A Life In Science,* London: Bloomsbury 1998/2019

Feynman, Richard P., *Surely You're Joking, Mr. Feynman: Adventures of a Curious Character,* New York: Bantam Books 1985

Fine, Melanie, *Fission Girl: Lise Meitner's Escape From Nazi Germany And Her Untold Role In The Manhattan Project,* Bolton, ON: Amazon.ca 2017

FitzGibbon, Constantine, *Secret Intelligence in the Twentieth Century,* New York: Stein & Day 1976

Flammersfeld, Arnold, *Lise Meitner* in *Gedächtnisausstellung zum 100. Geburtstag von Albert Einstein, Otto Hahn, Max von Laue, Lise Meitner,* Berlin: Staatsbibliothek Preussischer Kulturbesitz 1979

Fleming, Donald and Bernard Bailyn, editors, *The Intellectual Migration: Europe and America 1930-1960,* Cambridge MA: Harvard University Press Belknap 1969

Fleming, Ian, *The Penguin 007 Collection: 14 James Bond Novels,* London: Penguin Books Ltd. 2006

Fleming, Kate, *Celia Johnson: A Biography,* London: Weidenfeld & Nicolson 1991

Fleming, Peter, *The Fate of Admiral Kolchak,* London: Rupert Hart-Davis 1963

Flannery, H.W., *Assignment to Berlin:* London: Michael Joseph Ltd. 1942

Fölsing, Albrecht, *Albert Einstein: A Biography,* New York: Viking Penguin 1997

Foot, M.R.D., *SOE: The Special Operations Executive 1940-1946,* London: British Broadcasting Corporation 1984

…, *Resistance: Europe Resistance to Nazism 1940-1945,* New York: McGraw-Hill 1977

Foot, M.R.D. and J.M. Langley, *MI9: Escape and Evasion 1939-1945,* Boston, Toronto: Little Brown & Company 1979

Ford, Henry, *The International Jew: Complete Four Volumes,* being editorials in *The Dearborn Independent,* Lexington, KY: Eternal Sun Books 2017

Forshaw, Barry, *The Man Who Left Too Soon: The Biography of Stieg Larsson,* Melbourne, Victoria: Wilkinson Publishing 2010

Fort, Adrian, *Prof: the Life of Frederick Lindemann,* London: Jonathan Cape 2003

Frank, Sir Charles, *Operation Epsilon: The Farm Hall Transcripts,* London: Institute of Physics Publishing 1993

Frank, Johannes, *Eva Braun: Ein ungewohliches Frauenschicksal in gesichtlich bewegter Zeit,* Coburg: NATION EUROPA Verlag GmbH 1999

Franks, Lucinda, *My Father's Secret War: A Memoir,* New York: Hyperion 2007

…, *Timeless: Love, Morgenthau and Me,* New York: Sarah Crichton Books, Farrar Strauss & Giroux 2014

Fraser-Smith, Charles, with Kevin Logan, *Secret Warriors: Hidden Heroes of MI6, OSS, MI9, SOE and SAS,* Crescent, Exeter: The Paternoster Press 1984

Frayn, Michael (1998), *Copenhagen,* New York: Anchor Books Random House 2000

Freeman, Kerin, *The Civilian Bomb Disposing Earl: Jack Howard & Bomb Disposal in WW2,* Barnsley, South Yorkshire: Pen & Sword Books Ltd 2015

French, A.P. and Kennedy, P.J., editors, *Niels Bohr: A Centenary Volume,* Cambridge: Harvard University Press 1985

Freud, Sigmund, *die Traumdeutung,* Frankfurt am Main: S. Fischer Verlag 1900/42/68

Friedlander, Saul, abridged by Orna Kenan, *Nazi Germany and the Jews 1933-1945,* New York: Harper Perennial 2009

Friedman, Ina R., *Flying Against the Wind: The Story of a Young Woman Who Defied the Nazis,* Brookline MA: Lodgepole Press 1995

Frisch, Otto R., F.A. Paneth, F. Laves and P. Rosbaud, *Beiträge zur Physik und Chemie des 20. Jahrhunderts: Lise Meitner, Otto Hahn, Max von Laue,* Braunschweig: Friedr. Vieweg & Sohn 1959

Frisch, Otto R. et al, *Trends in Atomic Physics: Essays dedicated to LISE MEITNER, OTTO HAHN, MAX von LAUE on the occasion of their 80th birthday,* New York: Interscience Publishers 1959

Frisch, Otto R., *What Little I Remember,* Cambridge: Cambridge University Press 1979

Fritz, Martin et al, *The Adaptable Nation: Essays in Swedish Economy during the Second World War,* Stockholm: Almqvist & Wiksell International 1982

Fry, Helen, *The Walls Have Ears: The Greatest Intelligence Operation of World War II,* New Haven: Yale University Press 2019

…, *MI9, A History of the Secret Service for Escape and Evasion in World War Two,* New Haven: Yale University Press 2020

Fullilove, Michael, *Rendezvous With Destiny: How Franklin D. Roosevelt and Five Extraordinary Men Took America into the War and into the World,* New York: The Penguin Press 2013

Gabrielsson, Eva with Marie-Francoise Colombani, translated from the French by Linda Coverdale, *Stieg & Me: Memories of my Life with Stieg Larsson,* London: Orion 2012

Gallagher, Thomas, *Assault in Norway: The famous commando mission that changed the course of history,* New York: Harcourt Brace 1975 and 2002 Lyons Press edition *Assault in Norway: Sabotaging the Nazi Nuclear Program*

Garbe, Detlef et al, *Gedenkstätten in Hamburg: Ein Wegweiser zu Stätten der Erinnerung an die Jahre 1933-1945,* Hamburg: KZ Gedenkstätte Neuengamme, Landeszentrale für politische Bildung 2003

Garcia, Juan Pujol & Nigel West, *Operation Garbo: The Personal Story of the Most Successful Spy of World War II,* London: Biteback Publishing Ltd. 2011 (1985)

Garlinski, Josef, *The Enigma War: The Inside Story of the German Enigma Codes and How the Allies Broke Them,* New York: Charles Scribner's Sons 1979

Gedye, G.E.R., *Fallen Bastions: The Central European Tragedy,* London: Victor Gollancz Left Book Club Edition, Not For Sale to the Public 1939

Gellhorn, Martha, *The Face of War,* New York: Grove Press 1959/1988

Gellhorn, Martha and Virginia Cowles, *Love Goes to Press,* 2nd edition, Lincoln and London: U of Nebraska Press 2008 (1945, introduction by Martha Gellhorn 1995)

Gellhorn, Martha, *Selected Letters of Martha Gellhorn, edited by Caroline Moorehead,* New York: Henry Holt and Company 2006

Gerlach, Walther and Dietrich Hahn, *Otto Hahn: Ein Forscherleben unserer Zeit,* Stuttgart: Wissenschaftliche Verlagsgesellschaft mbH 1984

Ghose, Shohini, *Her Space, Her Time: How Trailblazing Women Scientists Decoded the Hidden Universe,* Toronto: Penguin Random House Canada 2023

Gilbert, Martin, *Auschwitz and the Allies,* London: Michelin House 1981

…, *Kristallnacht: Prelude to Destruction,* New York: Harper-Collins 2006

…, *Churchill and the Jews,* Toronto: McClelland & Stewart Emblem 2008

Gill, Anton, *An Honourable Defeat: A History of German Resistance of Hitler, 1933-1945,* New York: Henry Holt 1994

Gilmour, John, *Sweden, the Swastika and Stalin: The Swedish Experience in the Second World War,* Edinburgh: Edinburgh University Press 2011

Gimpel, Erich, Agent 146, *Erich Gimpel: Spion für Deutschland,* München: Süddeutsche Verlag 1960

Giron, Aug., Editor in Chief (Huvudredaktor), *Kungl. Sjökrigsskolan 1867-1942 Minneskrift utgiven med anledning av Kungl. Sjökrigsskolan 75- årsjubileum hösten 1942, Första delen,* Eskilstuna, Sweden: Aktiebogalet L.D. Oberg & Sons 1942

Giroud, Francoise, translated by R.M. Stock, *Alma Mahler or the Art of Being Loved,* New York: Oxford University Press 1991

Glees, Anthony, *The Secrets of the Service: The Story of Soviet Subversion of Western Intelligence,* New York: Carrol & Graf 1987

Gleeson, James, *They Feared No Evil: The Woman Agents of Britain's Secret Armies 1939-1945,* London: Corgi Books 1978/76

Gold, Alison Leslie, *The Devil's Mistress: The Woman who lived and died with Hitler,* Boston: Faber and Faber 1997

Goldsmith, Maurice, *Frédéric Jolio-Curie: a biography,* London: Lawrence and Wishart 1976

Gordin, Michael D., *Einstein in Bohemia,* Princeton NJ: Princeton UP 2020

Gordon, David L., and Boyden Dangerfield, *The Hidden Weapon: The Story of Economic Warfare,* New York: Harper & Brothers 1947

Gosling, F.G., *The Manhattan Project: Making the Atomic Bomb,* Washington DC: Office of History and Heritage Resources, Executive Secretary, Office of Management, Department of Energy, January 2010

Goudsmit, Samuel A., *Alsos,* New York: Henry Schuman Inc. 1947

Gourley, Catherine, *War, Women and the News: How Female Journalists Won the Battle to Cover World War II,* New York: Atheneum 2007

Gowing, Margaret, *Britain and Atomic Energy 1939-1945,* Basingstoke, Hampshire: Palgrave, United Kingdom Atomic Energy Authority 1964

Gowing, Margaret and Arnold, Lorna, *The Atomic Bomb,* London: Butterworths 1979

Görtemaker, Heike B., translated from the German by Damian Searls, *Eva Braun: Life with Hitler,* New York: Random House Vintage Books 2012

Granatstein, J.L. & David Stafford, *Spy Wars: Espionage and Canada from Gouzenko to Glasnost,* Toronto: Key Porter Books Limited 1990

Graves, Diane, *In The Company Of Sisters: Canada's Women In The War Zone, 1914-1919,* Robin Brass Studio Inc. 2021

Griehl, Manfred and Joachim Dressel, *German Heavy Bombers,* Atglen, PA: Schiffer Military/Aviation History 1994

Gross, Leonard, *The Last Jews in Berlin,* New York: Simon & Schuster 1982

Groves, General Leslie M., *Now It Can Be Told: The Story of the Manhattan Project with a new introduction by Edward Teller,* Da Capo Press 1983.

Gregor, Neil, *Daimler Benz in the Third Reich,* New Haven & London: Yale University Press 1998

Grunwald, Max, *History of Jews in Vienna*, Philadelphia: The Jewish Publication Society of America 1936

Gubbins, Major-General Colin, *The Art of Guerilla Warfare,* SOE 1940

Gun, Nevin E., *Eva Braun: Hitler's Mistress,* London: Leslie Frewin 1968

Haffner, Sebastian (1979), *The Meaning of Hitler,* London: Phoenix 2003

Hager, Thomas, *The Alchemy of Air,* New York: Broadway Books 2008

Hahn, Otto, *Mein Leben: Mensch und Wissenschaftler Unserer Zeit,* München: Bruckmann 1968

Hahn, Otto, translated and edited by William Ley, *Otto Hahn: A Scientific Autobiography,* London: McGibbon & Kee 1968

Hahn, Otto, *My Life,* translated by Ernst Kaiser and Eithne Wilkins, London: MacDonald 1970

Haines, Joe, *Maxwell,* Boston: Houghton Mifflin 1988

Haldane, R.A., *The Hidden World,* London: Robert Hale & Company 1976

Halton, David, *Dispatches From The Front: Matthew Halton, Canada's Voice At War,* Toronto: McClelland & Stewart 2014

Halton, Matthew, *Ten Years To Alamein,* London: Lindsay Drummond 1944

Hamann, Brigitte, *Hitler's Vienna: A Dictator's Apprenticeship,* New York: Oxford UP 1999

Hambro, C.J., *I Saw It Happen In Norway,* New York: D. Appleton Century 1940

Hamilton, Janet, *Lise Meitner: Pioneer of Nuclear Fission,* Berkeley Heights, NJ: Enslow Publishers 2002

Handel, Michael J., editor, *Strategic and Operational Deception in the Second World War,* London: Frank Cass 1987

Hansen, Dr. Reimer, *Lise Meitner: Eine Würdigung,* Berlin: Hahn-Meitner–Institut 1989

Hansen, Ron, *Hitler's Niece: A Novel,* New York: HarperCollins 1999

Hardy Dorman, Angelia, *Martha Gellhorn: Myth, Motif and Remembrance,* Charleston, SC: JettDrive Publications 2015

Hardy, Ann and Lore Sexl, *Lise Meitner,* Hamburg: Rowohlt Taschenbuch GmbH 2002

Harling, Robert, *Ian Fleming: A Personal Memoir,* London: The Robson Press 2015

Harris, Larry and Brian Taylor, *Escape to Honour,* Toronto: Macmillan 1984

Harris, Robert, *V2,* London: Hutchinson 2020

Hartcup, Guy, *The Challenge of War: Britain's Scientific and Engineering Contributions to World War Two,* New York: Taplinger Publishing Company 1970

Hastings, Max, *All Hell Let Loose: The World at War 1939-1945,* London: HarperPress 2011

…, *The Secret War: Spies, Codes and Guerillas 1939-1945,* London: William Collins 2015

Haufler, Hervie, *Codebreakers: How the Allied Cryptographers Won World War II,* New York: Penguin New American Library 2003

Hauge, E.O. (1955), translated from Norwegian by Major Malcolm Munthe, *Salt Water Thief: The Odd Life of Odd Starheim,* Bungay, Suffolk: Richard Clay and. Co. Ltd. 1958

Haukelid, Knut, *Skis Against the Atom: The exciting first-hand account of heroism and daring sabotage during the Nazi occupation of Norway,* Minot, North Dakota: North American Heritage Press 1989

Hayes, Peter, *Industry and Ideology: IG Farben in the Nazi Era,* Cambridge and New York: Cambridge University Press 1987, 2001

…, *From Cooperation to Complicity: Degussa In The Third Reich,* Cambridge UK: Cambridge University Press 2004

Hayman, Ronald, *Hitler + Geli,* London: Bloomsbury Publishing 1997

Heiden, Konrad, translated by Ralph Manheim, *Der Fuehrer: Hitler's Rise To Power,* London: Victor Gollancz Ltd 1944

Heinemann-Grüder, Andreas, *Die Sowjetische Atombombe,* Münster: Verlag Westfälisches Dampfboot 1992

Heisenberg, Werner, *Physics and Beyond: Encounters and Conversations,* New York: Harper & Row Torchback 1972

Hellstedt, Leone McGregor, editor, *Women Physicians of the World: autobiographies of medical pioneers,* Washington and London: Hemisphere McGraw Hill 1979

Helm, Sarah, *A Life In Secrets: Vera Atkins and the Missing Agents of WWII,* New York: Doubleday 2005

Henderson, Sir Neville, *Failure of a Mission: Berlin 1937-1939,* New York: G.P. Putnam's Sons 1940

Hephaestus Books 2017, *Swedish Spies* (pamphlet)

Hepp, Ernst Adolf, *State Department Special Interrogation Mission,* Wiesbaden: U.S. Department of State Oct. 5, 1945, declassified December 1, 1950

Hermann, Armin, *The New Physics: The Route Into The Atomic Age, In Memory of Albert Einstein, Max Von Laue, Otto Hahn, Lise Meitner,* Munich: Heinz Moos Verlag 1979

…, *Die Neue Physik, Der Weg in Der Atomzeitalter, Zum Gedenken an Albert Einstein, Max von Laue, Otto Hahn, Lise Meitner,* München: Heinz Moos Verlag 1979

…, *Die Jahrhundertwissenschaft: Werner Heisenberg und die Physik seiner Zeit,* Stuttgart: Deutsche Verlags-Anstalt 1977

Hertig, Arthur T., M.D., *Human Trophoblast,* Springfield, IL: Charles C. Thomas 1968

Hewlett, Richard G., and Oscar E. Anderson, Jr., *The New World, 1939/1946: Volume I, A History of the United States Atomic Energy Commission,* University Park, PA: The Pennsylvania State University Press 1962

Hilmes, Oliver, translated by Donald Arthur, *Malevolent Muse: The Life of Alma Mahler,* Lebanon, NH: Northeastern University Press 2015

Himmler, Katrin, translated by Michael Mitchell, *The Himmler Brothers: A Family History,* London: Macmillan Pan 2008

Hinshaw, David, *Sweden: Champion of Peace,* New York: G.P. Putnam's Sons 1949

Hinsley, FH; Thomas, EE; Ransom, DFG; Knight, RC; *British Intelligence in the Second World War, Volume 1,* London: Her Majesty's Stationery Office 1979

..., *British Intelligence in the Second World War: Its Influence on Strategy and Operations, Volume II,* New York: Cambridge University Press 1981

..., *British Intelligence in the Second World War: Its Influence on Strategy and Operations, Volume III, Part 1,* New York: Cambridge University Press 1985

..., *British Intelligence in the Second World War: Its Influence on Strategy and Operations, Volume III, Part 2,* New York: Cambridge University Press 1988

..., *British Intelligence in the Second World War: Its Influence on Strategy and Operations, Volume IV,* New York: Cambridge University Press 1990

..., *British Intelligence in the Second World War: Its Influence on Strategy and Operations, Volume V,* Cambridge University Press 1990-07-01

Hinsley, F.H. and Stripp, Alan, editors, *Codebreakers: The inside story of Bletchley Park,* New York: Oxford University Press 1993/2001 paperback

Hirsch, Pam, *The Constant Liberal: The Life and Work of Phyllis Bottome,* London: Quartet Books Ltd. 2010 (dedicated and signed by the author)

Hirsch-Heisenberg, Anna Maria, editor, translated by Irene Heisenberg, *My Dear Li: Werner & Elisabeth Heisenberg,* New Haven: Yale University Press 2016

Hirschfeld, Wolfgang as told to Geoffrey Brooks, *Hirschfeld: The Story of a U-Boat NCO 194-1946,* Barnesly, South Yorkshire: Leo Cooper 1996

Hitler, Adolf, translated by Ralph Manheim, *Mein Kampf,* Boston: Houghton Mifflin 1943

Hitz, Frederick P., *The Great Game: The Myth and Reality of Espionage,* New York: Alfred A. Knopf 2004

Hodges, Andrew (1983), *Alan Turing: The Enigma,* London: Vintage Books 2014

Hoffman, Banesh, with the collaboration of Helen Dukas, *Albert Einstein, Creator and Rebel,* New York: Viking 1972

Hoffman, Klaus, *Otto Hahn: Achievement and Responsibility,* New York: Springer Verlag 2001

Hogg, Ian V., *German Secret Weapons of World War II: The Missiles, Rockets, Weapons and New Technology of the Third Reich,* New York: Skyhorse Publishing 2016

Holt, Thaddeus, *The Deceivers: Allied Military Deception in the Second World War,* New York: Scribner Lisa Drew 2004

Hopp, John, *Die Hölle in der Idylle: Das Aussenlager Alt Garge des KZ Neuengamme Erweiterte Neuausgabe,* Hamburg: VSA Verlag 1987 & 1993

Horn, Bernd, *A Most Ungentlemanly Way of War: The SOE and the Canadian Connection,* Toronto: Dundurn Press 2016

Houghton, Vince, *The Nuclear Spies: America's Atomic Intelligence Operation Against Hitler and Stalin,* Ithaca and London: Cornell University Press 2019+

Howard, Michael, *British Intelligence in the Second World War, Volume 5,* London: Her Majesty's Stationery Office 1990

Howarth, David, *The Shetland Bus,* London: Thomas Nelson & Sons 1951

Howarth, Patrick, *Intelligence Chief Extraordinary: The Life of the Ninth Duke of Portland,* London: The Bodley Head Ltd. 1986

Howe, Ellic, *The Black Game: British Subversive Operations Against the Germans During the Second World War,* London: Michael Joseph 1982

Howes, Ruth H. & Herzenberg, Caroline L., *Their Day in the Sun: Women of the Manhattan Project,* Philadelphia: Temple University Press 1999

Hoy, Hugh Cleland, *40 O.B., How The War Was Won,* London: Hutchinson 1932

Hughes-Wilson, *The Secret State,* New York: Pegasus 2016

Hunt, Sir David, *A Don At War: Revised edition with new introduction,* London: Frank Cass 1990

Huntford, Roland, *The New Totalitarians,* London: Alan Lane 1975

Hyde, H. Montgomery, *The Quiet Canadian: The Secret Service Story of Sir William Stephenson (Intrepid),* London: Constable 1962

…, *Room 3603: The Story of the British Intelligence Center in New York during World War II,* New York: Farrar, Strauss & Company 1963

…, *Cynthia: The Spy Who Changed the Course of the War,* London: Hamish Hamilton 1966

…, *The Atom Bomb Spies,* London: Hamish Hamilton 1980 (dedicated to Wm. Stephenson)

…, *Secret Intelligence Agent: British Espionage in America and the Creation of the OSS,* Foreword by Sir William Stephenson ("Intrepid"), New York: St. Martin's Press 1982

Hydrick, Carter Plymton (1998), *Critical Mass: How Nazi Germany Surrendered Enriched Uranium for the United States' Atomic Bomb,* third edition, Chicago: Independent Publishers Group 2016

Infield, Glenn B., *Eva and Adolf: The Strangest Love a Woman Ever Experienced,* New York: Ballantine Books 1974

Irons, Roy, *Hitler's Terror Weapons: The Price of Vengeance,* London: HarperCollins 2002/3

Irving, David, *The Mare's Nest,* Boston & Toronto: Little Brown & Company 1964

…, *The German Atomic Bomb: The History of Nuclear Research in Nazi Germany,* New York: Da Capa Press 1967

…, David, *The Virus House: Germany's Atomic Research and Allied Counter-measures,* London: William Kimber, 1967

Isaacson, Walter, *Einstein: His Life and Universe,* New York: Simon & Schuster 2007

Isenvberg, Sheila, *A Hero of Our Own, The Story of Varian Fry, How one American in Marseille saved Marc Chagall, Max Ernst, André Breton, Hannah Arendt, and more than a thousand others from the Nazis,* New York: Random House 2001

Isitt, Benjamin, *From Victoria to Vladivostok: Canada's Siberian Expedition, 1917-1919,* Vancouver: UBC Press 2010.

Ismay, H.L., Lord, *The Memoirs of General the Lord Ismay,* London: Heinemann 1960

Istria, Cico Jr., Natal, Rio Grande do Norte (Brasil): *Missione Alsos* 2016

Jackson, Sophie, *Churchill's White Rabbit: The True Story of a Real-Life James Bond,* Stroud, Gloucestershire: The History Press 2012

…, *SOE's Balls of Steel: Operation Bubble, 147 Willing Volunteers and 25,000 Tons of Ball Bearings,* Stroud, Gloucestershire: The History Press 2013

Jacobsen, Annie, *Operation Paperclip: The Secret Intelligence Program That Brought Nazi Scientists to America,* New York: Back Bay Books, Little Brown 2014

Jacobsen, Hans-Adolf, *Kriegstagebuch des Oberkommandos der Wehrmacht (Wehrmachtführungsstab) Band I: 1.August 1940 – 31 Dezember 1941,* Frankfurt am Main: Bernard & Graefe Verlag für Wehrwehsen 1965…, *1939, 1945, Der Zweite Weltkrieg in Chronik und Dokumenten,* Darmstadt: Wehr un Wissen Verlagsgesellschaft mbH 1959 (2 copies, 1959 & 1965 editions, different notes in each)

Jacobsen, Hans-Adolf and Hans Dollinger, *Der Zweite Weltkrieg in Bildern und Dokumenten,* München: Verlag Kurt Desch GmbH 1965

James, Robert Rhodes, *"Chips": The Diaries of Sir Henry Channon,* London: Weidenfeld 1993

Janik, Allan & Stephen Toulmin, *Wittgenstein's Vienna,* New York: Simon & Schuster 1973

Jeffery, Keith, *The Secret History of MI-6, 1909-1949,* New York: Penguin 2010

Jeffreys, Diarmuid, *Hell's Cartel: IG Farben and the Making of Hitler's War Machine,* London: Bloomsbury 2008

Johnson, Brian, *The Secret War,* London: British Broadcasting Corporation 1978

Jones, R.V., *Most Secret War: British Intelligence 1939-1945,* London: Hodder & Stoughton 1979

…, *Reflections on Intelligence,* London: Mandarin Paperbacks 1990

Jörgensen, Christer, *Hitler's Espionage Machine: German intelligence agencies and operations during World War II,* London: The Brown Reference Group 2004

Josephs, Jeremy, *Swastika Over Paris: The Fate of the Jews in France,* New York: Little, Brown Company 1989

Jung, Carl G., translated by R.F.C. Hull, *Aspects of the Feminine,* Princeton, NJ: Princeton University Press 1982

…, *Modern Man in Search of a Soul,* London: Harcourt, Brace and Company 1933

…, *The Wisdom of Carl Jung, Edited by Edward Hoffman, Ph.D.,* New York: Citadel Press Kensington Publishing Corp. 2003

Jung, Emma, translated by Cary F. Baynes and Hildegard Nagel, *Animus and Anima,* Putnam, Connecticut: Spring Publications 1957

Jungk, Robert, English translation by Victor Gollancz, *Brighter than a Thousand Suns: a Personal History of the Atomic Physicists,* New York: Harcourt 1956

Jungk, Peter Stephan, translated from the German by Anselm Hollo, *Franz Werfel: A Life in Prague, Vienna and Hollywood,* New York: Fromm International 1991

Kahn, David, *The Code Breakers: The First Comprehensive History of Secret Communications from Ancient Times to the Threshold of Outer Space,* New York: Macmilland & Co., Inc. 1967

…, *Hitler's Spies: German Military Intelligence in World War II,* New York: Macmillan 1978

Kant, Immanuel, *Kant's Critique of Judgement, translated by J.H. Bernard,* London: Macmillan 1931/1892, inside cover "Arthur K. Davis London September 27, 1944" – Art was in US Naval Intelligence then.

Karlbom, Rolf, *Sweden's iron ore exports to Germany, 1933-1944,* Scandinavian Economic History Review, 13:1, 65-93, DOI:10.1080/03585522.1965.10414365

Karlsch, Rainer, *Hitlers Bombe: die geheime Geschichte der deutschen Kernwaffenversuche,* München: Deutsche Verlags-Anstalt 2005

Karlsch, Rainer & Zbynek Zeman, *Urangeheimnesse: Das Erzgebirge im Brennpunkt der Weltpolitik 1933-1960,* Berlin: BEBUG mbH/Edition Berolina 2016

Kean, Sam, *The Bastard Brigade: The True Story of the Renegade Scientists and Spies Who Sabotaged the Nazi Atomic Bomb,* London: Hodder & Stoughton 2019

Kelly, Cynthia C., editor, *The Manhattan Project,* New York: Black Dog & Leventhal Publishers 2003

Kennedy, J.F. *Why England Slept,* New York: Wilfred Funk 1940

Kennedy, Ludovic, *Pursuit: The Sinking of the Bismarck,* London: Book Club Associates 1975

Kennedy, Michael, *Mahler,* London: J.M. Dent & Sons 1990

Kennedy, William P., *United States Historical Museum: Yearbook 1947,* Washington DC 1948

Kerner, Charlotte, *Lise, Atomphysikerin: Die Lebensgeschichte der Lise Meitner,* Weinheim und Basel: Beltz Verlag 1986

Kerner, Charlotte, *Lise, Atomphysikerin: Die Lebensgeschichte der Lise Meitner,* Weinheim und Basel: Beltz Verlag 1986

Kerr, Philip, *Prussian Blue,* New York: G.P. Putnam's Sons 2017

Kershaw, Ian, *Making Friends With Hitler: Lord Londonderry, the Nazis and the Road to War,* New York: The Penguin Press 2004

Kiernan, Denise, *The Girls of Atomic City: The Untold Story of the Women Who Helped Win World War II,* New York: Touchstone 2013

Killen, John, *A History of the Luftwaffe: From Richtofen's Flying Circus to the Cockpit of the Me262,* Toronto: Bantam Books 1967/86

Kilzer, Louis, *Hitler's Traitor: Martin Bormann and the Defeat of the Reich,* Novato CA: Presidio 2000

Klein, Alexander, *The Counterfeit Traitor,* New York: Henry Holt and Company 1958

Klinkenberg, Wim, *De Ultracentrifuge 1937-1970: Hitlers bom voor Strauss?,* Amsterdam: Boekhandel Van Gennep NV 1971

Knopp, Guido, *Hitler's Women – and Marlene, Translated by Angus McGeoch,* Thrupp, Stroud, Gloucestershire: Sutton Publishing Limited 2001/2003

Koblik, Steven, *The Stones Cry Out: Sweden's Response to the Persecution of the Jews 1933-1945,* New York: Holocaust Library 1988

…, *Sweden: The Neutral Victor,* Stockholm: Scandinavian University Books 1972

Koblik, Steven, translated by Joanne Johnson and Steven Koblik, *Sweden's Development from Poverty to Affluence, 1750-1970,* Minneapolis: University of Minnesota Press 1975

Kokoschka, Oskar, translated from *Spur Im Treibsand* by Eithne Wilkins and Ernst Kaiser, London: Thames & Hudson 1962

Kokoschka, Oskar, translated from the German by David Britt, *My Life,* London: Thames & Hudson 1974

Krafft, Fritz, *Im Schatten der Sensation: Leben und Wirken von Fritz Strassman,* Weinheim: Verlag Chemie 1981

…, *Ein frühes Beispiel interdisziplinärer Teamarbeit : Zur Entdeckung der Kernspaltung durch Hahn, Meitner and Strassman, (I) Phys. Bl. 36 Nr.4 and (II) Nr.5,* Weinheim: Physik Verlag GmbH, 22 Februar 1980

…, *Im Schatten der Sensation – Tabellarischur Lebenslauf,* Weinheim: Verlag Chemie 1981

Krafft, Prof. Dr. Fritz & Prof. Dr. Adolph Meyer-Abich, *Grosse Naturwissenschaftler: Biographisches Lexikon,* Frankfurt am Main & Hamburg: Fischer Bucherei GmbH 1970

Kragh, Helge, *Quantum Generations: A History of Physics in the Twentieth Century,* Princeton, NJ: Princeton UP 1999

Kramish, Arnold, *Griffin: The Greatest Untold Espionage Story of World War II,* Boston: Houghton Mifflin 1986

Krause-Brewer, Fides, editor, *Als Hitler kam: 50 Jahre nach dem 30.Januar 1933: Erinnerungen prominenter Augenzeugen,* Berlin: Herder Taschenbuch 1982

Krenz, Kim, *Deep Waters: The Ottawa River and Canada's Nuclear Adventure,* Montreal & Kingston: McGill – Queen's University Press 2004

Krosby, H. Peter, *Finland, Germany and the Soviet Union 1940-1941,The Petsamo Dispute,* Madison, WI: U of Wisconsin Press 1968

…, *Finland, Germany and the Soviet Union 1940-1941, The Petsamo Dispute,* Madison, WI: U of Wisconsin Press 1968

Kunetka, James, *The General and the Genius: Groves and Oppenheimer-the Unlikely Partnership That Built the Atomic Bomb,* Washington DC: Regnery History Salem Communications 2015

Kurowski, Franz, *Allierte Jagd auf deutsche Wissenschaftler: Das Unternehmen Paperclip,* München: Kristall be Langen-Müller 1982

Kurzman, Dan, *Blood and Water: Sabotaging Hitler's Bomb,* New York: Henry Holt 1997

Labatut, Benjamin, *When We Cease To Understand The World,* New York: New York Review of Books 2020

Lagercrantz, David, continuing Stieg Larsson's Millennium Series, translated from the Swedish by George Goulding, *The Girl in the Spider's Web,* Toronto: Viking 2015

Lambert, Angela, *The Lost Life of Eva Braun,* New York: St. Martin's Press 2006

Lampe, David, *The Last Ditch: Britain's Secret Resistance and the Nazi Invasion Plans,* Barnsley, South Yorkshire: Skyhorse Publishing 1968/2007

Lampton, Christopher, *Wernher von Braun,* New York: Franklin Watts 1988

Langer, Walter C., *The Mind of Adolf Hitler: The Secret Wartime Report,* New York: Basic Books 1972

Langley, Mike, *Anders Lassen, VC, MC of the SAS: The story of Anders Lassen and the men who fought with him,* London: Hodder & Stoughton 1988

Lanouette, William with Bela Silard, *Genius in the Shadows: A Biography of Leo Szilard, the Man Behind the Bomb,* New York : Skyhorse 2013

Laqueur, Walter, *A World of Secrets: The Uses and Limits of Intelligence,* New York: Basic Books 1985

Laqueur, Walter and Breitmen, Richard, *Breaking The Silence: The story of Eduard Schulte, the German industrialist who risked everything to oppose the Nazis and was the first to tell the world of the fate of the Jews in Hitler's Europe,* New York: Simon & Schuster 1986

Large, David Clay, *Nazi Games: The Olympics of 1936,* New York: Norton & Company 2007

Larson, Erik, *In The Garden of Beasts: Love, Terror and an American Family in Hitler's Berlin,* New York: Crown 2011

Larsson, Stieg, translated from the Swedish by Reg Keeland,*The Girl With The Dragon Tattoo,* Toronto: Viking 2008

..., translated from the Swedish by Reg Keeland, *The Girl Who Played With Fire,* Toronto: Penguin Canada 2010

..., translated from the Swedish by Reg Keeland, *The Girl Who Kicked The Hornet's Nest,* Toronto: Viking 2009

Latimer, Jon, *Deception in War,* London: John Murray 2001

Le Carré, J., *Tinker, Tailor, Soldier, Spy,* New York: Bantam 1975

..., *A Perfect Spy,* Markham, ON; Penguin Books 1986/7

Lee, Sabine, *Sir Rudolf Peierls: Selected Private and Scientific Correspondence, Volumes 1 & 2,* London: World Scientific 2009

Leitz, Christian and David J. Dunthorn, *Spain: In An International Context 1936-1959,* New York: Bergbahn Books 1999

Lemmerich, Jost, *Mass und Messen: Ausstellung aus Anlass der Gründung der Physikalisch –Technischen Reichsanstalt am 28.März 1887,* Berlin: Staatsbibliothek Preussischer Kulturbesitz 1987

..., *Die Geschichte der Entdeckung der Kernspaltung,* Berlin: Technische Universität 1989

..., *Bande der Freundschaft: Lise Meitner-Elisabeth Schiemann Kommentierter Briefwechsel 1911-1947,* Wien: Österreichische Akademie der Wissenschaften 2010

Lett, Brian, *Ian Fleming & SOE's Operation Postmaster: The Untold Top Secret Story,* York-Philadelphia: Penn & Sword 2012/2020

Levine, Paul A., *From Indifference to Activism: Swedish Diplomacy and the Holocaust 1938-1944,* Uppsala: dissertation for PhD degree, Uppsala University 1996

Lewin, Ronald, *Ultra Goes To War: The Secret Story,* London: Hutchinson 1978

..., *Ultra Goes To War: The First Account of War II's Greatest Secret, Based on Official Documents,* London: Hutchinson 1978

Libby, Leona Marshall, *The Uranium People: The human story of the Manhattan Project by the woman who was the youngest member of the original scientific team,* New York: Crane, Russak & Company, Charles Scribner's Sons 1979

Lidegaard, Bo, *Landsmänn: De Danska Judarnas Flykt 1 Oktober 1943,* translation to Swedish by Margareta Eklöf, Pössneck, Germany: Albert Bonniers Förlag 2013

Lindberg, Hans, *Svensk flyktingpolitik under internationellt tryck 1936-1941,* Stockholm: Allmänna Förlaget 1973

Lochery, Neill, *Lisbon: War in the Shadows of the City of Light, 1939-1945,* New York: Public Affairs Perseus 2011

Lockhart, R.H. Bruce, *Memoirs of a British Agent,* London: Macmillan 1932 and 1974, Folio Society 2003

Lockhart, Sydney, *First in Her Class; Pioneering Feminist Grace Lockhart,* Alliston, ON: Canada's History magazine Dec. 2021-Jan, 2022, pages 38-41

Lockot, Regine, *Errinern und Durcharbeiten: Zur Geschichte der Psychoanalyse und Psychotherapie im Nationalsozialismus,* Frankfurt am Main: Fischer Taschenbuch Verlag 1985

Lodenius, Anna-Lena, and Larsson, Stieg, *Extremhögern,* Stockholm: Tidens Förlag 1991

Loftis, Larry, *Code Name: Lise,The True Story of the Woman Who Became WWII's Most Highly Decorated Spy,* New York: Simon & Schuster Gallery 2019

Loggie, Ruth, edited by Ross Hebb, *A Canadian Nurse in the Great War: The Diaries of Ruth Loggie, 1915-1916,* Halifax, NS: Nimbus Publishing Limited 2021

Lovell, Mary S., *Cast No Shadow: The Life of the American Spy Who Changed the Course of World War II,* New York: Pantheon 1992

Lownie, Andrew, *Traitor King: The Scandalous Exile of the Duke and Duchess of Windsor,* New York: Pegasus Books, Ltd. 2022

Lucas, Amand, translated from the French by Milton W. Cole and Stéphane Coutu, *The Bomb and the Swastika,* Middletown, DE: Crossocean Publishing 2011

Lundmark, Thomas, *The Untold Story of Eva Braun,* USA: Thomas Lundmark 2010

…, *Eva Braun: Her Life and Times, 1912-1945,* Roseville MN: Birch Grove Publishing 2019

Lycett, A., *Ian Fleming,* London: Phoenix 1996

Macdonald, Bill, *The True Intrepid: Sir William Stephenson and the Unknown Agents,* Surrey, BC: Timberholme Books 1998

Machtan, Lothar, *The Hidden Hitler,* translated by John Brownjohn, New York: Perseus Books 2001

Macintyre, Ben, *Agent Zigzag: A True Story of Nazi Espionage, Love, and Betrayal,* Crown Publishing Broadway Paperbacks, 2007

…, *Double Cross: The True Story of the D-Day Spies,* New York: Crown Random House 2012

…, *For Your Eyes Only: Ian Fleming & James Bond,* New York: Bloomsbury USA 2008

…, *Operation Mincemeat:* New York: Harmony Books 2010

…, *Rogue Heroes: The History of the SAS, Britain's Secret Special Forces Unit That Sabotaged the Nazis and Changed the Nature of War,* New York: Ben MacIntyre Books Penguin Random House 2016

MacKenzie, Norman & Jeanne, *The Time Traveller: The Life of H.G. Wells,* London: Weidenfeld & Nicolson 1973

Mackenzie, W.J.M., *The Secret History of S.O.E.: Special Operations Executive, 1940-1945,* London: St. Ermin's Press 2002/2000

MacLaren, Roy, *Canadians Behind Enemy Lines 1939-1945,* Vancouver: U of BC Press 1981

MacPherson, Malcolm C., *Time Bomb: Fermi, Heisenberg, and the Race for the Atomic Bomb,* New York: Berkley Books 1986

Macrakis, Kristie, *Surviving the Swastika: Scientific Research in Nazi Germany,* New York: Oxford UP 1998

MacRae, Stuart, *Winston Churchill's Toyshop,* Kineton, Warwickshire: The Roundwood Press 1971

Mahan, J. Alexander, *Vienna Of Yesterday And Today,* Vienna: Vienna Times 1928

…, *Famous Women Of Vienna,* Vienna: Halm and Goldmann 1930/29

Mahl, Thomas E., *Desperate Deception: British Covert Operations in the United States,1939-1944,* Washington and New York: Brassey's 1998

Mahler, Alma (1940), translated by Basil Creighton, *Gustav Mahler: Memories and Letters,* London: Cardinal 1990

Mahler-Werfel, Alma, selected and translated by Anthony Beaumont, *Alma Mahler-Werfel: Diaries 1898-1902,* London: Faber & Faber 1998

Mailer, Norman, *The Castle in the Forest,* New York: Random House 2007

Manchester, William, *The Arms of Krupp 1587-1986,* New York: Bantam Books 1968

Manchester, William and Paul Reid, *The Last Lion: Winston Churchill Defender of the Realm, 1940-1965,* New York: Little, Brown and Company 2012

Marks, John, *The Search for the Manchurian Candidate: The CIA and Mind Control; The Story of the Agency's Secret Efforts to Control Human Behavior,* New York: Times Books 1979

Marks, Leo, *Between Silk and Cyanide: A Codemaker's War 1941-1945,* New York: The Free Press 1998

Marneffe, Francis de, *Last Boat from Bordeaux: War Memoirs of Francis de Marneffe,* Cambridge MA: Coolidge Hill Press 2001

Martin, Roy V., *Ebb and Flow: Evacuations & Landings by Merchant Ships in WW2,* Southampton: Aerial Edition 2020

…, *The Suffolk Golding Mission: A Considerable Service,* Great Britain: Brook House Books 2014

Masterman, J.C., *The Double-Cross System in the War of 1939 to 1945,* New Haven & London: Yale University Press 1972

Masters, Anthony, *The Man Who Was M: The Life of Maxwell Knight,* London: Grafton 1984/86

Matthews, Jason, *Red Sparrow,* New York: Scribner Simon & Schuster 2013

…, *Palace of Treason,* New York: Scribner Simon & Schuster 2015

…, *The Kremlin's Candidate,* New York: Scribner Simon & Schuster 2018

Maugham, Somerset, *Ashenden,* London: Vintage Books 2000 (Heinemann 1928)

Max-Planck Gesellschaft, *Mitteilungen Heft 4, 1960,* Göttingen: Max-Planck Gesellschaft Zür Förderung Der Wissenschaften, Juni 1960

McCormick, Donald, *17F: The Life of Ian Fleming,* London: Peter Owen 1993

McCormick, Donald and Katy Fletcher, *Spy Fiction: A Connoisseur's Guide,* Oxford UK: Facts on File Limited 1990

McKay, C.G., *From Information to Intrigue: Studies in Secret Service based on the Swedish Experience, 1939-1945,* London: Frank Cass & Co., Ltd. 1993

…, *Emperor Of Spies: Onodera's Wartime Network In Europe,* Stamford, England: EOinx Books Historical Studies in Secret Intelligence 2019

McKay, Sinclair, *The Secret Life of Bletchley Park: The WWII Codebreaking Centre and the Men and Women Who Worked There,* London: Aurum Press 2010

…, *The Lost World of Bletchley Park,* London: Aurum Press 2013

McLachlan, Donald, *Room 39: Naval Intelligence in Action 1939-1945,* London: Weidenfeld and Nicolson 1968

…, *Room 39: a study in Naval Intelligence,* New York: Atheneum 1968

McLain, Paula, *Love and Ruin,* Canada: Bond Street Books 2018

McRae, Stephanie T., *World War 2 History's 10 Most Incredible Women,* PSIA 2016

Mears, Ray, *The Real Heroes of Telemark: The True Story of the Secret Mission to Stop Hitler's Atomic Bomb,* London: Hodder & Stoughton 2003

Medawar, Jean & David Pyke, *Hitler's Gift: The True Story of the Scientists Expelled by the Nazi Regime,* New York: Arcade Publishing 2012/2000

Menkis, Richard & Harold Troper, *More Than Just Games: Canada and the 1936 Olympics,* Toronto: University of Toronto Press 2015

Meitner, Lise, *Erinnerungen an Otto Hahn,* Stuttgart: Hirzel Verlag 2005

Middlebrook, Martin, *The Battle of Hamburg: Allied Bomber Forces Against a German City in 1943*, New York: Charles Scribner's Sons 1980

..., *The Peenemünde Raid: The Night of the 17-18 August 1943*, London: Penguin 1982

Middleton, W.E.K., *Physics at the National Research Council of Canada, 1929-1952*, Waterloo, ON: Wilfrid Laurier University Press 1979

Miller, David, *Athens to Athens: The Official History of the Olympic Games and the IOC, 1894-2004*, Edinburgh: Mainstream Publishing 2003

Miller, Joan, *One Girl's War*, Wolfeboro NH: Brandon 1987

Milton, Giles, *Churchill's Ministry of Ungentlemanly Warfare: The Mavericks Who Plotted Hitler's Defeat*, New York: Picador 2016

Milward, Alan S., *War, Economy and Society 1939-1945*, London: Allen Lane Penguin 1977

Minshall, Merlin, *Guilt Edged*, St. Albans, Herts: Granada Panther 1977

Monk, Ray, *Inside The Centre: The Life of J. Robert Oppenheimer*, London: Jonathan Cape 2012

Montagu, Ewen, *The Man Who Never Was: The classic story of the most daring spy plot of World War II*, Philadelphia and New York: Lippincott 1954 and London: Corgi Books Transworld Publishers Ltd. 1953/79 (also Bantam paperback 1965)

Moore, Ruth M., *Niels Bohr: The Man, His Science, and the World They Changed*, New York: Alfred A. Knopf 1966

Moore, Walter, *Schrödinger: Life and Thought*, Cambridge UK: Press Syndicate of U of Cambridge 1989

Moorehead, Caroline, *Gellhorn: A Twentieth Century Life*, New York: Henry Holt and Company 2003

..., *Selected Letters of Martha Gellhorn*, New York: Henry Holt & Company 2006

Mosley, Leonard, *The Reich Marshall: A Biography of Herman Goering*, New York: Doubleday 1974

Moss, Norman, *Klaus Fuchs: The Man Who Stole The Atom Bomb*, London: Grafton 1989

Moyzisch, L.C., *Operation Cicero: The Espionage Sensation of the War*, London: Wingate 1950

Mulley, Clare, *The Women Who Flew For Hitler: A True Story of Soaring Ambirion and Searing Rivalry*, New York: St. Martin's Press 2017

..., *The Spy Who Loved: The Secrets and Lives of Christine Granville*, New York: St. Martin's Press 2012

Mundy, Liza, *Code Girls: The Untold Story of the American Women Code Breakers of World War II*, New York: Hachette Books 2017

Munson, Kenneth, *Die Weltkrieg II – Flugzeuge: Alle Flugzeuge der Kriegführenden Mächte*, Stuttgart: Motorbuch Verlag Stuttgart 1972

Nehring, General Walther K., *Die Geschichte der Deutschen Panzerwaffe 1916-1945*, Stuttgart: Motorbuch Verlage Stuttgart 1974

Neufeld, Michael J., *The Rocket and the Reich: Peenemünde and the Coming of the Ballistic Missile Era*, New York: Simon & Schuster 1995

Newman, Bernard, *Epics of Espionage*, New York: Philosophical Library 1951

Nichols, Maj.Gen. K.D., U.S.A. (Ret.), *The Road to Trinity: A Personal Account of How America's Nuclear Policies Were Made*, New York: William Morrow 1987

Nietsche, Friedrich, translated and edited by Walter Kaufmann, *On the Genealogy of Morals & Ecce Homo*, New York: Vintage Books Random House 1967

Nolan, James L., *Atomic Doctors: Conscience and Complicity at the Dawn of the Nuclear Age,* Cambridge MA and London: Belknap Press of Harvard University Press 2020

Norman, Andrew, *The Amazing Story of Lise Meitner: Escaping the Nazis and Becoming the World's Greatest Physicist,* Barnsley, South Yorkshire: Pen and Sword Books Limited 2021

Norris, Robert S., *Racing for the Bomb: General Leslie R. Groves, the Manhattan Project's Indispensable Man,* South Royalton, Vermont: Steerforth Press L.C. 2002

Nowak, Jan, *Courier From Warsaw,* Detroit: Wayne State University Press 1982

O'Connor, Bernard, *Churchill's Most Secret Airfield: RAF Tempsford,* Stroud, Gloucestershire: Amberley Publishing 2013

O'Donnell, Patrick, *The Brenner Assignment: The Untold Story of the Most Daring Spy Mission of World War II,* Philadelphia: Da Capo Press 2008

…, *Operatives,Spies, and Saboteurs: The Unknown Story of the Men and Women of WWII's OSS,* New York: Free Press 2004

Ogilvie, Marilyn and Harvey, Joy, editors, *The Biographical Dictionary of Women in Science, Volume 2 L-Z,* New York: Routledge 2000

Öhman, Suzanne, *Wortinhalt und Weltbild: Vergleichende und methodologische Studien zu Bedeutungslehre und Wortfeldtheorie,* Stockholm: Kungl. Boktrykeriet P.A. Norstedt & Söner 1951

Oliphant, Mark, *Rutherford: Recollections of the Cambridge Days,* Amsterdam & New York: Elsevier 1972

Olsen, Oluf Reed, translated from the Norwegian by F.H. Lyon, *Two Eggs on My Plate,* Chicago: Rand McNally & Company 1953

Olson, Lynne, *Troublesome Young Men: The Rebels Who Brought Churchill To Power And Helped Save England,* Canada: Anchor Canada of Random House 2008

…, *Citizens of London: The Americans Who Stood With Britain In Its Darkest, Finest Hour,* New York: Random House 2010

O'Keefe, David, *One Day in August: The Untold Story Behind Canada's Tragedy at Dieppe,* Toronto: Alfred A Knopf Canada 2013

Ondrack, Jack, *Gold Medalist: The Annotated Autobiography of Leone McGregor Hellstedt, MD, MSc, PhD, Med.lic., DSc,* Edmonton: Alberta Bound Books 2013

Ordway, Frederick I. III and Mitchell R. Sharpe, *The Rocket Team,* William Heinemann Ltd. 1979

Overy, Richard, *Why The Allies Won,* London: Jonathan Cape 1995

Owen, David, *Battle of Wits: A history of psychology and deception in modern warfare,* London: Leo Cooper 1978

Owings, Alison, *Frauen: German Women Recall the Third Reich,* New Brunswick NJ: Rutgers University Press 1993/2011

Pais, Abraham, *Niels Bohr's Times, In Physics, Philosophy and Polity,* Oxford: Clarendon Press 1991

Parker, Matthew, *Goldeneye Where Bond Was Born: Ian Fleming's Jamaica,* New York: Pegasus Books LLC 2015

Parkin, Simon, *A Game of Birds and Wolves: The Secret Game That Won The War,* London: Hodder & Stoughton 2019

Parkinson, F., editor, *Conquering the Past: Austrian Nazism Yesterday & Today,* Detroit, MI: Wayne State University Press 1989

Pash, Boris T., *The Alsos Mission,* New York: Charter Books, 1969/80

Pauley, Bruce F., *From Prejudice to Persecution: A History of Austrian Anti-Semitism,* Chapel Hill & London: The University of North Carolina Press 1992

Payn, Graham and Sheridan Morley, editors, *The Noel Coward Diaries,* Boston Toronto: Little Brown 1982

Pearson, John, *The Life of Ian Fleming,* London: Jonathan Cape 1966

…, *Ian Fleming: The Notes,* London: Queen Anne Press 2020

Peierls, Rudolf, *Bird of Passage: Recollections of a Physicist,* Princeton: Princeton University Press 1985

Percy, Antony, *Misdefending the Realm: How MI5's Incompetence enabled Communist Subversion of Britain's Institutions during the Nazi-Soviet Pact,* Buckingham: The University of Buckingham Press 2017

Persico, Joseph E., *Piercing The Reich: The Penetration of Nazi Germany by American Secret Agents During World War II,* New York: The Viking Press 1979

…, *Roosevelt's Secret War: FDR and World War II Espionage,* New York: Random House 2002

Persson, Sune (2002), translated by Graham Long, *Escape from the Third Reich: The Harrowing Story of the Largest Rescue Effort Inside Nazi Germany,* New York: Skyhorse 2009

Petrie, Sir Charles, *King Alfonso XIII and His Age,* London: Chapman and Hall 1963

Petropolous, Jonathan, *Royals and the Reich,* New York: Oxford University Press 2009

Pfundner, Martin, *Alpine Trials & Rallies: 1910 to 1973,* Dorchester: Veloce 2005

Philipps, Roland, *A Spy Named Orphan: The Enigma of Donald MacLean,* New York: W.W.Norton 2018

Picker, Dr. Henry, *Hitlers Tischgespräche im Führerhauptquartier: Hitler, wie er wirkilich war,* Stuttgart: Seewald Verlag 1977

Picker, Dr. Henry and Heinrich Hoffmann, *Hitlers Tischgespräche im Bild,* München Berlin: F.A. Herbig Verlagsbuchhandlung 1980

Pilapil, Vicente R., *Alfonso III,* New York: Twayne Publishers 1969

Pile, Jonathan, *Churchill's Secret Enemy,* Bolton, ON: Amazon.ca, May 24, 2012

Pincher, Chapman, *Too Secret Too Long,* New York: St. Martin's Press 1984

…, *Their Trade is Treachery,* London: Sidgwick & Jackson 1981

…, *Traitors: The Labyrinths of Treason,* London: Sidgwick & Jackson 1987

Pincock, Stephen, *Codebreaker: The History of Codes and Ciphers from the Ancient Pharaohs to Quantum Cryptography,* New York: Walker & Company 2006

Polley, Von Otto M., text, and Dr. Siegfried Hartwagner, *Klagenfurt: Die Stadt Am Wörthersee,* Innsbruck-Klagenfurt-Linz: WUB 1959

Popper, Karl, *Conjectures and Refutations: The Growth of Scientific Knowledge,* London: Routledge 1963/2002

…, *The Open Society and Its Enemies: Vol. II The High Tide of Prophecy Hegel and Marx,* London: Routledge & Kegal Paul 1945/73

Powers, Thomas, *Heisenberg's War: The Secret History of the German Bomb,* New York: Alfred A. Knopf 1993

Price, David A., *Geniuses At War: Bletchley Park, Colossus, and the Dawn of the Digital Age,* New York: Alfred A. Knopf 2021

Purnell, Sonia, *A Woman Of No Importance: The Untold Story of WW2's Most Dangerous Spy, Virginia Hall,* London: Virago Press 2019

Purser, Philip, *Lights in the Sky,* New York: Severn House 2005

Ramsay, Archibald Maule (1952), *The Nameless War,* Milton Keynes: Revisionist Books 2016

Ramsay, David, *'Blinker' Hall, Spymaster: The Man Who Brought America Into World War I,* Stroud, Gloucestershire: Spellmount Limited 2008

Rankin, Nicholas, *Ian Fleming's Commandos: The Story of 30 Assault Unit In WWII,* London: Faber & Faber 2011

…, *A Genius for Deception: How Cunning Helped The British Win Two World Wars,* Oxford, New York: Oxford University Press 2008

…, *Churchill's Wizards: The British Genius for Deception 1914-1945,* London: Faber & Faber Limited 2008 (this is the same book as the one above, different title and publisher)

…, *Telegram From Guernica: The Extraordinary Life of George Steer, War Correspondent,* London: Faber and Faber Limited 2003

Rayner-Canham, Marlene and Geoffrey, *Women in Chemistry: Their Changing Roles From Alchemical Times To The Mid-twentieth Century,* American Chemical Society and Chemical Heritage Foundation 1998

…, *A Devotion to Their Science: Pioneer Women of Radioactivity,* Montreal: McGill-Queen's University Press 1997

Read, Anthony and David Fisher, *Operation Lucy: Most Secret Spy Ring of the Second World War,* London: Hodder & Stoughton 1980

…, *Colonel Z: The Secret Life of a Master of Spies,* New York: Viking Penguin 1984

Read, Conyers, *Mr Secretary Walsingham and the Policy of Queen Elizabeth,* Cambridge MA: At the Harvard University Press 1925

Rees, P., *Fascism in Britain: An Annotated Bibliography,* Hassocks, Sussex: Harvester Press 1979

…, *Biographical Dictionary of the Extreme Right Since 1890,* New York: Simon & Schuster 1990

Reginbogin, Herbert P., translated by Ulrike Seeberger and Jane Britten, *Faces of Neutrality: A comparative Analysis of the Neutrality of Switzerland and other Neutral Nations during WW II,* Piscataway, NJ: Transaction Publishers 2009

Regnat, K.H., *Vom Original zum Modell: Heinkel He 111:* Bonn: Bernard & Graefe Verlag 2000

…, *Vom Original zum Modell: Dornier DO17,* Bonn: Bernard & Graefe Verlag 2005

Reid, R.W., *Tongues of Conscience: War & the Scientists' Dilemma,* London: Readers Union Constable 1970

…, *Tongues of Conscience: War and the scientist's dilemma,* London: Panther paperback 1971

Reyburn, Wallace, *Some Of It Was Fun,* Toronto: Thomas Nelson & Sons (Canada) Limited 1949

…, *Rehearsal for Invasion: An Eyewitness Story of the Dieppe Raid,* London Toronto: George C. Harrap & Co. Ltd. 1943

Reynolds, Quentin, *Dress Rehearsal: The Story of Dieppe,* New York: Random House 1943

Rhodes, Richard, *The Making of the Atomic Bomb,* New York: Simon & Schuster 1986/2012

Richards, Pamela Spence, *Scientific Information in Wartime: The Allied-German Rivalry 1939-1945,* Westport CT, London: Greenwood Press 1994

Richelson, Jeffrey T., *A Century of Spies: Intelligence in the Twentieth Century,* Oxford: Oxford University Press 1995

…, *Spying on the Bomb: American Nuclear Intelligence from Nazi Germany to Iran and North Korea,* New York: W.W. Norton & Company 2006

Richelson, Jeffrey T., and Desmond Ball, *The Ties that Bind: Intelligence Cooperation Between the UK, USA, Canada, Australia and New Zealand,* Winchester MA: Allen & Unwin 1985

Ridley, Norman, *The Race for the Atomic Bomb,* Barnsley, South Yorkshire: Pen and Sword Books 2023

Riehl, Nikolaus and Frederick Seitz, *Stalin's Captive: Nikolaus Riehl and the Soviet Race for the Bomb,* Washington DC: The American Chemical Society 1996

Rife, Patricia, translation by Peter Jacobs, *Lise Meitner: Ein Leben für die Wissenschaft,* Düsseldorf: Claasen 1990

…, *Lise Meitner and the Dawn of the Nuclear Age,* Boston: Birkhäuser 1990/92 (also a paperback)

Rings, Werner, translated by J. Maxwell Brownjohn, *Life With the Enemy: Collaboration and Resistance in Hitler's Europe 1939-1945,* New York: Doubleday & Company, Inc. 1982

Rippon, Anton, *Hitler's Olympics: The History of the 1936 Nazi Games,* Barnsley, South Yorkshire: Pen & Sword Books 2006

Robinson, Andrew, *Einstein on the Run: How Britain Saved the World's Greatest Scientist,* New Haven and London: Yale University Press 2019

Rollyson, Carl, *Nothing Ever Happens to the Brave: The Adventurous Life of America's Most Glamorous and Courageous War Correspondent,* New York: St. Martin's Press 1990

…, *Beautiful Exile: The Life of Martha Gellhorn,* London: Aurum Press 2001

Romanones, Aline, *The Spy Wore Silk: Further Adventures of an Undercover Agent,* New York: G.B. Putnam's Sons 1991

Rosary, Edward Michael, *Fleming's Wars: The History Behind the Fiction of Ian Fleming's James Bond,* Rune Orcadia Publishing 2020

Rose, Paul Lawrence, *Heisenberg and the Atomic Bomb Project: A Study in German Culture,* Berkeley Los Angeles London: University of California Press 1998

Rose, Sarah, *D-Day Girls: The True Story of the Women Who Helped Win the Second World War,* London: Crown Publishing Group 2019

Rosental, S., editor, *Niels Bohr: His life and work as seen by his friends and colleagues,* New York: Interscience Publishers 1964

Rossiter, Mike, *The Spy Who Changed The World: Klaus Fuchs, Physicist and Soviet Double Agent,* New York: Skyhorse Publishing 2015/2017

…, *The Spy Who Changed The World: Klaus Fuchs and the secrets of the nuclear bomb,* Great Britain: Headline Publishing Group 2014

Rosso, Diana de, *A Life of Intrigue,* Harpenden, Herts: Lennard Publishing 1991

Rout, Leslie B. and John F. Bratzel, *The Shadow War: German Espionage and United States Counterespionage in Latin America during World War II,* Frederick MD: University Publications of America 1986

Rowan, Richard Wilmer, *The Story of Secret Service,* New York: The Literary Guild of America 1937

…, *Terror in Our Time: The Secret Service of Surprise Attack,* London: Hutchison & Co. Ltd. 1945.

Rudberg, Pontus, *The Swedish Jews and the Holocaust,* London and New York: Routledge 2017/2019

Rudel, Hans-Ulrich, *Stuka Pilot,* Costa Mesa, CA: The Noontide Press 1987/1990

Russell, Emily, editor, *A Constant Heart: The War Diaries of Maud Russell 1938-1945,* Dorset, UK: The Dovecote Press 2017

Russell-Jones, Mair and Gethin, *My Secret Life in Hut Six: One Woman's Experiences at Bletchley Park,* Oxford: Lion Hudson 2014

Sabourin, Gilles, *Montreal and the Bomb,* translated from the French by Katherine Hastings, Montreal: Baraka Books 2021

Salewicz, Chris and Adrian Boot, *Firefly: Noël Coward in Jamaica,* London: Victor Gollancz 1999

Sanders, Ian L. and Lorne Clark, *A Radiophone in Every Home: William Stephenson and the General Radio Company Limited, 1922-1928,* Twyford, Reading, Berkshire: Loddon Valley Press 2012

Sastamoinen, Armas, *Nynazismen: Tillägnas alla bortglömda antinazistiska kämpar,* Stockholm: Tr.-AB Federativ 1961

Sayer, Ian and Douglas Botting, *The Women Who Knew Hitler: The Private Life of Adolf Hitler,* New York: Carroll & Graf Publishers 2004

Scalia, Joseph Mark, *Germany's Last Mission to Japan: The Failed Voyage of U-234,* Annapolis, MD: Naval Institute Press 2000

Schaaf, Michael, *Der Physiochemiker Paul Harteck (1902-1985),* Stuttgart: Historisches Institut der Universität Stuttgart 1999

Schachtman, Tom, *Laboratory Warriors: How Allied Science and Technology Tipped the Balance in World War II,* New York: HarperCollins 2002

Schellenberg, Walter, translated by Louis Hagen, *The Schellenberg Memoirs: A Record of the Nazi Secret Service,* London: Andre Deutsch 1956

…, *Invasion 1940: The Nazi Invasion Plan for Britain,* London: St. Ermin's Press 2000

Schenzinger, K.A., *I. G. Farben,* München & Wien: Wilhelm Andermann Verlag 1953

Schmelzer, Janis, *IG Farben: vom "Rat der Götter" Aufstieg und Fall,* Stuttgart: Schmetterling Verlag 2006

Schneier, Bruce, *Applied Cryptography: Protocols, Algorithms, and Source Code in C, 2nd ed.,* New York: John Wiley & Sons 1996

Schonland, Sir Basil, *The Atomists (1805 – 1933),* Oxford: Clarendon Press 1968

Schorske, Carl E., *Fin-de-Siècle Vienna: Politics and Culture,* New York: Vintage Books Random House 1981

Schramm, Percy Ernst, with Hans-Adolf Jacobsen, *Kriegstagebuch des Oberkommandos der Wehrmacht (Wehrmachtführungsstab) 1940-1945, Band I: 1. August 1940 – 31. December 1941,* Frankfurt am Main: Bernard & Graefe Verlag für Wehrwesen 1965

Scott, Franklin D., with an epilogue by Steven Koblik, *Sweden: The Nation's History,* Carbondale and Edwardsville IL: Southern Illinois University Press 1988

Seaman, Mark, editor, *Special Operations Executive: A New Instrument of War,* London: Routledge 2006

…, *Garbo: The Spy Who Saved D-Day,* Richmond, Surrey: Public Record Office 2000, summaries by Tomas Harris

Sebag-Montefiore, Hugh, *Enigma: The Battle for the Code,* Hoboken, NJ: John Wiley & Sons 2000

…, also a Folio Society edition, London 2005

Seelig, Carl, *Helle Zeit – Dunkle Zeit: In Memoriam, Albert Einstein,* Zürich: Europa Verlag 1956

Segrè, Gino, *Faust in Copenhagen: The Struggle for the Soul of Physics and the Birth of the Nuclear Age*, London: Jonathan Cape 2007

Segrè, Gino and Hoerlin, Bettina, *The Pope of Physics: Enrico Fermi and the Birth of the Atomic Age*, New York: Henry Holt & Company 2016

Sencourt, Robert, *King Alfonso: A Biography*, London: Faber and Faber Limited 1942

Sereny, Gitta, *Albert Speer: His Battle With Truth*, London: Macmillan Picador 1995/96

Sexl, Lore and Ann Hardy, *Lise Meitner*, Hamburg: Rowohlt Taschenbuch Verlag 2002

Shakespeare, Nicholas, *Ian Fleming: The Complete Man*, New York: HarperCollins 2023

Shilton, A.C., *Can America's Supercomputers Defeat Covid For Good?*, New York: *Popular Mechanics* September/October 2021

Shirer, William L., *The Rise and Fall of the Third Reich: A History of Nazi Germany*, London: Martin Secker & Warburg 1959

…, *The Nightmare Years, 1930-1940: a Memoir of a Life and the Times*, Boston: Little Brown 1984

Sime, Ruth Lewin, *Lise Meitner: A Life In Physics*, Berkeley: University of California Press 1996

Siney, Marion C., *Raoul Wallenberg: Swedish Diplomat In Hungary: A Little Known Story of WWII Heroism*, Michigan Quarterly Review, Vol. III, No. 1, January 1964

Singh, Simon, *The Code Book: The Evolution of Secrecy from Mary Queen of Scots to Quantum Cryptography*, New York: Doubleday 1999

Skoglund, Elizabeth R., *A Quiet Courage: Per Anger,Wallenberg's Co-Liberator of Hungarian Jews*, Grand Rapids, MI: Baker Books 1997

Smith, Chris, *The Last Cambridge Spy: John Cairncross, Bletchley Codebreaker and Soviet Double Agent*, Stroud, Gloucestershire: The History Press 2019

Smith, Edward Abel. *Ian Fleming's Inspiration: The Truth Behind the Books*, Barnsley, South Yorkshire: Pen & Sword Books 2020

Smith, Michael, *Foley: The Spy Who Saved 10,000 Jews*, London: Hodder & Stoughton 1999

…, *Six: The Real James Bonds 1909-1939*, London: Biteback Publishing 2010/2011

…, *The Secrets of Station X: How Bletchley Park Helped Win the War*, London: Biteback Publishing 2011

…, *The Debs of Bletchley Park*, London: Aurum Press 2015

…, *Bletchley Park: The Codebreakers of Station X*, Oxford: Shire Publications 2016

Smith, Richard Angus, *Spying and Surveillance in Shakespeare's Courts*, PhD thesis, Department of English, University of Sydney 2014

Smyth, H.D., *Atomic Energy: A General Account of the Development of Methods of Using Atomic Energy for Military Purposes under the Auspices of the United States Government*, United States of America Government Printing Office, reprinted by His Majesty' Stationery Office, London, 1945

Soames, Mary and Wally Ross et al, *The Heroic Memory: The Memorial Addresses to the Rt.Hon. Sir Winston Churchill Society Edmonton, Alberta, 1965-1989*, (dedication to Jack Ondrack signed by Mary Soames), Edmonton, AB: The Churchill Statue and Oxford Scholarship Foundation 2005

Sokolov, V.I., translated from the Russian by NACA, *Critical Velocities of Ultracentrifuges*, Washington: Technical Memorandum 1272, National Advisory Committee for Aeronautics 1951

Solomon, Flora, and Barry Litvinoff, *A Woman's Way*, New York: Simon & Schuster 1984

Sontag, Raymond James and James Stuart Beddie, editors, *Nazi-Soviet Relations 1939-1941,* Washington DC: Department of State Publication 3023 1948

Sorel, Nancy Caldwell, *The Women Who Wrote the War,* New York: Arcade Publishing 1999

Spaight, J.M., *The Battle of Britain 1940,* London: Geoffrey Bles 1941

Spears, Sir Edward, *Assignment to Catastrophe: Vol. I, Prelude to Dunkirk July 1939 – May 1940,* London: William Heinemann Ltd 1954

Speer, Albert, *Inside The Third Reich,* London: Sphere Books 1970

Speer, Albert, Translation by Joachim Neugroschel, *Infiltration: How Heinrich Himmler Schemed to Build an SS Industrial Empire,* New York: Macmillan 1981

Stafford, David, *Camp X: Canada's School for Secret Agents 1941-1945,* Toronto: Lester & Orpen Dennys Limited 1986

…, *Churchill and Secret Service,* Toronto: Stoddart 1997

…, *Britain and European Resistance: A survey of the Special Operations Executive, with documents,* Toronto: University of Toronto Press 1983 (also a second paperback edition issued 2022)

Stein, Leon, *The Racial Thinking of Richard Wagner,* New York: Philosophical Library 1950

Steiner, Prof. Michael, *Lise Meitner zum 125. Geburtstag,* Berlin: Staatsbibliothek Preussischer Kulturbesitz 2003

Steinert, Harald, translated and adapted from the original German by Nicholas Wharton, *The Atom Rush: Man's quest for radio-active materials,* London: Thames and Hudson 1958

Stephenson, Wm., Highet, G., Hill, T., Dahl, R., with an Introduction by Nigel West, *British Security Coordination: The Secret History of British Intelligence in the Americas, 1940-1945,* New York: Fromm International 1999

Stern, Fritz, *Einstein's German World,* Princeton, NJ: Princeton University Press 1999

…, *Dreams and Delusions: The Drama of German History,* NY: Alfred A Knopf 1987 (signed by author)

…, *Einstein's German World,* Princeton NJ: Princeton UP 1999

…, *Five Germanys I Have Known,* New York: Farrar, Straus & Giroux 2006/2007

Stevenson, Wm., *A Man Called Intrepid: The Secret War 1939-1945,* London: Macmillan/Book Club Associates 1976, also Harcourt Brace 1976

…, *Intrepid's Last Case,* London: Sphere Books 1984 and copy Lyons Press 2002

…, *Spymistress: The True Story of the Greatest Female Secret Agent of World War II,* New York: Arcade 2011

Stoltzenberg, Dietrich in German and several translators to English, *Fritz Haber: Chemist, Nobel Laureate, Jew,* Philadelphia, PA: Chemical Heritage Foundation 2004

Stolz, Werner, *Otto Hahn/Lise Meitner,* Leipzig: BSB B.G. Teubner Verlagsgesellschaft 1983

Strecker, Edward A., *Their Mothers' Sons: The Psychiatrist Examines an American Problem,* Philadelphia and New York: J.B. Lippincott 1951/46

Strevens, Michael, *The Knowledge Machine: How Irrationality Created Modern Science,* New York: Liveright Publishing 2020

Ströman, Jan, *Svenska Korosserimakare: Berättelsen om ett hantverk,* Stockholm: Centrum för Närungslivshistoria och Ekerlids Förlag 2009

Sturrock, Donald, *Storyteller: The Life of Roald Dahl,* London: Harper Press 2010

Svedberg, The and Kai O. Pedersen, *The Ultracentrifuge,* Oxford: The Clarendon Press 1940

Svedberg, The, editors Tiselius, Pedersen et al, *The Svedberg 1884 30/8 1944,* Uppsala: Almqvist & Wiksells Boktrykeri AB 1945

Swedish Ministry for Foreign Affairs, *Sweden and Jewish Assets (World War II,* Stockholm: Swedish Ministry for Foreign Affairs 1999

Szilard, Leo, editors Bernard T. Feld and Gertrud Szilard, *The Collected Works of Leo Szilard: Scientific Papers,* London & Cambridge MA: The MIT Press 1972

Talty, Stephan, *Agent Garbo: The Brilliant, Eccentric Secret Agent Who Tricked Hitler & Saved D-Day,* Boston: Houghton Mifflin Harcourt 2012

Teller, Edward, *Memoirs: A Twentieth Century Journey In Science And Politics,* Cambridge MA: Perseus 2001

Tennant, Peter, *Touchlines of War,* Hull: The University of Hull Press 1992

Thiessen, Vern, *Einstein's Gift,* Toronto: Playwrights Canada Press 2015

Thomas, Gordon and Max Morgan Witts, *Guernica: The Crucible of World War II,* New York: Stein & Day 1975

Thomas, Gordon, *Secret Wars: One Hundred Years of British Intelligence Inside MI5 and MI6,* New York: St. Martin's Press 2009

Thomas, John Oram, *The Giant Killers: The Danish Resistance Movement 1940/5,* London: Michael Joseph 1975

Thunberg, Anders, *Karin Lannby: Ingmar Bergmans Mata Hari,* Stockholm: Natur & Kultur 2009

Time-Life Editors, *Barbarossa,* Alexandria, VA: Time-Life Books 1990

…, *Lightning War,* Alexandria, VA: Time – Life Books 1989

Toeppel, Roman, *Kursk 1943: The Greatest Battle of the Second World War,* Warwick, England: Helion & Company 2018/21

Tooze, Adam, *The Wages of Destruction: The Making and Breaking of the Nazi Economy,* London: Penguin Allen Lane 2006

Torekull, Bertil, translated by Joan Tate, *Leading By Design; The IKEA Story,* New York: Harper Business 1999

Toynbee, Arnold, J. *A Study of History, Volume II,* London: Oxford University Press 1934/63

Trevor-Roper, H.R., editor and commentator, *Blitzkrieg to Defeat: Hitler's War Directives 1939 – 1945,* New York: Holt, Rinehart & Winston 1964

Trevor-Roper, Professor Hugh, editor, translated from the German by Richard Barry, *Final Entries 1945: The Diaries of Joseph Goebbels,* New York: G.P. Putnam's Sons 1978

Trevor-Roper, H.R., English translation by Weidenfeld and Nicolson 1953, *Hitler's Table Talk 1941-1944: His Private Conversations,* London: Phoenix Press 2003

Troy, Thomas F., *Wild Bill Donovan, Stephenson, and the Origins of CIA,* New Haven CT: Yale UP 1996

…, *Donovan and the CIA: A History of the Establishment of the Central Intelligence Agency,* Frederick, Maryland: University Publications of America, Inc. 1981/1984

Tsouras, Peter, *Disaster at D-Day: The Germans Defeat the Allies, June 1944,* London: Greenhill Books 1994/2004

Tuccille, Jerome, *Hemingway and Gellhorn: The Untold Story of Two Writers, Espionage, War, and the Great Depression*, Baltimore MD: WinklerMedia Publishing Group 2011.

Turner, Des, *Aston House Station 12: SOE's Secret Centre*, Thrupp Stroud Gloucestershire: Sutton Publishing Limited 2006

Turner, Henry Ashley Jr., *German Big Business & The Rise of Hitler*, New York: Oxford University Press 1985

Urbach, Karina, *Go Betweens for Hitler*, Oxford UK: Oxford University Press 2015

Valloton, M. Henry, *Alfonso XIII, Traduccion del Marques de Morella, Prologo del Condo de Romanones*, Madrid: Editorial Tesoro 2nd edition 1945

Van Calmthout, Martijn, *Sam Goudsmit and the Hunt for Hitler's Atom Bomb, translated and edited by Michael Horn*, New York: Prometheus Books 2018

Vance, Jonathan F., *The True Story of the Great Escape: Stalag Luft III, March 1944*, Barnsley, Yorkshire: Greenhill Books c/o Pen & Sword Books Ltd. 2019

Vansittart, Lord, *The Mist Procession: The Autobiography of Lord Vansittart*, London: Hutchinson 1958

Venezia, Mike, *Lise Meitner*, New York: Scholastic 2010

Villiers, José, *Granny Was A Spy*, London: Quartet Books 1988

Vincent, Isabel, *Hitler's Silent Partners: Swiss Banks, Nazi Gold and the Pursuit of Justice*, New York: William Morrow & Company, Inc. 1997

Volkman, Ernest, *Spies: The Secret Agents Who Changed the Course of History*, New York: John Wiley & Sons 1994

Von Ardenne, Manfred, *Memoiren: Ein Glückliches Leben für Technik und Forschung*, Zürich und München: Kindler Verlag 1972

… Erinnerungen, fortgeschrieben, Ein Forscherleben im Jahrhundert des Wandels der Wissenschaften und politischen Systeme, Düsseldorf: Droste Verlag GmbH 1997

Von Below, Nicolaus, *Als Hitlers Adjutant 1937-1945*, Mainz: Pour le Merite 1999

Von Lang, Jochen, *Bormann: The Man Who Manipulated Hitler*, London: Book Club Associates 1977/79

Von Schirach, Richard, *Night of the Physicists Operation Epsilon: Heisenberg, Hahn, Weizsäcker and the German Atomic Bomb*, translated by Simon Pare, London: Haus Publishing 2015

Von Willamowicz-Moellendorff, Fanny Gräfin, geb. Baronin von Foch-Stockholm, *Carin Göring*, Berlin: Martin Warneck Verlag 1934

Walden, Geoffrey R., *Hitler's Berchtesgaden: A Guide to Third Reich Sites in the Berchtesgaden and Obersalzberg Area*, Stroud, UK: Fonthill Media 2014

Walker, Mark, *German National Socialism and the Quest for Nuclear Power, 1939-1949*, Cambridge: Cambridge University Press 1989

Walker, Mark, *Nazi Science: Myth, Truth and the German Atomic Bomb*, New York: Plenum Press 1995

Waller, Douglas (2011), *Wild Bill Donovan: The Spymaster Who Created the OSS and Modern American Espionage*, New York: Simon & Schuster Free Press 2012

Walters, Guy, *Berlin Games: How the Nazis Stole the Olympic Dream*, New York: HarperCollins 2006

Wark, Wesley K., *The Ultimate Enemy: British Intelligence and Nazi Germany 1933-1939*, Oxford: Oxford UP 1986

Warlimont, Walter, translated from the German by R.H. Barry, *Inside Hitler's Headquarters 1939-1945*, Novato CA: Presidio, Weidenfeld & Nicolson 1962/1964

Warwicker, John, *Churchill's Underground Army: A History of the Auxiliary Units in World War II*, Barnsley, S. Yorkshire: Frontline Books 2008

Weale, Adrian, *The SS: A New History*, London: Little Brown Abacus 2012

…, *Science and the Swastika*, London: Macmillan 2001

Weart, Spencer R. & Melba Phillips, Editors, *History of Physics*, New York: American Institute of Physics 1985

…, *Scientists In Power*, Cambridge, MA: Harvard University Press 1979

Weaver, Denis, *On Hitler's Doorstep*, London: Hodder & Stoughton 1942

Weidinger, Alfred, translated from the German by Fiona Elliott, *Kokoschka and Alma Mahler: Testimony to a Passionate Relationship*, Munich & New York: Prestel 1996

Weisskopf, Victor, *The Joy of Insight: Passions of a Physicist*, New York: Basic Books Harper Collins 1991

Welchman, Gordon, *The Hut Six Story: Breaking the Enigma Code*, Cleobury Mortimer, Shropshire: M&M Baldwin 2016

Wellerstein, Alex, *Restricted Data: The History of Nuclear Secrecy in the United States*, Chicago and London: University of Chicago Press 2021

Wells, Mark K., *Courage and Air Warfare: The Allied Aircrew Experiences in the Second World War*, London: Frank Cass Co. Ltd. 1995

West, Doug, *Dr. Wernher von Braun: a Short Biography*, Doug West 2017

West, Nigel, *MI6: British Secret Intelligence Service Operations 1909-1945*, London: Weidenfeld and Nicolson 1983

…, *MI5: British Security Operations1909-1945*, Barnsley Yorkshire: Pen & Sword Books 2019 (Bodley Head 1981)

…, *GCHQ: The Secret Wireless War 1900-1986*, London: Weidenfeld & Nicolson 1986

…, *Secret War: The Story of SOE, Britain's Wartime Sabotage Organization*, Barnsley Yorkshire: Pen & Sword Books 2019 (Hodder & Stoughton 1992)

…, *Counterfeit Spies*, London: St Ermin's Press 1998

…, *At Her Majesty's Secret Service: The Chiefs of Britain's Intelligence Agency, MI6*, London: Greenhill Books 2006

…, *Black Ops: Secret Military Operations From 1914 to the Present*, London: Welbeck Publishing Group 2020

West, Nigel, Introduction by, Foreword by William Stephenson, *British Security Coordination: The Secret History of British Intelligence in the Americas 1940-1945*, London: St. Ermin's Press 1998

Weston, Tom, *Fission: Based on a True Story*, San Bernardino, CA: Weston Media 2011

Whiting, Jim, *Otto Hahn and the Story of Nuclear Fission*, Hochessin, Delaware: Mitchell Lane Publishers 2004

Widfelt, Bo and Rolph Wegmann, *Making For Sweden: Part 2 the United States Army Air Force*, Surrey, KT: Air Research Publications 1998

Wiessenthal, Simon, *Justice Not Vengeance*, London: Weidenfeld and Nicolson 1989

Wigner, Eugene P., *The Recollections of Eugene P. Wigner, as told to Andrew Szanton,* New York: Plenum Press 1992

Wilcox, Robert K., *Japan's Secret War: Japan's Race Against Time To Build Its Own Atomic Bomb,* New York: Marlowe & Company 1995

Wilgress, Dana, *Memoirs,* Toronto: Ryerson Press 1967

Wilgress, Leolyn Dana, *The Trade of South China,* Ottawa: Bulletin of the Department of Trade and Commerce Oct. 1918 – Jan. 1919

Williams, Robert C. and Phillip L. Cantelon, editors, *The American Atom: A Documentary History of Nuclear Policies from the Discovery of Fission to the Present,* Philadelphia: U of Pennsylvania Press 1984

Wilkinson, Peter, and Joan Bright Astley, *Gubbins & SOE,* London: Leo Cooper 1993 and Pen & Sword Books 1997

Williams, Robert Chadwell, *Klaus Fuchs: Atomic Spy,* Cambridge: Harvard UP 1987

Williams, Robert C. and Philip L. Cantelon, *The American Atom: A Documentary History of Nuclear Policies from the Discovery of Fission to the Present 1939-1984,* Philadelphia PA: University of Pennsylvania Press 1984

Wilson, James, *Hitler's Alpine Headquarters,* Barnsley, UK: Pen & Sword Military 2013

Winant, John Gilbert, *Letter from Grosvenor Square: An Account of a Stewardship,* Boston: Houghton Mifflin 1947

Winder, Simon, *The Man Who Saved Britain: A Personal Journey into the Disturbing World of James Bond,* London: Picador 2006

Winks, Robin W., *Cloak & Gown: Scholars in the Secret War, 1939-1961,* New York: Quill Wm Morrow 1987

…, *The Historian As Detective: Essays On Evidence,* New York: Harper & Row 1968

Wingate, Sir Ronald, *Lord Ismay, a biography,* London: Hutchinson 1970

Winslow, Pauline Glen, *The Windsor Plot, a Novel,* London: Arlington Books 1981

Winterbotham, F.W., *The Ultra Secret,* New York: Harper & Row 1974

…, *The Ultra Spy: An Autobiography,* London: Macmillan 1989/1991

Wirtz, Karl, *Im Umkreis der Physik,* Karlsruhe: Kernforschungszentrum Karlsruhe GmbH 1988

Wohlfarth, Horst, editor, *40 Jahre Kernspaltung: Eine Einführung in die Originalliteratur,* Darmstadt: Wissenschaftliche Buchgesellschaft 1976

Wouk, Herman, *The Winds of War,* Boston: Little, Brown 1971

Young-Bruehl, Elisabeth, *Anna Freud: A Biography,* New York: Summit 1988

Zentner, Dr. Christian, chief editor, *Das Dritte Reich: Zeitgeschehen in Wort, Bild und Ton Nr. 29,* Hamburg: John Jahr Verlag KG ca. 1975

Ziegler, Philip, *King Edward VIII,* New York: Alfred A. Knopf 1991

Zimmerman, David, *Top Secret Exchange: The Tizard Mission and the Scientific War,* Montreal-Kingston: The McGill-Queen's University Press 1996

Photo Credits

Page/Note

21/43 Photo courtesy of the DGL Historical Foundation

21/44 Photo courtesy of the US Library of Congress LC-DIG-ppmsc-09214, commons.wikimedia Universitaet Wien 1900 and the University of Vienna, Austro-Hungary LCCN20022708401

23 Ondrack/Hellstedt

24 Ondrack/Hellstedt

25/45 Photo courtesy of Max Planck Gesellschaft, Alamy HRNP53

25/46 Photo courtesy Archive of the University of Vienna/Originator/R.Fenzl/135.608 1898

27 Ondrack/Hellstedt and Ondrack

30 Ondrack/Hellstedt

31 Ondrack/Hellstedt

32/48 Photo courtesy of the University of Calgary, from Toronto Public Library Accession Number TSPA_0051081F from the Toronto Star Photograph Archive, in the public domain

33/49 Photo with caption courtesy of David Halton

34-66 Ondrack/Hellstedt

66/70 Photo of Jack's Lagonda taken by Jack Ondrack. Photo of lady golfer Alamy F2AYCN.

67/71 Photo of Buick Alamy 2RCTCWA

70/72, 71 Photos courtesy of the National Museum of Sweden, Stockholm

75/89 Photo from Dalzel-Job, p.108+

76/90 Photo from Dalzel-Job, p.108+

85/131 Photo page on p.230+ in William Stevenson, *A Man Called Intrepid*; also in the Harcourt Brace Jovanovich edition, courtesy of BSC Papers, Station M Archives

99, 100/200 Photos courtesy of the Max Planck Society, Alamy C45COW and 2CBCEN4

103/215 Alamy TA2XDR

104/216 Photos courtesy of Basque Library, University of Nevada, Reno

104/217 Photos Alamy 2M96Y5H and 2HK3MFY

105/218 Photos courtesy of Postal Service of Spain, London Graphic(TIME cover) and Dellach Golf Club

111 Ondrack

112/221 Photo courtesy The Telegraph UK Red-Duchess

114/227 Alamy 2R3901J Opening ceremony. Alamy FD833A. Hitler Goring saluting

114/227 "Photo of TV camera in Bildarchiv Preussischer Kulturbesitz, Alamy CDJ132J, Alamy 2R3901J, Alamy FD833A, Alamy M9MF57

114/228 Alamy DMWMKE

115/229 Courtesy of Bundesarchiv Berlin

115/230 Photo courtesy of Lacombe and District Historical Society

117/231 Alamy KWC3DH

117/232 Alamy 2J33H3G and 2J33K5C

117/233 Alamy 2J33N28

117/234 Bayerische Staatsbibliotek, Heinrich Hoffman hoff.27389 and Alamy DB3PEC

119/244 Alamy 2J33WCJ

121/245 Photo courtesy of Aertzteblatt.de.archiv/36954/60

123/250 Hitler in Wien. Bundesarchiv – Bild 146-1978-028-14

123/251 Alamy 2AECRPD, inv. 1YO3298560

124-131 Ondrack/Hellstedt

138/267 Photo courtesy of the Archives of the Max Planck Society, Berlin

140/276 Photo courtesy of the Archives of the Max Planck Society, Berlin

142/284 Photo of Leo Szilard courtesy of the Argonne National Laboratory

142/285 Photos courtesy of the Atomic Energy Foundation

144/295 Alamy 2H45DF2

148/312 Photo courtesy of the Deutsches Museum, Munich

162/358 Photo courtesy of David Halton

163/362 Image courtesy of David Halton

165/364 Photo courtesy of Niels Bohr Archive, Copenhagen

169/375 Photo courtesy of the Max Planck Society, Berlin

170/377 Photo courtesy of the Archiv zur Geschichte der Max-Planck-Gesellschaft, Berlin

170/378 Photo of Fritz Haber in WWI courtesy of the Archives of the Max Planck Society, Berlin

170/379 Photo courtesy of the Archiv zur Geschichte der Max-Planck-Gesellschaft, Berlin KWI_f_Chemie_I_3, Alamy 2T3J6JY

171/383 Photo courtesy of the Archiv zur Geschichte der Max-Planck-Gesellschaft, Berlin KWI_f_Chemie_II_11

171/384 Photo courtesy of the Archives of the Max Planck Society, Berlin

174/392 Harteck photo courtesy of the Archives of the Max Planck Society, Berlin

174/393 Heisenberg photo courtesy of the Emilio Segre Visual Archives AIP

179/408 Photo courtesy of the Archives of the Max Planck Society, Berlin

181/417 Photo courtesy of the Archives of the Max Planck Society, Berlin

185/434 Photo courtesy of the American Institute for Physics Emilio Segre Archives

186/435 Denham photo courtesy of Churchill Archives Centre, Churchill College, Cambridge

186/436 Corcoran photo courtesy of the Corcoran Archives, Stanford University Library

199/486 Photo courtesy of the Norsk Industrial Museum, Vemork

199/487 Photo courtesy of the Norsk Industrial Museum, Vemork

206/516 Ondrack/Hellstedt

216/538 Emily Blunt Alamy M378W4

216 Clara Leone photo from Ondrack/Hellstedt

216/539 Julia Roberts photo Alamy H82D9B

216/540 Lise Meitner photo *MaxPlanckMeitnertoLaue.jpg* courtesy of the Max Planck Society, Berlin

216/541 Talia Shire photo Alamy PNTPMA

Cover: Jack Ondrack drawings; Alamy C5HH47; Meitner from Max Planck Society, Berlin; Clara Leone from Ondrack/Hellstedt

List of photos used courtesy of the Archives of the Max Planck Society, Berlin:

- for_page_181_Hahn_XVII_24_2
- Hahn_XVII_24_23_Farmhall
- Harteck_Paul_2
- KWI_f_Chemie_I_3
- KWI_f_Chemie_II_11
- Laue_I_3_65
- Meitner_I_27_Copyright_Lotte_Meit...
- Meitner_II_2
- Meitner_II_4
- Meitner_III_3
- R_1_10_49
- Strassmann_I_3

Index

The End